CW00474250

THE PATHLESS WAY

Also by Adam Nichols

The War of the Lords Veil

THE PATHLESS WAY

Adam Nichols

MILLENNIUM

An Orion Book
London

Copyright © Adam Nichols 1996
All rights reserved

The right of Adam Nichols to be identified as the author of
this work has been asserted by him in accordance with the
Copyright, Designs and Patents Act 1988.

This edition first published
in 1996 by Orion Books Ltd
Orion House, 5 Upper St Martin's Lane
London WC2H 9EA

A CIP catalogue record for this book is available
from the British Library

ISBN: (Csd) 1 85798 434 X
ISBN: (Ppr) 1 85798 435 8

Typeset by Deltatype Ltd, Birkenhead, Merseyside

Printed and bound in Great Britain by
Clays Ltd, St Ives plc.

This book is for Ellen Shizgal, best of friends,
and for
Gaile, Jade and Martin
with love

No book is ever finished without help. I'd like to say thanks to Caroline Oakley, my editor, for her patience, sanity and skill.

I

Guthrie Garthson squinted up through the rain at where the lookout stood perched atop the small, cedar shingle roof of the Closter's Bell Tower.

'I see something!' the lookout shouted down hoarsely, his words all but drowned by the wind and the driving rain. 'Along by the trees on the river's far shore.'

The crowd of folk that packed the Closter's entrance yard below shifted nervously along the yard's log walls. The cold rain came down in sheets, and the people were muddied and shivering, voices raised in an anxious chorus.

'What do you see?' Guthrie Garthson shouted up, forming a trumpet of his hands, trying to make himself heard above the wind and the noise of the crowd. 'Who is it?'

But the man above made no reply, his attention riveted on what only he could see.

'What's *happening*, man?' This from barrel-chested Hone Amis Latirson at Guthrie's side, a shout loud enough to startle those clustered nearby.

But the lookout stayed deaf to their inquiries. He stood unmoving, perched like a gull atop the Bell Tower roof, peering intently through the pelting rain out over the height of the Closter's walls.

Reeve Guthrie wiped cold water from out of his eyes, twisted his long, pale hair into a rough knot to keep it out of the way, shook himself. 'I'm going up there.'

Hone Amis put a beefy, restraining hand on Guthrie's arm. 'No. Show some patience, lad! There's only room enough for one man atop that tower.'

Guthrie swung loose. 'I'm not going to stand here, waiting like some patient dog while that fool up there stares off into the clouds and says nothing. I *will* know what is happening!'

'No,' Hone Amis repeated. 'It's too dangerous. There may be

1

archers.' He took Guthrie by the shoulders. 'Your father commanded me to keep you safe.'

'Damn what my father commanded.' Guthrie wrenched himself loose once more. 'Damn my father for a fool!'

'Guthrie!' Hone Amis hissed. 'Mind your tongue! There's folk about.'

Guthrie gestured at the milling, anxious people who filled the Closter's high-walled entrance yard all around; most of the ordinary folk of the settlement were crowded in here, in a space far too small to hold them comfortably, complete with soggy bundles of hastily gathered belongings, shrieking fowl, and bleating, frightened sheep – all fled here to escape the violence. 'They have more on their minds right now,' Guthrie said, gesturing to the packed folk, 'than anything *I* might happen to say about my father.'

Hone Amis scowled. He wore a padded leather helmet with a low brim that came down like a thumb to protect his nose. On the helmet's brow gleamed the metal badge of the Reeve Vale Militia – crossed spears above a sword blade, surmounted by a half-circle of gleaming brass stars that were the mark of his rank as Militia Master. Hone Amis pointed to the badge. '*This* is my duty. You are the Reeve's son and heir. That is *your* duty. And you know it brings both privilege and responsibility. You must never –'

'Second son,' Guthrie interrupted. '*Second* son.'

A sudden burst of rain hit, silencing them. It was the first of the autumn storms, this, come roaring in from off the western sea like a great cascading wave through the sky, and it was cold as ice; both men could only stand as they were, spluttering and shaking, until the force of it should abate.

'Makes no difference,' Hone Amis gasped out once the rain had let up enough. The oiled, sleeveless chainmail byrnie he wore streamed with water and he slapped at his torso irritably, trying to squelch out the rainwater that had soaked him. His thick grey whiskers lay slicked fast to his cheeks, giving him an oddly deflated look. 'Second son or not, it makes no difference! You must –'

'It makes *all* the difference,' Guthrie spat. 'As you *well* know, Hone Amis Latirson!' He glared at the other man, blinking water out of his eyes. 'And don't *lecture* me! I'm no longer a little lad you can push about.'

'Then *act* like a grownup!' Hone Amis spat back. He shook his head. 'You haven't seen your twentieth summer yet, and you think you know it all. How do you expect to ...'

2

Guthrie spun on his heel and would have sprinted off through the crowd except that Hone Amis gestured quickly to a contingent of Militia standing nearby.

'Stop him!'

There were only five of Hone Amis's men within hailing distance, the majority of the Militia being engaged in the defence of the settlement or else keeping what semblance of order they could here in the Closter's yard. The five barred Guthrie's way like a fence.

'Out of my way!' he commanded them, placing his hand threateningly on the hilt of the sword he wore. It was a longer, more ornate weapon than the plain Militia-issue, short-bladed ones they carried, and he still felt self-conscious wearing it, for it was a named blade – Tusk, one of the five tempered-iron swords his father owned – and Guthrie's through blood inheritance rather than any especial need or skill; he knew himself to be an indifferent swordsman at best, despite all Hone Amis's tutelage. But Guthrie relied upon the effect such a blade could have, even if only half-drawn as it was now.

The men facing him were roughly uniformed in leather byrnies and padded leather caps, each cap bearing the crossed spears and sword blade insignia of the Militia. They were armed not only with short-bladed swords but also with stout, Militia-issue spears. These were farm lads, however, conscripted under the terms of their tenancy, only half trained as of yet. They held the spears like hoes.

'Master Amis?' one of them asked uneasily.

'Guthrie!' Hone Amis snapped. 'It is your father's command that you stay here safe, and that I keep you so. Do you think I *like* being here, cooped up like a hen in a hutch, blind to what is happening outside? I ought to be out there with the Militia. It's *my* men out there risking their necks. But I do as your father commands. I do what I am duty bound to do!'

Hone Amis stepped closer towards Guthrie and lowered his voice. 'Stop acting like an impatient fool of a boy and grow up, lad! You have responsibilities. You have ...'

Guthrie turned his back on the older man and strode towards the Militia arrayed before him. 'Get out of my way!' He straight-armed the nearest aside and brazened his way through. The men hesitated, caught between Hone Amis's instructions and respect for who and what Guthrie was.

'Idiots!' Guthrie heard Hone Amis say.

For it was too late to stop him. Guthrie vaulted across a

dilapidated cart somebody had brought in and thrust into the wet chaos of the crowd. Skidding through mud and braided sheep droppings, his long legs scissoring, he made for the yard's back wall where a set of stairs led upwards to the bell tower. The sword nearly tripped him twice, catching between his legs, and he cursed the stupid thing – it was all very well to wear one in the controlled circumstance of the practice yard, but this moving chaos was an altogether different situation.

Folk stared; he could see uneasy speculation on their faces as they watched him – the Reeve's second son – splash hastily past. Eyes were turned to the gateway, up to the bell tower, uncertain. Most of the settlement had found safety here, yes, but it was a blind, anxious safety, what with the Closter's high log walls and that stupid, unanswering lookout.

And meanwhile ...

'I see them!' the lookout cried suddenly from above.

Guthrie had reached the stairs at the back wall by now. He leaped up them, three at a time, skidding atop the platform at their head. The sword caught unexpectedly between his legs, spilling him painfully up against the wooden wall. He scrambled up, unbelted it, and flung sword, sheath, harness and all to the plank floor in a sudden spasm of irritation.

Looking up, he saw that the bell tower's little roof was no more than fifteen paces above him now. 'What's happening?' he shouted as loudly as he could. When that produced no response, he hammered the side of the tower's wall with his fists and shouted anew: *'What's going on out there?'*

The man above craned his neck over the eaves and looked down, surprised. His hair was plastered slick by the rain, his face white and stricken.

Guthrie felt his heart turn in his breast, seeing that stricken face. 'What?' he demanded. 'What is *happening* out there, man?'

The lookout's mouth worked, but the words would not come. He jerked back from the roof's edge, disappearing from view, and Guthrie heard him drop through the trap door which led from the rooftop into the upper reaches of the tower. An instant later the great bell began to ring.

Gong gonggg! Gong gonggg!

The folk packed into the courtyard below surged in sudden panic. *Gong gonggg!*

Guthrie flung himself through the small door leading into the

4

tower and leaped up the circular interior steps. On the floor above him, the lookout hauled blindly away at the bell rope and would not answer his hail. The Bell Tower shivered with the volume of that *gongging*.

Cursing the man for a fool, Guthrie dashed past and up through the trap door to the little roof. The rain struck him in the face like a solid thing, and he stood, panting, balanced uneasily on the slick, uneven surface of the cedar shingles. Up here above the protection of the walls, the cold storm wind shoved at him like a hard wet hand. Struggling to keep his balance, he squinted into the distance.

The Closter was situated well up the River Esk from Riverside, Reeve Vale's main settlement. Riverside lay nestled between the grey sea and the dark mountains, ringed by cleared and ordered fields, the white of sheep flecking the grassy slopes of the hills. Here up-river, however, the dark mass of the wild lands was close about. The Closter stood on a promontory above the river. The land about the walls had been axe-cleared, but beyond that, in all directions, rose the stone surge of the mountains – rock and tree and rain and cloud all tangled together now in the downpour. From the Closter's walls, a sweep of cleared slope led down to the river, muddied and swollen and surging now. Guthrie could make out the trees along its far bank, a dark, tossing mass. But for long moments he could make out nothing else.

What had the lookout seen?

Then, through the confusing skirl of the rain, he saw it too.

Men were fleeing in a ragged wave from out of the trees on the Esk's far bank, struggling to reach the swollen ford, willy-nilly splashing. Guthrie felt a stab of sick panic go through him. It was Vale men he saw, ordinary farmer folk and Hone Amis's Militia together in panicked flight, fleeing for their lives.

Behind them, he made out dim, leaping shapes. Guthrie gasped and sketched a quick warding sign with his fingers, for it seemed to him of a sudden that the men below were being pursued by the very Fey themselves – the elemental inhabitants of the wild lands that old Bowin, his father's bard, sang stories about ... risen in a fury of vengeance against the men who had felled their trees and broken their soil.

But no.

It was mortal enough men who came leaping out of the trees – the marauding Sea Wolves, bounding down to the river's bank, tall, grim men garbed in darkly oiled chainmail, round shields glimmering in the rain. They wore ivory and iron helms crested with stiff horsehair and wielded wicked, long iron war-spears. They howled like very wolves as they fell upon the backs of the fleeing Vale men.

The Closter bell was still ringing, and Guthrie saw white faces turn at the *gong gong*, heard faint shouts as the Vale men struggled to cross the Esk. Guthrie saw a Sea Wolf impale one of them, the poor soul thrashing like a gaffed fish, saw another cut down like a butchered sheep, a third skewered as he tried to scrabble up the Esk's muddy bank. The river ran dark with blood and flailing bodies. Those Vale men who made it across the water bent themselves and ran desperately towards the protection of the Closter's walls.

Since boyhood, Guthrie had listened to the heroic tales old Bowin told – Great Owen's story, or the saga of Egil Bloodaxe – but what was taking place before him resembled not at all the battle scenes described in old Bowin's tales. There was no heroism here. It was like the autumn butchery of sheep – blood and cries and wet meat.

Guthrie turned from the sight, his belly knotting sickly, and shouted down into the Closter's yard, 'Open the gate!'

But the great *gong gonggg* of the Tower bell drowned him out. He could feel the very roofbeams underfoot vibrate with it. The folk below were shouting, half a hundred conflicting voices, milling about in frightened confusion in the rain.

Gong gonggg! Gong gonggg!

'Open the gate!' Guthrie cried again. 'Open the gate!' But it was no use. No one could hear.

Below, near the foot of the bell tower now, he made out Hone Amis staring up at him. Guthrie waved his arms, gesturing, pantomiming the opening of the gate. Hone Amis made a trumpet of his hands and shouted something, but Guthrie could not make it out.

Despairing, Guthrie cast one last glance over the Closter's walls, seeing the poor remnant of Vale men scrambling desperately over the grassy slope leading to the Closter, with the Sea Wolves howling in close pursuit, and then he flung himself back through the roof's trapdoor and inside the bell tower. Careering down the inside steps, his skull ringing with the bell's thunder in the tower's enclosed space, he thrust the lookout away from the bell rope, sending the man sprawling across the floor. 'Fool!' he hissed. 'Leave it be.'

The man stared up at him, stunned. 'I only thought ...' he sputtered.

6

Guthrie ran on.

The yard was a seething chaos. Folk tried to halt him, shouting questions, and Guthrie had to beat his way through. He skidded to a stop in front of the gateway. 'Open the gate!' he called to the four Militia men who stood guard there, swords unsheathed and ready.

One of the four stepped towards him. 'The Militia Master gave orders that —'

'Fool!' Guthrie shouted. From the outer side of the wall came the sound of shouting, and fists thumped against the gateway's wooden doors. Guthrie reached impulsively for his sword, remembered with a curse that he had flung it aside, and leaped forwards unarmed, trying to shoulder his way through the Militiamen and lift the locking bar that kept the oaken gateway doors closed.

Hands wrenched at him from behind and he was flung heavily to the sodden ground. A blade was at his throat. 'We have *orders*,' one of the Militia hissed into Guthrie's face. 'Nobody is to open this gate without direct permission from Master Amis or the Reeve himself.'

'Fools!' Guthrie spluttered, struggling against the men as they strove to hold him down in the mud. He felt the chill bite of the blade against his neck. The pounding on the wooden door was a desperate tattoo now. 'There's men out there will *die* of your stupidity. Let me free! Do you not know me for who I am?'

'Let him up!' a voice shouted in command.

The men fell away and Guthrie struggled to his feet. Hone Amis stood there. 'The gate!' Guthrie panted. 'The Sea Wolves have routed our men. Open the gate or the survivors will be caught against the walls and slaughtered like so many sheep!'

Hone Amis paused for an instant, listening to the shouts and pounding from outside, then turned to the Militia men. 'Open the gate.'

'But, sir,' one of the men said. 'What if ...'

'*Now!*'

Two of them lifted the locking bar up and swung open one half of the double-doored gateway. Men came pouring through in a chaotic swirl of wind driven rain and blood and screaming.

In the whirling confusion, something struck Guthrie, hard and unexpected, in the pit of his belly and he doubled over, gasping. On his knees, he saw only a blurred rush of limbs and legs and bodies, too overwhelmed by the cramping pain in his middle, the struggle to get breath, by the noise and confusion and the drumming rain to be able to make any real sense out of what was passing all about him.

7

And then there was the sudden slamming of the gates and relative quiet was restored.

Guthrie struggled to his feet, his breath coming in painful gasps. For one terrible moment he thought to see a blade through his guts. But no. Whatever had hit him had left no mark. The butt end of something, then or simply a knee or elbow.

'They took us by the hot springs,' he heard someone say, in a hoarse, panting voice. 'Never even saw them till it was too late.'

Crowded up against the now closed gateway doors was a group of perhaps two dozen ragged, white-faced, battle-haggard men. Many were wounded, some so badly they could not stay upright save with the support of a comrade. Three Sea Wolves lay dead in the gateway, and the mud under the survivors' feet ran brightly wet with crimson blood. Guthrie stared, shocked. Was this all that remained of the force his father had led against the Sea Wolves? He could not believe it.

From the other side of the gate came triumphant howls and shouting.

'There's none left out there alive now,' one of the shattered newcomers gasped as folk looked fearfully towards the gate. The crowd had gathered tight in a nervous mass about the survivors.

'Back off!' Hone Amis yelled at them. 'Back away and give us room here.'

'What happened out there?' a voice shouted.

'Where's Mally?' somebody else shrieked. 'Where's my Mally?'

'Back off, I say!' Hone Amis repeated. 'We must have order here!' He stood surrounded now by a dozen or so of his Militia, and he directed them to push the crowd away. Folk backed off grudgingly.

The man was continuing his story, half doubled over, hands against his thighs, pausing every few words for breath. 'The bastards came over ... over the side of Roary's Hill. We never saw them till ... it was too late.'

'The Reeve,' Hone Amis demanded. 'What of the Reeve?'

The man went silent, then shivered. 'Killed. I saw ... saw the Sea Wolf Chieftain take him through the ... belly with a spear.'

Hone Amis stared.

'It was within the first moments, almost before ... before we knew what was happening. It was uncanny. How did they know about that short cut across Roary's Hill? How did they *know*?'

'What about the younger Reeve, man?' Hone Amis asked. 'What about Garrett?'

'Dead as well,' somebody else replied. 'Both of them dead.'

Hone Amis went pale. '*Both?*'

A great *thwump* suddenly shuddered the stout gateway doors.

'Battering ram,' somebody muttered.

A wail went up from the crowded folk, and they surged away from the gateway in a panicky rush.

'What do we do *now?*' somebody wailed. 'Powers preserve us. Everything's taken from us. It's the end!'

'No!' Hone Amis shouted. He looked across to Guthrie.

Guthrie shivered. His father and Garrett dead? Impossible! Not his father, wide chested and strong as any bull; not Garrett, quick and sure. No. It could *not* be true.

But a part of him believed. And that part of him took a certain bitter satisfaction in the news. He felt a shiver go through him. All his life he had lived as second son, while Garrett the elder took all the privileges. All his life Guthrie had yearned against his second son's fate, neglected, unimportant.

And now ...

'Listen to me!' Hone Amis called out to the crowd. '*Listen to me!*' He stood, arms raised in the rain, shouting at them till they began to listen. 'Reeve Garth is killed. Reeve Garrett Garthson too. But we still have a Reeve. Garth's second son, Guthrie, still lives! These bastarding Sea Wolves have *not* taken everything from us yet.'

All eyes turned on Guthrie. He shivered self-consciously, wiping a muddy string of hair out of his face. This moment was the sudden fulfilment of a thousand adolescent fantasies: his father and elder brother somehow gone, only he remaining, taking for himself the power and the privilege.

But he stood frozen by the very shock of it, sick in his belly.

About him, Militia men waited, the crowded folk waited, expectant. He felt, suddenly, as if he were the axle of some great wheel that had ground to a halt. All the weight of it was balanced upon him alone.

And he knew not what to do.

It was not fair! Garrett would have known how to cope with this situation. Garrett had been properly trained for such things, had the experience for such things. But nothing had ever given the second son that sort of experience.

The crowd shifted, uneasy. The insistent *thwump thwump* of the battering ram against the gate sounded ominously through the rain, and Guthrie felt his heart beating in panicky counterpoint to the ram's rhythm.

This was not the way he had dreamed it would be. This was not the way it was *supposed* to be.

Hone Amis stepped closer towards him. 'The walls,' he said, voice lowered.

'What?' Guthrie responded, not understanding.

'Order them to the walls. Pelt the bastards from above as they batter the gateway.'

Guthrie blinked, shook wet hair out of his face, blinked again. He turned to the gathered people. 'Come away ...' but his voice gave out unexpectedly, becoming a mere croak, and he had to begin again. 'Come away from the gate,' he commanded.

For a long moment, nobody moved. Hone Amis turned to give an order but Guthrie gestured him desperately to silence.

'We will put men up on the walls, pelt them from above as they batter the gateway.' His voice was coming stronger now. 'You can serve no good milling about here. To the walls. The walls!'

He saw the relief now on their faces, as they found a centre to things once again. For an instant he felt a rush of sheerest joy. He was the Reeve at last. He was the hub to their wheel, he the mind, they the limbs. Men sprinted away to do his bidding, heading towards the ladderworks that led up to the crest of the Closter's wooden walls.

But then a voice shouted, '*No!*'

Everybody turned.

From the rear of the yard, walking in measured pace through the cold swirl of the rain, came a procession of grey-robed Closterers. The clustered people made hasty way, backing off to give them a clear road. A double handful of grey-robed figures walked calmly out – the full membership of the Closter as far as Guthrie knew. At their head was the Abbod, hands tucked in the wide sleeves of his robe, face quiet.

'You will never stop the Sea Wolves that way,' he said, drawing to a halt in front of Guthrie and Hone Amis.

'Abbod,' Hone Amis said, sketching a brief, formal bow. He took a breath, glanced quickly at Guthrie, turned back to the grey-robed man before him. 'I did not look to see you out here in the yard, especially not now. For allowing us to take refuge in your Closter, we thank you. But, Abbod, you must continue to stay indoors with your folk, as we agreed. This is no place for you or yours.'

The Abbod shook his head. 'On the contrary, Master Amis. Now is the time you need us most.' The Abbod was tall, overtopping husky Hone Amis by a full head and shoulders. He was not a young man, but neither was he exactly old. His face was framed by the hood of his grey robe, soggy now in the rain like all else, but his eyes shone bright as stones in a sunlit stream.

Guthrie regarded the Closterers uneasily.

The Abbod and his kind were a mystery. A small, quiet group of men and women, they lived here away from the main settlement, in this Closter they had built, and none knew for certain what it was they occupied themselves with behind the high wooden walls here. There were some folk in Riverside who insisted that Reeve Gram, Guthrie's grandfather, had made a mistake in ever giving them permission to build here when Riverside was hardly begun and the first small band of them had walked up from the settled lands southwards. Old Merith Osbart's son, Jon, had been seduced away by them and never seen again, or so it was claimed. And there were stories of Closterers possessing secret teachings. It was known that other Closters existed in the south, and that there was a sometime traffic between the Closter settlement here and those others. Folk had prophesied dire consequences from such southern connections ...

The Closterers, however, did harm to none – quite the opposite in fact, for some of them seemed possessed of healing skills which they plied willingly enough. They minded their own business, punctually contributed the tithes that old Reeve Gram had insisted upon.

Yet they were decidedly not like normal folk. Shepherds spotted them sometimes wandering the hills like sleepwalkers, or seated upon some rock staring into vacant sky for whole days on end ...

Guthrie swallowed, facing them unexpectedly now, trying to reckon what might have spurred the Abbod into coming out into the yard like this after he had agreed it best to keep the Closterers separate from ordinary Vale folk. Guthrie hesitated, not knowing quite how to proceed. Would this Abbod accept direction? There was altogether too much unknown about these Closterers ...

The *thwump* of the battering ram continued to sound through the wind and rain like a great drumbeat.

'Can you not hear *that*, Abbod?' Guthrie demanded. 'It's dangerous out here. Best that you and yours return to shelter.'

The grey-robed Abbod drew closer to Guthrie and looked him – the two were of almost the exact same height – directly in the eye.

11

'Ye have grown quickly accustomed to giving commands, Reeve Guthrie Garthson.' He spoke with a southern accent, yet not nearly as thickly as some of the other Closterers Guthrie had heard. 'But it has been written: "The best of rulers utters no word lightly. He is but a shadow, barely seen. The best of rulers hesitates rightly, seeing what he has foreseen."'

Hone Amis moved up. 'You heard the Reeve. Get back indoors where you and yours belong. As we *agreed*, Abbod!'

But the Abbod stood as he was, and the silent, grey-robed group of men and women behind him. 'Ye will not stop the Sea Wolves by what ye plan here.'

'Go!' Guthrie ordered. 'Get back indoors, to safety, where you ought to be.'

But the Abbod only smiled. He took two steps towards Guthrie, leaned forward, and said, 'Yer self or yer lived life ... which is most near? Yer goods or yer lived life, which is more dear?'

Guthrie shook his head, confused.

'This is no time for silly *talk*, man!' Hone Amis snapped. He glared across at Guthrie. 'I never did hold with this lot being allowed to settle here in the first place. Nothing but a pack of sneaky mumblers ... I've had enough of this!' He turned on the Abbod. 'Get back inside as the Reeve commands!' In a quick rush, he moved forwards and shoved at the grey-robed figure, hard.

The Abbod did not appear to do anything special, yet somehow Hone Amis tumbled awkwardly, flat onto his face in the mud.

Guthrie made a quick warding sign with his fingers, as did several other Vale folk nearby.

Hone Amis scrambled to his feet, scarlet with anger and mortification. He drew his short sword from out of its scabbard at his hip, moving in menace towards the Abbod.

'No!' Guthrie commanded. 'Amis! Leave him be.' He gestured at the sword. 'And put that away.'

For a moment, Hone Amis stood as he was, face clenched, glaring at the Abbod. Then he did as he had been ordered, reluctantly, slamming his blade home in the sheath with an angry *thwunk*.

Guthrie stared uneasily at the Abbod and his folk. The Closterers lived here peaceably enough, apparently doing harm to none ... all that might be true enough. But none knew, truly, what uncanny acts they might be capable of ...

The Abbod raised his hand mildly, palm out. 'Master Amis,

forgive me. I meant no disrespect. But neither I nor mine will return indoors as ye insist.'

Hone Amis stared.

'You would defy me?' Guthrie demanded. He felt his own face flush with anger.

A sudden sheet of cold rain swept across them all, leaving folk spluttering and shivering.

The Abbod shrugged, seemingly no more affected by the rain than by Hone Amis's attempt at attack. 'If that is the way ye wish to see it ... then yes, I must defy ye, young Reeve. But it is for the good of the whole that I do so.'

'How so?' Guthrie demanded.

'Ye will never stop the Sea Wolves by doing as ye plan.'

The battering ram went *thwump thwump*, and the oaken timbers of the gate groaned.

The Abbod raised a hand towards the gateway. 'The gate might hold. Or it might not. But if it does hold, and these Sea Wolves lay siege to the Closter, the advantage is still all theirs. This is no military structure we have built here.' He gestured to the tops of the Closter's wooden walls. 'With no proper walkways, ye cannot place enough men up there to be able to do any serious damage to those outside. And we have no food to feed yer folk. We have scant water supply. They can starve us out easily. Or burn us out, come to that.'

'Not in this rain!' somebody called out.

There was a splutter of nervous laughter from the folk gathered about.

The Abbod smiled. 'Not in this rain, agreed. But the rain will not last forever. Tomorrow, or the next day, all they need do is torch the walls. There is little ye could do to prevent them.'

Guthrie wiped cold water out of his face. 'We could try!'

The Abbod smiled once again. 'A laudable sentiment, my young Reeve. But hardly practical.'

The battering ram continued its hammering against the gate. *Thwump! Thwump! Thwump!*

'So what are *you* suggesting we should do?' Guthrie demanded.

'Let me talk with them.'

Hone Amis snorted. 'And you will do what? Tell them to go home and leave us alone. And I suppose they will just turn about, return to their ships, and leave behind all they have taken from us just because you ask?'

13

The Abbod turned to Guthrie. 'I am no ... ordinary man, young Reeve.'

Looking at the tall, grey-robed figure of the Abbod, standing there as calmly as if this were any ordinary, sunny afternoon, Guthrie felt a shiver go through him.

'Have a man call to them from the walls. Suggest a truce. Say ye wish to talk with them.'

Guthrie hesitated.

The Abbod drew close to him and leaned forward. 'It is yer only hope, young Reeve. I *know*. Ye must trust my knowledge on this.'

Guthrie looked around. Every eye was upon him. He glanced at Hone Amis, hoping for some sort of support, indication of a sensible course, something ...

But Hone Amis only glowered at the Abbod suspiciously, his fist still clenched about the hilt of his sheathed sword.

This was most decidedly *not* as Guthrie had imagined it. He was Reeve, yes – finally! – but there was no joy in it. He was wet through and chilled to the marrow, and he felt sick in the pit of his belly, thinking on what hammered at the Closter doors trying to get in at them. And the folk gathered about him looked, every one, to him for the answer that would save their lives.

At that moment, he did not feel himself possessed of any answers.

'Let me talk with them,' the Abbod insisted.

Guthrie hesitated, despairing.

'Trust me, young Reeve.'

The Abbod's look was clear and compelling. After one last, painful moment's uncertainty, Guthrie nodded. 'Aye ... All right.'

'Send a man to the walls.'

'I shall go myself,' Guthrie replied.

'No!' Hone Amis put in. 'It's too dangerous.'

Guthrie was in no mood to brook constraints from Amis. 'I will do as I wish, Master Amis. And neither you nor anyone else will gainsay me.' He glared at the older man. 'Is that *clear*?'

Hone Amis swallowed, face puckered with surprise. 'Aye ... Reeve.'

'Good.' With that, Guthrie strode towards one of the ladders leading to the wall's top. The gathered folk hovered, uncertain at this sudden and unexpected turn of things, muttering amongst themselves. But Guthrie strode through them without pause and they quickly shifted back out of his path.

Atop the wall, the wind blew in fierce gusts, and Guthrie had to

14

hold up a hand, sheltering his face. There was barely room for him to place his feet upon the narrow little walkway up here, and he had to lean into the wall for support, the wet, weathered roughness of the log framework against his chest. Perched like that, he gazed downwards at the Wolves. There were perhaps six or seven dozens of them, perhaps more. It was difficult to count, what with the still swirling rain and their moving about so. The ram was a great tree, slung between two columns of men. *Thwump! Thwump!*

'Heya!' he shouted down, as loud as he might. '*Heyaaa!*'

He had to shout himself nearly hoarse before attracting their attention. 'We wish a parley,' he called to them then.

Pale, helmed faces stared up at him. Rain glinted off polished iron blades. Guthrie shivered. These men had killed his father, his brother, the Powers alone knew how many others. Out of the rolling sea they had come in their three long black ships, without warning, destroying crops, slaughtering livestock and women and men. And the Abbod wished to *talk* with them? A quick, violent anger choked Guthrie. If he had the power he would have smashed these cursed Sea Wolves to a bloody pulp already. If he were a giant, he could stride through them, like a man through a chicken yard, and crush them utterly.

But such impossible, storybook options were not open to him, and he could think of nothing else to do save what the Abbod insisted.

'We wish a parley,' he called out once more, trying to swallow his anger. 'Who amongst you speaks with authority?'

Below, several of the Sea Wolves had clustered together, their faces tipped up towards him. He saw one of them lift a hand in a gesture. Faintly, he could make out the sound of them talking amongst themselves in their own language, harsh and guttural as the cawing of crows.

What if none of them could understand him?

'We wish a parley,' Guthrie called out one last time. If none down there understood him, then this parley of the Abbod's was obviously not meant to be.

Below, a tall, burly man with a vivid scarlet crest along his helm stood slightly away from the rest. He was mail clad like the others, with a long sword slung about his waist and a long iron war spear in his hand. 'I doo,' he shouted up, brandishing the spear. 'I be Kawdeer, Cheeftann. I vill speek.'

Guthrie almost laughed at the outlandish sound of the other's words. But the man below him shook his spear and glared upwards and that would-be laughter died in Guthrie's throat.

'I be Kawdeer,' the man named himself again, 'Cheeftann of zhe Loong Courrunt Sea Volfes. Call yer own Cheeftann, boy, to coome und speek vith me.'

It took Guthrie a few moments to sort out the Sea Wolf's words. He flushed, understanding. 'I ... I am ...'

Chieftain, he had been about to respond, but at his side, suddenly, he felt the Abbod draw nigh.

'We will open the gates to ye,' the Abbod called down. 'We will talk.'

'No!' Guthrie hissed.

The Sea Wolf Chieftain laughed and brandished his spear triumphantly. 'Ve vill oopen yer gates oorselfes!'

'But at a price,' the Abbod shouted. 'A high price, perhaps. And there is nothing here of value to ye.'

'I shall be zhe joodge of zhat.'

'Ye will lose men. There will be death. And ye will gain nothing here.' The Abbod spoke with such forceful, calm-voiced authority that the Sea Wolf Chieftain paused.

'Und joost who be ye, grey-roobed man? Doo ye speek for zhis place?'

'I am Abbod of this Closter. I speak for all who shelter here within our walls.'

'Ve vill breek yer valls, Grey Roobe!'

The Abbod merely gazed down at him.

Abruptly, the Sea Wolf Chieftain darted forwards and, with a grunt and a quick snap of his arm, flung his spear straight up at the Abbod.

Guthrie threw himself backwards, ducking behind the protection of the wall and hanging there, one-handed. But beside him the Abbod shifted position not at all, merely stood as he was.

With a sick certainty, Guthrie looked up, expecting to see the spear shaft protruding from the Abbod's breast. So much for trying to parley! But no. Incredibly, the Abbod must have somehow plucked the cast spear from out of the very air, for Guthrie saw him standing there holding the Chieftain's weapon up in one hand.

Calmly.

Guthrie felt the hairs along the back of his neck rise like a dog's hackles. Pulling himself to his feet, he peered over the wall's top.

16

Below, the Sea Wolves and their Chieftain were staring, mouths agape.

The Abbod smiled. 'Shall we talk, then?' he called down.

The Chieftain remained silent for long moments, staring upwards, his face clenched with sudden uncertainty. Those about him burst into startled chatter. He silenced them with a barked command. One came up and said something in his ear. He nodded, muttered a response, gestured with an arm in a sweeping motion, and the man backed off. The Chieftain then raised his arms, palms out, looking up at the Abbod. 'Ve vill talk, Grey Roobe. As ye vish it. Oopen yer gates as ye proomised.'

'No!' Guthrie said in the Abbod's ear. 'We cannot trust them. Open the gates and they will rush in and slaughter everybody!'

'Trust me, young Reeve,' was all the Abbod said. 'I have seen into this.'

Guthrie did not know what to do. Open the gates to such men as those below? It was insanity! 'But, Abbod ...'

'*Trust* me, young Reeve.' The Abbod looked at him, a compelling, dark-eyed gaze. 'There is more at stake here than ye can understand.'

Guthrie swallowed. 'I ...'

But the Abbod, with surprising agility, was already descending the ladder groundwards. Of necessity, Guthrie followed after, to find the Abbod waiting for him at the gate, the Sea Wolf's spear held casually still in his hand.

Hone Amis pulled Guthrie a little to one side. 'What is it? What has he said to them?'

Guthrie shook his head. 'He told them we would open the gate.'

'*What?* Is the man mad?'

Guthrie shrugged uncomfortably. It did indeed sound like madness. But Amis had not heard the certainty with which the Abbod spoke, had not seen him somehow snatch that spear out of the very air. 'I think we must do as he says.'

Hone Amis started to remonstrate, but Guthrie cut him off with a sharp gesture. 'We have little choice, Amis. It is as he said. Those cursed Sea Wolves can starve or burn us out as they please. My father and brother are killed. Your Militia is all but shattered. What other option do we have save to trust this Abbod?'

Hone Amis looked unconvinced. 'It is *madness!*'

Guthrie pointed at the Abbod. Folk had backed uneasily away from him. He stood calmly, alone before the gateway but for the

17

Militia that still guarded the doors. The other Closterers remained quietly as they were, unmoved from where they had first come to a halt. They stood as calmly as the Abbod, as if the panic and chaos about them were nothing unusual. 'It is mad times,' Guthrie said uneasily. 'Perhaps it is mad solutions we need.'

Hone Amis shook his head.

Guthrie looked uncertainly at the Militia by the gateway. Would they obey him if he gave them this crazy order to open the doors? And what would the anxious folk crowded in here do? How could he expose them to such danger?

The Abbod, spear still in hand, looked to him with calm, expectant certainty.

Shivering, Guthrie stepped forwards. Ordering the Militia men aside, he slipped the great locking bar from the gateway doors himself.

'It is all right!' he cried at the wail that went up from the gathered people. 'The Abbod will talk with them. The Abbod will *deal* with them!'

Guthrie backed quickly away, dropping the heavy wooden locking bar, and the doors slammed open. The Sea Wolf Chieftain came striding through, laughing, the sword that had hung scabbarded at his waist out now and swinging in his hands. Behind him, bottlenecked in the entrance way, a bristling mob of mailed and crest-helmed Sea Wolves pushed in after him.

Folk faltered back, hands white knuckling weapons. Guthrie backed off with them, cursing himself for a fool to have dropped his sword back where he had and thus leave himself defenceless in the face of what stood now inside the opened gate.

The Abbod strode forwards, alone, barring the Sea Wolves' way.

A hush settled over all. The rain, that had beaten down insistently all day, slackened suddenly away to nothing. A wavery shaft of pale sunlight lit the Closter's yard. Even the wind seemed stilled for the moment.

The Sea Wolf Chieftain paused, looking about. The sunlight caught the scarlet horse hair crest of the war helm he wore, painting the stiff bristles with the shining, living red of fresh blood. 'Soo, Grey Roobe, ye be a man of yer voord.'

The Abbod shrugged, standing his ground. 'And ye, Sea Wolf?'

The Chieftain threw back his head and laughed loudly. 'Ye have nerve, man. I vill grant ye zhat.' He stood staring at the Abbod for a moment. Then, 'Zhat be a good speer ye hoold zhere. I vould have it back.'

'Ye threw it away. Why should I return it to ye?'

'It be Biter. A loongtime companion of mine. I value it, Grey Roobe. Give it back to me und I vill spare yer life.'

The Abbod smiled and hefted the spear casually. 'There is one manner in which I might return it to ye that ye would not like, perhaps.'

The Chieftain took an instinctive step backwards. A tense jitter passed through his men. One of them flung a spear abruptly at the Abbod, a blur of movement. But though the Abbod appeared hardly to shift, the weapon missed, skittering aside him to stick in the mud beyond.

'Enough!' the Sea Wolf Chieftain shouted. He stared at the Abbod. 'Ye said ye vished a parley. Vhat have ye to say, zhen, Grey Roobe?'

The Abbod proffered the spear, held horizontally before him. 'Would ye have yer weapon back?'

The Sea Wolf Chieftain nodded.

'I propose a contest, then. Ye and I.'

'Speer to sword?' the Sea Wolf replied.

The Abbod shook his head.

'Vhat, zhen?'

'A simple contest.'

'*Vhat?*'

'Whichever one of us, unarmed, can make the other do what he wishes, shall have the spear.'

'No veapons?'

'Exactly.' The Abbod smiled. 'But perhaps we should raise the stakes in this game. Whichever one of us wins gains not only yer spear, but all else in this Closter. If ye win, all here is yers ...'

A clamour of sudden dismay went up from the Vale folk gathered at the Abbod's back. But he held up his hands, quieteningly, and such was the presence of him that the hubbub fell way into silence.

'If ye win,' he repeated, 'everything here is yers, buildings, people, livestock, all. To do with as ye wish. But if *I* win ...'

'Everyzhing here, it be myne already,' the Sea Wolf said.

'Not *yet*,' the Abbod replied, hefting the spear. 'And ye would pay a high price for it, believe me.'

The Sea Wolf Chieftain paused. Behind him, his men shifted uneasily. 'But if I can force ye to doo as I vish, zhen all is myne. Freely?'

19

The Abbod nodded, thrusting the spear he held point first into the mud, letting it stand there beside him.

The Sea Wolf Chieftain regarded the Abbod, tall in his grey robes, but thin and light boned. He squared his own thick muscled shoulders and laughed. 'So be it.' Shrugging out of the scabbard's harness, he gave it and the sword he still held into the keeping of a man at his side. His helm, too, he handed over, revealing a craggy face and a head as round and bald as an egg.

'Come, then ... *Egg*,' the Abbod said.

The Sea Wolf Chieftain bristled at the name, his face clouding with quick anger.

'*Egg*,' the Abbod repeated.

The Sea Wolf snarled. 'Ye vill pay for those vords, little man!' He stepped forwards, arms out and reaching. 'Let zhis contest of yers begin.'

But the Abbod held up his hand. 'I win.'

'*Vhat?*'

'I have made ye take part in this contest of mine. I have already made ye do as I wish.' He smiled. 'According to the terms of the contest, I win.'

The Sea Wolf's face crimsoned.

'We made an agreement,' the Abbod said. 'Ye must abide by yer part in it. Yer spear is mine. This place is mine. Ye have lost, *Egg*.'

The Chieftain shook his head angrily. 'I vill have no part in such a shtewpid, *cheating* game as zhis!' Quick as a cat, he whirled about, snatched up the long sword he had given up, and came at the Abbod.

Witnessing this sudden treachery, Guthrie felt his heart kick in his breast. At his side, Hone Amis made to leap forwards, gesturing his Militia to follow. 'No!' Guthrie hissed, for he remembered the thrown spears, and the Abbod saying, *I am no ordinary man*.

Trust me, the Abbod had said.

Guthrie hauled Hone Amis back by the arm. 'Let him be. He knows what he is about.'

And sure enough, the Sea Wolf's rush had slowed to a wary scuttle, for the Abbod stood before him as calm as ever, not even bothering to reach for the spear that still stood planted point first in the mud by his side.

The Sea Wolf raised the long sword two handed.

Still the Abbod stood unmoved.

Weapon up, the Sea Wolf Chieftain hesitated. He looked the

20

Abbod in the face, snarled as if he were indeed a wolf in flesh and not merely name, brandished the blade menacingly. The Abbod flinched not at all. The Chieftain's shoulders slumped. The long iron blade began to droop.

Guthrie let out a sigh of relief.

'*Egg*,' the Abbod said.

Sudden as a lightning clap, the Sea Wolf let out a curse and struck, bringing the blade up in a great, sweeping, crossways slash.

The Abbod moved not at all, save perhaps to lift his chin a little higher, baring his neck more clearly to the blade so that the single stroke decapitated him cleanly.

The head flew sideways, driven along by the force of the blow, and the grey-robed body collapsed, in a scarlet fountaining of blood, to the mud.

Guthrie stared, unbelieving, as the Sea Wolf Chieftain retrieved the severed head. Holding it aloft by the hair, he laughed at the stricken Vale folk. 'Soo much for yer precious vizard!' He turned the limp thing in his hand and looked into the slack white face. 'Zhat is what ye get for trying *tricks*, little man. And foor calling me names.' He laughed again. 'I vin. *Ye* lose!'

The Abbod's dead eyes blinked. The dead mouth, dribbling blood and spittle, opened. In the sudden, stunned hush that enveloped all, the Abbod's head spoke in a harsh, gasping voice: 'Ye are wrong. There is more at stake here than ye will ever know.'

The Sea Wolf Chieftain flung the head away, as if it had bitten him. 'Vizard!' he shrieked, his voice cracking.

From where it lay on the ground, the head smiled – the Abbod's familiar, calm smile – and said, 'Wrong again, *Egg*.'

The Sea Wolf Chieftain howled.

As if that howl were somehow a signal, a great sheet of rain came down upon them in a sudden, drenching burst. The wind screeched through the gateway like a live thing, driving the rain before it, blinding all within. A bolt of blinding lightning struck the wall next to the gate with a great, sizzling *CRAACKKK* and an explosion of thunder that brought folk to their knees. The gateway doors collapsed sideways upon the mass of Sea Wolves clustered there.

Where the bolt itself had struck, the wall beside the gateway splintered, riven like so much kindling, and collapsed outwards in whirling furious sparks.

The Closter's yard erupted into shrieking chaos.

Guthrie stumbled and went down, his ears ringing in pain, half blinded. Somebody fell heavily over him and he pushed the person off, rolling away to come up on his hands and knees. Under his hand, he suddenly felt something round and hard and wet. For a long instant, he could not think what it was. Then he knew, for he heard it speaking in the Abbod's voice. 'Guthrie,' he heard it say. 'Guthrie ...'

There was movement all about him, a frantic scramble of people outwards through the break in the wall the lightning had made. Guthrie could not think clearly. It had all happened too suddenly. Like a leaf in a strong river current, he found himself carried along in the rush, the dead Abbod's head clutched in his hand, stumbling over the charred wall beams, skidding along wet grass, the rain like a solid wall in his face, blinding him.

And then he was away and running, his heart clamouring in his breast, running like a wild thing, mindless and stricken.

II

By the time Alia Bowriss knew anything to be amiss, it was too late.

She was working her way down through the Salter Pass, returning from the high shoulders of the Slate Peaks. On any normal day, coming down through the pass as she was, Alia ought to have been able to gaze out from atop the stone spur of Tally's Bluff and along the curve of the Mira Hills' pine-clad slopes into Reeve Vale itself and the gleaming heave of the sea beyond. But the autumn had commenced early this year, and the intervening distance was shrouded in storm clouds thick as dark wool.

This high, she walked through the bellies of the clouds themselves, along tree-clad slopes shrouded in tendrils of slow-dancing, glowing cloud-mist. A chill glamour was cast upon the silent forest, and Alia slowed suddenly, catching slight, supple movement at the edge of her vision.

Tall, half-glimpsed, gliding shapes, pale and ghost-silent.

Forest Fey.

Or nothing at all, perhaps.

Alia stood transfixed near a small stand of ancient, mossy mountain beeches, still as a tree herself. She blinked, shivering a little in the cloudy dank, staring into the pearly mist.

It was in hopes of just such a communion as this that Alia had taken to the wild Heights; she had been away longer than ever before, long enough utterly to lose track of the days, and had gone far and been alone enough to slide a little out of the ordinary world.

She could perceive the elegant, moving shapes of the Fey more clearly with each breath. Her pulse beat suddenly fast.

All her young life she had yearned, knowing in her heart that the wild lands held a world of hidden wonders, yet never quite able to cross over to them. Sometimes she felt like a crippled bird, trying to learn how to fly, yearning, despairing. At others, she felt it almost happening, felt the mysterious wonder opening to her like a delicate, complex flower.

23

Like now.

She stood unmoving, poised, yearning.

It was said the Fey sometimes gathered ordinary mortal folk to them, across the threshold.

Twice already in the past days had she caught brief glimpses of these pale, elegant-limbed shapes. But none this clear. They were gliding closer to her, and she saw them truly for the first time: tall, pale beings, impossibly thin, with large, unblinking dark eyes and calm faces.

Alia let out a long, sighing breath.

One seemed to draw closer towards her, moving like a great crane in a dance, legs lifting with slow, unhuman grace, stepping towards her, away, towards ...

Alia's heart shivered with a great hope.

And then, in an eyeblink, the Fey were disappeared.

Alia gasped.

And was taken as she stood, shaken and part-way blind to the ordinary world.

Half a dozen ragged men came leaping suddenly out of the beech trees in the fog and tumbled her roughly to the leaf-soaked ground. By instinct, she managed to bring her knee up into the groin of one of them, so that he grunted and fell away from her. And she bit another so that he howled. But there were too many of them. Two pinned her down, while a third methodically smacked her into submission.

'Pull his teeth, ye two,' she heard a voice say.

Hard hands jerked her to her knees and she felt her bow and her quiver of arrows stripped from her. Her sleeping roll, small travel-pack, and belt knife followed. One of her captors yanked her arms painfully up behind her back and twisted them so that she was held there on her knees, head down, half bent over and helpless.

Alia was consumed by a blind rage of frustration at such stupid, interfering fools whose presence had driven the Fey off, ruined *everything*. She tried to twist away from the painful hold on her arms, tried to shout her anger at them. But her mouth was filled with blood and she choked, gagging.

'What's in the bag?' one of the group demanded of the man now holding Alia's travel-pack. 'Anything good?'

'Bet there ain't nothing worth shit in that pack,' put in another. 'This one don't seem no better off than a bush tramp by the looks of 'im.'

'It's yer opinion on the matter that ain't worth shit,' the man holding Alia's pack responded.

'Open the pack, Shadders,' another said.

Alia shuddered. She blinked, shook her head, took a long, shuddering breath, trying to clear her mind. The rage fell away from her, giving way to the first cold shivers of fear. Her heart laboured. Who *were* these men? Not Vale men, certainly. They had the breathy accent and queer speech of Southerners, and they were ragged and thin and dirty. And each, she now saw, looking up at them through the disarrayed mass of her long auburn hair, was armed with sword or dagger, several carried crossbows, and one now her own hunter's longbow. Their faces had the hard look of desperate men.

Alia's own face throbbed painfully where they had hit her and her mouth was still full of the wet-iron taste of blood. She felt a cold shudder go through her guts.

Bandits, sure as sure.

'Kill the bastard now, I say, and have done with him,' muttered the man rummaging through Alia's pack. He was the youngest of the lot, this one, not much older than Alia herself. His face was partly covered with the pale, wispy beginnings of a beard through which a scattering of inflamed pimples showed. Out of Alia's pack he drew the small rack of jerked venison she had been saving. He squinted at it for a moment with weak blue eyes, and then began to chew on it.

'Gimme a bite, Shadders,' one of the others demanded.

The younger man shrugged and took another chew of the venison. 'When I'm ready, Gill. When I'm ready.'

The man named Gill took a menacing step forwards. He was grey-grizzled and husky, with a noticeable limp, his face hard and twisted as an old tree. 'Don't mess me about, ye pup. I want ...'

For a moment, Alia hoped that these men would go at each other tooth and nail, like mangy hill rams so caught up in bashing horns at each other they were blind to all else. She held her breath, hoping. Only let her luck hold here, and perhaps the rest would join in too – they were a ragged, angry enough looking lot. She might have a chance to escape away in the mêlée ...

But it proved a forlorn hope.

'Shut up, the two of ye!' cried the man who had slapped Alia. He was a thin fellow with a jagged scar marring the left side of his face

25

from chin to forehead. 'I'm sick of ye two chivvying each other. We got to get this boy here trussed up and back to camp.'

'Kill 'im ... mumphh ... now,' repeated the one chewing the venison. 'Don't see why ... mumphh ... we should have to ...'

''Cause that's what we been told to do!' snapped Scarface. 'Torno's orders.'

'Feck Torno!'

Scarface rounded on him. 'Ye stupid little shit! Ye don't understand nothing, do ye, Shadders? This ain't no little cut and run caper we're part of here. It's the likes of *ye* that'll ...'

'Hoi!' one of the others said, and Alia felt sudden hands at her breasts under the brown-green dyed leather of her jerkin. 'This ain't no boy.'

Scarface whirled.

'Have a feel.'

Scarface did. Then he jerked Alia's auburn hair out of her face and yanked her head back so that her features were revealed clearly. 'Young. And a nice enough looking little bitch under the dirt, I reckon, once a man sees what she rightly is.'

Alia spat in his face.

'But with a temper.' Scarface back-handed her, hard, and Alia tasted more blood. 'Mind yer manners, girl!'

'Been a *long* while since I had me a woman,' the one named Shadders said, chewing still at Alia's venison. He eyed Alia hungrily. ''Specially a ... mumphh ... young firm one like this.'

The grey-grizzled man who had earlier demanded a piece of the venison laughed. 'Ye? Ye ain't never no much as come within *sniffin'* distance of a real woman, ye puppy.'

Young Shadders reddened. 'Watch yer tongue, Gill, or I'll –'

'Ye'll what? Ye little snot-nosed git.'

'Enough!' snapped Scarface. 'If ye two don't –'

A sudden call sounded from beyond the beeches. Alia started, as did the men about her. After a moment's pause, however, Scarface replied, a ululating, wordless cry. A new group came out from amongst the cloud-shrouded trees, more of the same ragged, armed, hard-faced sort, making perhaps a dozen and a half all told, now. Perhaps more.

There had been bandits in the wild hills beyond the borders of Reeve Vale ever since Alia could remember, harrying the outlying farms occasionally, taking unwary travellers if they could. Human

26

wolves they were, and in bad seasons Master Hone Amis Latirson would take his Militia out and run them off.

But it had been long since any hunter had been taken by a bandit. Hunters' vengeance was swift and certain, and the hunters knew these hills like nobody else. Hill bandits were aware of this well enough in the ordinary course of things.

Alia only hoped this lot were aware of it.

But she felt a sickening uncertainty.

One of the newcomers stood in advance of the rest, hands on hips, looking down at Alia. He was a short man but thick-set, with long arms and a black spade of a beard above which were dark, calculating eyes. 'And what have we here?' he demanded.

'We found this ... *boy* trying to sneak up on the camp,' Scarface replied.

The word 'boy' evoked a suppressed titter from the men clustered about Alia.

The bearded man eyed the lot of them suspiciously. He took a step forward.

'Looks like he might be one of them hunters ye told us to look out for, Sethir,' Scarface said.

'He weren't much, though,' young Shadders spoke up quickly. 'He were just standing here in the mist, trying to get a bearing on our camp clearing, I reckon. We took him before he knew what was happening.' Young Shadders walked over and offered the newcomer some venison. 'No need for ye to worry yerself about him, Sethir. Here. Take the rest o' this jerky. We'll truss this boy up proper and bring him on into camp for ye.'

'That's right, Sethir,' one of the others put in quickly. 'No need for ye to worry yerself. We'll bring him in. He's just a no-account boy. Ye can go on about yer rounds.'

The bearded man they had named Sethir ignored the proferred venison and stood as he was, long arms crossed over his thick chest, staring down at Alia. 'Hunter?' he demanded of her.

Alia nodded. Without thinking, she twisted her right arm as far as she might in the painful grip her captors still had on her, and lifted it to try to show him the embroidered image of a stag's head on her upper sleeve. She was prouder of that small image than of anything else in her life, and she displayed it to him triumphantly before realizing that he could know nothing about what the image meant.

But to her surprise he nodded stiffly. 'Hunter indeed.'

Alia blinked. How could this outland bandit know about the stag

27

crest of the Reeve Vale hunters? She scrutinized him more closely. He was indistinguishable from the others, ragged as any of them. Only his manner set him apart a little, and the fact that his accent was noticeably less southern.

'If you recognize me for who and what I am,' she told him defiantly, 'let me go.'

At the sound of her voice, the man's face darkened. He looked at the men about her. '*Boy*, you say! Do you think me stupid? Let her up.'

The men muttered sullenly.

'Let her up!'

Grudgingly, they obeyed.

Alia scrambled awkwardly up from her knees, her heart beating hard with sudden hope. She flexed her arms experimentally, wincing at the stab of pain the movement caused. 'Let me go,' she said to the bearded man. 'I don't know who you are or what you want, but you can only bring trouble to yourselves by troubling me. If you know what I am, you *know* that. Beware hunters' vengeance! Leave me be if you value your lives.'

Such was the certainty in her voice that some of the men clustered about her muttered amongst themselves in momentary unease. But the only response Sethir showed was a slow stare and a scratch at the thick bush of his beard. Then he smiled, a predatory flash of yellow teeth under black moustaches. 'Bring her along to camp,' he said, gesturing to the men at his back. 'Torno likes them young.'

A chorus of disgruntled mutterings greeted this from those clustered possessively about Alia.

'You didn't think you were going to have her right here on the ground, did you?' Sethir laughed. 'All of you together in the fog under the beeches? Wouldn't have been much left for Torno, would there?'

'*We* found her,' complained young Shadders. 'Why should Torno get her?'

'Because,' said the bearded man, 'that is the way of it, boy.'

'Just like that?'

Bearded Sethir nodded.

'Torno gets her,' Scarface said, 'and the rest of us who *found* her, we get nothing?'

'Exactly,' Sethir replied.

'And ye calls that fair?'

28

'Fair enough. Unless ...' quick as a heartbeat, Sethir drew the long knife that hung on his belt and padded forwards, light on his feet for all his thicksetness. 'Unless you want a blade in the guts for your pains.'

Scarface backed quickly off. 'Take her, then. Damn ye!'

The bearded man executed a deep, mock bow. 'Such generosity touches my heart.' He gestured to the men at his back once again, and two of them came forwards and made to take Alia by the arms.

She managed to elbow one of them in the throat, twisted free from the other, and made a dash for freedom through the curling mist.

Panic gave her wings. Things were gone terribly wrong, that bandits such as these should show no fear of hunters. And they seemed far too organized than mere bandits had any right to be. It was not just herself she had to save now; she must get back to Hunters Camp and pass the warning on to Reeve Vale.

But the bandits were too many and too close. She stood no chance. They ran her down all too easily, and her attempt at freedom gained her nothing but more bruises.

The bandit camp was far, far larger than Alia had anticipated. Seeing it come out of the mist suddenly clear below, she felt her guts twist in alarm. From the looks of things, there might easily be over a hundred men here. More. What was happening? It was unheard of, so many being gathered together like this in the wild border country of the Hills.

The new lot under the orders of bearded Sethir had bound her hands tight behind the small of her back and looped a length of coarse, braided rope about her neck. One of them tugged at her now, her original captors left behind, jerking her along downslope between the screen of mountain beeches that partly shielded the hollow where the camp was. The ground was thick with shed beech leaves, and their feet swished soggily as they walked. Alia shook with the indignation of it, being led along like a tethered beast.

A man stepped up beside her, matching his pace to her stumbling one. He grinned at his companions. 'Shame to let Torno be the only one having all the fun,' he said, wheezing foul breath into Alia's face. He cupped a hand quickly about one of her breasts, squeezing it with painful force through the leather of her hunting shirt. 'Oooh ... Ye ought to feel that, lads.' He made an exaggerated, blissed-out face. 'Like a soft little animal, that is.'

29

Sethir shoved him aside. 'She's not your meat. Leave her be.'
Alia shuddered.

Down they dragged her, helpless, into the camp.

From every corner, men came up – only dim moving shapes in the cloud mist at first, and then, suddenly, ragged and hungry faced and all too clear. They surged forwards like ants to honey, calling out questions, making comments, all eyes upon Alia.

Bearded Sethir himself took hold of her tether and hauled Alia quickly away and into a canvas tent at the camp's far edge. Once inside, he tripped her, shoving her roughly, face first into the ground. Before she could do anything, he was upon her, one knee jammed painfully against her back, a hand forcing her face into dank, root-laced earth. She felt something cold press against her wrists. Unexpectedly, her hands dropped free. He pulled away from her then, leaving her in a heap, gasping. 'Stay here. Inside,' he ordered, 'if you value your safety.' Without another word, he turned and quickly ducked back out of the tent.

Alia lay as she was, too shaken and sick and quivery for the moment to try moving. Her arms throbbed with pain, and she could still taste the blood from where Scarface had slapped her. Her heart beat like a crazy thing.

From outside, she could hear the noise of the camp, an aggressive, communal buzz, as from so many aroused bees in a hive.

It was all she could do, for a moment, not to burst into hysterical weeping. She was alone, far from her own folk, and helpless. She curled up foetally, hugging herself, sobbing in heaves. Closing her eyes, she wailed in silent distress, calling out to any wandering hunter that might be in the vicinity, calling desperately for succour.

But such a call was, of course, no use whatsoever. Only in child's tales were folk able to call spirit to spirit in that manner. This was no child's tale she was now in the midst of. She was all alone.

Fear gripped her like a live thing in her guts.

'Torno likes them young,' the bearded man named Sethir had said. It was all too clear what *that* meant. Alia shuddered, thinking on what manner of man it would take to lead the kind of brutish, rag-tag mob she had seen in this camp.

'Calm,' she told herself, trying to take long, slow breaths. '*Calm.*'

But it seemed impossible to still her frantic heart. Her breath came in painful gasps, as if somebody had cinched a cord too tightly about her ribs. She felt the world around her grow dark, pulsing, a great dark current that swept her along, whirling, swirling ...

30

Then a pale globe of some sort was hovering inexplicably above her, like a little moon, mottled as a moon might be, dark and light and ...

Alia blinked and shook herself. No moon at all.

A man's face.

'She'll do,' somebody said.

'Aye. I thought so the moment I saw her.'

Alia recognized this second voice: bearded Sethir.

The face above her drifted away.

Alia swallowed. She felt sick and dizzy, as if somebody had slipped her some strong potion. Yet she had imbibed nothing. She blinked, squinting to focus on her surroundings, fighting the strange disorientation that had overcome her until the dim interior of the tent began to take proper shape about her. She made out Sethir by the tent's entrance, his dark, calculating eyes intent upon her. Between him and her stood another man.

He was not young, this other, but he stood slim and elegant for all that. He was dressed in a tunic of soft, shining material, crimson as good wine, and flowing satin breeches that were charcoal black, tucked into high-topped, finely crafted leather boots of a rich mahogany hue. A long traveller's cloak, black with crimson lining, hung from his shoulders. His face was clean shaven and extraordinarily handsome, with high, well-formed cheek bones, eyes blue as a summer morning sky, and long hair black as the cloak and breeches he wore.

But the most striking aspect to him was the jewels: each of his ears was studded with multiple gold plugs in which rubies sparkled; he wore necklaces, bracelets, rings; his boot tops were interlaced with gold filigree work; his cloak was stitched through with small, glittering precious stones. As he moved, all this jewellery tinkled softly, like tiny wind chimes, a subtle, extraordinary sound.

Alia stared, not knowing what to make of such a figure. He stood out amongst the rest of the men here like a sleek hound amongst tatty rats.

He bowed to her, an elegant, mocking motion. 'Ye is welcome to our humble camp.' He spoke with a southern accent, his voice as mocking as his movements. In his right hand, he held a small linen poesy bag, sweet smelling, which he lifted to his nostrils. The other hand held a short, stout staff of some strange sort, with a largish, round object attached to the top of it.

Alia stared, wide-eyed, at that staff. Some smooth, oiled wood

31

formed the haft, gleaming in the tent's dim light. An intricate tanglewood of carvings twined up it. But it was the round thing capping the haft that suddenly had all Alia's attention.

A dead man's skull, dark with age and wear.

Against the peat-brown bone, gold filigree work glinted. A myriad little jewels beaded that filigree, like shining, rainbow-tinted water droplets sparkling on a gilded spider's web laid across the dead bone.

It was beautiful and terrible, and it made Alia's stomach curdle just to look upon it.

She turned away, the small hairs on her neck bristling, and focused instead on Sethir – his was the more comfortable direction.

Her heart was somehow more calm now than it had been, and her breathing too. She knew this Sethir to be a figure of at least some authority here. She took a long breath, gathering herself. 'Let me go,' she said to him, determined to brazen things out. 'You know me for what I am. Let me go if you value your own safety. Hunters' vengeance is swift and certain.'

The jewelled man laughed, a cold sound.

Sethir smiled in his beard. 'I know you, all right. One of Charrer Mysha's brats for certain. Daughter of some grubby crofter, or shepherd, no doubt. Your father beat you, or some such, and you used to run off into the hills, aching and bruised, and yearning for escape. And when you were old enough, you fended off the fumbling advances of the sweaty boys, knowing yourself destined for better things, hating the narrow little life you had been born into, yearning for something better, freer, finer.' Sethir laughed a mocking laugh. 'And so, when you could, you ran off into the wilds to Mysha, like the others of your sort.'

Alia felt herself flush. It was a humiliatingly accurate portrait, that, twisted and mocking though it might be.

'Aye, I *know* you all right, girl,' Sethir went on. 'I know your type well enough. Whiners and losers, self-indulgent complainers who think they're better than ordinary folk. Well, the world is changing, girl. *Your* time is passing.'

Alia stared. 'Who *are* you?'

Sethir stared her back, his face dark with emotion. 'One who knows the Vale all too well.'

'But how do you –'

'Enough!' Sethir snapped. 'I have no intention of *discussing* matters with you.'

The jewelled man laughed his chill laugh once more.

Alia tried to ignore him.

'So ye deem ye know this girl, Sethir?' the jewelled man asked.

Sethir nodded. 'Well enough.'

Again, came the chill laugh. 'She is far more than ye can guess.'

Sethir scowled. 'Meaning what?'

The jewelled man put aside the poesy bag he had been holding and stroked the dome of the skull that adorned his staff, running his long pale fingers across the dark bone in a languid caress. Alia tried to look away from him but, to her consternation, found she could not. 'She is one who sees into the dim edges of the world. One who sees what others cannot.'

Alia shivered. The man's eyes held steady on her, unwavering, the intensity of that gaze somehow a kind of violation. And yet ... yet there was something compelling, something inviting about that gaze as well.

What manner of man was this?

'Isn't that right, girl?' he persisted.

Alia was not sure what he might mean. Surely he could not know of her ability – half-ability, rather – to see the wild forest Fey?

The jewelled man slowly canted the staff in his hands until the face of the skull directly fronted her. The gold filigree work glinted mesmerically on the old bone. Alia gasped. For a moment, it seemed that a pair of softly luminous eyes had stared at her from out of the skull's empty, dead sockets.

The jewelled man gazed at her. He licked his lower lip, slowly. ''Tis a shame to have to sacrifice ye. I could use such a one as ye. Ye has been underrated, girl.'

Alia shuddered. This strange man repelled and yet somehow attracted her at the same time. He seemed to see into her as none other ever had ...

'What are you on about?' Sethir demanded irritably. 'You know what we must do here, what we *agreed* to do here. This is too good an opportunity that's been handed to us. You're not going to back out of this now, Tasamin!'

The jewelled man raised one dark eyebrow. 'And if I decide to? What could ye do about it?'

Sethir scowled. 'Do not underestimate me.'

The jewelled man smiled thinly. 'That, never. But see ye does not commit the same mistake.'

Sethir glared at him for a long moment, then shrugged. 'Well enough.' He gestured to Alia. 'We are agreed, then, upon her?'

The jewelled man hesitated, looked sideways at Alia for a long moment, then shrugged, nodded. 'Agreed.'

'And you will back me, afterwards.'

'As we agreed.'

Sethir nodded in satisfaction. 'Good!'

Alia looked from one to the other, uneasy. She reached a hand surreptitiously down to her right leg, to the top of the high, doeskin hunter's boot she wore. Her bow, her quiver of arrows, her belt knife, all had been taken from her. But her captors had overlooked the slim little blade she kept sheathed in her right boot. She was not altogether helpless.

The jewelled man turned, his dark, unwinking eyes fixed on her.

Alia did not know if he had understood the movement of her hand. She tried to keep still, her fingers curled about the knife's hilt under the lip of her boot-top. Her heart beat painfully hard. Just let him come a little closer, or Sethir ...

But the jewelled man kept his distance. His gaze went from her face to the hand at her boot-top and back to her face once more, slowly. He smiled a thin, humourless smile. 'Sleep, girl,' he said. He wafted his skull-topped staff at her, while from his other hand a twinkling network of glinting jewellery had appeared, pulsing, eye-catching ... 'Sleep.'

Alia struggled, her heart thumping in fright. The eyes in the skull seemed to gaze at her, luminous as if clusters of fireflies nested in the dead sockets.

'Sleep ...'

She let the boot knife go, rubbed at her eyes, feeling them heavy, heavy.

'*Sleep* ...'

Slowly, heartbeat by heartbeat, Alia came back to herself.

The tent's interior was very dim now. She stretched, groaning, for she had slept twisted somehow, and tried to sit up. Her head throbbed and her face, where she had been slapped, was puffy and stiff and sore. Her mouth felt dry as tinder-bark.

With a start, she recalled Sethir and the jewelled man and all. The remembrance made her shudder. She reached a quick hand down to her boot top, but the little knife was still there. She sighed, shook her head, hunched where she was near the tent's back wall, too stiff to move further for the moment, cold and shivering, miserable and achy and confused.

Time dribbled by. Alia's arms ached sullenly. Her bruised face throbbed. She shifted, trying to sit up, grunted at the pain the movement caused her stiffened limbs. Weariness gripped her. Her thoughts were fuzzy, vague, like small creatures lost in a muddy current ...

And then the sudden rasp and flap of canvas brought her alert with a start.

It was dusk outside, just this side of the night's true dark. Through the tent's entrance way, his form lit by the glow of a small, hand-held candle-lantern, a great bear of a man came stumping in. A dark thatch of beard covered his chest, coming up over his cheeks almost to his eyes, and long, unruly hair came down low over his brows, so that his eyes seemed to peer at her from hedges of dark hair. And he stank, a cheesy, rank odour, strong as cow shit in a barn.

He held up the candle-lantern and stood silent, scratching vigorously at his armpit with his free hand, staring at her hungrily. The arm holding the lantern was thick around as one of Alia's thighs. He gazed at her for long moments, like a farmer studying a brood cow, then grinned, a mere gap-toothed hole in the beard.

Alia had expected some word from him, command, threat, question. Something. But he remained dead silent. Putting the lantern down, he shrugged out of the leather jerkin he wore.

His torso and arms were covered in dark, wiry hair. In the lantern's wavering candlelight Alia could see the gleam of sweat through it. He began to undo his leggings.

Shuddering, Alia tried to slither as far from him as she could in the confines of the small tent. She reached a shaking hand down to her boot knife. It was no dreadful weapon, her little blade, but it was enough to plant between a man's ribs or up under the hollow of his chin and send his spirit off into the Shadowlands.

Still without a word, the man slid out of his leggings and stood before her, naked and hairy and huge, disgusting as any troll out of a child's story.

The rank smell of him nearly made her gag.

She gripped the hilt of the knife hard. Panting a little still, she got her feet under her.

He came at her, arms out, male member up and swinging like a club.

She struggled to her feet and backed away from him, her legs shaky and weak enough to make her ridiculously awkward. Her

35

beating heart faltered. He towered over her like some huge, predatory beast. Her head came no higher than to his sternum. The little knife clutched in her hand suddenly seemed a pitiful thing against him, and she felt momentarily paralysed, like a hapless bird before some huge serpent.

He grinned, gap-toothed and ugly, and reached out a hairy paw to her.

Alia lashed out instinctively with the knife, slashing him across the palm.

He snatched the hand back, grunting. For an uncertain moment he paused, eyes on the knife. Then he came at her again, bleeding hand out for her, grinning no longer.

Alia tried to duck past him and out the tent, but he moved with unnerving quickness for such a huge man and caught her by the shoulder. She stabbed at him, felt the blade bite, but her knife hand was engulfed in one of his and the little weapon was ripped from her grasp. She beat at him with her fists, but he merely laughed.

Grabbing her by the length of her hair, he hauled her to the back of the tent, flung her down, dropped next to her, and began tearing at her breeches. Desperate, she tried to pull his hands away. It was no use. She was helpless.

But before he had managed to yank her breeches more than part way down her thighs, a sudden sound from the tent's entrance way made him turn.

'Torno!' somebody said.

'Out!' he grunted over his shoulder, the first word Alia had heard from him. 'I said I wasn't to be disturbed!'

Squinting past a naked, hairy shoulder, Alia saw bearded Sethir standing in the tent's entrance.

Torno twisted about, one hand still holding Alia pinned squirming to the ground. 'Sethir! I don' care what ye mights be wantin'. Get *out*. Now!'

But by way of response, Sethir drew the long knife that hung on his belt and leaped into the tent. Naked blade in hand, he flung himself upon Torno. The force of his sudden attack dragged Torno from Alia, leaving her abruptly free.

The two men tumbled across the tent. Sethir's blade came up to strike, but a hairy hand stopped it short. Torno grunted, thrusting Sethir down. The sheer brute strength of the man seemed unstoppable.

It was long moments before Alia could regain possession of her wits and her limbs. Hitching up her breeches, she stumbled across to where her own little knife still lay on the ground and grabbed it up.

'Help me, girl,' Sethir gasped.

He was by far the smaller man, and struggling against Torno's greater weight and strength. But he managed to slide half out from Torno's grip. Quick as an eel, he twisted himself about and took the bigger man from behind, holding him by the matted hair and one huge arm. He had no breath left for words, but Alia saw the appeal in his face. Sethir's blade had been flung out of his hold and halfway across the tent.

Torno thrashed about like an enraged bear, and already Sethir's desperate grip was loosening.

Alia slipped forwards, her heart thumping. The two men lay virtually still now, grunting and hissing, locked and straining against each other.

Then Sethir heaved, and for a moment Torno was exposed to her, belly and throat. She saw the animal flare of rage in Torno's eyes. Dodging sideways, she darted in, took her knife in both hands, and drove it up under his chin with all the strength she had, feeling the thrust of the blow all the way up to her shoulder joints as the little blade grated against bone.

Torno thrashed like a stranded fish, but she held on, twisting the knife, forcing it up and up, her hands buried under the dirty mat of his beard, hard up against his chin.

When it was over, she pulled away, gasping, hands and forearms sticky wet with hot blood. She felt a thrill of sudden, terrible satisfaction, seeing the still, hairy body before her.

Sethir rolled to his knees, his head hanging, breath coming in ragged, heaving pants. He looked up at her. 'Go! Get ... get away from here ... fast ... fast as you can.'

Alia stared at him.

He struggled to his feet, snatched up his blade where it lay on the ground, and made a long, vertical slash through the tent's back wall. 'Go!' he hissed, lifting one side of the slash.

Alia made to retrieve her own knife, but he gestured her impatiently on. 'No time for that,' he gasped, his chest heaving still. 'Quick! Get ... get *out* of here.'

She stood shivering, panting, heart still beating hard, staring at the hulk of the dead bandit Chief.

'Go!' Sethir repeated, reaching for her.

Alia went, letting him thrust her out through the tear in the

37

tent's canvas wall, and then stumbling confusedly off through the darkness.

Dank cloud mist still hung thick over everything, and within instants the tent was obscured behind her. She slowed, shivering in the cold, wet night air, unsure which way to go. She had the whole of the encampment to slip through before she might gain the safety of the forest itself. But as long as nobody came to investigate the sounds of the struggle in the tent, she reckoned to have time enough to get away. With luck, any who might have heard would just accept such a ruckus as the throws of passion.

Alia stood as she was, breathing soft as she could. Her heart beat painfully hard still, and her legs quivered. It took real effort to keep her breathing quiet. She could not understand why this Sethir had come to her aid. It seemed to make no sense.

As her eyes grew accustomed to it, Alia realized that the night's dark about her was laced with an uncertain luminescence. The moon was only a few days from full, and it seemed as if the veil of cloud mist somehow trapped the silvery moonlight in a shifting, gossamer web. Alia could make out dim man-shapes in that strange, glowing, mist-shifting not-quite-darkness. Away to her left, she heard muffled voices. The dim brassy flicker of a watch fire showed. Quiet as could be, feeling a cautious way through the soaked beech leaves underfoot, she began to creep off in the opposite direction.

All was silent. All was well. She quickened her pace a little, beginning to feel now that she could indeed make good on this unlooked chance for escape.

And then, from behind her, a shout went up. 'She's killed him! The little bitch has *killed* Torno!'

Sethir's voice.

Alia's first instinct was to turn and flee, but she held herself in check. The tent was still scarce a score of paces behind her, and she had most of the camp yet to negotiate. The enshrouding mist was her best ally here now. So she crouched where she was, held herself still as a hunted fawn, heart pounding, and listened.

Shouts and callings. The slap of running feet. Near her, a dark form came rushing past, slipped, and stumbled to his knees. Cursing, he scrambled up in a shower of soggy leaves and continued on, like all the rest, towards Torno's tent.

What was Sethir about?

The hubbub rose to sudden, noisy shouting, then died away into nothing. 'I was passing by,' Alia heard Sethir telling them, 'and heard a strange noise. Inside the tent, I found Torno like this. Look! See the wound in his throat under the beard? Stuck it to him while he mounted her, the little bitch!'

And angry chorus of mutterings greeted this.

'How could a mere girl ... a *girl* do for Torno?' somebody demanded querulously.

'She was a hunter,' came Sethir's quick response. 'You've been told about them. And she was armed. Those fools who took her didn't search her properly. She had a blade in her boot. Look! See? That's her blade.'

'How do ye know that?' somebody demanded.

'Torno was still alive when Sethir found him.' This was another voice, one it took Alia a few moments to identify: the jewelled man's.

'He told me ...' Sethir was saying. 'He told me to take charge.'

A sputter of uneasy mutterings.

'I was there,' Alia heard the jewelled man say quickly. 'I heard! Torno gave the leadership over to Sethir.'

'And he told me to *get* that little bitch for him!' Sethir added quickly.

More mutterings, angry this time.

'Look at him!' Sethir cried. 'Look at what she *did* to him.'

Alia crouched, frozen. What was the man on about?

'She cut it right off!' somebody said.

'Must'uv took it as a trophy.'

'The sick little bitch!'

'We'll *get* her for this!'

'Oh, we'll get her all right!' Sethir's voice once more. 'She can't have got far. Torno was still alive when I found him. She can't have got out of camp yet.'

'After the bitch!' a dozen voices chorused.

Alia leaped to her feet and fled, crashing blindly through the edge of a fire-pit, heedless of whatever noise she might make.

From behind, the shout went up as they heard her.

A tree reared up unexpectedly in front of her through the mist and Alia carommed painfully off it, cartwheeling to her knees before she could gain her balance again.

Behind her, men howled like demon hounds.

Something hissed by her left cheek and *thwunked* into the bole of the tree against which she had stumbled – a quivering crossbow bolt. Scrambling desperately to her feet, Alia skittered away, putting

39

the tree behind her for cover, running hard as she could, her lungs burning, half blind in the mist, hoping some Power might guide her feet so she did not step into a badger hole or trip unexpectedly to land sprawling, head first against some tree's unyielding root.

'There she is!' Sethir's voice again. 'She's getting away. Catch her, you fools, before she reaches the cover of the trees. *Catch her!*'

Alia was running downslope, her feet skidding wildly on the treacherous, leaf-slicked ground. She heard again the nasty hissing of crossbow bolts through the mist and the *thwunk* as they struck wood. Before her, she could just make out the rearing, twisted columns of the beeches bordering the camp's verge. She fell amongst them, bouncing from one wet trunk to another, hauling herself along and through them.

She stumbled, gasping, her side stitched up with pain from this mad running. She heard shouting – behind her, on either side. There were too many, too close. She had not got enough of a head start.

Desperately, she flung herself down a dark slope, heedless of the possibility of a fall, and into a thicket. Deeper she wormed herself, hugging the wet ground, hoping against hope that her pursuers might dash right past.

And they did just that. Or so it seemed. The sounds of pursuit dwindled.

But then, through the thicket's screen of braided limbs, she caught a quick glimpse of movement in the mist off to her left.

Utterly silent movement.

Huge dark eyes gazed at her from a moon-pale face, a shimmering, half-guessed visage, almost transparent at moments, wavering in and out of solidity.

Alia gasped.

The Fey glided close to her thicket, its dark eyes unblinkingly fixed on her. Alia felt the hairs at the back of her scalp shiver queerly. She could read no familiar, human expression on that strange, intent face. It was like a man's face, and yet it was not. Pale as new bone, long jawed and hairless. The pale skin glimmered softly, like pearl in the faint moon-glow of the cloud mist.

Alia stared, her heart in her mouth.

But the Fey turned from her abruptly, flicking its dark gaze across the far slope with a quick, fluid motion of its head. Just that quick gaze, and then it was gone from her sight like a curl of smoke whipped away by the wind.

Gone so utterly, she was not certain it had ever, in fact, been more than a figure of her own imagining.

Something crashed suddenly near her and she scrunched up small as could be, trying to bury herself deeper in the thicket's protection.

A dark figure, half glimpsed, bounded past.

But before she could let out a breath, it skidded, whirled, turned back. It hesitated for one long instant, then plunged unerringly into her thicket, hands reaching for her.

Alia felt herself torn out of her concealment and hauled aloft as if she were no more than a little child. She beat at the hands that held her, but it was like beating at a tree, so hard and unyielding were they.

And then, in the dim, uncertain luminescence of the night-mist, she saw what it was that had hold of her. Her heart kicked against her ribs.

A thing out of childhood nightmare, it seemed. No manner of creature at *all* like the Fey ...

A demon face. Glittering, inhumanly huge eyes. Bared tusks the length of a grown man's fingers.

Impossible, terrible thing ...

Shouts and callings began to sound suddenly in the near distance as her pursuers beat their way back, growing louder each moment. Alia heard a crackling of branches on the far side of the thicket in which she had crouched.

The demon-creature that gripped her glanced quickly about, its yellow eyes shimmering eerily in the misty half-dark, then bounded away. Alia twisted and struggled desperately in its grip, but it merely clamped an arm about her more tightly and she gasped, feeling her ribs compressed painfully.

It was a wild, downslope dash, branches slapping into her, the demon leaping in great, inhuman strides, sure footed in the half-dark as any cat.

Behind, the shouts of her pursuers began to fade.

Abruptly, they shot out of the cloud-mist, which fell rapidly away behind, transforming to a moving ceiling lit by pale moon-glow. The demon-creature slowed its impossible speed a little, moving through the dark at a more nearly human pace.

It shifted her, swinging her onto one shoulder like a sack of beets. Alia did not try to resist; there was nothing she could do against such strength.

41

Onwards it went, well beyond the beeches now, into the long sweep of pines that covered most of the hillslopes. It was no longer raining here on the lower slopes, but the woods were soaked. The creature vaulted rain-slicked rock, skidded through puddles, burst through screens of pine bows in explosions of water, seemingly indefatigable.

And then it paused, going still, listening.

Silence, save for the little normal sounds of the forest.

The demon peered along their back-trail in the dark, obviously listening. It snuffled, shook its ugly head. Alia heard it sigh a long, slow breath. After all the mad dash they had made, it seemed not to be breathing hard at all.

Alia shuddered. What manner of creature was this?

Unexpectedly, it slipped her from its shoulder and placed her on her feet on the wet, needle-thick ground. One hard hand rested on her shoulder for a long moment, then lifted.

Alia stood unmoving, her heart hammering, not knowing what to expect.

The great, inhuman eyes gazed at her. For a moment, the shifting clouds overhead thinned, and the woods were lit by a brief, moving glow of moonlight. The demon's eyes glowed yellow and eerily shining as a cat's. Alia felt a sick panic. It was impossible to read any truly recognizable human emotion on that demonic face, but the way it stared at her made her shiver. It was a hungry look, an open-mouthed, covetous look.

She tried to dart away, but it grabbed for her, catching her by the arm. Its free hand came up, and Alia saw something glint suddenly in the dark – a blade! She tried to wrench free but the thing's strength was far too great.

The blade hovered before her face, scintillating strangely, as if it were composed of little jewels along its length. The creature's huge yellow eyes held steady on her, unwavering, the intensity of that gaze somehow a kind of violation. And yet there was something compelling, something inexplicably ... *inviting* about that gaze as well.

The hand holding her let go, dropping her arm. Alia wanted to turn and flee, but somehow she could not. Instead, she found herself merely standing there, slack jawed and helpless and shivering. The demon took her left hand, turning it until her palm was exposed. The blade came down in a quick, complex, darting jab, and Alia felt the cold bite of it against her flesh. She shuddered, helpless, gasping.

42

Then, unexpectedly, it thrust her away.

'Go,' it said. The voice was guttural and deep, and echoed somehow like a voice in a cave.

Alia stared, shivering. The palm of her left hand stung like fire.

'Run,' it said, waving her off with one hand. 'Run away!'

Alia stumbled back a few paces.

'*Run!*'

As if a chord had abruptly been severed, Alia turned and ran, understanding none of this, but running, running downslope till her lungs ached fiercely and her legs burned, running till she fairly flew along, running, running in the dark till she fell, gasping painfully, her heart tremoring, and she collapsed in a soaked, shivering heap.

She lay for a long time, only half aware, folded in upon herself.

And then, blinking, she grew aware that dawn was coming upon the world. She started up in a sudden panic, cold and shivering and painfully stiff, realizing she must have slept, cursing herself for the utter, mindless stupidity of such a thing ...

But the forest was silent save for the ordinary, pre-dawn callings of the birds. She listened to the *cheep cheep* of a white tail, the little *willa woo, willa woo wooo* of a pair of hill doves. The feathered folk all seemed calm enough.

Alia groaned, stiff and sore and exhausted to her very bones. Yesterday's storm was blowing away, the clouds shredding into tatters in the pewter morning sky, but all was wet and dripping about her, and Alia was soaked and shivering and miserable. The dawn breeze cut her like a knife.

She blinked, seeing the dark, jumbled shapes of the pines all about her slowly taking on colour as the light increased. She could smell the resiny scent of them. A tufted-eared squirrel skittered by on a limb overhead, stared down in sudden shock at her, standing still and silent below him, and whisked away.

Birdsong, the whispering of the dawn breeze in the pines, the forest folk going about as usual. Another rising of the sun ...

But Alia's heart did not lighten, for all the comforting normality of the world beginning another, ordinary new day.

Her left hand throbbed painfully. Looking down, she saw that her palm had been scored in an intricate pattern – a series of small, interlocking curves, or an intricate rune of some sort, or a kind of face, perhaps ... She could not tell.

She saw the huge-eyed, tusked, inhuman face in her mind's eye. She had never heard tell of any such creature like it. Demon-faced, human of limb, incredibly strong. And it had carried her away from the bandit camp to safety. Why? Impossible creature! None of it made any sense she could see.

What kind of horrible craziness had come into the world?

Alia felt a fit of the shakes take her, so strong she could do nothing but lie doubled over, hugging herself, waiting till they should go. She did not feel she had the strength to move ...

But she had to make it back to Hunters Glade to tell Charrer Mysha and the rest about what she had seen up here: the bandit stronghold ... the man Sethir's wretched conniving, the jewelled man with his bizarre, bejewelled skull.

Alia shook her head, disbelieving.

It was all too *strange*!

But the memory of Torno's hands upon her was simple enough. She shook, recalling the greasy feel of the bandit leader's beard, the hot thickness of his life's blood. The remembrance set loose an angry shudder of outrage in her. In all the incomprehensibility and impossible strangeness of that which had happened, what he – and the others – had tried to do to her stood out clear. She clung to her anger as a kind of anchor, focusing on it, thrusting the creeping strangeness of events from her mind.

The sooner she made it back to Hunters Glade the better.

They would get Hone Amis and the Reeve Vale Militia out along with the hunters, and then these ragged scoundrel bandits would be taught the hard lesson they so much deserved.

Rout the lot of them out. Send them fleeing. Smash them like one would smash a nest of hornets in a barn.

Return things to what they were supposed to be.

Alia struggled shakily to her feet. Hugging herself against the chill of the early morning, she limped onwards, aching with exhaustion and cramp, waiting for movement to loosen the stiffness that made each step a painful stagger. She felt a little rush of grim satisfaction go through her as she struggled on. She knew these hills well enough to be able to find her way back to this bandit camp once again, and could lead a retributive force up here.

She would look forward to *that*.

Oh *yes*.

III

Guthrie Garthson stood, numbed and shivering. He stared vacantly about, seeing a rock-studded, grassy slope up which he must have walked. The slope's crest, where he now stood, was crowned by stone slabs, splintered with age and weather, moss slicked and wet and chill. The eastern sky glowed with faint dawn light. The morning wind was cold as ice. No rain any longer. Above him, the storm clouds were shredding away into tatters. The teeth of the Slate Peaks showed against the glowing sky in the eastern distance. Below them lay the dark folds of the Mira Hills. Below them, in turn, lay the glinting ribbon of the River Esk. And on the river's bank in the distance, dim in the half-light but clear enough to be seen nonetheless, lay the Closter.

Made little by distance, it lay like some child's discarded plaything, broken and still. Guthrie could see no sign of life, no movement. Nothing.

Unable to bear the sight, he turned away and collapsed back against a mossy boulder, utterly spent. He had no notion as to where exactly he was, no clear recollection of how he had got here, whatever place this might be.

Hunched there, gasping, he lifted what he held in his hands and gazed at it. The Abbod's dead face stared back at him, eyes open, unblinking. Guthrie knew not what had possessed him to bring the gruesome thing along.

In the dawn's grey radiance, it looked pale and pitiful.

But staring down on that slack white face, Guthrie felt only bitter anger. 'I trusted you!' he hissed at it. 'I *trusted* you! And you ...' the words died unspoken. There was no way strong enough to say what he felt.

Gone, all gone. Everything destroyed.

Thrice cursed, damnable fool of an Abbod!

After convincing Guthrie to open the gates, after having got him

45

personally to open the gates to the cursed Sea Wolves ... To just stand there, utterly defenceless, and let himself be killed.

When everything pointed to his being able to do ... *extraordinary* things to protect himself.

Without even trying to resist.

Accomplishing *nothing!*

Guthrie raised the decapitated head in rage and disgust and would have hurled it from him.

But could not.

This was not the first time he had tried to rid himself of it. But he seemed under some uncanny compulsion; try as he might, he could not bring himself to hurl the thing away.

Guthrie shuddered.

Wearily, he struggled to his feet. It was pinching cold, the bite of autumn in the dawn air. His breath made little clouds of vapour, and he could not stop the shivering that took him now he was no longer moving. He had been travelling all night, empty minded as a beast whose nest had been destroyed, restless, looking for he knew not what. He felt utterly spent, but that restless drive was still upon him.

So on he went. Turning his back on the sad, distant shape of the shattered Closter, he staggered blindly away from it, stumbling through the splintered stone slabs at the crest of the slope and over to the other side, where he saw more grassy slope, downwards leading now, and continued on for a weary time until he saw a cluster of silver birch glowing palely in the dawnlight a ways off from the course he had been blindly taking. The trees' branches, naked but for a few ragged yellow leaves fluttering in the breeze, formed a stark, knuckly web against the sky. Guthrie made for them, plodding through wet, knee-high yellow grass.

The birches were clustered about a gleaming pool, rock rimmed. Pushing through the white trunks, the last few leaves whispering about him, Guthrie came to stand unsteadily on a grassy, leaf-strewn bank at the water's verge. The pool lay still and clear as glass. Guthrie saw the moving clouds reflected in it, the shining, pale cobalt of the new morning sky, the wavery, naked arms of the birches themselves. Leaning over, he saw his own shape, stricken faced and weary, the foul head clutched to him. Like a very spectre he looked.

He stumbled back, shaken, and caught his heel unexpectedly on some hidden snag. With a little cry, he sprawled backwards, landing heavily enough to drive the wind from him. Bruised and panting, he lay spread where he had landed, his cheek pressed against cold, wet leaves and grass, too exhausted and shaken to move further.

Before him, nested some little distance away in the ochre-leaf-littered grass, lay the head.

Guthrie stared at the thing and laughed weakly. This chance slip had accomplished what all his will had been unable to do. He had dropped the head. He was free of the uncanny thing!

He tried to stand then, but found to his dismay that he simply could not. He had no strength left but to lie there, gasping. The head seemed to stare at him. He looked away uneasily. Overhead, he saw the last of the clouds boil away with ponderous grace. Around him, the dawn breeze whispered incomprehensible things in the dying leaves. The head stared its unblinking stare. He could feel its dead gaze like a cold draught upon his back.

Guthrie shuddered. The world about him seemed to shimmer unaccountably.

Like a clod of earth dropping away into a deep pool, he dissolved into exhausted sleep.

But sleeping, he dreamed.

Guthrie was in a dark, winding place. Before him stood the Abbod in his grey robe, head tucked underneath his arm. And the head was speaking, calmly. But Guthrie could understand nothing, for the words were merely an incomprehensible mumbling, like the burble of a stream.

And then he began to feel the place about him start to come apart, like some great, complicated tapestry unravelling, with him caught helpless in the midst. He turned from the Abbod and fled, skittering along from one disintegrating pathway to another, feeling the very ground under his feet shredding away, as if he ran on a canopy of brittle autumn leaves with nothing whatsoever underneath.

And the decapitated Abbod followed him. Where Guthrie ran flat out, skidding along in frantic haste, the Abbod walked leisurely. Yet those leisurely steps kept him somehow abreast of Guthrie's desperate pace. The Abbod held the head out in one hand, as if it were some precious offering, and the head kept on talking its incomprehensible talk.

'*Help* me,' Guthrie implored. 'Tell me how to get away from this place before it comes apart entire. Make *sense*, curse you!'

47

But the head's watery mumblings became no more understandable.

Guthrie screamed at it, but it only talked on, the headless Abbod striding easily along at Guthrie's side, while the place they were in came inexorably apart about them.

And then, with a terrifying abruptness, the last shreds of firmness fell away and Guthrie found himself groundless in a black void, a great, empty gullet into which he was plunged. The last thing he saw before that great void swallowed him whole was the head, held up to him on an open palm, shining like a lantern, smiling the Abbod's calm smile.

Guthrie screamed.

And awoke on the leafy grass, sunlight blindingly bright in his eyes.

He scrambled to his knees, panting, his heart thudding. The head lay as it had been amongst the leaves, staring at him still. He glared down at it, shuddering, and had an urge to fling the wretched thing into the pool. But he dared not touch it.

Guthrie ran his hands over his face, blinking. He limped down to the water, sank his whole head into it, and came up spluttering, long pale hair spun across his eyes in a wet tangle, icy water sliding down his spine. But he sighed gratefully, needing the good shock of it.

Looking about, Guthrie saw that it was still morning; he could not have slept long. The sky was shining blue and clear and bright. On the branches of the birches, the remaining yellow-brown leaves danced and twirled softly in the sunlight. It was a good place, this. He breathed a long sigh and let himself down on the grass by the water's edge. His arms quivered even with that simple effort. His belly was cramped with hunger, and he felt weak as any abandoned barn kitten.

What was he to do now?

A simple, terrible question, that. He was alive. The world went on. But there was nothing in that world left for him now. All had been taken. He felt a sudden, returning pang of rage and turned towards the head. 'Cursed *fool*!' he hissed at it. 'Why did I listen to you?' Reaching down, he dug up a hand-sized pebble and flung it at the staring, dead eyes. The stone missed, and he fell to cursing some more.

But it was scant relief.

And what was he to do?

48

Lie here, perhaps, and never get up.

There was an attractiveness about that, achingly weary as he was. The final dropping away into the Shadowlands. An ending. Why had he not died back at the Closter? All his yearning, adolescent dreams come true, only to turn into terrible nightmare. Everything gone and destroyed. He felt like a stranded fish, washed ashore by currents beyond his control, gasping and stricken.

Yes ... to lie here until the end came.

But his belly was knotted with hunger cramps, and the wind blew cool and clear in his lungs, and something there was in him that would simply not lie down.

Guthrie sighed wearily. Levering himself to his knees, he looked about. The pool was large enough to have trout in, perhaps. But there was precious little chance of him being able to take any. And there was nothing else he could discern about him that might be edible. He licked dry lips, crouched over the pool and drank. The water tasted of rock and moss, and was cold enough to make his teeth ache. But it filled him like ballast, and he turned back to the bank feeling more solid than he had.

And there sat the head, staring at him still. He scuttled away from it, then stopped himself, cursing. He had had *enough* of the foul, uncanny thing. He stalked a few paces off, tore a dead limb from one of the birches and stripped the branches from it in a ragged sweep. Clutching that like a club, he returned and swung at the head, hitting the back of the dead skull solidly and sending it rolling with erratic bounces across the leafy grass towards the pool's verge. It teetered there, then plopped into the water and lay bobbing sluggishly, face down, like some grotesque fisherman's float.

'Cursed, *fool* Closterer,' Guthrie said to it, shivering. Then he flung the branch aside and stumbled away through the screen of whispering birches as quickly as his unsteady legs would take him.

He moved at a staggering run, away from the pool along through a grassy stretch of hillside, blindly forcing himself onwards and onwards until his lungs ached for air and his side was stitched up painfully.

He stopped then, bent over with his hands on his knees, gasping. When he had hold of himself, he straightened, trying to think more clearly. The great stone upthrust of the Slate Peaks was at his back, and all about him lay rolling, grassy slopes clotted here and there with stands of trees. Though he still had no clear notion of where he might be – his blind wandering had carried him well beyond any

49

part of the country he recognized – he reckoned he could not have walked so terribly far. It was only a matter of time before any downslope took him inevitably to either the River Esk or the sea itself, and from either of them he felt fairly sure of his ability to locate himself.

Besides, downslope walking was about all he felt he could manage at this point, so that was where he headed.

He walked for the whole of the morning through sloping, hummocky meadow and thin patches of forest, immobilized at times by cramps and very weariness, his pace slowing to a stagger, without seeing sign of anything familiar. And not a living soul did he see, either. The land was empty and silent. No wavering threads of hearthsmoke marked the horizon. There was no distant sound of ploughman or horse, no shouts of shepherd children herding sheep. It was as if he moved through a ghost land. Even the very beasts themselves seemed mute. And not a bird marked the sky save, now and again, a carrion crow.

The terrible silence of it made him shudder.

And then, rounding an outcropping of splintered stone, he saw a small farmstead a ways ahead. Sobbing with relief, he staggered downslope, calling out to the farm's inhabitants.

But the house was empty, the interior a shambles. He could not tell if the mess had been caused by Sea Wolves ransacking the place or by the farmer and his family taking all they could as they fled in haste. It mattered little which. The place stood sad and abandoned.

It had been a nice small house, with a central live-in room, a sleeping loft, and a flagstone kitchen off to one side. Guthrie turned towards the kitchen, his mouth watering involuntarily at the possibility of what he might find there. But as soon as he passed the threshold, he heard the scuttle of rats. Little dark eyes glared up at him from the room's corners. He felt his belly cramp up. What food there might have been was gone now, or spoiled by the rats well past his ability to stomach it.

He turned and staggered away. There was nothing here.

But halfway out the door, he heard a soft noise from the room at his back, a little whimper, like a sick puppy might make. He turned and looked back at the room. A trestle table lay on its side in the far corner. Three chairs stood in a group, one tipped over, legs up as if it were dead. The fireplace was cold and black. An empty scuttle sat

50

next it. Guthrie stood for long moments, listening, but could hear nothing save the stealthy sound of the rats in the kitchen.

And then he heard it again, from the room's far corner, behind the tipped-over trestle table. A little whimper. His heart thumping, he made a careful way over, not at all sure what it might be that made the sound.

Two young children sat scrunched up against the corner behind the table, arms wrapped tight about each other. They stared up at him with terror-wide eyes, shaking.

Guthrie felt a surge of relief. 'It's all right,' he assured them. 'I'm not going to hurt you. You're the first people I've seen since ...'

They only stared up at him, shaking against each other, white faced and terror ridden, like mice helpless before a marauding cat.

'I won't harm you,' Guthrie repeated. He could not tell the ages of these two, five or six, perhaps. One was bigger than the other, though not by much. They were filthy, their clothes ripped and fouled, hair hanging in tangled knots about their faces. He could not see if they were boy or girl. Guthrie's heart went out to the poor things. 'What happened here? Do you know where your mother and father are? Are you hurt, either of you?'

Still, they only stared at him.

He reached a hand down. 'Come now, let me ...'

The bigger of the two bit him, sinking sharp little teeth painfully into the flesh at the base of Guthrie's thumb.

'Aieee!' Guthrie snatched his hand back, blood dripping.

The two children darted away between his legs, scuttling across the room and out the door.

'Come back!' he shouted. 'Come *back*!' He ran after them. From the doorway, he saw them skitter across the top of a grassy knoll beyond the house and disappear down the knoll's far side. 'Come back!' he shouted again. 'Little fools! I am your Reeve. I will not harm you. *Come back*!'

But it was no use. They were gone.

Guthrie stood staring at where they had disappeared, sucking at his torn hand, cursing silently. He was Reeve, oh yes. Reeve of a land of the dead, a land of children so terrified they bit the hand offered to them in aid.

Tears filled his eyes, blurring his vision. How could such terrible things happen? Not two days ago, life was normal, everything sensible. Now, nothing made sense any more. He felt a thrust of

51

bitter, impotent anger go through him at those who had caused this.

Blinking his vision clear, Guthrie stood staring at the green slope of the knoll where the children had vanished, staring until his eyes throbbed, hoping that they might return. Having encountered human company in this empty land, he desperately did not want to find himself alone again. He called reassurances to them. He went over and stood near the house's well, drew up a dipper of cool water and held it in the air for them to see, if they were looking. 'Water,' he called, trying to entice them back. 'Sweet, cool water.'

But all in vain.

Finally, he had to give it up. He was far too weary to try chasing after them. 'Little fools,' he grumbled, then felt a quick sting of remorse, thinking on what they must have endured, those two.

He drank from the dipper in his hands, drew more water, splashed his face, drank again. Then, having little other choice, he turned his back and moved wearily off.

He walked on and on, his mind hazed with weariness, head hung, watching one foot come down after the other, the grass swishing about his knees. He knew he could not be all that far from the coast and Riverside, the main settlement of Reeve Vale, where the River Esk came down to meet the sea. But though he kept looking for familiar landmarks, he found none. Somehow, he had managed to lose the river, lose his bearings, lose his way completely. He had never travelled these slopes above the coast alone before, and never on foot; his ventures out here had been on horseback, as part of larger companies. His only clear memories of such journeys were the staring faces of the farmers and their raggedy-clothed families as he and the rest rode past in their equine splendour, for horses were a rarity in the Vale and only the ruling families possessed them. Gazing about him now in fruitless quest for anything familiar, he wished he had paid more attention to his surroundings on those trips.

Onwards he staggered, his legs a tormenting ache, half lamed by a sharp stone he had not seen which had all but sliced through his left bootsole, bruising his foot cruelly. Onwards. And onwards still. Like a man in a dream, an endless walking dream ...

And then, how much weary time later he was not sure, he rounded the slope of a steep, grassy hillside and found himself gazing down across a bluff. Below him lay Riverside, and the glistening coils of the River Esk where it came down to meet the sea.

Guthrie blinked, shivered, shook himself, blinked again unbelievingly.

From what he had glimpsed of the Closter from the crest of the slope where he had paused in the early dawn, it had been dead and deserted. But for all their brokenness, the walls had been recognizable enough. Here, that was not the case. Where he would have looked, only a day past, to see the well-known shapes of familiar buildings – the Sollydes' family mill, the Loews' smithy, Obart Hall, the great peaked roof of Reeve Hall itself – there was now naught but charred and sodden ruins.

Looking on what remained, Guthrie felt sick with rage and grief.

His grandfather had founded this place, built it up from nothing, enticing homesteaders up from the south, opening sea-trade routes with distant Long Harbour down the coast, fighting hardship and storm and calamity, forging a thriving, growing, altogether successful settlement in these northern wilds where others before him had failed. Riverside was the northernmost steading of all, the furthest from settled lands. And it had looked to be one of the wealthiest.

Gone, now. All gone. Folk killed, buildings burnt, valuables stolen away. Guthrie felt painful tears fill his eyes. It was impossible. It was unforgivable. He wanted to lash out at those who had done this, to smash them as they had smashed everything below. He wanted revenge.

But there was nobody to revenge himself upon.

And then he saw human movement amongst the ruins. At first, he took them to be survivors and his heart lifted in momentary relief. But the sunlight glinted on polished metal, and he saw the bright gleam of horsehair crests as a line of Sea Wolves moved slowly through the shattered remains of the buildings, weighed down with bundles and bags.

Following their movement with his eye, Guthrie saw they were headed towards the harbour. He lifted his gaze and squinted into the distance. There lay the Sea Wolves' three long black ships, looking like great sea beasts basking in the calm waters of Reeve Bay. He saw rowboats passing back and forth, loading men and booty.

They were leaving, then. Taking their ill-gained spoils and sailing away.

Something snapped in Guthrie then. The very injustice of it burned him, that these raiders should get away thus freely, leaving behind naught but misery and ruin and death. He let out a snarl like an animal and skidded down the steep slope of the bluff before him, unthinking, blind, furious. He lost his footing, tumbling heels over head downwards to smack up painfully amongst some bushes at the slope's base. Fighting himself clear of these, he struggled on.

Through more tangled bushes he forced a way, then across a knee-deep, rushing stream, a tributary to the Esk. He ran up and across the stream's far bank, panting, staggering, wild with fury, and thence on through trampled fields and into the settlement's outskirts.

The place stank of charred wood and burnt meat. The very thought made Guthrie gag. Away to his left he heard the cawing of crows. As he looked, one came spiralling upwards and flapped past overhead. It gazed down at him insolently, slow and sated and secure. Guthrie shook his fist up at the bird, turned, and made for the spot where he had seen it arise. He stumbled along through the littered dirt laneways linking the shattered houses together until, turning a corner, he saw what had drawn the crows.

The bodies lay in a disorderly heap. How many, he could not easily tell. He did not have the stomach to move closer and count. The crows, and other scavengers, had been at them. Pale bone showed here and there, sticking out through ribboned wet flesh.

They were Vale men, that was clear enough by their clothing. And at least one woman lay amongst them; he could see the folds of her dress. And he made out the little limbs of children.

Guthrie was not near enough to recognize anyone. It made no difference. Reeve settlement was no larger than three or four hundred souls all told. And Riverside held less than half that. No matter who might lie here in this sorry human pile, he would know them, or at least recognize their features.

Head bowed in stricken grief, Guthrie recited the death litany for them, giving them soul's release: 'A scathless journey in the darkness, friends. A scathless journey and fruitful ends. Gone from the world of living ken. Into the Shadowlands ... to begin again.'

He stood for a long, shattered moment, staring at the pitiful remains, then turned and staggered wildly away towards the harbour.

There was no clear thought in Guthrie's mind. He did not know what he planned, alone and entirely unarmed as he was. The anger and despair in him had poisoned sanity. He was like a rabid dog, vicious in his madness, ready to bite any he came upon.

But when he arrived finally at the harbour, panting and furious, it proved too late. Three dark ships were coasting slowly out to sea, red sails snapping in the offshore breeze. Guthrie raged and screamed, shaking his fists, running down to the strand and flinging rocks that came to hand, leaping up and down on the gravelly shore. He ran along the shingle, paralleling the ships' progress, shrieking, until he missed his footing and plunged head first ignominiously into the surf.

Leaned against the gunwale of the nearest ship, a row of Sea Wolves laughed, their mocking voices floating across the water, small with distance but all too clear.

Guthrie dragged himself weakly to his knees, the icy water breaking about him, and wept, helpless, as the Sea Wolf ships glided away with insolent ease.

It was near evening before he returned entirely to himself.

Struggling stiffly to his knees, Guthrie looked about. The sun hung red and swollen above the sea on the western horizon, partly buried in a hedge of dark cloud. He knelt on the Reeve Bay strand. Before him, the sea lay calm, stretching like a great smooth blanket from the cut of Reeve Bay away to the end of the world. Nowhere was there any sign of the Sea Wolves' ships.

At Guthrie's back, Riverside was silent as a burial yard.

Which was exactly what it had become, Guthrie reminded himself bitterly.

It was a long while before he could summon the energy to move. What was the point? Everything had been taken. He was alone amongst the dead.

Yet move he did, in the end. The chill of evening was coming on, and he shivered in the sea breeze. Slowly, staggering like an ancient, he made his way back towards the settlement's streets.

His mouth was parched as old leather, and he went to the community well first. It was shuddering strange, standing there in the semi-dark and the silence, sipping cool well water from the familiar ladle. There ought to be others about, women and girls gathered here at the well for gossip, young men nearby boasting casually to each other for the girls to overhear. The old familiar things were all so clear, so real, that Guthrie could almost believe that what he now lived was the dream.

But no. What he now lived was all too real.

He put down the ladle and turned away. Off to his right, he made out the remains of Reeve Hall. Even burnt and shattered as it was

55

now, it still dominated this whole side of the settlement. Guthrie swallowed, gazing at it. Slowly, he walked that way.

It stank like everything else here now, a stinging blend of odours that caught in the throat. Guthrie stood before the ruin and felt the tears come once more. He had loved this place and hated it, for it was both home and prison. But now it was the love that predominated. He had loved the fine, straight lines of it, the way the roof steeply sloped, the elaborate carvings on the eaves.

Stepping over the charred detritus that now filled the shattered entrance way, Guthrie walked slowly inside. The roof had partially collapsed, leaving a heaped mess in what had been the Great Hall. Guthrie put a hand out against a charred column. It leaned slantways now, splintered and bent, where once it had stood proud, one of the six pillars in the Great Hall. And each had been carved from base to top, intricate, exciting carvings that he had explored as a boy, telling himself stories to fit the figures he had seen carved there, men on horseback, soaring hawks, great spouting sea whales.

Guthrie traced the faint remnants of that charred carving. There was nothing he could recognize. Like everything else, this was taken too. And the Hall itself was wrecked as surely and utterly as the pillar under his palm. He remembered it all as it had been to him when he was young, the great hearthfire down the room's centre, the pillars seeming tall as trees, his father seated on the High Seat at the far end, holding session here as Guthrie's grandfather had before him. Here it was that the Moot had met every new moon, the Five families and the Seven, the leading families of the settlement, gathered together. Here it was that the settlement's decisions were hammered out, and that sentence was passed on those few who had committed unforgivable crimes.

Mostly, such men had been shamefaced and meek, accepting the Reeve's justice as their due. But Guthrie remembered one case when he was a boy, a short, thickset man with a black plank of a beard, who had raged and threatened when the sentence of full outlawry and banishment had been passed upon him. He had been a shepherd, and had murdered another man over a woman, or some such. Guthrie recalled the scene clearly, for all that he could not have been more than ten or eleven at the time, the man shouting, the struggle to get him out of the Hall. And Guthrie recalled clearest of all the shared satisfaction they had all felt afterwards, having acted together in their own protection and dealt with such a man.

Standing there in the shattered remains, Guthrie remembered

everything so clear it hurt. How folk had trooped in through the double doors for each Moot session, dressed in their finest clothes for the occasion. How tempers would rise in the midst of discussion. He remembered Reeve Garth, his father, shouting some obstreperous member into silence. He remembered the interchange of friendly insults between families, the laughing, the intricate, oftimes frustrating, but always stimulating interchanges that formed the social and political dynamic of the ruling families of Reeve Vale.

Guthrie shook his head and smiled and sighed and blinked back painful tears, remembering it all.

And somewhere under the heaped and smouldering mass before him lay the High Seat. He recalled all too clearly his own frustrations, second son as he was, forced to watch from the side as his elder brother Garrett took his place up there, standing behind his father during the sessions. Guthrie swallowed. Garrett had looked every inch the young Reeve, standing up there, scarlet cloaked, dark haired and thick boned like Garth himself, sharp eyed and canny. Guthrie had hated him with the black hate of adolescent jealousy. But he had loved him too, and loved the way he stood there, proud as a hawk.

Well ... all that was gone now, and he, Guthrie, was Reeve, as he had always hungered to be.

The cruel irony of it was like a blade in his guts. Every yearning adolescent fantasy he had ever dreamed focused on this place, with him in the High Seat.

Reeve Guthrie Garthson.

In a kind of daze, Guthrie staggered forwards towards where the Seat must lie. He scrabbled amongst the rubble, scooping away warm ash and splintered, black wood until he found it. Or what was left of it. The lovely carved arms were twisted and splintered and charred. The whole of the back had split apart. Only the seat itself, solid old oak and nearly sturdy as rock, had survived anywhere near intact.

Gingerly, Guthrie lowered himself to it and gazed slowly about the Hall.

It was growing dark, and the Hall lay shrouded in black shadows. But, in his mind's eye, he could see everything as it had once been, torches dancing, folk gathered eager and flushed, ready for the Moot's intricacies like so many young salmon ready for the sea. And he saw his father, seated as he was now, raising his arms to call the formal opening: 'This Moot is now in session. Are all present?' And then Reeve Garth would call the roll of the families, the Five first, the landowners, the Charrers, the Obarts, the Meriths, the Hones, the Tyllises. Then the Seven, the crafts-families, the Owins, the Villerings, the Loews, and so on until all had been accounted for.

And then Reeve Garth would stand, and all eyes turn to him as he called, 'I declare this Moot ... *open.*'

Guthrie took a ragged breath, another. Slowly, he stood on shaking legs, feeling the solid edge of the oak seat at the backs of his knees. He raised his arms, as he had watched his father do so many times, and said, his voice hardly more than a breathy, harsh whisper: 'I declare this Moot ... *open.*'

But the Hall lay drowned in silence, dark and dreary and sad. In the distance, a crow called, *haww haaaww*, as if in mockery.

'Father,' Guthrie whispered. 'Oh, *Father* ...' Then he flung himself from the Seat and stumbled away. He could not bear it. To be given everything. To have everything taken from him.

Somewhere, the dead body of his father lay, food for the crows and foxes and worms. His brother's body, too. And somewhere, also, lay his poor mother. And everyone else. Guthrie had seen no survivors. The Sea Wolves, it seemed, had killed all.

He recalled the fiasco of the Closter, damning the Abbod and his criminal foolishness yet again. Gone, all dead and gone.

Thought of the Abbod reminded Guthrie suddenly of the grisly, uncanny head, and of the dream he had had of it: him skittering along feeling the very ground under his feet shredding inexorably away while the head gibbered at him incomprehensibly. Guthrie shuddered, trying to put the recollection away from him. But he felt as if the ground were indeed shredding away from under him. There was only him left alive. Riverside, the whole of the Vale itself, had become a place of terrible death.

He staggered out through the Hall's shattered entranceway into chill air. Black night had fallen. Above Guthrie the stars hung spangled, cold and distant and still beautiful despite all, untouchable, eternal, unaffected by human misery.

Guthrie bowed his head and wept. The stars ought to tumble from their places, the world tremble into shards ... for it seemed to him that the very Powers themselves – those great life forces that moved the world, animating all – had to be fatally out of kilter for such terrible things as had occurred to happen.

He only wished it were so, that the Sea Wolves had indeed upset the multifold balance of the world so much that they would become the recipients of some great blacklash, some great rebalancing of Power. And Power to atone for what they had wrought at Reeve Vale.

But he knew in his heart that such would never be.

There were folk – simple shepherds and fishers and such for the most part – who made images, putting shape to this or that Power: Luan of the Wind, winged and fierce, or Sweet-water Kaila of the many forms. But Guthrie knew such images were not the truth. The Powers were greater, or lesser, than human images of them. The Powers were ... themselves.

Like strong currents under smooth water, save that the water was the world entire.

Guthrie shivered, half sensing them. The same Power that made the rivers run made his own blood pulse; that which drove the thunder clouds to violence fed his own tempers. But though the Powers, greater and lesser, moved him, as a wind moved a flapping pennant, there was nothing in them for him to appeal to. They were simply ... beyond his need. The easy appeals of simple folk over their little images – 'Revenge me, oh great-winged Luan,' – were not for him.

No great justice would descend upon the Sea Wolves. Those they had murdered would make the long, final voyage to the Shadow-lands – to be reborn again eventually into happier lives perhaps – and it would all be over: the Sea Wolves were come and gone, with impunity.

Guthrie staggered away from the shattered Hall. He felt his heart was like to break.

Riverside's once familiar laneways were become a black maze choked with rubble from the tumbled remains of fire-eaten build-ings. Guthrie lost his bearings, stumbling this way and that in the dark, until he found himself on the edge of the town, next to the Merith family Mill. That building had been gutted like everything else. All that remained was a charred skeleton of beams slumped about the big stone disk of the grinding wheel and spilling out across the laneway. Nearby lay a soggy heap of unmilled oats. The grain-bags had been torn apart, and the oats soiled. The whole area stank of piss.

Guthrie clenched his fists in impotent fury.

There was no need for such utter, senseless destruction! What manner of men were they, these sea raiders, that they were so unwilling to leave behind anything save total ruin?

What had he done in this life ... what had any of them here in the Vale done to bring such utter, inhuman destruction down upon themselves?

Guthrie thought of the crest-helmed Sea Wolves laughing mockingly at him from the gunwale of their ship as they sailed safely away, and he nearly gagged at the bitter outrage that filled him. They were gone and safe across the waters. And who knew where on the wide sea they were headed, or what land they might call home?

No doubt they were laughing at him still.

Standing there, hearing that mocking laughter in his mind, Guthrie felt the grief inside him harden into something else entirely.

They were men, these mocking, cursed Sea Wolves.

Where they went, he could follow.

It unrolled clearly in his mind.

Southwards. That first, yes. He would journey south to the settled lands. To Long Harbour, perhaps. Folk would know things down there. Somebody somewhere would have heard of these Sea Wolves.

Years, it might take to track them down. He groaned at the very thought. He wanted to destroy them *now*. But if it took years ... so be it. He would do it.

What else was there left in the world for him?

Guthrie felt his heart beating stronger. This was his land they had destroyed, his people they had killed. *His*. He would track them down as a hunter might track a pack of renegade wolves. He would be mercilessly persistent. He saw himself years hence, lean and dangerous, the Sea Wolves broken under the terrible force of his revenge.

He would make those bastarding raiders pay. He would make them rue the day they ever came to Reeve Vale. Oh yes ... He would be revenged upon them.

Revenge.

The word sang in his mind.

Revenge!

IV

Alia staggered along as best she could, making a slow progress through the bush-choked rills that ribbed the lower slopes of the Mira Hills. There were far easier paths to Hunters Glade, but this was the safest, for she reckoned none would be able to follow her. She was shivering with exhaustion, but at least there was no more rain, and the exertion of travelling had both dried and warmed her.

Before plunging through a particularly tangled thicket, she paused for breath, put a hand to her face and felt it stiff and swollen. The touch of her fingers made it throb like a rotten tooth. It had been years since she had felt the like. It conjured memories that churned her guts – her father's angry shouting, the hard smack of his hand.

Those cursed bandits would be sorry for what they had done. She swore that most solemnly. For their cruel intentions, for the physical injury they had done her, for the carefully buried memories they had shaken loose in her. And for their ill-timed interference.

Who knew what might have happened if that first raggedy lot had not come piling out of the cloud-mist to drive the Fey away? All her days, it seemed, she had yearned for just such a moment of communion. The dream of a lifetime. And the cursed fools had wrecked it!

But all the anger in her was mixed with exhaustion and horror and something else less identifiable. Her mind was aswirl with uncomfortable remembrances: the staring faces of the bandits in the cloud-mist; the troll-like bandit leader coming for her; the greasy feel of his matted beard; the hot, spurting wetness of his lifeblood; the elegant jewelled man and his queer, bejewelled skull; the lone Fey – had she truly seen such? She was no longer certain; and that uncanny and inexplicable demon-creature.

Of it she was certain enough. Her left hand throbbed painfully, and she kept peering compulsively at the design inscribed in her flesh there, attempting to make it out. But to no avail.

Over and over again Alia ran though events in her mind – the man Sethir's lying connivances, the demon-creature's appearance, its improbable rescuing of her – trying to make sense of things. But no sensible pattern emerged.

Alia shuddered, trying to push it all from her mind. It was too strange. She tried to force herself to focus on movement instead, on each footstep, each bend and shift and turn of the way ahead.

So she struggled on throughout the day, stumbling and half blind at times with the uncomfortable swirl of her thoughts and very weariness.

By the afternoon, the choking bush began to give way finally to more open woods on the lower slopes. Birch predominated here, with a few maples, stout trunked and tall, standing over them. The maples glowed like soft torches, red and purple and delicate gold with early autumn colour.

Alia made a stumbling way over a wearisomely long, sloping rise and down through a hedge of silver birch towards Birchleg Pool – a spot well known to hunters, quiet, away from the pathways most used by ordinary Reeve Vale folk. There was good clean water here, cold as ice, with rainbow-sided trout hiding back under the rocks if one knew where to look.

Panting, Alia leaned against one of the wispy-barked, whispering birches that hedged the pool. The afternoon sun swum half-hid amongst a hedge of clouds. Reflections of light danced across the water before her. She shivered, chilled now and utterly weary, but her heart gladdened at the pool's familiar sight.

Staggering down across the grassy bank, she sank to her knees at the pool's edge, cupped the icy water in her palms and splashed her face and neck, gasping at the shock. Then she drank and settled back on her haunches with a little sigh.

Food next.

She slipped quietly along the shoreline, careful not to make a sound or let her shadow fall across the water. Having fished here before, she knew the pool's secrets and headed for the narrower, deeper end where two large, flat stones intersected. Softly, she lowered herself down across her favourite of the two and let her right hand (not the scarred and still-throbbing left) slide into the water, making a careful, slow job of it, ignoring the numbing shock of the cold water.

Ever so gently, she reached fingers into the shadow the stone cast, in which she could glimpse a darker shadow hovering. Quick as thought, she jerked the trout out of the water by the gills in one smooth, cat-sharp motion.

Alia bowed her head in thanks, reciting the words softly, 'For the giving of your life, I thank you, friend.' Then she scooped the fish up, bit down sharply on the spine just behind its head and ended its flopping distress. She would have liked a fire, both for its warmth and because raw trout was far from being her favourite meal. But she had eaten worse on occasion, and she had no intention of wasting time here. Food and water and a few moments of rest, that was all she would allow herself. Then she must away once more. The travelling would warm her up, and, if she pushed herself, she was sure she could make Hunters Glade before nightfall.

She stripped away the wet fish flesh with her teeth and chewed gingerly, for the movement made her swollen face ache. Some little distance away, she spied a small patch of redberries half hidden in the grass. They were wrinkled and past ripe, but tastier than the fish. A little draught of icy water, more trout, the last of the berries, water again. She could feel the strength of it begin to seep into her.

Squatting on her heels, chewing, she gazed across the pool. The rocks on the far shore were reflected perfectly, like two halves of a single, joint entity. But looking at those rocks, Alia suddenly saw something else, something that bobbed sluggishly just below the water's surface. Curious, she rose, grunting with the discomfort of her sore limbs, and went over.

It hung submerged in the water, a dark, strange something, round as a largish squash. Alia flipped the bony remains of the trout back into the water for the teeny-weenies to scavenge, and reached for the thing.

At first, she thought it might indeed be a squash of some sort, slimy with corruption, and then that it might be some hapless, small furry creature that had fallen into the water and drowned.

It was neither.

Seeing the lank hair and the slack white flesh of the dead face, she flung it instinctively from her with a shudder.

What in the name of all the Powers was such a gruesome thing doing here? Alia felt a shudder go through her. It was like a creepy echo, this rotting head, to the jewelled man's uncanny skull.

The head bobbed sluggishly in the water just beyond her reach, and Alia cursed her own foolishness; once having found the thing, she could not just leave it there – no matter what uneasy feelings it might evoke in her. Murder had been committed here. She would

63

have to inform the Moot. There would be full outlawry and banishment for somebody over this.

She cast about her and saw the signs of where the small furred folk had come down to drink, scattered rabbit pellets, the delicate cloven print of a little deer in a patch of wet earth at the pool's side. But over there, something larger had come down the bank to the water, had lain stretched on the ground further up. Human, from the signs. This same morning perhaps. But she could see no blood or other indications of any struggle.

Shaking her head, Alia pulled off her high-topped hunter's boots and waded out into the icy water to retrieve the thing. It was far from pretty. The teeny-weenies and the crawdads had been at it. Flesh hung in ragged wet strips from the forehead and cheeks, and part of the bone of the jaw had begun to show along one side. The eyes were nothing but vacant, mucusy sockets. It stank, a wet, pungent, clinging odour.

It was impossible to tell who it might have been.

Alia felt a hot flush of resentment go through her. After everything that had happened ... and now she must cope with this! The thought of facing the Reeve Vale Moot made her shiver with unease. It had been three long years since she had last set foot in Riverside, and she had no liking to return to the town now. But she knew well enough what was required of her in a situation such as this: she must bear official witness to this killing at the Moot in Reeve Hall before Reeve Garth himself. And the severed head ... Unpleasant a burden though it might be, she must take it along with her as evidence.

But she felt a growing reluctance. Her hand, holding the head by its wet hair, began to shake. Almost before she knew she had done it, she had flung the head back into the pool.

Alia stared in unbelief as it rolled torpidly in the water. Why had she done such a ridiculous thing? She would only have to retrieve it again.

But now, though she tried to enter the water, she found that she could not, somehow, force herself to do it. She would feel the cold, slick surface of a submerged rock under one foot, bring the other foot up off the bank, and then find herself, unaccountably, standing with both feet on the leafy grass.

She stood there, shaken, cradling her scarred left hand, which hurt – quick flashes of pain as if someone were thrusting invisible needles through it. A cold shiver crawled along Alia's spine, and she felt her heart thump. She whirled. The hair on her scalp lifted. Almost, she expected to see the demon-creature hovering near, or some other such impossible being – a half-glimpsed, darksome shadow-shape under the birches perhaps.

But there was nothing, not even one of the faint, sideways glimpses of the Fey she sometimes experienced. The pool was empty of movement and still as glass again now, the whole area silent save for the soft whisperings of the birches in the afternoon breeze.

Quickly, her heart still thumping, she grabbed up her boots and hurried away through the trees.

Only when she had put the place well behind her did she pause to put her boots back on. By then she was feeling angered, and more than a little foolish. How would she explain any of it to Charrer Mysha and the rest? Or to the Moot itself, should it come to that.

She flexed her left hand, the discomfort of which had subsided to a dull, nagging throb. She turned back towards the pool, but found herself – she, who had been this route a half a hundred times! – suddenly unsure of the way.

The sheer ridiculousness of it enraged her.

She tried again, but somehow it was no use. Try as she might, she only ended up in stumbling confusion.

It gave her the shivering meemies.

Alia sketched a warding sign in the air, her fingers quivering. She understood none of this. It frightened and infuriated her. She stood there, shaking, loath in her very bones to give in helplessly to this uncanny compulsion that gripped her, but having no choice it seemed. There was nothing else left her to do save walk away.

So walk away she did, turning her back to the place, shaken and shivering and baulked. Her belly was cramped into a tight knot. Had the world gone entirely mad, then? The Powers shaken out of their proper kilter? If the very sun himself were to fall suddenly from out of the sky, she felt she would not be surprised.

But there was not a thing for her to do about any it.

Having no other option, Alia set herself for the last leg of her journey. If she pushed herself, she was sure she could still reach Hunters Camp before nightfall, just. She had had more than enough of fright and confusion, and she ached to be done with violent, lying bandits, impossible demon-creatures, mysterious severed heads and uncanny compulsions.

Alia set herself like a hound on a trail, thinking of fire warmth and hot mint tea and familiar faces, and staggered on, aching in her very bones to be back where everything was safe and normal.

But everything, it turned out, was not safe and normal.

Hunters Camp was hidden in a cleft on a spur of the Mira Hills that came down to the coast in a huge, sweeping tumble of rock and pine. Only those who knew well where to look stood any chance of finding the camp; so Alia was dismayed and shocked to see before her on the path the clear spoor of many feet – unmistakable prints of hobnailed boots, not soft-soled hunters' footwear.

She stood in the chill evening twilight and felt her belly cramp up in anguish. She could not believe it. Bandits? Could *that* be why those in the hills had shown no proper fear of her hunter status? Was she already too late with her news? Alia thought of the decapitated head left behind at Birchleg Pool and shuddered, seeing in her mind's eye the lean-tos and tents and drying racks of Hunters Camp in ruins, the dead sprawled about like so many torn and abandoned rag dolls, their heads taken. For what if these bandits collected such grisly trophies?

It did not bear thinking on.

After what she had endured, to reach the end of this exhausting journey, only to have the haven she had counted on snatched from her, was nearly too much. Almost, she collapsed then and there. She felt tears fill her eyes and blinked them back furiously.

What was she to do now?

The way ahead was clearly compromised. Who knew but that those who had made these tracks might not be only a little ahead, waiting in ambush for just such as her to come unwittingly along.

She felt a crawly shudder go down her spine. Perhaps, even now, some of them were spying on her from a distance.

The rising loop of the path curved away before her, winding like a little river, disappearing quickly into the pines. On either side, steep slopes reared up, thick with more pines. In the growing dimness of evening, the trees bordering the path were drowned in purple shadows. Her heart thumping, Alia scuttled into that shadowy dimness and scrambled hastily away from the path.

Feeling safer, she hunkered down against a pine bowl, gasping raggedly for breath. It made no sense, bandits invading Hunters Camp. She could not, *would* not believe it.

But the tracks had been there, too plain to deny.

Alia hung her head tiredly, uncertain what to do next. Her

swollen face throbbed with pain, her left hand had begun to itch maddeningly, and her limbs were leaden with weariness. Discretion suggested that she turn back and make for the security of Riverside, where she could certainly count on finding safety. No hill-bandit rabble, no matter how insanely ambitious or violent, could do aught seriously to threaten a whole town. But Riverside was a far walk from here, and she did not feel able for it, exhausted as she was and with night nearly here. Besides, she still could not quite bring herself to accept what those tracks seemed to confirm.

Alia hugged herself, shivering. It was chill here in the darkening woods, and would grow more so as night came on.

Perhaps there was some explanation for those tracks other than bandits.

Perhaps not.

Alia sighed. Shaking herself, she set off towards Hunters Camp, her pulse beating hard with hope and dread.

It was slow, exhausting work, for she dared not move too quickly. Having felt once already what it was like to fall into bandit hands, she was none too eager to repeat the experience. And she did not have even her little boot knife now. Upslope she wormed her way, pausing often to listen, her eyes flitting nervously this way and that, until eventually she struggled up over the sharp crest of Sundog Ridge and caught a glimpse through the trees of the beginnings of Hunters Vale on the other side below her.

Though the light was failing, she could see well enough to make out a portion of the path to Hunters Camp which lay a double score of paces to her left. There was no sign of hidden watchers or ambush, no indication anything was amiss. The world hung still and silent. The last of the day's light glowed beyond the spine of the further slopes, like a crimson veil flung across the sky.

Alia stayed as she was, bent over, trying to stifle her panting breaths, watching, listening, sniffing the air for any sign. But there seemed nothing.

Darkness ate up the wood.

Alia waited for moonrise. It took no great time – the moon was only a couple of days from full – and as the white-gold orb ghosted up over the horizon, she started onwards again. The silver half-light formed an intricate, mazey tapestry of shadows, and though it was better than no light at all, Alia was forced to move almost as much by touch as sight. She knew the area well, though, and was still able to advance at a fair pace, the dark and uncertainty and her own stiff, aching limbs notwithstanding.

After a time, she heard the murmurous sound of distant voices. With that as a guide, she soon spied the far-off glimmer of firelight below. Moving more carefully than ever, she crept onwards until, at last, she lay against the knobby root of one of the pines, shivering in the chill darkness, and peered into the firelit camp fifty paces below her.

Something was most definitely amiss.

A lattice of black, feathery pine boughs stood between her and the camp, making it hard to see things for certain, and the uncertain moonlight combined with the flickering light of the fires created a confusing dance of shadow shapes. But there were far too many folk moving about down there. Alia searched hopefully for familiar faces, but it was all too unclear. The sound of their voices was a sea sound, clamorous and distant, and she could make out no more detail with her ears than she could with her eyes.

But it was clear enough that this was not the familiar camp she knew. The worst had happened, then: the camp had been overrun. She felt her heart shudder in dismay.

Rising to a half-crouch, Alia turned and started to slink away. But her weary legs had stiffened and she stumbled, barking her shin painfully against an unexpected upthrust of stone and fell clumsily to her knees. She let out a little inadvertent cry of pain and surprise.

Upslope, a branch snappled suddenly.

Alia froze.

Again, she heard the snapple of little branches breaking, but softly this time. She shifted slightly to one knee, getting a foot under her. The sounds continued for a moment, softly, as something or somebody trod a careful, transverse way through the pine trees upslope from her in the moon-dappled dark.

Then silence.

Alia felt her pulse thump in her throat. In the uncertain tangle of moon radiance and black shadow, she could make out nothing. She held her breath, listening, trying to catch whatever it might be out there in movement, but there was only continued silence now.

With painful care, she got both feet under her, rose, and began to slip away, weaving from one patch of concealing shadow to another. She plied her stiff legs like a dancer, careful step after careful step, lifting her knees high, testing the needle-carpeted ground beneath her feet through the soft leather soles of her hunter's boots before placing her weight.

There was silence still about her, save for the thumping of her own heart, and she thought she was going to make it.

But her weary legs failed her for one brief, fatal moment, and she stumbled. In a sudden rush, something leaped at her from the dark and a hard hand took her by the shoulder, thrusting her backwards. She fell, and her attacker fell with her.

She heard hissing breath near her face and reached out, groping for the vulnerable softness of his eyes with her thumbs. But with a crash another body hit her unexpectedly from behind, thumping hard into her back. She gasped, struggling. A fist smacked her along the side of her face, making the bruises already there flare into agony, and her vision broke apart into whirling blots of light.

By the time she had recovered herself, they were hauling her stumbling along, one at each elbow, down towards the firelit camp. She tried to tear out of their grasp but it was no use. They pulled her inexorably in amongst the fires.

She could see the folk squatting about the flames look up, startled. Alia had never seen so many people in Hunters Camp. The place fairly swarmed with them. She felt suddenly weak with dismay. Hunters Camp was no place for crowds. It was a quiet place, and peaceful. A green haven.

But it was peaceful haven no longer: men and women were crowded in here like so many noisome, roosting fowl. And young children too, she now saw. Families.

But who had ever heard of bandit families?

Her two captors were armed and grim faced. Not hunters, certainly. Yet Alia's initial dread began to give way to confusion. The men hustling her along wore brimless leather caps, one with a weasel tail dangling behind, and in the firelight she could see an embroidered design on those caps: the crossed-spears-and-sword-blade insignia of the Reeve Vale Militia. Not bandits at all, then. And those about the fires ... Vale men and women all, Alia now realized.

Alia understood none of this. Nobody came to Hunters Camp save the hunters themselves. What were Militiamen doing, playing at sentry here?

On they dragged her, past the first of the fires. And now she saw something else: bandages, wounds, blood. She tried to stop, wrenching at the hold the two men had on her. 'What has happened here?' she demanded of them.

They gave her no reply.

'What has *happened*?' she repeated, her voice scaling up. She struggled to break free of their grip. 'Let me go. I'm a hunter. I belong here. Let me *go*!'

But the men only dragged her on.

'Alia!' a voice called out.

Craning her head, Alia spotted Orrin, his unruly red hair shining like a torch in the firelight as he came striding over. 'Let her go,' he called to her captors. 'She's one of us.'

But the two men merely hustled Alia onwards, ignoring him.

'Let her *go*, I said!'

'Walk away, boy,' one of the men replied. 'This is no concern of yours. We bring her to Hone Amis. If she is as you claim, she will come to no harm at his hands.'

Alia stared. Hone Amis? What was the Master of Reeve Vale's Militia doing here?

'Let her go!' Orrin repeated. He put two fingers to his lips and whistled the sharp, up-scaling distress call familiar to all hunters.

It took only a few heartbeats for aid to come.

Alia saw Patch one-eye and lean Tym appear at Orrin's elbow, and others behind.

'Let her go,' Orrin ordered. 'Now!'

An ugly tension had sprung up suddenly. Alia felt it clear as a kick in the belly. Somebody behind Orrin had brought a bow and stood with the arrow knocked and aimed at Alia's captors. The man with the weasel-tailed cap half let her go and drew his sword in a quick *whissk* of cold metal.

'Did *they* do that to her?' Alia heard somebody demand angrily.

It was a long moment before she could make sense of the question, remembering her battered face. 'No!' she gasped, intending *no* to the question, *no* to the bared sword, the drawn bow, *no* to the whole situation here. She had never, *never* seen a fellow hunter draw a bow in angry threat like this.

'Let her go!' the bowman snapped.

'*Enough*!' a voice shouted suddenly, loud enough to freeze them all as they stood.

Hone Amis himself came striding over. 'Put that weapon away, boy!' he snapped, pointing at the lad with the drawn bow. 'Now! Before you regret it.'

Slowly, the bow was lowered.

Hone Amis nodded. 'Good.' He turned to the men still holding

Alia. 'What is going on here?' He gestured to the one on Alia's left who still held his drawn sword. 'And sheath that blade.'

The man did as he was ordered. 'We caught this girl skulking about outside the camp in the dark, Master Amis, and were bringing her to you, as you ordered we ought with anybody we intercepted out there. But these ...' he glared at the hunters, 'madcaps took it into their stupid heads to try and stop us.'

'She's one of *us*,' red-haired Orrin snapped. 'You have no right to haul a hunter about like some sack of dirt.'

'She was an intruder, boy. Skulking about out there like any bandit. We have our orders.'

'Which you obey even in the face of all common sense?' Orrin demanded. 'How can you be so stupid? You can see she's dressed in hunter's greens. Look at the emblem on her sleeve. She's one of *us*. Any fool with half an eye can see that!'

'Orrin, calm yourself, lad.' It was Charrer Mysha, come padding up to join them. 'These are hurtful times. You do nobody any good by losing that temper of yours.'

'But they can *see* she's one of us,' Orrin snapped back. 'Are they *stupid?*'

'Ser Charrer,' Hone Amis said to Charrer Mysha by way of greeting, using the formal "Ser" of the ruling Families and making a short bow of recognition.

Mysha nodded back, silent.

Hone Amis glared for a moment, obviously offended by Mysha's offhandedness. Then he hooked a thumb at red-haired Orrin. 'Tell this foul-tempered boy of yours to watch his mouth, Ser Charrer, or one of my Militia will close it for him with a boot heel. What kind of a Commander are you that you cannot properly control your own people?'

'They are not *my* people, Amis,' Charrer Mysha replied. 'As I've already tried to make clear to you. They came here of their own will, and may leave as freely as they came. I am no sort of *Commander* at all.'

A small group was gathered about Hone Amis. Closest stood three in particular: a thin, grey-beared, dour man, sombrely yet finely dressed; a balding man with a plump, florid face; and a grey-grizzled Militia Captain, his cap-badge showing the single star of his rank, who stood at Hone Amis's right hand.

The Captain pointed an accusing finger at Charrer Mysha. 'So these hunters of yours just run about willy nilly, like so many

71

brainless hounds without direction? Have you gone completely mad, warped away in this wilderness?'

Hone Amis waved his Captain back. 'Hold your tongue,' he hissed.

But the only reply Mysha made to the Captain's remark was to shrug.

More folk were drawing in from other parts of the camp now. Militiamen took stance around Hone Amis, merging with those already there to enclose Alia and her captors and form a protective hedge for the Militia Master and the trio who stood close to him. The young hunters who had come at Orrin's call drew in protectively about Charrer Mysha in their turn. More joined them, till there were two sizeable groups confronting each other.

Alia looked uneasily at the Militia Master, who stood solid and unbending, his grey whiskers bristling about his jaw like a dog's raised hackles. He was shorter than Charrer Mysha by a full head, but thicker of build, with a bit of a belly. But there was no softness to him. He had a well-deserved reputation as a hard case. Alia knew the type – her father had been one such – a man who brooked no opposition to his will. He was kitted out as for a fight, in chainmail byrnie, sword, and padded fighting helm, all battered with use. Even in the flickering light of the fires, she could see the anger in him writ clear on his face. But there was something else, too. His face was haggard and pale. His eyes had a staring cast to them, and there were dark bruises of exhaustion under those eyes. He had the look of a man dangerously on the edge.

Charrer Mysha, in contrast to Hone Amis, was long limbed and thin and agile as a rangy pony, beardless, his long, grey-streaked dark hair pulled back from his face and tied in a knot at the back of his skull to keep it out of the way. He wore hunter's leathers and moved softly, talked softly. His dark eyes gazed unblinkingly at Hone Amis. He had far-seeing eyes, did Mysha, and saw things others could not. This evening, though, Mysha's eyes held the same sort of haggard look as Hone Amis's.

Alia shivered. Those gathered here seemed tense as so many coiled metal springs, ready to let go with a sudden, violent snap.

She did not understand any of this.

'You cannot command the waves, Amis,' Charrer Mysha was saying, but softly. 'And the autumn leaves will not return to the branch by your orders.'

Hone Amis frowned.

'Make sense, damn you!' the plump, balding man said irritatedly. 'This is no silly game we play here! You sound like a be-damned Closterer.'

'I *am* making sense, Merith Roul,' Mysha replied. 'You cannot make a thing so just by ordering it so. The world is not made thus.'

Hone Amis snorted. 'The world is as men *make* it.'

Mysha sighed.

'Ser Charrer,' the grey-bearded, dour man at Hone Amis's shoulder said with sudden, fierce earnestness, 'You are a member of one of the Five Families. It is a blood calling, that, for all that you ran away from it. It is a *responsibility*.'

'Aye!' plump, balding Merith Roul added. 'For all we know, Poll and your father are both dead and *you* are Head of Family Charrer now. Listen to what we've been trying to tell you, damn it. Listen properly as Ser Charrer, not some ignorant, ragged woodsrunner!'

Charrer Mysha stiffened. 'The accident of one's birth is not what matters here.'

'Accident of birth!' The grey-bearded man shook his head in disgust. 'You *have* gone mad!'

Charrer Mysha shrugged and executed a mock bow. 'Madness is as madness does, Ser Obart.'

The grey-bearded man spat. 'Fool!'

Hone Amis stabbed an accusing finger at Charrer Mysha. 'It may have been all right to play your little hunter's games up here in the hills till now. But *now* everything is changed!'

An angered murmur went up from the hunters gathered about in response to this.

'Wake up, the lot of you!' Hone Amis cried to them. 'The world has changed. The cursed Sea Wolves saw to that. The old Reeve is dead, Riverside is destroyed.'

Alia stared, stricken. Riverside destroyed? The Reeve dead?

'And good riddance to it, is what I say,' Orrin replied, to a surge of muttered agreement from those about him.

'*What?*' Hone Amis barked.

Orrin stepped forward, his unruly red hair bright as flame in the firelight. 'Good riddance to it!' he repeated.

The grizzled Militia Captain at Hone Amis's side glared at the young hunter, his face puckered with outrage. 'You ignorant, ungrateful *puppy*! You owe everything, *everything* to Riverside and to the Reeve and the Five Families and what they have wrought here in this wilderness through their own sweat and blood. Without them, you would have nothing save chaos and violence. Folk would be living in squalor, at the mercy of bandits.'

Alia shuddered. She felt as if she were in some queer sort of dream, the flicker of the firelight painting everything, faces about her all shadow and gleaming eyes and bared teeth. 'Riverside is destroyed?' she said haltingly into the silence that had now fallen. 'The Reeve is ... *dead?*'

'Aye, destroyed,' Hone Amis responded irritably. 'Where have you *been*, girl?' He glared at the hunters gathered against him. 'Are you all stupid? Everything is *changed!*'

A muttered growl came from the hunters. They closed ranks further, faces sullen with anger.

Hone Amis's Militia gathered closer to him, fists on the hilts of their short-bladed swords. Hone Amis pointed accusingly at Charrer Mysha. 'It was easy enough for you to flee away and start this little haven of yours in the wilderness, aye, and to leave the proper running of things to others for all those years. But now ... *now* you must forsake such self-indulgent foolishness. Surely you must see that? Surely! Or don't you care what happens to folk any more?'

Charrer Mysha sighed. 'I care, Amis. I *care*. But you are more right than you know when you say things have changed. The world we hunters knew may be dead and gone, but the same holds true for you. Your world is gone, too.'

Hone Amis bristled. 'Not unless I give in and abandon it! And *that* I will never do!'

Mysha sighed once more. 'How can I make it clear to you, Amis?' He gestured to the green-clad hunters clustered close about him. 'We came here because we wished to be free of your world.'

'Free!' Hone Amis snorted. 'You've run away from your responsibilities to play at being children in the woods. It's time you grew up! Winter will be upon us all too soon. We have work to do if we are to save the settlement.'

'What if we don't want to save it?' demanded young Orrin.

The Militia Captain took a menacing step forward, his hand on the hilt of his sword and his face lit with anger.

Hone Amis called him back with a muttered command. 'I lose patience, boy,' he said to Orrin. 'We *will* rebuild Riverside. We *will* save the settlement. You are either with us or against us. And if against us, you are no better than a common hill bandit and shall be treated as such.'

Orrin stepped forwards, bristling. Charrer Mysha tried to put a restraining hand on his shoulder but the younger man shrugged it off impatiently and faced Hone Amis and the three that still stood closest to him, glaring. 'You and yours are guests here at Hunters Camp, Hone Amis Latirson. What sort of a guest is it who threatens his hosts?' Orrin spat. 'You're as bad as dirty hill bandits, the lot of you!'

A strained, momentary hush settled over everything. Alia heard the snappling of the fires' flames, the *crunch* of a hobnailed bootsole across a twig underfoot as one of the Militia shifted position.

'Wait!' she called to them all.

It was like the moment in the Heights when she had watched the two bandits about to go for each other; they were like buck dogs facing each other, these two groups, hackles up, mindless to aught else. She could smell disaster here sure as sure if nothing interfered to prevent things from escalating.

'Let me *go!*' she ordered the men who still held her captive. She glared at Hone Amis. 'I'm a hunter. Surely you can see that.'

He hesitated for a long moment, then shrugged, nodded, gestured to the men. They released her.

Alia stumbled away. Orrin reached out and grabbed her by the hand. It was her left one he took, and sudden pain shot through her arm as he gripped it. For a brief, disorienting moment, Alia saw the demon-creature clear as clear in her mind's eye, driving the men, the argument, the camp itself from her awareness. She saw the huge inhuman eyes, beckoning, beckoning ...

'Alia!' she heard Orrin say. '*Alia!*'

He had his arms about her now, had gathered her to him protectively. 'What did you *do* to her?' he demanded over her head of the two who had dragged her in.

'No,' she said to him, gasping, shaking herself loose from the demon-vision – if vision it were. 'It's all right. I'm all right.' She fended him away, slipping from his grasp, turned to face the two conflicting groups. 'Listen to me!' she cried. '*All* of you, listen! I've just come down through the Salter Pass.' She pointed to her bruised face. 'Look at the state of me. How do you think I got like this?'

'*They* did it to you,' one of the hunters called, pointing accusingly at Alia's erstwhile captors.

'No!' Alia responded. 'Not them. Bandits. *Bandits!*'

They were staring at her now, Militia and hunters alike.

Alia stood, aching arms out to encompass both sides arrayed about her in the dancing flicker of the firelight. 'You stand here squabbling with each other, and meanwhile, in the Heights, bandits are gathering. I saw a hundred of them. More perhaps!' Alia paused self-consciously, then swallowed and continued. 'They have a camp set up in the Heights. And there was this leader ... Torno. And ...' The words came tumbling out now; it was such a relief to tell it. 'And there was this man called Sethir ... and he ... and I ... I ended up ... stabbing this Torno and then ... Then there was this strange jewelled man who had a skull ... with jewels on it. And I thought I saw eyes in the skull. Almost. But it must have been ...'

'Don't be *ridiculous*, girl,' Hone Amis interrupted. 'None of what you're saying makes any sense. And there's *never* been bandits in that number in the Heights.'

Alia glared at him. 'There are now.'

Hone Amis snorted. 'You panicked. You imagined things. I've seen it happen many a time, even to grown men, never mind a slip of a boy-dressed girl like you. Every stray sound in the dark becomes a lurking enemy. Got those bruises on your face running into a pine in the dark, most like. Next, you'll be telling me one of the Fey swooped into this bandit camp and whisked you away to safety.'

The Militia round about laughed.

Alia blinked. 'No,' she said, without thinking. 'It was something else entirely.'

'Entirely what?' Hone Amis enquired.

'That carried me away.'

The Militia Master looked at her and shook his head dismissively, as if she were some wayward, fibbing child. He closed his eyes, opened them, sighed. 'We have important concerns here,' he said, tight lipped. 'You try my patience. So be a good girl and don't distract us with childish imaginings. Run away now and leave us to our business.'

Alia began to panic, feeling things slipping away from her, feeling it all go wrong somehow. She was weary, sore, flustered. She looked across to Charrer Mysha. 'It's *true*,' she told him desperately. 'I ... I was up near Tally's Bluff. I caught a glimpse of ... *them*. And while I was trying to see them more clear, the bandits took me, brought me to their camp trussed like a hog.' She shuddered, remembering.

The Militia Captain at Home Amis's side took a step towards Alia. 'Them?' he demanded. 'And who is this *them?*'

Alia looked at him, at Hone Amis, looked away. 'The ... Fey.'

The Militia Master snorted in disgust. 'The Fey? You're telling silly *children's* tales, girl. Grow up!'

Alia turned to Charrer Mysha again. She did not know what to do.

One of the things that held them all together here in Hunters Camp was a shared experiencing of the deep mysteries of the wild lands. To some extent or other, every hunter had experienced something of the Fey, and of the mysterious, soul-shivering current of the great wild where Powers moved and the world became something *other*. It was this very experience, more than anything else, perhaps, that differentiated them from ordinary Vale folk – for Vale folk, walled away in their houses and orderly fields, experienced the great mysteries only in child's tales.

And so practical men like Hone Amis dismissed all such things, and accounts of them, out of hand.

Alia felt her belly tighten in anguish. How could she have been so stupid as to blurt things out like that? The Fey, ragged bandit hordes, lying Sethir and the elegant jewelled man with his uncanny skull; it all sounded so *improbable*. She was only thankful she had not said anything of (the very thought made her hand throb) that uncanny demon-creature ...

Mysha padded forwards out of the hunter pack that had surrounded him and came over to where Alia stood between the hunters and the Militia.

Hone Amis glared at him. 'Enough of this, I say, Ser Charrer. We have more important matters to contend with than this girl's silly ravings!'

Alia stood, stricken. Such was the forcefulness of the Militia Master, that she could see the beginnings of doubt in the eyes of the hunters gathered here. And for one long, terrible moment, Hone Amis's complete repudiation of all she had said worked upon her to such an extent that she almost began to doubt herself.

But she clenched her fists, feeling a thrust of pain in her left as the marks the demon had scribed into her palm were compressed. She turned to Charrer Mysha imploringly. 'It's *truth!*' Her voice cracked and she had to swallow. 'Everything I've said.'

Mysha's far-seeing eyes glimmered in the firelight like an owl's. Alia shivered. Surely he, of all folk, would not doubt her. Every hunter here might have experienced the wild's mysteries to some extent, but none like Mysha. Not only could he see the Fey; he could also *converse* with them. The very look of him was different from anybody Alia had ever known, as if he walked with one foot in the ordinary world and one in something *other*.

Mysha looked at her long and deep.

Then he nodded, put a hand on Alia's shoulder, and turned to Hone Amis. 'If Alia here says there are a hundred bandits up in the Heights, I believe her.'

Hone Amis glared at them in irritation. 'Don't be a fool, Mysha! The girl's a crazy adolescent. All this foolish talk. She's obviously lying, or demented. Or both!'

'She is neither,' Mysha responded quietly.

Alia felt a flush of warmth go through her, feeling Mysha's slim hand on her shoulder, feeling the support it offered.

Hone Amis frowned. He took a breath, clenched and unclenched his fists. 'Look, Mysha, we both know what being alone at night in the wild lands is like. The mind ... sees things that aren't there. This girl of yours no doubt means well enough. But you cannot ... *cannot* expect me to take what she says seriously when she starts talking about such things as the jewelled men and the Fey – about children's fantasies – as if they were real!' He turned to Alia. 'What manner of a witling do you take me for, girl?'

'There are more things in the world than you know, Hone Amis,' Charrer Mysha said. 'Or do you claim to know *everything* there is in the world?'

The Militia Master shook his head impatiently. 'Of course not! But I recognize adolescent nonsense when I hear it. Reeve Vale is in chaos. You've given us refuge here in Hunters Camp, but who knows how many folk may yet be left alive down in the Vale, or what state they may be in by now? Lost and half crazed the most of them, no doubt. We need to arrange food and shelter. We need to search for survivors. The young Reeve himself may still be alive and down there somewhere! Would you have us wasting time on some wild chase after this girl's fantasies?'

'I'm telling the truth!' Alia snapped.

Hone Amis scowled. 'What would so many bandits be doing up there in the Heights, girl?'

Alia shrugged uncomfortably. 'I don't know. But I fear the worst.'
'And that is?'

But before Alia could frame a reply, Orrin had stalked over to stand on the opposite side of her from Mysha. She felt his shoulder press up against hers.

'Don't take stupid risks, Militia Master,' Orrin said.

'Don't give me advice, boy,' Hone Amis snapped back. 'I was

ordering forays against bandits when you were still in your swaddling clothes puking over your mother's shoulder.'

Alia felt Orrin stiffen, but before he could respond, Mysha interceded. 'But the boy has the right of it, Amis. It *would* be a stupid risk for us to ignore the possibility of so many bandits in the Heights. You're a practical man. Think! What if Alia *is* right and we ignore what she says?'

The Militia Master shook his head. He glared at Charrer Mysha, hands on his hips, in truculent silence. Then, slowly, he shrugged, grimaced, sighed. Finally, he nodded with ill grace. 'All right! Agreed. If, and I say *if* there is any truth to this girl's story, we must find it out, if only to ...'

'So we organize a bandit hunt,' Orrin said, interrupting.

'Shut *up*, boy!' the Militia Captain snapped menacingly.

'Mysha,' Hone Amis demanded, '*why* can't you keep your people in line?'

Mysha sighed. 'They're not *my* people, Amis. How many times must we go through that?'

There was silence for a long few moments.

The two older men at Hone Amis's side – grey-bearded Ser Obart and pudgy, balding Merith Roul – drew close to him. The Militia Captain joined them, and, heads together, the four began a quiet-voiced conference.

Before they had more than just begun, however, Hone Amis shook his head, said something in a fierce whisper, then shrugged out and away from the others. He ran a hand wearily across his face, clenched his eyes shut for a moment, shook himself. 'Right. I've had enough of this. There is much to be done tomorrow. Even *more* now, with this girl's bandit scare.' He turned to the three behind him. 'We can talk tomorrow.' Grey-bearded Ser Obart glared daggers at him, but the Militia Master ignored it. 'For now ...' He turned back to Charrer Mysha and the hunters, ran a hand over his face once more, yawned a great, jaw cracking yawn. 'For now, good night, the lot of you.' With that he turned abruptly and stamped off, the trio with him following, his Militia falling in behind.

Alia sighed a great sigh of relief.

'Good riddance to him,' Orrin muttered. He made a rude sign in the Militia Master's direction. 'Arrogant arsehole!'

Charrer Mysha shook his head. 'One day that temper of yours is going to bring you to grief, lad, mark my words.'

'But not tonight,' Orrin replied, smiling triumphantly. He took

Alia by the shoulder and swung her along with him towards one of the fires. 'Come on, Alia my girl, tell us about these bandits of yours. What *happened* to you up there in the Heights? Did you really catch a clear glimpse of *them*?'

Orrin's exuberance, as always, was infectious, and Alia could not help but smile a little. But it did not last; there was too much of grief written on the faces round about for her to be able to listen easily to Orrin's usual animated prattling. What terrible thing had occurred in Reeve Vale while she had been away up in the Heights?

'What ... what has happened?' she asked, gesturing to the stricken folk all about.

'Raiders from out of the sea,' Orrin responded. 'Bringing fire and destruction and death.'

'And leaving this human flotsam washed up here.' It was lean Tym, come up to walk with them at Orrin's side. Tym was older than most of those who made their home in Hunters Camp, and embittered by some sad thing or other he had left behind – what, nobody knew, for none in Hunters Camp talked of their past lives in the Vale. He shook his head now, surveying the refugees that filled the camp.

Patch one-eye joined them. He patted Alia on the shoulder. 'Welcome home,' he said softly.

'Hunters Camp isn't meant to be a rabbit warren like this,' Tym was complaining.

'Should we have denied these poor folk sanctuary, then?' Patch demanded.

Tym shrugged. 'It only works to our own destruction.'

Patch shook his head.

'It does us no good!' Tym insisted. 'As long as none of the Vale folk could find us here, we were secure enough. There was no way in which they could fetch us back.'

'Leave it go, Tym,' Orrin said. 'Alia's too weary to ...'

But Tym went on. 'You *know* that's what they've always wanted to do, Orrin! They hate us getting away from them. When they didn't know where we lived, we could go down to Riverside and trade meat and hides, and there was nothing they could do to interfere.' Tym gestured at the crowded camp. 'Where's our safety *now*? What's to stop this Hone Amis Latirson from trying to march us all back down there to Riverside, with the point of a blade at our backs, and forcing us to do his will?'

'They're not the enemy, Tym,' Patch said. 'Be reasonable. They're our own folk. They needed help.'

'They're not *my* folk!' Tym said fiercely.

Alia stared at Tym's white, fierce face, at the stricken expressions of those huddled in refuge about the camp's fires, at worried, kind Patch. It was all so overwhelming. She faltered and stumbled, only Orrin's still firm grip keeping her from going to her knees. It was not just weariness and the uneven ground; the world as she had known it was shattered apart – overnight it seemed – in blood and violence. Everything broken by catastrophe. Sea Wolves and death and disaster. Bandits and bejewelled skulls and impossible demon-creatures in the Heights.

Her one moment of hope with the Fey up in the wild Heights wrecked. And what chance was there of ever finding herself again in that most special situation?

It felt to her as if a great black pit were opened before her and she stood staring down into it, an endless drop into empty, devouring darkness. For a moment, that pit had seemed utterly real ...

Orrin's firm hands held her upright, and the illusion dissolved away. He held her round the arms, leaving her sore left hand thankfully untouched, and guided her along. Alia shivered. She wanted the warmth of a fire, a mug of hot mint tea, familiar faces around her. She wanted not to feel the world coming apart. She wanted to sleep long and wake in the morning to find that everything was as it once had been.

But she felt, with a sinking certainty, that her old world was indeed gone forever.

And she did not know at all what might lie ahead.

V

Guthrie was floundering along through the wild woods that choked the hummocky slopes of the foothills, searching for a way back to the sea. Coming away from Riverside, he had followed what he took to be a simple short-cut southwards which ought to have saved him leagues of tiresome walking; instead, the maze of the hills had swallowed him up, and the sea, it appeared, had vanished. The sun seemed to play tricks with him, guiding him first one way then another. Every rise over which he had hoped to glimpse the sea's shining expanse proved a disappointment, revealing to him only more tangles of pine forest, more steep-sloped hillsides, more wearying, directionless travel.

It was his second day now of such fruitless wandering. His limbs shook as he trudged on, each step a weary effort. The revenge fire that had lit him in Riverside was burnt low now, but he could still recall clearly the Sea Wolves' mocking laughter, and that was enough, somehow, to keep him moving.

So Guthrie struggled weakly on. He did not know how many days it had been since last he had eaten properly, and these damnable hills seemed devoid of stream or brook. His mouth ached for water. His awareness was sputtering like a candle flame, and the world seemed strange about him. There were times he seemed to catch the trees in conspiracy, laughing softly at him behind his back, and he would shout at them, threatening, pleading ...

Until, at last, the clutching wood gave way abruptly to an expanse of undulating meadow.

Guthrie stared, open mouthed. The open slope before him hung like a great green wave, frozen in the very act of breaking upon the shore of the forest.

He walked out into the whispering grass, leaving the trees behind. Some little ways on, he found a grassy brook, drank greedily, stumbled on again. His body seemed to feel light as air now. The world appeared to glow with an inner radiance, as if stones and trees and slow flapping crows were naught but burning torches thinly dressed in illusion. He stumbled to a halt, entranced. The sky above him swirled and filled itself slowly with dark clouds, like a pouring of black dye into deep blue water. He spied a huge, plunging horse leaping across the sun. The sky itself seemed to thrum with a multitude of strange voices. But though he stood transfixed, listening, he could make no sense out of what he heard.

Such incomprehensible voices reminded him suddenly, uncomfortably, of the dream he had had of the dead Abbod: of him skittering along from one disintegrating pathway to another, feeling the very ground under his feet shredding away, the decapitated Abbod following him, the head talking its incomprehensible talk ...

Remembrance of that dream made Guthrie shiver. The trauma of Riverside had driven all else from his mind, and he had spared the unwholesome skull hardly a thought. He did not wish to think on it now.

He started onwards through the whispering grass. From behind him, he began to hear a faint mumbling. He walked quicker, trying to ignore it, broke into a shambling run.

'Guthrie ... Guthrie ... Guthrie ...'

He did not look back, afraid of what he might see.

'Guthrie ... Guthrie ...'

'Leave me *be*!' he cried, whirling. He saw the spectre of the head floating in midair, like a haunting moon, the dead eyes wide and shining like lamps, the dead mouth working. Guthrie struck out, trying to bat the foul thing down from the air, leaping and shrieking.

Then the spectre-head swooped, long dives like a hawk's. Guthrie fled, heart hammering in terror, flapping his arms awkwardly about him, stumbling, falling, dragging himself up and along, his ribs hurting with each gasping breath. A great hand seemed to be squeezing him in a choking grip. He could not get air. He could not see.

Overhead, deep thunder rumbled. Frigid rain hammered suddenly at him. The world shattered apart into black gulfs and splintering, painful jags of light. But neither the thunder's roar nor the great splashing downpour of the cold rain could obscure the head's insidious voice: 'Guthrie ... Guthrie ...' it repeated, mumblingly, over and over and over.

Guthrie let out a shriek of outrage and terror, the last shreds of his strength unravelling, and felt himself collapse down a long dark slope into nothingness.

The cawing of crows roused him. Painfully, Guthrie propped himself half up and gazed about, blinking. He was cold and stiff, soaked through all along his back and side, where he had been lying on the wet grass, and dried out to mere dampness where the light and air had been able to get to him. All about him stretched rolling meadow. He fell back, utterly exhausted, gazing blindly into the endless, clear, after-storm blue of the sky above. He felt the dry heat of the sun upon him. His lips were raw and cracked, his tongue pebbly it felt so dry.

Hearing the crows again, he craned his head to look. Three black shapes hopped agilely into the air at his movement. From the safety of the air they eyed him with insolent appraisal.

Carrion birds.

Guthrie shuddered.

He did not know where he was. The past lay on him like a dream – the broken Closter, burnt Riverside, the uncanny head swooping at him like a bird of prey while the voice of the thunder roared ... all was there, but distant, somehow. He felt very light, as if his bones were filled with air, as if a stiff breeze could send him tumbling off across the meadow grass like a huge thistledown. He no longer felt hungry at all.

But, oh, his mouth was cruelly dry.

He tore up a handful of the wet grass and sucked on it, but it proved no more than a tantalization. Gasping, he struggled stiffly to his feet and staggered off in search of water. There were trees ahead, far off on the edge of his sight. Hoping they meant water, he made towards them, feeling his knees squeak with each step.

It seemed to take forever, that journey, struggling on through knee-high, storm-wet grass. The day waned, afternoon light giving slow way to the glowing radiance of sunfall. Guthrie thought he heard the world fill with the slow *hisss* of the sun as it sank into the sea – for all that he could not see the sea. And he heard the first faint stars speak to each other in the pewter sky, soft voices like a distant wind. When he drew close enough, he could hear the trees, too, whispering amongst themselves. The secret voices made him recall the head's insistent mumblings, and he shivered, casting uneasy glances behind.

But he came to the trees unmolested, slipped past the whispering branches, and came out onto an outcropping of splintered stone. Spying no water, he scrambled awkwardly over the rock and saw before him more grassy slope, the distant crest of which was crowned with a cluster of silver birch glowing palely in the dimming silver light, the last of their autumn leaves twirling like little lanterns in the breeze. They seemed to beckon. Guthrie made for them, plodding wearily through the wet grass.

There was water ahead. He could smell it as he drew close. Guthrie swallowed, imagining the blessed, liquid coolth of it on his tongue, and his heart quickened.

But drawing nigh, he realized that the birches grew about an all too familiar, rock-edged pool. Pushing through their shimmering leaves, he came to stand unsteadily on the open, grassy space at the water's verge.

The surface of the pool lay still and clear as glass. Guthrie saw the reflection of the darkening sky in it, the wavery arms of the birches.

He had come full circle.

He shuddered and would have fled such uncanniness. But the sweet, irresistible call of the water came to him clear as a ringing bell. He fell to his knees at the pool's verge and drank, smashing his hand into the water's glassy surface first to shatter his own stricken-faced reflection as it stared up at him. The cool, liquid ecstasy of the water in his mouth was such that he nearly swooned away.

When he had had his fill, he collapsed weakly back on the grass. He blinked, staring abut him. All that struggle, only to find himself here once more.

The birches whispered secrets amongst themselves. There was an uncanny feel in the air. Guthrie shivered. He stared at the web of shifting, half-stripped branches across the pool from him and suddenly gasped, for there, amongst the dance and twirl of the autumn leaves, was a face staring at him. He could just make out one impossibly long-fingered, slim hand against the silver shreds of a birch trunk ...

Pale, that face, and dominated by huge, dark, unblinking eyes – an ethereal form, not much more than half glimpsed in the failing light.

One of the Fey.

Guthrie felt his heart turn in his breast. The dreaminess in which he had walked fell away from him and he scrambled backwards, away from such an impossible creature.

The Fey were nothing but children's tales!

85

He shivered, looking into those dark, half-glimpsed, unhuman eyes. Guthrie had heard Fey-tales as a child, huddled next to his mother in the darkness of the winter nights: the world of the Fey and the human world overlapped, yes, but the two were not the same, and little good ever followed for ordinary mortal folk from meetings with the ethereal Fey; the Fey were unpredictable, unknowable; they had been here long and long before folk came northwards to settle these wild lands and did not willingly accept the newcomers; sometimes, they would steal human children ...

So the children's tales ran.

The unhuman dark eyes gazed at him, never blinking, the long-fingered hand, where it rested against the trunk, stayed still as still.

Guthrie felt a shudder go through him. Once, it was said, the Fey had intervened in human affairs. During the great war in the south it had been, the Demon War. But that was long ago, when even his dead-and-buried grandfather had been but a small boy. And only a story in any case.

But what if ...

Guthrie felt his pulse suddenly jump. What if the tales he had heard as a child, of how the Fey had stepped into human affairs to do battle with Tancred Black Robe, the terrible southern Wizard, where truth after all?

What if they were to do the same again now?

He came up to his knees, facing those big, steady, utterly unhuman eyes. 'Help me,' he implored. 'It is said that your kind aided human folk once before. Aid us now. Help me in my revenge. Help me ...'

The Fey stepped softly out from amongst the trees, moving with the easy grace of the very breeze itself. It was pale as new bone, and seemed almost to glow softly in the dimming light of the evening. But Guthrie had to blink and stare to keep it in focus, for it seemed somehow to slide in and out of his sight in some uncanny manner. Silent as a thought, it glided along the pool's shore towards him.

Guthrie felt a surge of sudden panic. There was no human friendliness in that pale face. 'No ...' he protested. 'Keep away!'

The Fey stood quiet, still some distance along the shore line from him, impossibly long and slim of limb. The dark eyes stared unblinkingly at Guthrie.

He felt his knees shake, his belly cramp up.

Then the Fey turned and stepped delicately into the water at the pool's edge. It remained strangely difficult to focus on, fading in and out of clarity, but Guthrie was able to follow it, just. Moving with the deliberate, long-limbed grace of a crane, it stretched one long arm down into the water and came up with a round, pale, dripping stone in its clasp. Easing out of the pool, it glided silently over to Guthrie, the stone balanced on one of its long-fingered hands, offering it to him.

Guthrie reached his own shaking hand out. Any object given by the Fey would be potent indeed. He felt his heart swell. He felt like a hero in one of the child's tales ...

But he froze with his arm only partway extended. It was no water-smoothed stone the Fey offered to him. The pale, long-fingered hand supported a white human skull, picked shining clean by the little creatures of the pool.

The Abbod's head.

'No ...' Guthrie moaned.

But his hand reached, as if with a life of its own, and he felt the cold, dripping hardness of the thing settle solidly on his palm.

The Fey gazed at him in silence, then withdrew. One heartbeat it was there, the next gone. Like smoke, or a shadow. It might never have been, save for the thing left in Guthrie's hold.

Guthrie stared at it. Gingerly, he pivoted the skull until the face of it was towards him. The empty eye sockets seemed to stare at him. He shuddered and tried to fling it away.

But could not.

It was as before. The terrible, foul thing had an uncanny hold over him such that he could not, could *not* throw it away.

'What do you want with me?' he demanded of it. '*What?*'

The head gave no response.

'Cursed, foul *thing*,' he hissed at it. 'Leave me be!'

But the head merely sat in his palm, cold wet bone, inert as any stone.

Guthrie sighed wearily. The pool had grown silent as a grave about him. Even the trees' voices had been stilled. Darkness had all but fallen, and he had to squint to make sense of his surroundings.

He was gripped by a sudden and complete conviction that this place held nothing for him now.

He felt ... unwanted.

The first stars were out now, full night nearly here. Sighing again, not fully understanding what drove him, Guthrie turned and trudged away into the deepening dark, forcing his weary legs onwards. He cursed his ill luck – back where he had begun, all his weary travelling having got him nowhere. The utter futility of all he had done overwhelmed him.

But far down, like a spluttering little fire, he felt the anger alight in him still. And he could still hear the Sea Wolves' mocking, cruel laughter.

He would not be baulked.

He would *not*.

Southwards again. That was where he must go. As he had intended. Despite all obstructions. Foul, uncanny skull or no.

Guthrie shook himself. Lifting his head, he saw the great jewellery of the stars alight in the deep sky. The night air was chill and he shivered. The stars danced their slow, slow dance through the heavens. Their world had not changed, would not change. Each belonged as it was, and would for ever.

But not he. Not any longer.

Guthrie felt hollow. He had been wrenched from his world. There was nothing else left him, no hunger that mattered now, save the one thing.

Revenge.

VI

It was like a nightmare, an endless, walking nightmare, Guthrie placing one weary foot before the other. Step. Step. Step. He had woken, trudged off through grassy meadows, and then, somehow, the woods had swallowed him and he found himself helplessly wandering again. Sunlight spilling through the deep tree-green in clouds of dancing light. A quick, inhuman visage, gazing at him – great dark eyes in a pale face, there plain as plain, and then gone in a breath. The clipping whir of little bird wings over his head. The breeze amongst the trees, talking, talking. A squirrel in a tree, red face bracketed by a blue-green tapestry of leaf and branch. The indignant squirrel voice shouting at him: *chunna chunna chut chunna chunna chut chut!*

Guthrie found himself slumped back against the rough bole of a pine, legs splayed out before him. He blinked confusedly, having no clear recollection of how he had come to be where he was. He could smell the sharp, resinous scent of the tree at his back, feel the stickiness of dribbled sap smeared against his cheek. Somewhere in the distance, the squirrel chunnered on.

He looked down at the skull, smooth and weighty in his hands, the bone of it yellow-white and solid feeling. He felt along the curved length of the jaw, cupped the intricately jointed dome of the skullcap with his palm. The long, exposed teeth seemed to grin at him, or leer, perhaps.

Guthrie felt a quick stab of hatred for the thing, like a cramp through his belly. A more useless, ugly burden he could not imagine. It would not let go of him, yet it gave him nothing. For the dozenth time he attempted to throw it from him.

And failed.

'What do you want with me?' he demanded of it. '*What?* Tell me or let me be!'

But the skull merely sat in his hold like a stone, dead to any entreaty of his.

Guthrie sighed wearily. 'No matter,' he murmured. 'For soon I will be like you,' He was beginning to feel it in his guts now, that he would not be much longer for this world. Too much had been taken from him. He was dwindled into a mere shell of his former self, like the husk of an old, old fruit, shrivelled beyond any ability to bring forth anything of life.

Not a single living person had he seen since that morning after the siege of the Closter. He was Reeve of a dead people.

Fitting that he, too, should be numbered amongst those dead.

'Soon,' he repeated to the silent skull, letting himself slump back against the rough bole of the pine. The revenge lust in him had gone cold. Soon he would make that final journey into the Shadowlands, like all the others. Why continue on like this? It meant only more exhausting, aimless walking. He had had enough of walking. Much easier to simply lie here forever.

Much easier.

But some stubborn little spark within him had not quite guttered out. Not yet. 'Help me, you useless thing,' he demanded of the skull, holding it up before him. '*Help me!*'

Nothing.

Guthrie slumped back. He felt hope drain from him like blood from a wound. No more of hope, then. No more of struggle. He sighed, weary beyond belief, and let his head loll.

Across his arm, an iridescent beetle crawled, a little greenish living jewel. He gazed at it vaguely. The soft forest light glinted off the creature's oily green carapace. The little legs moved rhythmically, the long, agile feelers wavered out before the black head and beady little eyes. *Food food food*, that was what it was thinking. Guthrie smiled. Aye, *food food food*. A good thought, that. A pure thought. A pure little being, unsullied by hopes or fears or hopeless hungers for revenge.

Guthrie closed his eyes, lay back in utter weariness. He felt a little tickling across his palm. Another travelling beetle, perhaps. But, he realized suddenly, it was the palm on which the skull lay.

Again he felt it, a little shiver as if the skull itself had shifted ever so slightly in his hold. He opened his eyes, stared at it. For an instant, the empty sockets seemed to contain eyes again, bright with life and knowledge, and to stare back at him.

Guthrie blinked, shocked. His heart beat with sudden, nervous hope. But when he looked once more, the skull's eye sockets were blind and empty, as always.

90

Useless, burdensome thing.

But then he felt it shiver once more, only the faintest of motions, little shuddering movements tickling his palm – so faint that he was not certain whether the thing actually moved at all, or if it were merely his own imagination that made him feel it.

Hardly daring to draw breath, Guthrie kept his hand still, staring. It seemed as if the skull moved, swivelling in his palm, or his palm turned – he knew not which – until the skull's face was turned away from him, as if peering off through the trees.

Guthrie shivered. There seemed nothing special about that direction. It led simply to more trees, exactly the same as all the rest.

He struggled painfully up to his feet, paused, uncertain and shaken, his heart thumping. Then, shivering, holding the skull out before him, he staggered off in the direction towards which it seemed to be staring.

When he saw the figure ahead of him through the trees, Guthrie thought it only another vision – one of the Fey again, or perhaps one of the other shadowy beings that seemed to throng the wood, for he had seen more than one apparition. The skull gazed in the figure's direction. Or perhaps not. He could no longer tell for sure, and did not know if it had led him along this way, or if he had merely stumbled here blindly on a fool's desperate quest.

But the figure ahead seemed an altogether solider being than any he had so far encountered.

It stood quiet, only half seen in the tree-thick, green dimness of the forest, still as the very trees themselves. Human, it seemed, robed in grey.

Guthrie felt a jolt go through his belly, seeing that grey robe. It was towards the shade of the dead Abbod that the skull had led him, then. Like the figure he had encountered in the dreams. Only he was not dreaming now. The dead Abbod's spirit seemed to stand before Guthrie plain as plain, dressed in the grey Closterer's robe he had worn when he had been killed by the Sea Wolf Chieftain – when he had *let* himself be killed. A charge of quick anger shook Guthrie, filling him with momentary strength. All the vagueness fell from his mind.

'*You!*' Guthrie cried accusingly, to the skull, to the figure before him, to both. He thrust out the skull in his hand, as if brandishing a weapon at the grey-robed apparition. 'How *dare* you stand there before me like this after what has happened? Everything is taken and gone and killed now. *Everything!* And you might have stopped it. You were a man of power. I *saw* what you were capable of. And you ...' But here Guthrie faltered.

The grey-robed figure stood before him calmly. It raised slow hands, palms out in a quietening gesture. The head was covered by a hood, but Guthrie could see the eyes under that hood gazing at him with steady attention.

Steady eyes in a head shadowed by the grey cloak's hood ...

Guthrie took a sudden, shocked step backwards, realizing that this figure before him was clearly not that same, headless shade of the dead Abbod whom he had encountered in the dreams.

'Ye mistakes me,' the grey robe said softly. 'Peace, lad.'

Guthrie glared at it, losing the question of who or what he talked with in the anger that still flared in him. 'You dare talk to me of *peace*? After everything I ever held dear has been torn from me and destroyed? After fire and destruction and death ...'

'Yer self or yer lived life,' the grey robe recited calmly, 'which is most near? Yer goods or yer lived life, which is more dear?'

It was a breathy voice, high pitched, laced with a southerner's burry accent, so soft that Guthrie had to strain to hear.

'Desire or yer lived life, by which does ye steer?'

Guthrie only stared, mouth slack.

'Which, of loss or gain, shall prove the greater bane?'

Guthrie did not know what to do or say. The grey robe's questions might have been entirely gibberish for all the sense they made, but there was an uncanny calmness about the still-standing figure that made it somehow difficult for Guthrie to hold on to the anger that had lit him.

'I knew him,' the grey robe said.

'Who?'

The figure pointed to the skull in Guthrie's hand. 'Abbod Rianna.'

Guthrie stared. 'Who ... *are* you?'

The figure bowed to him. 'I am a member of the Order of Closterers.'

Guthrie swallowed. 'You escaped safely from the Closter, then, after the Sea Wolves' attack?' He took a step forward eagerly. 'Are there more of you? What of the ordinary Vale folk? Did they too escape?'

The grey-robed figure shook its head. 'I have just arrived in this place. Through the mountains, from southwards.'

'Then you know nothing of ... of what has happened here?'

Pointing to the skull in Guthrie's hand, the figure sighed. 'I see ye half-starved and stricken and lost. I see an old friend dead.'

Guthrie felt a shiver go through him. 'How can you ... *recognize* him?'

The grey shoulders lifted in a shrug. 'We were friends.'

'But ...' Guthrie started, and then went silent. There was no telling what these Closterers might or might not be capable of. He had seen the Abbod do incredible things.

Guthrie stared at the figure before him, standing with the same stillness he had witnessed in the dead Abbod, arms tucked into the sleeves of the grey robe, with none of the homely little fidgety movements one expected in ordinary folk. Abruptly, Guthrie found that calm stillness utterly offensive. 'Riverside is destroyed,' he said bitterly. 'The Vale folk are destroyed. The Closter itself is destroyed!'

The grey-robed figure gazed at him calmly.

'Are you deaf?' Guthrie cried. 'Destroyed. *Destroyed!* Everything is destroyed!'

The Closterer sighed. 'Aye, I hear ye, lad. I hear ye. Such news saddens my heart. But 'tis not altogether unexpected.'

'But I thought you said ... Did you know?'

'Nay, lad. Nay. I did not *know*. But something drew me here. There is a patterning in all this.'

Guthrie stared, confused. 'Patterning?'

'I was ... channelled here.'

'Channelled?' Guthrie felt like a simpleton, repeating each time what this Closterer said, but he could make no sense of it.

'There are patterns in the world, lad. One learns to be ... sensitive to such things.'

Guthrie felt the irritation rise in him. 'Speak plain, can't you? If you came here with a purpose, tell it to me. I am the Reeve of this Vale. You trespass upon *my* lands when you walk here!'

The instant he had said it, Guthrie felt bitterly foolish. Reeve, indeed! Dying Reeve of a dead Vale. Dying fool, more like!

The Closterer gazed at him as calmly as ever. Under the shadow of the hood, Guthrie saw the eyes move in a solemn blink, like an owl's.

Silence.

Guthrie let out a long, weary breath. He would never be Reeve. It was all silliness and pretence. He would die here in these woods. He shook his head, shrugged. 'Go back from where you have come. There is nothing for you in Reeve Vale, friend. There is nothing for anybody here.'

The Closterer did not move.

'Go, I said. *Go!*'

The grey-robed figure said, 'Does ye know aught about the Closterers' Path, lad?'

Guthrie shook his head.

'If ye knew, ye would not try to tell one such as I to turn aside. I did not ... decide to come here.'

'Somebody sent you, then?'

'Nay. Nobody sent me.'

'But if you didn't decide. And nobody sent you ...'

'One does more and more each day in the pursuit of knowing,' the Closterer said. 'But follow the Pathless Way, the goingless going, and each day one does less, until one reaches fundamentalness.'

Guthrie shook his head. *Goingless going?* What nonsense was this?

'Trading all for none, leaves nothing undone.'

Guthrie stared.

'Ye does not understand,' the Closter said, calmly.

'No. I do not! You recite gibberish to me. Do you deem me a fool? Speak plain or don't speak at all!'

'I spoke to ye plain as I know how.'

'You spoke like ...' Guthrie began, but suddenly faltered. What mattered it, what this queer Closterer might say or not say? Nothing mattered. Not any more.

He felt dizzy and weak and suddenly unutterably weary.

The world seemed to slide past him, tilting. The ground smacked into his face, an unexpected, sharp blow, like a great, leaf strewn fist.

'Easy, lad,' a voice said, and he felt an arm about his shoulder, helping him to a sitting position. 'There's water not so very far off.'

Guthrie felt sinewy arms lifting him to his feet.

'Come on, lad. 'Tisn't far.'

Tottering like a babe, Guthrie let himself be led along through the trees until, eventually, he and the Closterer came out on the rock-bound shore of a little lake. The Closterer let him down, and he drank gratefully of the cold water.

'Here.' A hand took him gently by the shoulder, turning him. The Closterer held out a journey cake – baked oatmeal, honey, wild berries.

Guthrie took it in a shaking hand. He could smell the goodness of it. His mouth watered. He took a bite. It was tough and chewy, but more flavoursome than anything he could ever remember tasting in his entire life. He took it in small bites, chewing each to juice in his mouth before swallowing. His jaws ached from the sheer unaccustomedness of eating.

Finished, finally, he glanced up and saw the Closterer gazing at him.

'Good,' the grey-robed figure said. 'Ye looks in need of a little feeding.'

Guthrie grunted. He felt the wholesome energy of the journey cake begin to fill him. Drawing back his matted hair, he knelt at the water's verged and dunked his head, coming up spluttering. He did it again, shaking the water off like a hound. He felt his mind beginning to clear.

Sitting back, panting, feeling cleaned and chilled by the water, he looked up at the Closterer, not knowing what to say next. 'Tha ... thank you,' he managed to stammer after a little.

The Closterer nodded.

Silence.

Guthrie looked around him. He saw he was squatting at the verge of a little rock-bordered lake. A dark mass of trees crowded the rocky shore. The water lay still as glass. The silence of the place was almost complete, save for the soft sounds of a family of ducks bobbing and splashing about on the lake's far shore. High overhead, a lone hawk wheeled. Shreds of sunlit clouds filled the sky. The air in Guthrie's lungs was crisp and fresh. He felt more alive, suddenly, than he had in long days.

'Mirrormere,' the Closterer said, gesturing to the lake.

Guthrie leaned out over the water. It was a proper enough name. The perfectly still water below reflected sky and clouds and bordering trees, clear as clear. He leaned over.

It was a stranger's face, almost, that stared up at him, gaunt and haggard-eyed. He drew back with a shudder, remembering the last pool where he had looked at his own reflection.

And then, recalling that birch-encircled pool, Guthrie realized that he no longer had the skull with him. For several heartbeats, he felt only relief at being rid of the thing. But then he felt an unaccountable unease come over him. His palms itched for the skull's familiar weight.

He surged to his feet. 'Where is it?' he demanded of the Closterer.

The Closterer pointed, and there, not five paces off, the skull sat in the grass.

Guthrie scurried over and picked it up, cradling it in his arms like a little babe.

Looking across at the grey-robed, silent figure, he felt abruptly, self-consciously idiotic. What must he seem like to this stranger, clutching after a dead skull? Guthrie shivered. Was he gone mad, then, that he behaved this way?

'I ...' he started, trying to explain. But he could think of no way to explain it.

'The Abbod was no ordinary man,' the Closterer said then.

They were the very words the Abbod had used to describe himself. Guthrie felt a shiver of anger. 'Yet he died a very ordinary death, did your Abbod. Cut down like a silly hen.'

'I doubt that, lad.'

'You weren't *there*!' Guthrie snapped. 'I was. I *saw*! He stood there, unmoving, and let the Sea Wolf Chieftain cut him down. He never lifted so much as a finger in his own defence! And all after ...' Guthrie found he was panting with the intensity of telling it. 'After promising me ... *promising* me that I could trust him. Well, I *trusted* him. And what happened? The Closter was destroyed and my folk slaughtered like so many sheep.'

'Abbod Rianna was no ordinary man,' the Closterer repeated.

Guthrie glared. 'Your Abbod was a cheat and a liar!'

The Closterer merely shrugged. 'Then why does ye cling to his dead remains as if yer very life depended upon it?'

Guthrie looked down at the skull. 'I ...' There was no easy answer to that question.

'Sometimes,' the grey-robe said, 'a death serves a purpose the living cannot see.'

Guthrie shook his head. 'Are you suggesting that the Abbod allowed the Sea Wolf to kill him *on purpose*?'

'Perhaps.'

'That's madness! What purpose could his death serve? The Vale folk *died* because of his foolishness.'

'But ye is alive and standing here talking with me.'

'But that's ...'

'How did ye come here to me?'

'I didn't come to *you*. I was lost, couldn't find the sea. I was simply stumbling along aimlessly.'

'And yet ye *aimlessly* walked straight to me.'

Guthrie shivered, recalling the way in which the skull seemed to had led him along.

96

'There are more things in the world, lad, than ye might think.'

The very idea of what this Closterer was suggesting made Guthrie dizzy. The Abbod dying for *him*? For a second son? Why not for Garth, his father? That would make sense, dying to save the Reeve himself. But to let his father and Garrett die and he live ... That was unthinkable.

Guthrie took a ragged breath. 'If the dead Abbod did ... guide me here, why would he guide me to *you*?'

The Closterer shrugged. 'I do not know.'

Guthrie snorted in irritation. 'That is no answer!'

Again, the Closterer shrugged. 'Perhaps I have something that ye needs. Perhaps ye has something I need.'

'Such as what?'

'I don't know, lad. How could I?'

'What of the hidden knowledge you Closterers are supposed to have? I saw the Abbod do incredible things, catch thrown spears out of the very air ... And you recognized a dead man from his cleaned skull. You *must* know things ordinary folk do not. If the Abbod did indeed die for my sake ...' Guthrie paused. The idea was still too absurd for him to be able to put it easily into words. 'If he died ... on purpose, what was that purpose?'

The Closterer shrugged a third time. 'I do not know.'

Guthrie stood as he was, shaking with frustration. He wanted to throttle this grey-robed idiot who refused him the answers he needed.

The Closterer came forward and reached out to him. 'Come, lad, ye've had a trying time of it. What ye needs now is ...'

Guthrie wrenched away from the Closterer's hold and lashed out angrily. Unthinking, he aimed a backhand fist at the Closterer's hooded face. But the blow never connected. Instead, in some queer manner he could not understand, Guthrie found himself suddenly flat on his back at the water's edge.

The Closterer stood calmly over him. He looked up, angry, but the anger fell abruptly away into shock. The grey hood had slipped back, revealing the figure's face clearly for the first time. Guthrie stared. An old woman gazed down at him. Her hair was silver-grey, short cropped. Her eyes were bracketed by a web of wrinkles, her face folded into an intricate network of them. She smiled a lopsided smile at him, showing crooked teeth. Her eyes were sea green and steady as could be.

Guthrie shook his head. A woman. He had been dumped to the

ground by a wrinkle-faced old grandmother! He remembered the Abbod catching the Sea Wolf Chieftain's thrown spear, dumping Hone Amis in the mud of the Closter's yard. Shivering, he wondered what strange powers these Closterers commanded. No ordinary man had a chance, it seemed, if they willed against him. Stupid of him to have lashed out at one of them so, even against a mere old woman.

But it made the anger in him surge up again all the hotter, for it meant the Abbod *could* have prevented his own death.

The Closterer reached a hand down to help him to his feet.

Guthrie sighed, took the hand. His elbow hurt where he had landed on it. With the woman's help, he got to his feet. He retrieved the skull from where it lay a few paces off in the grass, having dropped it in his fall, and stood where he was, uncertain.

He was completely in this strange Closterer woman's power, he realized.

It was not a comforting notion.

Suddenly, all he wanted was to get away, to slip off into the screening trees that came down near the lake shore and to be rid of this unnerving Closterer for good.

But what then?

Aye, there was the rub all right. What path was left to him now? Accomplishing a fine revenge upon the Sea Wolves was all very well, but he could not even make his way successfully out of the forests that surrounded Reeve Vale, never mind find the south and manage to accumulate the wealth and the skills and the men needed. If he were only like these Closterers, now, he could ...

The thought struck him like a blow.

If he possessed the skills a Closterer did, none would be able to stand against him.

Guthrie saw it clear in his mind's eye: him striding up to the Sea Wolf Chieftain in the man's own home, the Sea Wolf thrusting at him with a spear, him doing whatever sleight of hand motion it was that spilled the man onto his back. Guthrie saw himself standing there, laughing over his fallen foe.

It was a *good* feeling.

He turned to the Closterer. The woman was old and frail seeming, yet she had dealt with him easily. She must be possessed of years of strange learning. 'Teach me!' he demanded of her. 'Teach me how to do the things you can do.'

For a long moment, the grey-robed woman gazed at him. Then, 'Ye wishes to follow the Pathless Way?'

98

'I wish to be able to do what you can do.'

'Why?'

Guthrie shied away from the other's questioning gaze. 'I ... I admire what you are able to do.'

The woman smiled her lopsided, crooked-toothed smile at him. Her eyes seemed to glimmer in an odd way, like bright stones glimpsed under a depth of water. 'I think ye has hidden motives, lad.'

'What if I do? Listen! Why else would the dead Abbod have guided me so that the two of us meet like this here in the middle of absolute nowhere? It must be so that you can teach me the Closterer's tricks.'

The woman snorted. 'Tricks? The Pathless Way is not composed of tricks.'

'Teach me.'

'It may not be the path ye thinks it to be, lad.'

'Teach me!'

The woman looked at the skull in Guthrie's hands. She sighed. 'Are ye certain sure this is what ye wishes to do?'

Guthrie nodded. 'Aye. *Certain* sure.'

For the space of a dozen heartbeats, the woman hesitated. Then she nodded slowly. 'So be it, then. Ye is here and I am here. I will teach ye.'

'Good,' Guthrie said. 'Good!'

'But be warned. There is no turning back. Treading the Pathless Way *changes* one.'

Guthrie smiled. 'It is a change I welcome.'

'Perhaps. We shall see.' The woman regarded him soberly. 'My name is Rosslyn. And yers is?'

'Reeve Guthrie Garthson.'

'And what do I call ye, Reeve Guthrie Garthson? That is a name of too many parts for the likes of I.'

Guthrie shrugged. 'Just ... Guthrie will do.'

'Right then, young Guthrie, gather yerself together and we shall find a place to camp.' She turned and reached up a dilapidated shoulder bag that had been sitting on the sod near her. It was, Guthrie realized, the only bit of luggage she carried. Rosslyn smiled. 'I see ye travels light. That is good.'

'It wasn't *my* choice,' Guthrie replied, 'to travel like this. I see nothing especially good about it.'

99

'Ah, but ye has learned to give things up. A very important lesson, that.'

Guthrie shrugged morosely. 'A lesson I would rather have learned in a less painful manner. Or not at all.'

Rosslyn smiled. 'A lesson ye will have to continue to learn if ye wishes to follow the Pathless Way, lad.'

Guthrie looked at her uncertainly, not knowing what to say.

'Come,' Rosslyn urged. 'Let us find a campsite.' And with that, she led him up from the lake's verge and away into the shadowed screen of the trees.

VII

'Along there,' Alia said, pointing through the rough pines to a long, up-sloping ridgeback that lay a ways ahead of them.

Hone Amis, standing near her, said nothing. Behind him, in two orderly files, four dozen Militia crouched, waiting. Fanned out amongst the pines were a score or so of hunters.

Alia glanced back at this little armed force uneasily; she did not feel it was near large enough. But Hone Amis had begrudged even so many, brushing aside the details of her story as exaggerations.

Alia sighed and ran her fingers gingerly over her bruised cheeks. Her face ached. 'Once on the other side of that ridgeback,' she told the Militia Master, 'we ought to come to the high lip of the beech hollow, and through the beeches be able to see down into the clearing where the bandits have their camp.'

Hone Amis merely grunted.

Alia sucked her sore lip, trying to keep her temper in check. This was their second day on the trail – the bandit camp being a fair ways up into the Heights as it was – and it had been no less than four days since her return to Hunters Camp. Hone Amis had stalled all through the first day, teasing out the details of organizing his men till it was far too late to leave; and then a great beast of a storm had come roaring in from the ocean on the second day, giving him yet another excuse for delay. And all yesterday and throughout this morning's march the Militia Master had been dropping snide remarks about wild goose chases and silly girl's fantasies. Alia felt about ready to throttle the man.

She tried to push back the memories all this evoked in her. Her sore face throbbing, this man ridiculing her ... It was all too uncomfortably close to her girlhood. She had a sudden, appallingly clear memory of her father, hand raised, face contorted with anger. Alia shuddered and pushed it resolutely from her. She had escaped all that, vowing to herself to put it behind her for ever. A vow more easily kept at some times than others ...

101

Two Militiamen slipped down towards them from the trees upslope. Unlike the ordinary Militia, these two wore mottled leathers and tight-fitting, brimless little caps with the Militia symbol embroidered on the front and a weasel tail dangling from behind. Alia recognized one from the duo who had dragged her into Hunters Camp.

Hone Amis had refused to use hunters as scouts on this foray – the utter height of foolishness as far as Alia was concerned – but these two, at least, seemed somewhat woodwise. And they walked the uneven, sloping ground with a certain light-limbed sureness.

'No sign of bandit lookouts this side of the ridgeback,' the taller of the two reported to Hone Amis. 'Everything's quiet as could be hoped.'

Hone Amis grunted an acknowledgement.

'Couldn't see sign of any camp on the far side,' the other added.

Hone Amis said nothing, merely raised an eyebrow.

Charrer Mysha came padding up to them and stood at Hone Amis's elbow, silent.

The Militia Master turned, spluttered a curse as he found Mysha unexpectedly there. '*Must* you sneak around like some thief?'

Mysha said nothing.

'This is no *game* we're playing here!' Hone Amis snapped, glaring at Charrer Mysha and drawing his sword.

For one crazy, heart-stopping instant, Alia thought Hone Amis was actually going to attack Mysha.

But no. The Militia Master only lifted the weapon above his head and silently gestured with the blade to his right and then to his left. Without a word, he set off upslope.

Alia heard the soft *shruusk* of blades leaving sheaths, and the two files of Militia followed Hone Amis up the ridgeback, slowly.

She looked across at Mysha. He rested a hand on her shoulder, a momentary, light touch of reassurance, then padded off along with the rest.

Alia followed after.

There was something a little creepy, almost, about the way the Militia moved. The hunters involved in this expedition went in no especial order, simply slipped along silently through the trees within hailing distance of each other, as they might on any ordinary hunt. But the Militia travelled as if one long cord attached them all together, as if they were being pulled along by some giant, invisible,

102

controlling hand; and Hone Amis kept them ordered thus with hardly more than a whispered instruction now and then.

With their iron-bound leather helms, short-bladed swords, and Militia spears, Alia had to concede they looked a competent and formidable lot, for all that they had been so soundly thrashed by the Sea Wolves.

But they made far too much noise marching in their ordered lines.

Red-haired Orrin came up alongside Alia for a moment. He gestured at the orderly Militia and shook his head. 'Fools!' he hissed into her ear.

Alia shrugged, knowing no other answer.

Up-slope they went, Militia and hunter alike. Alia felt her pulse begin to thump in her throat. Her left palm was slippery-damp on the haft of the bow she held – a replacement for the one the bandits had taken from her – and it itched maddeningly where the demon-creature had marked her. She tried not to think on it. But the itch grew until she had to stop momentarily, shift the bow, scratch. Sighing with relief, she stood still for a long few moments, blinking. Her eyes felt scratchy; she ached from cheek to shins; she had not slept at all well ...

Days now, and the strange, intricate pattern the demon-creature had carved in her flesh was still not properly scabbed over. In her mind, she saw the fearsome, unhuman face. It had haunted her sleep, that face, calling to her, beckoning.

Alia shook her head. Simple aftershock, she told herself. A natural reaction. Nothing more. Anybody would respond the same, seeing the uncanny creature again in her dreams.

But the dreams had given her no rest.

The great yellow, inhuman eyes wide and intent, the tusked mouth open, calling, calling to her ...

She felt a fit of the shakes go through her.

Alia shook herself together, pushing it all determinedly from her mind, and continued on at a quickened pace upslope through the trees, catching the others up.

She thought of how it would be once they reached the crest of the ridge – the look on Hone Amis's face when he gazed down across the far side of the ridgeback and saw the size of the bandit camp down below on the far side. Those scouts of his must not have gone far enough across the ridge to see properly what was on that far side.

No matter.

Upwards they went, on hands and knees now, creeping through the trees the scouts had declared free of bandit lookouts, upwards till Alia was panting and damp with sweat, upwards till, finally, they crept towards the keel of moss-dappled stone that formed the ridge's crest.

Alia scuttled along cross-slope, so as to be next to Hone Amis when he crested the ridge's rock spine and was able to look down beyond. It was painful movement, weary and stiff and sore as she was, but she clenched her teeth and moved quick, low, and quiet.

Crouching next to the Militia Master, Alia laid aside her bow momentarily and rested her itching left palm on the moist coolth of the moss covering the stone. She was shaking with exertion, excitement, anticipation. 'Down there,' she whispered to Hone Amis, who crouched a few paces away. 'On the other side of this rock, way down below amongst the beeches. You ought to have a clear enough view from here.'

Hone Amis peered round the rock's side.

Alia watched his back intently. She could not see his face, but he would betray the act of seeing the camp down there in some way. He would stiffen, or hunch up, or roll sideways. Something. Not even he could look upon the sight of a hundred and more hill bandits quietly making themselves at home on the border of his lands without showing some sort of reaction.

But he did none of the things she expected. Instead, he pushed back from the rock's edge, stood up and glared at her, his face darkening with anger. 'Bandits! Ha!'

Alia did not understand.

The Militia Master reached over to her and plucked her bodily up from the ground. 'Look, stupid girl. *Look!*' He swung her round over the stone crest and faced her in the direction of the valley on the other side below.

Alia felt her bruised face throbbing painfully. It was the right place. She knew it! She could see the screen of old beech trees, and, through their leaf-stripped branches, the clearing where the fires had been, where the bandit leader's tent had stood. Though her vantage point up here did not give her an altogether clear view of the area below, Alia could see enough through the intervening webbery of branch and limb to make out that there was no tent down there, no men, no fires.

Nothing.

'I ... I don't ... understand,' she stammered. 'Where have they all gone?'

Hone Amis shook her, his thick fingers digging painfully into her sore arms. '*Stupid* girl! There are no bandits down there. There never *were* any bandits down there.'

He thrust her from him in disgust. 'I've asked around about you, girl. You're a dreamer, one of those who wastes her life gazing off into nothing. I know your sort. Always looking for something better, seeing great wonders all about. Painting the world with your own imaginings, more like! And that's what these bandits of yours are. Nothing! And all the rest of your story. *Nothing!* Night flitters and vapours and a stupid, frightened girl's imagination.'

The Militia Master turned his back on her. 'It's all right,' he called to his waiting men. 'There's nothing down there. We've been led on a wild goose chase. As I expected.'

There was a chorus of grumblings from the Militia. They rose to their feet, sheathing blades, muttering to each other and glaring at the hunters who had materialized out of the trees at the sound of Hone Amis's voice.

'Can't trust any of them,' Alia heard one Militia man grumble. 'They're all misfits and nutters, these hunters.'

'What d'you expect?' said another. 'They're runaways, the lot of them. Look at 'em! Scruffy, dimwitted lot of scallywags.'

The gathered hunters bristled, but Alia only hung her head in mortification.

She turned her back on them all and gazed down into the valley on the other side of the ridgeback. It was the right place. It was! But no sign of the bandit camp could she see. They must have decamped, then, after her escape. And if that were so, there would be some sign of the camp left behind down there. There *had* to be. They might not be able to see it in the distance from up here, but the sign ought to be obvious enough down below. All she need do was get Hone Amis down there and she could show him the signs of the camp. Then he would *have* to believe her.

But when she suggested it to him he refused bluntly to have anything to do with the notion.

'Admit it, girl! You imagined it all. Jewelled men and skulls and the killing and all the rest of it. Don't compound the thing by lying about it.'

'I am *not* lying!'

Hone Amis glared at her. 'You've already wasted more than

105

enough valuable time. We could have been down in Reeve Vale, searching for survivors, for the young Reeve himself. We could be in Riverside itself by now. I could have have been doing half a dozen needful things. But no! Instead, I end up traipsing around through this forsaken bit of hill forest at the mercy of your foolish girl's fancy.'

Alia stood her ground. 'It *isn't* foolishness! If you'd only go down there and look, you'd see that –'

'Shut *up*, girl!' He stepped towards her, menacingly. 'Just shut up and do as you're told. Or I'll –'

'You'll what?' said a voice from behind Alia's shoulder.

Red-haired Orrin appeared at her side, Patch and lean Tym with him.

Orrin faced Hone Amis defiantly. 'Like to bully people smaller than yourself, do you?'

'Arsehole,' Tym added.

Hone Amis flushed with anger. He stabbed a finger at Orrin. 'Stay out of my way, boy, or you'll regret it.'

'It's you will have the regrets,' Tym said, coming to stand with Orrin. Patch moved up so that the three of them formed a kind of fence between the Militia Master and Alia.

'Arsehole,' Orrin said, repeating, for good measure, the insult that had provoked Hone Amis.

The Militia Master clenched his fists. His men had moved closer at the beginning of the altercation, but he waved them back irritably. He took a long, laboured breath, closed his eyes, opened them again. 'I have better things to do than stand here and listen to insubordinate *puppies* while ...' He whirled as Charrer Mysha come padding silently up. 'Keep these *adolescents* away from me! Do you hear? I'm fed up to the back teeth with them!'

Mysha held up his hands, palms out, in a gesture of calm.

But Alia plunged right ahead. 'Why shouldn't the bandits have decamped?' she demanded of Hone Amis. 'Knowing I'd escaped, knowing I was a hunter, they would have assumed I'd bring back a force to rout them out. Moving their camp is the obvious thing for them to do. Especially since they've had *four* days in which to do it. All we need to –'

'I will *not*,' Hone Amis interrupted, 'be lectured to on tactics by a boy-dressed girl frightened by her own imaginings!'

'You're the one who's frightened,' Tym said. 'Frightened to admit you might be wrong.'

106

'Enough!' Hone Amis cried. 'I *refuse* to discuss this further. There are pressing tasks needing to be done. I have the good of a community to consider. Something which you hunters know nothing about!'

'We have our *own* community,' Orrin said angrily.

Hone Amis threw back his head. 'Ha! A rag-tag group of scoundrels and cowards who would rather run away and play in the woods than face their responsibilities at home. You have no rules, no organization. And Ser Mysha is laughable as a leader.'

'How *dare* you?' Alia cried, furious. 'You ... you ignorant ...' Words failed her.

'Enough!' Hone Amis all but shouted. 'I will not argue this with a lying strayaway such as yourself.' With this he whirled and stalked off, gesturing his Militia along behind.

'But you can't just walk away!' Alia called in dismay. 'Those bandits are out there still, somewhere. They *are*, I tell you!'

The only reply was a chorus of mocking guffaws from the disappearing Militia.

The hunters gathered about hesitated uncertainly, but seeing the Militia march off, they too began to follow after.

'Wait!' Alia cried, moving to go after them.

'Let them go,' Charrer Mysha said softly.

'Arseholes!' Tym spat in the direction of the retreating Militia.

'I'll make that man pay for his arrogance one day,' Orrin fumed, glaring daggers at Hone Amis's retreating back.

'Let it be,' Mysha said.

'How could you just listen calmly while he said what he did, Mysha? The man's got his head up his arse 'cause he likes the view!'

Mysha shook his head. ''T'won't do any good to think like that.'

'But he ...'

'Let be,' Mysha repeated.

'We can't just let them all walk away like this,' Alia said. 'Mysha! Those bandits are camped here in the Hills somewhere. They *are*!'

Charrer Mysha shrugged. 'Perhaps, but ...'

'*Perhaps?*' Alia snapped. 'Do *you* think I imagined everything?'

Mysha looked at her for a long moment. His far-seeing eyes made her shiver a little; there were depths to Mysha nobody quite understood. 'I see no bandits and no camp, Alia.'

'But how can you ...' Alia began.

Mysha held a hand up, quietening her. 'I do not know what may or may not have happened.' At Alia's stricken look, he smiled

107

reassuringly. 'I am not as quick as some to draw my conclusions. The Militia Master is ... hasty in his judgements at times.'

Orrin snorted.

'But ...' Mysha gestured back the way the Militia Master and his men had gone. 'My way is that way.'

'And us?' Orrin asked.

'Have I ever forced any of you to anything?' Mysha inquired. 'Do what you feel to do.'

With that, Mysha turned and slipped away.

'We should go with him,' Patch said after a long moment's silence.

But Alia was not listening. She felt shaken, confused. She thought of what it would be like to return to Hunters Camp now, utterly discredited, the butt of people's jokes, the silly girl who imagined silly things. For a sudden instant, completely unexpectedly, she saw the demon-creature clear in her mind. The image of it beckoned, tusked mouth open, calling to her. The mark on her palm flared in a sudden torment of itching.

With a shock, she realized she ought to have shown her scarred palm to Hone Amis. There was proof of her story. But she felt a strange reticence; she had neither shown the scarring to anybody since her return nor so much as mentioned the demon. Alia shook her head, trying to clear it of the queerly compelling demon-vision that had come upon her. There must be some practical way to prove to Hone Amis and the rest that she was right. There *must* be!

'It's only sensible,' Patch was saying in his soothing manner. He put a hand on Alia's arm. 'Maybe ... maybe we should just ...'

But Alia had had enough of talk. She pulled abruptly away from Patch, vaulted across the stone keel of the ridge behind which they had crouched, and skittered precipitously down the other side. She heard shouts behind her, and ignored them. Her only focus was the area below. There *had* to be some sign of the camp down there. By the Powers, she had not imagined the whole thing. She had not!

Panting, she stumbled through the last of the screening beeches and came to a skidding halt. She turned a full circle, surveying the place. Leaves *scrushed* under her feet. She heard the soft crashing of the others as they followed her down the slope.

There must be some sign here. There must!

But she could see nothing.

'Alia!' she heard Orrin call.

She hurried instinctively away from him through the leaves,

stubbed her foot on some hard, hidden thing, and tumbled to her knees with a little cry.

It was the stones of a fire pit she had stumbled over, buried under the crumply mass of yellow-brown beech leaves.

'There,' she cried triumphantly as the others came to her across the clearing. 'What did I tell you?'

On her hands and knees, she scrabbled away at the ground before her, thrusting aside handfuls of brittle leaves to reveal the circle of blackened stones.

She stood up, sucked leaf-dirt from her sore left palm, and glared at her companions. 'I *told* you!'

They stood staring at her.

'Well don't just stand there like stupid geese,' Alia snapped. 'Come help me look!' She kicked about through the leaves and uncovered a second fireplace near the first.

The others too started thrashing about, kicking leaves right and left in droves, until they had uncovered no less than the remains of seventeen blackened hearths.

'So many ...' Orrin said uneasily. 'It's never been heard of, this many.'

'Poor souls,' Patch said in his kindly way.

Orrin looked at him sharply.

'The Vale folk, I mean,' Patch added. 'First the Sea Wolves ravage their homesteads, and now this bandit force comes like a wolfpack to take the rest.'

'Ill luck indeed,' Tym grumbled, shaking his head.

There was a long moment's silence between them.

'Right,' Orrin said. 'Let's get out of here and catch up Hone Amis and the rest and tell them what we've found. I'm looking forward to seeing the expression on the Militia Master's face when he's forced to eat his words to you!'

But Alia was looking about her at the remains of the bandit camp. 'They're not stupid, these bandits.'

'So?' Tym replied. 'Neither are we.'

'They knew I'd bring an armed force back up here.'

Orrin grabbed for Alia's hand, but she flinched away. He took her by the arm instead. 'Come *on!*' He dragged her along a few steps until she was able to wrench clear of his grip.

Alia thought of Sethir and the jewelled man. 'These aren't fools we're dealing with. *Think* about it! If you knew I would be coming with an armed force to roust you out, what would you do?'

Tym shrugged. 'Depends on how many men I had.'

'Depends on how many men *you* had,' Patch added, pointing at Alia.

'Sensiblest thing,' Orrin said, 'would be to do what they seem to have already done. Disappear off into the high country and cover their tracks.'

'And then what?' Alia pressed.

'Leave a few scouts about, I suppose,' Orrin said, 'to see if anybody finds the old camp.'

'And then what?' Alia pressed.

The three before her were glancing about uneasily now.

'They might be watching us as we speak,' Patch said softly.

Alia shook her head. 'It's not *us* they're interested in.'

'Not likely there's *anybody* about here,' Tym snorted.

'Suppose they *did* leave scouts,' Alia said. Orrin made an impatient gesture and tried to interrupt, but she cut him off. 'Over there perhaps,' she waved to the far side of the hollow in which the camp was situated, at right angles to the side from which they had approached the camp. 'They could sit up there, far enough away to remain unseen, yet close enough to spot us.'

Alia turned to her companions. 'If you moved your camp, covered your tracks, posted scouts up there ... What would you tell those scouts to do?'

Patch was the first to get it. Alia could see the realization hit him like a physical blow. 'Follow Hone Amis and his Militia back to their camp. Back to *our* camp.'

'Exactly,' Alia said. 'Track them to their home camp. Once they've found that out, these bandits can attack us in any way that suits them.'

'And we still have no idea where *their* camp may be located.'

Alia nodded.

'Powers preserve us,' Patch said, shaken. 'I think you've the right of it, Alia. It makes *sense*. And that Militia party would be dead easy to track.'

'I *told* you giving refuge to those Valers would work to our undoing!' Tym said sourly.

Orrin pivoted. 'We've got to warn them!'

'No!' Alia said. 'Wait! Hone Amis will never believe us. Never believe *me*.'

Tym spat. 'She's right. That arsehole won't believe a thing unless it's what he likes to see.'

Patch was pale. 'So what do we do, then?'

'Go after the scouts!' Orrin said. 'If Alia's right, they're following behind Hone Amis and the Militia. We can trail them and take the bastards from behind.' Orrin nodded his satisfaction with the idea. 'I don't *like* people pulling tricks on me.'

'You're crazy,' Patch said, and Tym nodded agreement.

'Got a better idea?' Orrin demanded.

'There must be some way to ...' Patch began.

'Think on it!' Orrin said, the excitement growing visibly in him. 'We can take them. We *can*! We'll save Hunters Camp, just the four of us.'

Alia was inclined to side with Tym and Patch in this. It seemed a mad, rash idea all right. Typical of Orrin. One did not simply go off hunting after men like this. And yet ... She ached to be vindicated, to be able to look Hone Amis straight in the eye and show him how wrong he was.

'Orrin's right,' she said, going to stand next to him. 'There's no time for anything else.'

'But ...' Patch started.

'We've got to stop them, Patch.'

'Aye!' Orrin agreed, grinning fiercely at Alia. 'We'll stop them all right. Stop them *dead*!'

Tym grunted.

Patch looked uncertainly from Alia, to Orrin, then back to Alia again. He sighed and turned imploringly to Tym.

But Tym only shrugged and said, 'I've seen that look on Orrin's face before.'

Patch sighed once more. 'All right. All right! But if we do this mad thing,' he said, 'we've got to go carefully.' He pointed at Orrin. '*Carefully*! Do you hear?'

Orrin nodded. 'Aye. Carefully. Agreed.'

But when he took the lead, Orrin was grinning like a wolf. Patch looked at Alia and shook his head.

They left at a fast trot, moving along in a single file column, just within sight of each other.

VIII

It was a hunt.

Alia moved with the same attentive care, the same heart-thumping concentration, bow half drawn, arrow nocked to the string, two more arrows held slantwise in the fingers of her still-sore left hand where she held the bow.

But it was men she hunted this day.

She ignored the continuing itch in her left palm, the aches and little stabs of pain her movement caused, the throb along her jaw where her cheek pained her. Her entire self was focused, her mind clear as mountain water, her senses open. She placed each foot with careful attention, her whole being straining like a great ear for any sign of movement nearabouts.

Drawing closer to the trail of Hone Amis and the Militia, Alia and the others had slowed their advance and spread out. She could see none of her companions from where she stood at the moment. The forest about her was silent.

She cut across a steepish slope, ducked behind the waist-high bole of an ancient, fallen pine, pulpy and green with moss, and peered cautiously beyond. She scanned for movement first, movement being always easiest to spot. Then she searched for shapes, edges, colours, anything that did not fit with the forest as it ought to be.

And there it was, not twenty paces away.

A man, crouching at the base of one of the pines, his back to her. He was dressed in raggedy clothing, baggy trousers, tattered jumper, grey-brown in colour and black with dirt. A crossbow lay cradled in his arms. He was no Vale man, and certainly no hunter.

Alia found it suddenly hard to get proper breath.

The man's attention was directed away from her, along the path the Militia had travelled. Alia could see plain enough the marks of their too-orderly passing. The man below her, no doubt, could see them just as plainly.

112

Alia felt her heart thump hard. This man had to be one of the bandit scouts. *Had* to be. She had been right!

Placed as she was, her shoulder against the pulpy bole of the downed pine, Alia had a clear sight of him. And a clear shot, too.

Slowly, she drew the arrow she had already nocked to the string. The rasp of the shaft against the bow sounded impossibly loud, and she expected the man to whirl about.

But no. He remained as he was, peering into the tree-thick slope in front of him, oblivious to her.

Alia anchored the arrow shaft, right thumb firmly up against her cheek bone – ignoring the twitch of pain that evoked – and sighted. The bow she held did not have the comfortable, familiar feel of her own, which lay now in bandit hands. Her left palm still throb-itched irritatingly ...

She let go the tension for a moment, took a breath, sighted again – there, in the middle of his back, just off centre from where a twisted leather cord crossed from shoulder to waist to support a short quiver of crossbow bolts. She could see the ragged cloth of his jumper rise and fall with his breathing.

As a hunter, Alia had killed, but always in the proper manner, and never a man. She felt her belly flutter. What did one say? The ordinary hunter's litany seemed altogether inappropriate: *For the giving of your life, I thank you, friend.*

The man below her was not giving of his life in the manner of a trout or deer or partridge, to feed and to clothe. His death would add no good thing to the world.

It seemed ... obscene.

Alia blinked the sweat out of her eyes. Her hands shook. Any instant, the man below would hear her, or feel her eyes upon his back and whirl about. She must do it, and do it quickly.

But she could not.

Where were her companions? She looked around desperately, but could see no sign of them.

The man below shifted position, and Alia shrank back, hiding herself behind the bole of the pine. Softly, she eased up on the bow and let the arrow out. Then, hunkering down, she peered around the tree. The man still had his back to her, still seemed oblivious.

Alia sighed. She could not do it. Perhaps this man deserved death. Perhaps he did not. How was she to know? Who was she to be the one to bring that final journey down upon him?

No. All she wished was to creep away, leave the man be.

But what of Hunters Camp? She could not simply allow this bandit scout to slip back in safety with the knowledge he gained here.

Carefully, she peered around the mossy edge of the pine. Below, the man lay as he had been, position unchanged, still peering before him into the trees.

Suddenly, the man stiffened.

Alia's heart came up into her throat and she froze, breathless. But he did not turn. Instead, he hunkered closer to the bole of the tree against which he lay and scrutinized the pines intently. Alia followed his line of sight.

At first, she could neither see nor hear anything save the ordinary, soft sounds of the wood. But then she caught a glimpse of movement. Little more than a mere shifting of the forest light at first, it was almost too subtle to catch. But as she watched, it slowly resolved itself into some creature, moving slow and silent through the trees in the distance.

Orrin! Alia recognized him clear.

The bandit below shifted his position slowly, bringing up the crossbow he was armed with. And now Alia realized one of the benefits of such a weapon over her own longbow; he would not have to stand, or even kneel, to shoot. He could lie there, unseen, and fire at Orrin from where he lay, safe on his belly.

Alia opened her mouth to shout a warning, but stopped herself. She did not know what the range of one of these southern crossbows might be. If she shouted, she might simply prompt the bandit into shooting. And Orrin, startled momentarily by her call, would prove an easy target.

Orrin was no more than thirty-five paces or so away from the bandit now, moving cross-slope through the trees. He paused, stared about, listening, tense and careful as a hind, but unaware all the same that he had been sighted.

Alia shivered. She saw the bandit below her sight along the stock of the crossbow. She brought her own bow up, drew, let loose, all in one quick, unthinking motion.

It was a bad shot, taking the man through the shoulder. He let out a shriek like a stricken hound, and twisted about on his knees to face her.

Alia nocked another arrow, her fingers clumsy with panic. There was still time for him to try to use the crossbow against her. She drew, let fly, all with the same unthinking, desperate haste as before.

Her aim, this time, was truer.

The broad-bladed hunting arrow pierced him through the ribs, coming out his back to pin him to the tree bole against which he knelt.

The man looked down in disbelief at the shaft protruding from his breast. With a cry, he dropped the crossbow, clutched the shaft that impaled him, and wrenched himself free from the tree. He staggered to his feet. The bladed end of the arrow stuck out from his back, runnelling with crimson blood. He stared up at Alia, white faced.

Alia stared back, stricken.

As a novice hunter, she had been shocked to discover that death from one of the sharp-bladed, deadly hunting arrows was far from instantaneous. Unless a hunter was lucky or skilful enough to make a clear heart shot, a mere rent in the body was not enough to kill immediately. It was loss of blood, the agony and shock of the wound that eventually killed. But it took time to die. Alia had tracked a gut-shot deer for leagues once – they all had done the same sort of thing, the younger ones, until they learned to be patient and wait for the right moment in order to be mercifully precise with their shot.

The man below her was dead. She had killed him. No doubt about that. But it would take time for him to die, long, slow, agonizing time, the blood seeping from him inescapably until the final moment.

Alia stepped slowly downhill. The bandit stared at her, one hand gripping futilely at the feathers of the shaft that stuck out through his ribs. 'You're ...' he gagged, spitting up frothy blood. 'You're just a ... a stupid *girl*.'

There was a sudden crash, and Orrin came bounding up to them, bow drawn, arrow nocked. He took in the scene before him in a quick glance, then paused, uncertain.

The bandit turned. 'She's killed me,' he said, hoarse voiced. 'This ...' he coughed more blood, drooling. 'This ... *girl* has ki ... *killed* me!'

The man fell to his knees with a groan.

'What *happened?*' Orrin demanded of Alia.

It was a long moment before she could bring herself to speak. 'He was ... was lying here in ambush. He saw you, would have ... killed you. So I ...' she broke down into sobs and could not go on.

Orrin came to her and put his arm about her shoulders protectively. 'My brave girl. Don't think about it now. I'm here.

Everything will be all right now. You did *right*. You did the brave thing, girl.'

Alia pushed him from her, blinking back tears. 'I *know* what I did. I'm nobody's little *girl*, Orrin!'

'Then don't make such a fuss about it all! He's a bandit, girl, a ruffian. He'd have had his way with you and then killed you afterwards, sure as sure. You *know* that. He deserved it, girl.'

Alia felt her bruised face throb. She shook her head. 'He's a man, Orrin. An ordinary man! How does any man *deserve* death?' She dropped her bow and knelt beside the man she had shot.

The bandit turned to her and spat full in her face. '*Bitch!*' he hissed, and then fell back. She tried to catch him, but he wrenched himself away from her hold.

He hit the ground face first. Alia heard the terrible grating wrench as the arrow was forced deeper through his chest. He shrieked, thrashing like a fish out of water.

Alia turned aside and was hopelessly sick.

'Come away from him,' Orrin urged, taking her by the shoulders, 'Come away. There's nothing you can do for him.'

Alia considered the man's agony. 'You're wrong, Orrin. There's one thing I can do.'

She shook Orrin's hold from her. With the back of her right hand she wiped the vomit away, spat the foul-tasting stuff from her mouth. With the same hand, she reached for her belt knife. It was new, and did not have the comfortable, worn feel of the one the bandits had taken from her up in the heights, but it was still a nicely made blade, sleek and sharp and well oiled.

She walked towards the bandit.

'Alia?' Orrin said. '*Alia!*'

She ignored him. Reaching down with her left hand – ignoring the thrust of pain that shot though it – she lifted the bandit's head by his tangled and greasy hair.

He stared at her, his face bone white with terror and pain and rage.

'A scathless journey in the darkness, friend,' she began.

'No!' he croaked. '*No!*'

'A scathless journey and a fruitful end. Gone from the world of living ken ...'

She wrenched his head back, exposing his throat.

He struggled, kicking like a stricken rabbit, but his strength was all gone.

'Into the Shadowlands ...' She brought the knife down. 'To begin again.'

He shrieked once, but the cry was drowned in blood.

Alia shuddered, feeling the wet warmth of his blood, remembering the other time she had felt such warm man's blood upon her hands.

He shook and twisted under her hold, and then, with a wet gush of bright blood and a final shuddering sigh, went utterly still.

She had freed him.

Alia let him drop, then turned aside and stumbled away to be sick again, dry heaves that left her sore and gasping.

Orrin stared at her, open mouthed.

Despite everything, Alia could not help but smile weakly, for poor Orrin looked at her as if she were transformed into one of the Fey before his very eyes. She wiped her mouth with her hand, then shuddered, tasting the man's still-warm blood on her fingers. She got to her feet.

'Are you ... all right?' Orrin asked.

Alia did not know how to answer. She wiped her knife clean, sheathed it, feeling numbed.

Orrin stared at the dead bandit, lying there in a little bloody swamp. He came over to Alia and put his arms about her. 'My *brave* girl,' he said softly.

Alia looked up at him, his face bent so close to hers she was almost cross-eyed, focusing. His green eyes were wide with wonder and ... and something Alia suddenly realized was passion. She felt a momentary throb of response, his strong hands pressed against the small of her back, her own eyes locked on his.

'Alia,' he whispered, hoarse. 'My Alia ...' Abruptly, he bent his head and kissed her, warm tongue and lips pressed hungrily against hers.

'No,' she said, straight-arming him off. 'No!'

He stumbled back.

Alia stood, panting. It had happened too suddenly, too unexpectedly. She had never looked for such an advance from Orrin.

He stood staring at her accusingly, like a small boy who had been abruptly denied a piece of sweetmeat.

'Alia ...' he said. 'Don't ... don't push me away.'

She shook her head. 'I can't do it, Orrin.'

'Why *not?*'

Alia sighed. How could she explain it to him?

117

A part of her wanted him, wanted the feel of his fine, strong hands, the solid sense of his long strong body against hers. But she had seen all too often what happened when women gave themselves over to a man. The man loved them, oh yes, but that love all too easily became a kind of trap.

In Orrin's eyes, and everybody else's, she would become Orrin's woman. No more easy banter with Tym and Patch, no more free hunts on her own when and as she wished. Orrin would worry over her, eye other men with suspicion, spend his time planning her life for her. He would watch her like the hawk in the proverb, sensitive to everything she said and did, and bristle like a hound if she dared to be resentful of his solicitude.

And there would be no more journeying alone into the high hills for her, no more glimpses of the Fey, no more teetering on the edge of the mysterious world of wonders that called to her so – that had always called to her so.

He would weight her like a great, heavy rock.

And he would get her with child, and strut and boast about it like a farmer with a new brood mare. Alia had seen it happen.

Alia sighed. It ought not to be like this.

She did not know how to say any of it to Orrin. Even to herself, it sounded pompous and silly when she tried to put it into words.

It was the call of the wild lands that had brought her out of her old life to salvation and heart's ease up here in the Heights: as a girlchild, she had sat for whole days on end, far from her family's overcrowded little cabin as she could get, hugging herself, sore from some beating, gazing up into the far, wild Heights, yearning, *yearning*. She had heard the faint voice of the wild's mysteries calling to her then; and it called to her now still, real as anything, real as the wind to a hawk, or the rushing stream to a trout.

She would never willingly jeopardize that. It would be like putting herself back in the miserable cage of her childhood once again.

Having once escaped that crippling cage – the smothering pack of rough brothers, her father's domineering violence – she was perhaps oversensitive ...

Orrin was still staring at her, the hurt look still plain on his face. 'It's ... it's not *you*, Orrin,' she began. 'I just ...'

'We fit well together, you and I,' he said. 'We would be good for each other.' He took a step nearer to her. 'I worry about you, Alia. Let me look after you. You need somebody to look after you.'

Alia backed away from him. There it was, the seductive offer:

118

somebody to care for her, to look out for her, look after her. But it was the door to the cage he was holding open for her.

And yet, he was a handsome man, and kind enough. Many a woman would think her mad to reject him.

He moved towards her.

Alia shook her head, held up her hands to halt him. 'No, Orrin. No.'

'Why *not?*'

He looked at her, and the genuine tenderness in his gaze touched her. But it was no use. She would not, *could* not give in to him. 'I'm ... I'm just not ... ready,' she told him lamely. 'Besides,' she pointed at the dead man. Already, the first flies were beginning to buzz interestedly about him. 'This is *not* the time for such matters!'

Orrin took a long breath, sighed. 'Aye, I suppose you're right, girl.'

Alia turned and retrieved her bow from where she had let it drop. She looked about her, took a breath. 'What next, then?'

But Orrin was still looking only at her, puppy-eyed. '*Orrin!*' she snapped. 'Be sensible.' She gestured to the dead man, the forest all about. 'What next? Do you know where Tym and Patch are likeliest to be?'

Orrin shook himself, looked about with sharper eyes. 'I've no notion where they might have got to,' he said to her query. Then he sighed. 'We didn't plan this very well. We should have stayed closer together. In pairs perhaps. I just went running off ...'

'We must find them, Orrin. I reckon this one,' she gestured to the dead bandit, 'isn't the only scout they had out.'

He nodded. 'Aye. My guess is Tym and Patch'll be across the ridge over there.' He pointed away to the left of where they stood. 'Let's be off and try it.'

They set out carefully, keeping a distance, yet staying within sight of each other.

Alia's hands were shaking now as she held the bow, and her feet were unsteady. She felt sick and confused. Death and passion, blood and kisses. It was all too much. She only wanted to be away from all of it.

The demon-creature suddenly appeared before her in her mind's eye, beckoning as it had before. She drove the image from her thoughts in irritation. A momentary, tearing thrust of pain went through her sore left hand, right up the arm. She halted, worried that she might have torn open the slow-forming scabs. But no. She

119

stood, panting, trying to flex some of the nagging soreness out, thinking on what might lie ahead, wishing she were somewhere else, *anywhere* else.

Alia took a long breath, let it out, took another, willing herself to go on. There were no easy choices left.

She heard Orrin whistle suddenly – the sharp hunter's whistle of distress – and her heart kicked. More bandits? Peering through the screen of trees, she saw him gesture, index finger up in a circle, then folding down to a point – hunter sign for quarry ahead.

What? she signed back, clenching and unclenching her hand to form the silent query.

He shook his head to show he did not know. Then, still silent, he hooked a thumb at himself, leftwards, then at her, to the right.

Alia nodded. Silent and careful as could be, she moved off rightwards, slipping along with her heart in her mouth.

She crouched behind a chest-high upthrust of lichen-covered rock, scanning the forest ahead. Past that, she padded around the thick bole of a pine, peering into the slanting forest light, looking for movement, shape, watching her footing, keeping the bow half drawn, swinging her head back and forth, scanning, scanning ...

And there it was suddenly, off to her left and in front, a man whirling to face her, bow up and drawn. Up came Alia's bow. She had drawn, anchored the arrow against her cheek, was about to let fly, all in one desperate instant.

Almost, she could not stop herself.

'Alia!' the man facing her hissed.

Almost, she had shot Patch.

Alia lowered her bow, hands shaking. She did not know whether to cry or laugh. 'Patch,' she breathed. '*Patch!*'

Silently, he motioned her over. He was white faced, and she could see his hands shake. 'I nearly shot you, girl,' he whispered as she approached. 'Thought you were one of *them*.'

She nodded. 'I too.'

'Look,' he said then, pointing to the ground with a hand that still quivered. 'Two of them at least.'

Alia looked down. The sign was plain enough: two men had crouched here, no doubt conferring, then headed off. Their trail, what she could make of it from here, led cross-slope and down towards the way Hone Amis and the rest had taken.

'We must find them,' Patch said.

Alia nodded.

'Where are the others? Do you know?'

'Orrin is near.'

'And Tym?'

'You don't know?'

Patch shook his head, his face pinched with worry. 'I left him over there.' He gestured ahead and to the left. 'He was headed up the other side of the slope. I don't know whether he's aware of these two. He may be ahead of them by now.'

Alia shivered. She turned and put her fingers to her lips, blowing the bird-call summons the hunters used.

In a few moments they heard Orrin's reply.

'What is it?' he asked when he had met up with them.

Patch showed him the sign. 'Two of them, following after Hone Amis and the rest.'

Orrin nodded. 'That makes three so far.'

'Three?' Patch said.

'Alia already took one.'

Patch stared.

Orrin told him the story quickly.

'Are you ... all right?' Patch asked her quietly, once he had heard the tale.

The simple concern on his face warmed her. She nodded. 'As possible.' She saw him look down at her hands, and realized that they were still blood stained.

Patch put a hand on her arm, a brief, comradely gesture of sympathy. 'Bad times, we're living.'

'Sympathy later,' Orrin said, slipping between Patch and Alia and breaking the contact between them.

Alia winced.

'Where's Tym?' Orrin asked of Patch.

'Ahead somewhere, far as I can tell. He might be in front of those two bandits. He might not know they're behind him.'

'We'll follow along and take *them* from behind,' Orrin said, his face grim. 'Patch and I first, you behind as a backup, Alia.'

Her initial instinct was to argue, resenting his protectiveness.

But Patch said, 'Good enough. Alia's done her part already.'

To that, she had no easy response.

So off they went, careful and quiet, Orrin and Patch ahead by thirty paces or so, she behind, so that the three of them formed a moving triangle.

Across a low ridge, they went, and down through a shallow gully.

And then Patch stopped, abruptly.

After a moment, he motioned them over.

Alia came up last, being further off than Orrin, and found the two men staring down at something that lay folded up against the roots of one of the pines.

It was the still form of Tym.

Alia sucked in a painful breath. Tym's eyes stared up blindly at her, the normal, living glisten of them gone dull and dusty with death. His chest was collapsed in a bloody ruin, where somebody had attacked him with a blade, stabbing again and again and again, shredding flesh and splintering bone.

Alia thought she was going to be sick.

'We should never have tried this,' Patch said. His voice broke and he hung his head. 'It was a mad notion, chasing after bandits by ourselves. We should never have –'

'We had no other choice,' Orrin answered gruffly.

But Patch shook his head, his face crumpled with grief. 'We should *never* have tried it. Look at poor Tym. Look at him!'

'Enough of that!' Orrin snapped, elbowing Patch aside.

'What are we going to do?' Patch demanded. 'We can't just *leave* him here!'

Orrin put a hand down to Tym. 'He's warm.' Orrin's face was white, grim, clenched. 'I'll tell you what we're going to do. Come on! They can't be far.' He leapt off like a hound after a hare.

'Wait!' Alia called, but Orrin was already gone. She looked at Patch. 'He'll get himself killed, running off crazy like this.'

Patch nodded, stricken.

'Come on,' she said.

They ran, caring more for speed than quiet now, zigging and zagging through the trees.

Ahead, Alia heard a sudden shout. She sprinted towards the sound, her heart hammering.

And there was Orrin, down in a little hollow between a brace of old pines, grappling with two ragged men.

It was Patch who reached them first, skittering desperately down the slope. Dropping his bow, he flew upon one of Orrin's assailants, dragging the man to his knees by main force.

Alia stood, bow up and drawn, helpless. The four struggling men were a desperate whirl of limbs and grunts and drawn blades. She had nothing clear to shoot at.

And then, with terrible suddenness, it was over. She saw Orrin drive his knife into the side of the man he fought with. Again and again, spattering blood with each blow now, till the man collapsed, howling. But it was Patch who went down under the other bandit. Alia saw Patch slip, tumble hard onto his back. But though he had dragged his opponent down with him, the bandit rose to his knees. The blade in the man's hand lifted, came down, once, twice.

Alia put an arrow through his spine and he crumpled.

'Patch!' she cried, and rushed to him.

Patch lay on his back, gasping. Blood pumped from an ugly gash across his left shoulder, and his jerkin was rent and bloody along the left side of his ribs.

'Oh, Patch,' Alia moaned.

Orrin came up, pale and panting. 'Is he ...'

Alia knelt down and probed at Patch's wounds, delicately. The shoulder gash looked nasty, but she thought it something a man might survive, if it were bound quickly to staunch the blood. But the ribs ... She feared to look there.

'It's ... it's gone numb,' Patch breathed. His face was white as bone. He motioned to his ribcage. 'How ... how bad is it?'

Alia bent to look. For a long instant she could make out nothing but blood and tattered cloth and dirt. Then she saw the long, wet slice along Patch's side and breathed a gasp of relief. The knife had skittered across the ribs rather than punching through them.

'It's all right,' she told Patch.

He looked up at her, eyes wide and staring. His hand clutched painfully at her arm.

'It's all *right*,' she reassured him. 'It's only a gash. The blade didn't drive between the ribs. We just need to get you bound up and stop the bleeding. You'll be fine.'

He lay back limply, gasping, letting go of himself at the news.

Alia turned and looked up at Orrin. Her hands were stained with blood, and blood still welled up out of Patch's shoulder wound. She gnawed at her lip worriedly. 'We've got to bind him, quick, before he loses too much blood. *Quick!*'

She lifted off her quiver, shimmied out of her leather jerkin and then out of the linen undershirt she wore. Working with desperate haste, ignoring the twinges from her sore left hand, she used her belt knife to rip the undershirt into strips. She then folded what remained of it into a pad, placed that over the wet gash of Patch's shoulder wound, and bound it tight as seemed right with several strips. Blood seeped through the makeshift bandage like water

123

through a sponge at first, and Alia had a moment of sickening fear that she would not be able to staunch the flow.

But it slowed as the pressure from the bandage began to do its work.

She turned to the cut along his ribs. It was the lesser of the two wounds, and easier to bind.

When she was done, Patch lay unmoving, white, still.

'We need to get him away from here,' Orrin said.

Alia nodded. She hugged herself, shivering. Naked as she was from the waist up, her skin was pimpled with gooseflesh. Orrin looked at her, seemed about to say something, closed his mouth instead. Silently, he handed her jerkin over. She shrugged it on, feeling the chill leather slide uncomfortably across her bare skin.

'I'll go for help,' Orrin said. 'You stay here with him.'

Alia shook her head. 'No. *You* stay here.'

'Listen, girl, I'm a better runner than you. I don't want ...'

'I've the stamina to make it, Orrin. You know that.'

'It's not stamina I'm worried about, girl. What if you meet more of them out there? What will you do then?'

'Run,' Alia replied. 'But what would I do here, with Patch, if some of them came past. I'm a *much* better runner than I am a fighter.'

Orrin shrugged uncomfortably.

'You're the better shot with a bow, Orrin. I'll leave you my bow and quiver.'

'No, girl! I don't like you running around by yourself in the forest. Stay here with Patch. Together, the two of you ...'

'Don't be *stupid*, Orrin! What I'm saying is the sensiblest course. You stay here with Patch. You're the better shot. You can protect him better than I. I go for help because that's what I *can* do. It's the only way!'

Orrin shook his head, not liking it.

She offered him her bow and quiver, but he refused.

'Right. I'm off,' she told him then, after a long moment of uncomfortable silence. 'Watch the bleeding. Get him some water. Find a better place for him to rest. No telling when I'll be back. Tomorrow morning at the earliest, most like. Hone Amis and the rest are well ahead by now, and the day's on the wane. Keep him still. Try not to ...'

'I know as well as you, girl, what to do and not do for him!' Orrin snapped in irritation. 'Don't try to –'

'I'm off, then,' Alia repeated awkwardly. She looked at Orrin for a moment in silence. 'Wish me luck.'

Orrin opened his mouth to say something, shook his head, sighed. 'Luck.'

Before he might say anything further, Alia turned and ran.

She pushed herself to the limit, skittering downslope, casting about for the best route that would leave as little trail as possible – in case there were indeed more bandit scouts around – but trying most of all for speed, running till her legs ached and her lungs burned.

On she raced, and on, through the endless maze of the pines, vaulting over fallen trunks, splashing across the little rills that occasionally crossed her way, hoping she had gauged her route correctly, desperate to catch up with Hone Amis and the Militia before dark made it near impossible.

But there came a moment when she simply could not run any further. Evening was descending, inexorably. The footing became treacherous. Alia's leg muscles went into spasm, and she tripped, sprawling face first, her chest heaving painfully. She spat out a mouthful of pine needles, shook herself. Her head swam. The darkening forest air about her seemed filled with glowing, wriggling snakes and she reared up, frightened, until she realized it was only her own exhaustion that was responsible. Her mouth now was full of a bitter, coppery taste. She breathed in heaving gasps. Her heart hammered so, she feared it would fail her.

In her mind's eye, she kept seeing the poor, bloody form of Tym. And she thought of Patch and Orrin, alone, bandit fodder, and felt a sick shiver go through her. Every moment wasted meant that much more danger for them.

But she could not yet get her limbs to move, could only lie prostrate where she was, exhausted, gasping, shivering, helpless as any babe.

In every direction, the pines were dark shapes, rearing up into obscurity. The dying evening light filtered through them like pale water through a web, highlighting a barky elbow here or the knobbly joint of a wooden limb.

Darkness crept over the world. Alia's heart ceased to beat so frantically, her breathing began to settle. She tried to stand, but her shivering, over-wearied legs were still too wobbly.

The silver glow of moonrise started to fill the eastern sky, no more than glimpsed through the web of trees at first. Then, through the dark spikes of the pines, Alia saw the glowing orb of the moon, full now, ghosting through the darkened sky like some disembodied, staring face.

An owl hooted, making Alia start. Close on that, she heard the sound of movement – some forest creature padding away from her. Then silence.

Alia shivered. There seemed, somehow, an uncanny feel to the air. She stared about her apprehensively.

Through the trees, something was making its way towards her, softly. Her heart clenched. Trembling, she tried to force herself up; it was still all she could do just to haul herself shakily to her knees. She attempted to knock an arrow to her bow, but her fingers quivered so she could not set the arrow properly to the bowstring.

Then she made out what it was coming towards her, and the bow fell from her hold.

Out of the tree-shrouded dark, the pale form of a Fey stepped into the slanting moonlight. It came towards her in utter silence and with utter grace, its impossibly slim limbs moving as if it traced the steps of a slow, intricate dance towards her. The dark eyes in its pale face gazed at her unblinking.

Alia shivered. It was hard for her to focus: one instant, the figure was pale and vague as a ghost, the next solid seeming as her own self.

The Fey had drawn close to her now. One of the slim arms reached out, like a shaft of very moonlight suddenly embodied before her. Fingers brushed her face. Cool and dry, they felt, palpable as any human touch, yet light as the kiss of the evening breeze. The dark, unhuman eyes stared down at her. The touch left her cheek. The Fey's long-fingered, pale hands reached for hers.

Her sore left hand flared into sudden agony as the Fey gripped it. Alia groaned, trying to wrench free. But the grip upon her was remorseless.

She sensed ... she was not sure what she sensed: a stomach-wrenching sinking away, as if she were a rock wobbling down through dark water. A thrust of panic went through her and she struggled to rise up.

The hands of the Fey, holding hers, were cool and light, insubstantial as the touch of a feather, yet incontestably powerful for all that. She felt like a little child being pulled down into deep, deep water, dark and endless and aswirl with strange currents. Down. Down ...

126

Alia shrieked.

She had *yearned* for this moment of communion, the very thought of which had been her secret hope and secret salvation. But this sickening, plunging sensation that overwhelmed her was nothing like the young girl's dream she had lived for all these years. And the Fey was too *strange*. As a girl-child, heart-sick and bruised, she had imagined some wonderful combination of strength and complete gentleness, of great power and greater understanding.

Instead, the remembrance struck her suddenly of the trout she had hooked out of Birchleg pool, flopping about helplessly, torn from its natural element. That was how she felt – torn from her natural place and plunged into dark, frightening chaos.

She had put the fish out of its misery as quickly as she could. Alia felt a cold thrust of utter panic go through her. Was the Fey now to do the same for her? Had it hooked her out of her natural element only to dispatch her to the dark landscape of the Shadowlands?

She felt a terrifying sense of dissolution overwhelm her. It was all a mistake! She did not want this. This was *terrible* ...

But then the churning chaos about her began to settle, as if she had been tumbled through the edge of some great, roiling current and brought back out.

But brought back out *where?*

Alia stared about her, shaken. It was the world she had always known, tree and rock and ground, moon in the star-strewn sky over head.

Yet it was not that world *at all*.

She seemed to hear the stars singing – clear bright voices in complex, ethereal harmonies. And that harmonic web wove in and around the flying moon. And the moon laughed, or howled, or simply sang. Alia could not tell.

The very world sang. Alia could feel it in her bones, a great, thrilling, complex chord.

The trees danced in an intricate pattern of limb and leaf and trunk. The air swirled. Moonlight flooded all in a great, pouring wash of soft radiance.

She made out the moving shapes of Fey – more than she could easily count – circling in a slow, impossibly graceful dance. There was no music save that of the stars and the moon and the very world herself, yet the dancers moved in perfect, unforced rhythm. The Fey tugged at Alia, guiding her towards that circling dance with insistent strength.

127

But her left hand now was a great torch of pain, an agonized flaring she could almost see as throbbing, ethereal light. She tried to wrench herself from the Fey's grip, but she was helpless against its strength. 'My hand ...' she gasped.

The Fey turned and regarded her silently for long, long moments. Its hands, holding hers, were still cool and light. Soothingly cool. She felt that coolness flowing into her suddenly, drowning the burning pain in her left hand like water poured upon flames.

Alia sighed, relieved, and was able to look about. The flooding moonlight was like a great current of radiant water. And the dancing Fey moved with the slow, weightless elegance of water-creatures, swirling on long-boned legs, arms waving like sea kelp in a gentle current, circling, pausing, circling ...

The Fey pulled her into the midst of it.

But it was no good. She could not hope to emulate the high-stepping elegance of the Fey. She was too sore and stiff, too disoriented, too self-conscious and shaken to be able to do more than stumble awkwardly after. The being holding her moved with such uncanny grace, each little motion a perfection of balance. She felt a stab of despair. It was impossible. She was too clumsy, too lumbering, too *human*.

The Fey tugged at her in an abrupt, hard jerk, nearly pulling her off her feet. She felt suddenly panicked. Was it losing patience? What would it do to her, pitiful, awkward thing that she was turning out to be? She could read no clear expression on that strange, almost-human face. Beautiful, yes. It was that. But it was a terrible, *other* beauty for all the humanness of its features.

The dark, unblinking, unhuman eyes stared into hers.

Alia shivered.

The Fey's dance wove on, and she found herself and her companion somehow in the middle of it, with Fey gracefully aswirl all around, their long, pale limbs moving still in that uncanny, perfect unison. The stars sang overhead, the moon wailed, the trees fluttered. Everything seemed in motion. Alia felt a great surge of something go through her, like a flood of water going through a chute. It passed through her, yet it filled her somehow at the same time. Her limbs tingled with it. Her very mind ... shivered. As an overly bright light might temporarily blind the eyes, so this great *something* pouring through her seemed to momentarily blind her mind.

And then, only half aware, she found herself dancing in slow, ecstatic perfection with them. Her limbs moved effortlessly, all her hurts and weariness somehow gone, each movement, each breath a simple joy.

Alia's mind emptied, a slow spilling away of thought, like a basket being tipped so that all its contents tumbled out, rolling haphazardly away.

She experienced one last, fragmentary, frightened moment of uncertainty. What were these beings doing to her? What was she *allowing* them to do to her?

And then, like a seal slipping smoothly into the green waves of the sea, she slipped entirely into the timeless, flowing pattern of the dance.

A slow, flowing ecstasy of movement, white, long-fingered hands in rising motion, the moon's shining face, singing stars in the velvet dark, the bobbing pines, the soft rush of the wind, the earth a great, soft drum under their moving feet, the swirl of pale, graceful limbs in perfect unison ...

Alia sat up with a panicky start.

She clutched her head, groaning at the pain her sudden movement had caused her – a stab of agony through her skull, her left hand throbbing, her legs stiff as if they were bound tight with wire.

The Militia! she thought. Poor Orrin and Patch. She had to ...

The Fey!

Alia groaned again. Her mind reeled. What had happened to her? She knew not what to think.

Where *was* she?

Blinking to try and clear her vision, she looked about her. It was early morning, the air still carrying the night's chill, and she shivered with the cold of it. Sunlight filtered through rustling, pale gold leaves all about her. She realized she was lying in the midst of a small, steep-sloped, grassy clearing, ringed by slender, high-mountain ash trees. The air here had that clean, ice-blue feel of the upper slopes. A little stream bubbled and danced across rocks draped in glistening emerald moss. On the stream's far side ...

The Fey.

Where *was* this place? How had she come here? Alia ran her trembling hands over her face, winced, for her face was still swollen and sore, and her left hand throbbed bad as ever.

She eyed the Fey uncertainly. It must have brought her here. What did it want with her now?

In the slanting early-morn light, the Fey appeared transparent almost, like a figure fashioned of palely tinted ice, but clear enough for all that. Though it looked very human-like in its exotic way, it made no simple human gesture, no fidgeting or blinking, no little human motion of nervousness or uncertainty, not even the shifting of a tired limb. When it stood still, it stood utterly still. And now, looking at its long, slender, pale body, Alia saw suddenly, clearly, that it was male.

How had she not noticed immediately?

For long moments the Fey stayed unmoving, watching her with its huge dark eyes. The morning breeze lifted the leaves. A hidden bird whistled a small song, all innocence: *Te weet te weet te weet te whoo!*

The Fey stepped over the stream, lifting long legs with the careful delicacy of a fishing heron, and bent down next to her. Alia stayed as she was, frozen. The Fey reached a slender-fingered hand to her face.

Alia shied back, her heart beating suddenly fast.

The Fey leaned closer, reaching for her. His fingers traced the slope of her brow, moving like so many trailing feathers, to rest upon her eyes. She felt a tingling jolt sing through her skull.

Frightened, she tried to skitter away. But he kept a grasp upon her, light but unbreakable.

Opening her eyes, Alia gasped. She could somehow see the Fey clearer now – elegant sinew, impossibly long of bone, impossibly slim, impossibly beautiful. And the very world was changed. The morning light was glowing silver, like bright moonlight. The ash trees sang a little leaf-song. Almost, she could catch ... words, or almost-words: *leaf and wind and water flowing, light and warmth and season's going* ... But there was too much else. She felt the great *thrummm* of the earth in her bones. Saw dawn clouds embrace overhead in a slow swirl of fleecy limbs. The little bird's song chimed clear as clear: *I meet I greet I meet with you! I meet I greet I MEET with you!*

Alia knelt where she was, frozen, staring.

It was the wondrous world of the Fey's dance. Her own familiar world and yet not ... most definitely *not* her own world.

How was it possible?

The Fey, who had kept his hold upon her, swept one graceful, slim hand before Alia's face. The fingers fluttered, as the wings of a bird might. And suddenly Alia saw the hand as a gliding ivory bird, riding the wind to great heights, up and up in ascending spirals, weightless as air, weightless as very moonlight itself. She felt herself the bird, felt the light, strong fingers of the wind upon her.

And below lay the world, spread wide in all ways.

The bird's eyes – her eyes – were incredibly sharp; she could see ... *everything*: the little bobble of an individual leaf in the wind, the slow, stone sigh of a great mountain, the whirl and dance of a stream over rocks, the white splash of a feeding trout. And she saw other, less familiar things: the pale, elegant form of a Fey dancing along the steep cleft of a green mountain valley, a pale flurry of movement under the cover of softly singing trees, a long neck and bright eyes belonging to no manner of creature she recognized, a veil of green light moving across the mirror-calm surface of a little lake like a graceful, glowing serpent.

It was a whole other world below her, like nothing Alia had ever experienced.

And then the bird shook and dived and it was fingers not feathers that fluttered in the morning breeze and she was back in the little mountain clearing with the Fey's hand still upon her brow.

Alia sighed.

The Fey reached its free hand – that had been the bird-hand – to her. The skin was like new bone, white, yet with a hint of ivory warmth to it. Alia felt the cool fingers trace the line of her cheek, gentle as a butterfly's wing brushing her skin.

She did not know what to do. The unhuman black eyes gazed at her steadily, only a hand's span or two away from her own. No recognizable human sentiment could she read in that steady gaze, nor in the beautiful, almost-human face. The fingers slid along the underside of her jaw. Alia started uncomfortably. But the touch was light and hurt her not at all.

Down to her throat his fingers moved, and from there they traced across her sternum, across the swell of her breasts, back up along her throat once more and across the other side of her face. Then, slowly, she felt the Fey let go his hold upon her.

The world fell out of its glamour and became once again the familiar place she knew. The Fey rose to his full height in one easy motion. He glided a few steps away from her, then stood stock still, gazing at her with his huge dark eyes. She saw him now as she had at first, translucent almost, yet clear for all that.

He lifted a long slim hand in a familiar human gesture made bizarrely elegant.

Suddenly, it was all Alia could do just to get breath.

Come, the gesture beckoned, the long pale fingers curling gracefully.

Alia felt her heart beat in terror and yearning.

In some manner she could not quite grasp, the Fey had made it clear to her what he was offering: a whole other world, a whole other life.

But at what price?

That, too, he somehow had made clear. When she had been at one with the great, soaring white bird, she had looked down upon a world unlike any she knew – an utterly changed world. But it was not, Alia somehow understood, the world itself that had changed. The world remained forever. It was she who had changed. And because she had been so transformed, so had the world been so. The world was the world. But the world of a bird was not that of a fish, and the world of a Fey was not that of an ordinary woman such as herself.

To enter the world he was offering, his world, she would have to *change*.

Come, his slender, unhuman, beautiful hand beckoned her. *Change.*

Alia shivered. She took a step towards him.

But then she shook herself.

No.

No!

Orrin and Patch! How *could* she have been so empty headed as to not even think ...

With a shudder, she looked at the Fey. Had he cast some sort of glamour over her? Turned her mind?

He was so beautiful ...

Alia felt a great confused shudder of feeling go through her. She ached to go with him, to undergo the change he offered, to put aside all the longings of her life and experience ... fulfilment.

But there was so much else pulling at her. Orrin, and poor, hurt Patch. The bandit threat. The hunters, who were all the family she had.

How could she forsake them?

How could she not? she thought, gazing at the wondrous Fey.

But the remembrance of Orrin and Patch would not let her be.

Each moment she stood here indecisive, they were put in more danger. Already, she had lost far too much time. Their lives were in her hands. It was like a hook in her guts, pulling at her.

Alia took a first hesitant step away, another. She glanced away from the Fey uneasily, glanced back.

The beckoning hand went slowly still.

Alia felt her heart rise in her throat. She took another step away, another still. Off nearby to her left, she spotted her bow and quiver lying on the grass. Would the Fey let her pick it up? Would he let her leave, or did he consider her his ... possession?

Slowly, she stepped towards the bow. The Fey moved not at all. With one eye on him, Alia stooped, snatched up both bow and quiver.

He merely stood, watching in silence.

Alia breathed a sigh. She shrugged into the quiver.

'I ...' She did not know what she wanted to say, or even if the Fey was able to comprehend.

'Tha ... thank you,' she stammered finally. 'Thank you for your ... invitation.'

The dark eyes did not so much as blink.

Alia felt a complete fool. 'I'm ... I'm sorry. I have ... friends who are relying on me to ... I cannot go with you. I'm sorry. It's very nice of you to ask me, but ...'

The words trailed away. How did one talk with a being such as the one before her? Everything she said felt like the prattlings of a stupid child.

Alia took a steadying breath. Slowly, she moved away from the clearing and the stream. 'I ... I must go.'

Still, he made no visible response.

'I'm sorry,' Alia repeated. Seeing him stand there so still and silent, she felt a great wash of unbearable sadness go through her. Almost, she returned to him. If he had beckoned at that moment, or made any recognizable human gesture, she might have.

But he did not. He merely stood, still as a pale statue, his unblinking, unhuman eyes fixed upon her face.

Alia shivered. 'I'm ... sorry,' she said yet again.

It was a lame goodbye.

Turning, she hurried off through the whispering, white-gold ash trees. She could feel his gaze still upon her from behind, but she resolutely refused to look back.

She broke into a fleeing run, ignoring the stiff agony of her legs.

133

Her heart thumped in earnest now, for she feared suddenly that he might try to stop her. Who knew the power of the Fey?

But nothing happened, and eventually she slowed her pace, walking along until she was able to get her breath back properly.

He had let her go. He had made her an invitation – that was clear as clear – and he had let her accept or not. That was what she should have truly thanked him for, she suddenly realized. He had let the decision be hers, and had abided entirely by her choice.

Alia halted and gazed back at the silent, empty wood that lay behind her. Her eyes were suddenly filled with tears. 'Thank you,' she said softly. 'But I ...'

As before, she felt like a fool. More so now, talking to empty air. There was no sign of him. She remembered the touch of his fingers across her face. She would, most like, never see him again.

At that thought, Alia felt a pang of sudden and complete dismay.

How many folk received the sort of invitation she had? It was a great gift.

And she had refused it.

For an instant, she felt the call of him again, and almost wheeled about and ran back the way she had come. It was what she had yearned for all her life.

But she could not. There were too many other demands upon her.

Alia turned resolutely, wiped away her tears, and gazed around to try to orient herself so that she could make the quickest route possible back to Hunters Camp. The palm of her left hand itched, and she scratched at it absently. She had no notion of whereabouts, exactly, the Fey's small clearing lay in the Heights, but she felt confident in her ability to orient herself once she was able to spot familiar landmarks.

Day was drawing on, the uncertain dawn-time of transition well over. There would be no trouble finding landmarks of some sort, Alia felt certain. But as she began to scrutinize things, the world suddenly seemed ...

Instead of the ordinary world she knew, Alia found herself gazing at something more nearly resembling a half-translucent façade. The trees, the blue-glowing sky overhead, and brown, needle-thick ground underfoot, all seemed to be ... merely a face. It was the only word that seemed to fit the uncanny perception she was experiencing. It was as if, at some deep level, she could no longer accept the world of things with the same certainty she had once had. She had seen the face of the world change. Now she suddenly was finding it difficult to focus clearly on the familiar face she had once so innocently and completely taken for granted.

Alia shivered, blinked, rubbed her eyes with the heels of her palms, hard. What if the Fey had taken her too far? What if she were never able to get back wholly again into the ordinary world? Heart thumping, she stared, focused, concentrated. Long, tormenting, slow, moments it took before the world began to settle into its familiar, comfortable pattern.

But settle it did, eventually.

Alia sighed, shook herself. She tried not to think. She forced herself to search about with a practical eye, looking for some sort of landmark. Precious time was passing.

That way and this she looked, but the trees were too close. Finally, she had to scramble up one of them. Only then, clutching the swaying limbs near the tree's top, her left palm throbbing painfully, did she sight anything at all familiar: a snowy peak that might be Mount Weem. Or might not. It was far from easy to be certain. But if it were Weem she saw, that placed the direction of Hunters Camp downslope and westwards.

Downslope she went then, running.

IX

Guthrie sat, legs tucked up uncomfortably underneath him. He arched his back, trying to ease weary muscles, opened his eyes, squeezed them shut again. The wind chittered through the trees about him. He shivered. His shoulders ached. His buttocks, too.

This was the second day he had sat thus.

Doing nothing.

He was very near to panicking.

Guthrie had imagined how it would be: himself and the old Closterer woman going through a series of esoteric movements, a deadly, graceful dance of secret Closterer knowledge and power.

Instead, all she had done so far was make him sit here amongst the trees at the edge of their makeshift camp, silent, unmoving, till he wanted to scream.

All his hopes were faltering. It seemed a ridiculous sham, this Closterer business. The Abbod had been of precious little use, after all, despite all his boasting about being no ordinary man. And this Rosslyn had shown him completely nothing.

Guthrie glanced surreptitiously at her. She sat a little ways off from him, calm as could be. Her eyes were half open, showing only whites. A little string of spittle dribbled from the corner of her mouth. Guthrie could not help but wonder if the old woman's mind might be failing her. He had seen it often enough in the old, that fatal fuzzy mindedness from which there was no return.

The thought made him go cold.

After everything he had survived, to have his cherished hope of revenge torn from him, to have the unexpected promise that had been born in him come to *this*. Sitting here while the days passed, doing *nothing!*

'Let your mind settle,' Rosslyn had told him. 'Like a lake calming after the wind goes.'

But he could not get his mind to settle. He yearned to be accomplishing something – anything! His back ached. His bent-up knees throbbed. He looked again over at silent Rosslyn, sighed quietly. Overhead, the clouds flowed free. He watched the little twirling movements of a nearby leaf. His restless glance moved sideways to where the dead Abbod's skull lay on the sod near him; he found himself to be strangely uncomfortable unless it was within his sight.

Upon which Rosslyn made no comment whatsoever.

That skull ... The uncanny thing was neither fish nor fowl nor good red meat, as the old saying went. Guthrie could not understand the hold it had over him, nor why it should have come to him, of all folk. It had to be more than mere dead bone, yet it lay inert. The bony face was turned his way; the empty eyes seemed to regard him with silent mockery. 'What are *you* staring at?' he demanded of it under his breath. The skull, as usual, stayed silent as any stone.

Guthrie felt a twinge of pain shoot through his knee. He shifted position, but the shifting only made the ache in his back worse. Suddenly, he could endure none of it any longer.

With a grunt, he unbent his legs and struggled to his feet.

Rosslyn's sea-green eyes opened on him.

He stood, legs and feet tingling unpleasantly as the blood returned to them, and stared at her. He took a breath, trying to keep his frustration from getting the better of him. 'Please, Rosslyn,' he began. '*Please!* I swear to you ... I *swear* I cannot take any more of this wretched *sitting!* It's completely wasted time. Give me something to *do*. Something I can *learn!*'

'Ye must learn first not to whistle while ye piss,' Rosslyn said calmly.

'What's *that* supposed to mean?' Guthrie snapped.

The frustration reared up in him like a needle-toothed little beast, and under its pricking he would have said more. But he paused at the sharp look Rosslyn gave him, closed his mouth. This old Closterer woman was his last chance. To such had his fortunes fallen. He took a breath, tried for calm. 'You said you were going to teach me, Rosslyn. So *teach* me. Please!'

'As long as ye persists in yer blindness,' Rosslyn said, 'I will do whatever I see fit to try to make ye see.'

Guthrie took another breath. 'See *what?*'

'What ye refuses to see.'

'And just what is it that I ... *refuse* to see?'

Rosslyn's voice took on a kind of sing-song cadence: 'The five true colours clog the eyes and blind us to the wondrous skies that lie about us. The five true notes will make us deaf to talking wind in bough and leaf that laugh about us. The five true tastes will blind the tongue, in very old or very young.'

Guthrie crossed his arms, took a breath, released it. '*That* is supposed to explain everything?'

Rosslyn shook her head and sighed. 'Impatient, blind boy.'

The two regarded each other for long, silent moments.

'Who ... what *are* the Closterers, then?' Guthrie demanded.

This was the first time Rosslyn had shown any willingness at all to talk with him. Until now, she had either ignored any queries of his entirely or told him to keep his mouth and his mind empty. He might or might not get her actually to teach him anything here, but he was determined to use this opportunity to at last get a few simple answers from her.

And if those answers turned out to be incomprehensible, as he feared they might ... His gut knotted at the very thought.

Rosslyn gazed at him unblinkingly. Her age-lined face was calm as calm, her sea-green eyes bright and clear and unwavering, like small, shining orbs lit from within. For the instant they seemed hardly human eyes at all. Guthrie shivered, but he pressed on. 'Rosslyn, you've told me *nothing!*'

The old Closterer sighed and nodded. 'Very well. We will have question and answer then, for a while.' She paused, continued. 'The Closterers are an Order. Men and women who live apart. Those for whom the world is not enough.'

'Not enough?'

'There are those who look through the face of the world, beyond it, who cannot turn away from the world's mysteries, who do not take well to the tasks of ordinary life. Does ye know the sort of folk I mean?'

Guthrie tugged at an ear, thinking. 'There was one such amongst the Five Families, perhaps. One of the Charrers. A dreamer. He ran off up into the hills. Caused no end of confusion and bad temper at the time. I was only a little lad when it happened, but I remember it clear. My father called the man a fool. Hone Amis despised him.' Guthrie shrugged. 'He collected a rag-tag group of misfits around him, others like him. Lived up in the hills and hunted. Some of them used to come into Riverside and trade fresh meat for flour or iron or such. A raggedy, thin looking lot they seemed. Surely it's not such as *them* who make up the Closterers?'

138

'No. But 'tis folk such as this hunting man of yers who are drawn to the Closterers' path, to the pathless way.'

Guthrie sighed. 'I don't ...'

'Hush now,' Rosslyn said. She rose to her feet in one simple, graceful movement. 'What do you think it is I will teach ye?'

'I ...' Guthrie shrugged. 'Some sort of ... secret knowledge. The Abbod,' he gestured to the skull on the ground near him, 'he could ... do things. Uncanny things.'

'Such as?'

'He could ... defend himself. He threw Hone Amis to the ground, caught the Sea Wolf's thrown spear. With ease. I never saw how. No ... ordinary man could do such things. Not like he did.'

Rosslyn merely smiled her crooked-toothed smile.

'Teach me how to do those things,' Guthrie implored. 'Teach me, Rosslyn!'

The old Closterer nodded finally. 'Come here, then.'

Guthrie moved forwards till he stood only a few paces from her.

'Find yer balance. Stand easy so ye feels yer body evenly weighted. On the balls of yer feet now.'

Guthrie's heart beat suddenly fast. He tried to focus. This was what he had been waiting for – at last! He set his feet, trying to find his balance the way Rosslyn had directed.

She examined his stance. 'That will do nicely enough. Does ye feel centred? So that ye can move suddenly in any direction?'

Guthrie swayed this way and that, testing the feel of it. 'Aye, I think so.'

'Try to strike me, then.'

Guthrie hesitated.

'Go on.'

The situation suddenly reminded Guthrie of his boyhood sword lessons with Hone Amis out in his father's arms yard. 'Keep your eyes on your opponent's,' the Militia Master had always said. 'Hold his attention. Then strike. Hard. But keep your gaze steady and don't betray the move beforehand.'

Guthrie stared intently into Rosslyn's green eyes. He was determined to impress her. Moving in a little half-circle closer towards her – she stood perfectly still – he kept his gaze steady, unwavering, giving away no betraying anticipatory flicker.

Then he struck.

And found himself face first on the ground, his mouth full of dirt. From behind, he heard Rosslyn laugh.

139

Furious, he whirled.

And stopped, frozen.

The old Closterer sat cross-legged, *in mid-air*, gazing calmly down at him.

Guthrie felt his stomach lurch. Rosslyn hovered in the empty air, perfectly still, perfectly calm. This was not anything he had anticipated. This was simply not *possible*.

Rosslyn laughed again, softly. 'Ye should see yer face, lad.'

Guthrie shivered, his belly twisted up painfully. He felt as if he had just plummeted from some great height. 'How ... how do you *do* that? Is it some ... some form of illusion?'

'Not at all,' Rosslyn replied.

'But how ...'

'Shush for the moment,' she told him. Then, as Guthrie watched, amazed, he saw the simple satchel that was all her baggage rise slowly into the air from where it had rested at the foot of one of the trees. From out of the satchel, a small bundle emerged. Rosslyn held it a moment. Then she beckoned him towards her. 'Here, take this.'

Guthrie had to reach up to take the little bundle from her hold. His hand shook as he did so.

'Unwrap it,' Rosslyn directed.

The bundle felt heavy for its small size. Unfolding the cloth wrapping, Guthrie found a little book. The cover was formed of thin wooden planks sheathed in pebble-grained leather dyed a rich crimson. The stitching along the cover's seams formed perfect edges, each stitch exactly in place, and the red leather shone softly, without blemish of any sort. There was no title.

Guthrie had seen few books in his life, and none even remotely like this fine little thing he held gingerly in his hands. It was a lovely piece of work.

'Open it,' Rosslyn said.

Guthrie did so. The pages were of excellent vellum parchment. About a third of the way down the first page, across the centre of it, in large, elegant, hand-drawn letters, was written: *The Pathless Way*. And underneath that, in smaller letters: *The Seer sees but does not seize.*

'The *Seer*?' he said.

'One who sees,' Rosslyn replied, 'where others are blind.'

'Sees *what*?'

The only answer the old Closterer gave was to gesture for Guthrie to turn the page of the book in his hands.

Hesitantly, he did so. The page he turned to was taken up by a single verse:

> Silent and still,
> And the crest of the hill,
> The Seer sees
> A motionless motion,
> A soundless commotion,
> A greatness receding,
> A far away seething,
> Returned with his breathing
> Gone silent and still.

'Well?' Rosslyn asked.

Guthrie gnawed at his lip.

Rosslyn laughed. 'Ye thinks it foolishness, doesn't ye? A waste of good sheepskin.'

'It's just ... It doesn't mean anything to me, Rosslyn. How can you expect me to *learn* anything from meaningless verse like this?'

'Look again,' Rosslyn said.

In Guthrie's hold, the pages of the book began abruptly to turn on their own, *snick, snick, snick,* as if an invisible hand were whiffling quickly through them. He half dropped the book in his surprise, grabbed at it awkwardly, managed to keep a grip.

Rosslyn merely smiled her crooked-toothed smile. 'Read,' she said.

Guthrie looked down at the page the book was now open to:

> The name that can be spoken
> Is but a token:
> A cloud across a star,
> A doorway and a bar,
> A shackle to be broken.

Guthrie looked up, dismayed. 'It's ... nonsense, Rosslyn.'

The old Closterer sighed. 'Guthrie! The name is not the name. That which is named as the name is never the name.'

Guthrie screwed his eyes up in frustration. 'It's just *words!*'

'Exactly,' Rosslyn said with satisfaction. 'Well answered.'

Which left Guthrie staring at her, open mouthed.

From her mid-air position, Rosslyn gestured to the book in Guthrie's hands. 'It is called simply *The Book*. It contains the Closterer teachings.'

'Did you write it?'

Rosslyn laughed. 'I? Never! 'Twas written before I was born.'

'Who wrote it, then?'

'Ye has heard of the Demon War? Long ago in the settled lands southwards?'

Guthrie blinked. 'Aye. Like everybody, I heard the stories when I was a child. About Tancred Blackrobe, the terrible sorcerer, and the Lord Vile, who could be in two places at the same time. About Bloodaxe, the hero, and the great army he commanded.' Guthrie shrugged. 'Children's tales, full of wonder and terror.'

Rosslyn smiled. 'As with many such tales, though, there is more than a little truth in this one.'

Guthrie ran a hand over his eyes. He found it hard to think with Rosslyn sitting calmly, impossibly, cross-legged up in the empty air. 'Could you ... come down?' he asked her. 'It makes my belly cramp, your sitting up there.'

Rosslyn smiled. Gently, she floated back down to the ground. 'Three generations gone, that war,' she said. 'Yer father's father was no more than a little lad, if he were born into the world at all by then.'

'So?' Guthrie replied, struggling to grasp the thread of all this.

'So *The Book* was penned by a man who took part in the Demon War, a man who was responsible, in part, for the defeat of the demons who invaded the Wold from the far south.'

'Do you mean to say those folk actually existed? Bloodaxe and Tancred Blackrobe and the rest? And one of them penned the Closterers' *Book*?' Guthrie shook his head. 'Are you trying to tell me the children's tales were all true?'

'There is more in the world than ye thinks, lad. A young man, there was, at the time of the War, driven from his home, kin slaughtered, cast into the wild lands which border the settled Wold. Like so many others of that time, he was human flotsam. But this young man had a special gift ...'

Rosslyn paused, gazing at Guthrie. 'Has ye ever heard, in these childhood tales of yers, of a man named Seer Tai?'

Guthrie shook his head.

'As a little lad, Tai had fits. He would fall out of the world ...' Rosslyn sighed. 'The Powers move us human folk in strange ways. We Closterers struggle half a lifetime to achieve what Seer Tai struggled half a lifetime to deny.'

The old Closterer went silent for a little. Guthrie waited, uneasy, feeling more and more confused.

142

'The book ye holds,' Rosslyn went on finally, 'is a copy of a copy of the original, penned by Seer Tai himself. And Seer Tai it was who built the first Closter and began ... everything.'

'But what do you Closterers *do?*' Guthrie demanded.

'Ye've just seen a little of what we are capable of.'

Guthrie ran a hand over his eyes. He was beginning to doubt already what he had seen Rosslyn do. It had to be some sort of illusion. 'Is it ... mind control, then?' he asked. 'Do you control the way others see the world, feeding them illusions as you wish?'

'Not at all.'

'But ... you couldn't just have *floated* there!'

'And why not?'

'It's just ... You can't ... The world isn't made so!'

'Oh? And how, then, is the world made?'

'The world is as the world is.'

'But *how* is the world?'

Guthrie shook his head. His stomach still felt cramped up. He clenched and unclenched his fists. 'Rosslyn ...' he began.

She silenced him with a gesture. 'Suppose ye tells me, then, how the world is.'

Guthrie only stared.

'Tell me the names of the five true colours,' Rosslyn said.

'I don't see ...'

'Tell me!' she ordered, her voice suddenly gone hard.

'All right.' Guthrie swallowed, took a breath. 'The five true colours are red, orange, yellow, green, and blue. You can see them in any rainbow.'

Rosslyn nodded. 'And the five true musical notes?'

'Od, Al, Oss, Imna, and Eir.'

'And the five true tastes?' Rosslyn continued.

'Sweet, sour, hot, salty, and savoury.' Guthrie sighed. 'What's the *point* of all of this, Rosslyn? *Everybody* knows these things. It's how the world is made. Five senses. Five fingers, five toes. Five elements. Five colours. Five tastes. Do you think me so *stupid* that I would be ignorant of the basic facts of life?'

'How else is the world made? Explain it to me.'

'Explain what every child knows?' Guthrie demanded petulantly.

'Aye, exactly.'

Guthrie sighed. 'The great, nameless Powers move the world,

weaving all together like a ... a tapestry. They are greater and lesser than anything we can imagine them to be.'

Guthrie paused. It had been many years since he had learned all this, struggling with his letters as a boy under his mother's tutelage. He recalled the times he had had to stand nervously before the critical eye of his father, reciting word for word the things he had been taught. It all came back to him in a sudden rush of memory – the resinous scent of the hearth fire in the Great Hall, his father's steady, demanding gaze, the snuffle of sleepy hounds under the table, his mother's hand resting gently on his shoulder in mute support – and he recited for Rosslyn the words he had learned at his mother's knee:

'Powers move me as they move the sun, Powers many and Powers one ...' Guthrie faltered for a moment before the rest came to him. 'Starlight and moonshine and endings begun, so each to each the web is spun.'

Rosslyn laughed. 'A verse I have never heard before. Where did ye come by it?'

Guthrie shrugged self-consciously. 'A childhood verse I learned from my mother.' He swallowed. 'I did not realize I could still recall it all with such clarity.'

Rosslyn nodded. 'The things we learn in childhood stay with us all our lives.' She gestured around them. 'And the world?'

Guthrie sighed. 'The world is composed of the five true elements – Earth, Water, Air, Fire, and Spirit. Each has its place in the pattern ...' Suddenly, he recalled another of his childhood's verses. 'Earth below, supporting all. Water next, in a waterfall. Air above, so free and clear. Fire higher, far and near. Spirit last and first as well, for in all the others does it dwell.'

Rosslyn nodded. 'Yes, I know that one.'

Guthrie shrugged. 'It's as I said. *Everybody* knows this. Each element has its rightful position and place. Earth is primary, the base, supporting all else. Next comes water, free-flowing, halfway between earth and air. Air above water, then fire highest of all save for spirit, which is both highest and lowest, completing the circle.'

Guthrie paused self-consciously.

'Very good,' Rosslyn said. She reached to one side of where she sat and plucked a small stick from the ground. 'And so, if I let go this stick, what will happen?'

'It will fall.'

'And why is that?'

'It's wood. Wood is Earth.' Guthrie held his hands up, palm out, and shrugged. 'Lift any Earth-thing and let it go. It will dive to its proper place because it *belongs* there. Just as the flames of a fire will always lift upwards, seeking their proper place above, where they belong. It is the manner in which the world is ordered.'

Rosslyn nodded. 'So it is said.'

'So it *is!*' Guthrie reached up a little stick of his own, held it up, dropped it. 'See! It dives back to where it belongs. I could stand here all day, doing the same thing over and over, and each stick would still dive downwards, every time.'

Rosslyn nodded. She opened her hand and let her own stick go. It moved not at all.

Guthrie stared, open mouthed. He knew it had to be an illusion of some sort: one simply could not ignore the fundamental realities of the world at one's convenience. But it seemed a very excellent illusion. 'How do you *do* that?'

In his hand, the book – which he had all but forgot – moved, to open at a new verse:

> *Face and hands and legs and arms,*
> *Fears and joys and spells and charms,*
> *Warp and woof and nothing more,*
> *Threads to clothe us, nothing more*
>
> *Tree and rock and cloud and stream,*
> *Are never what they look to seem.*
> *Mind nor self nor leg nor star,*
> *Nothing's what we say they are.*
>
> *Lift the cloth, the threads unwind,*
> *And something other will you find,*
> *Nothing what it seems to be,*
> *Neither ye and neither me.*

Rosslyn was looking at him.

'What am I supposed to make of that?' Guthrie asked, pointing an accusing finger at the verse. 'Nothing's what we say they are,' he read. 'It isn't what we *say* that makes the world what it is.'

'*The Book* is plain as plain can be,' Rosslyn replied. 'For those with the eyes to see.'

'Then I must be blind!' Guthrie snapped. He felt panic grip him. It was all slipping away. He needed something palpable. 'You promised to *teach* me, Rosslyn.'

145

'The name of the name is not ...' the old Closterer started.

'*Rosslyn!*' Guthrie cried in exasperation. 'I'm begging you, *please!* Show me something real. Show me something I can *do*. No more illusions. No more gibberish!'

Rosslyn shook her head. 'Impatient, blind boy.' She sighed, waved him off with a little motion of one hand. 'Put the book down and go, then.'

Guthrie stared.

'Go,' she repeated softly. 'Ye is not the sort to follow the Pathless Way. Leave it to others better suited.'

'No,' Guthrie said. '*No!*' He felt suddenly sick. 'Rosslyn ... *please!* You're my only chance now. There's nothing else left for me!'

Rosslyn said not a word.

'Please!' Guthrie repeated. 'Do you wish me to beg? I'll do that if I must. On my knees if I must. Rosslyn, teach me. *Teach* me!'

Rosslyn sighed. 'Ye has no notion of what ye asks.'

'It's my very life, Rosslyn.' Guthrie took a ragged breath. 'I have nowhere to go. There is nothing left me now but this.'

'Ye has no ... patience to grasp what must be grasped.'

Guthrie took a step towards her eagerly. 'Show me. Let me learn by *doing!*'

Rosslyn shook her head. 'And does ye think yerself ready for such *doing* without proper preparation? Would ye throw a child into a deep lake and say, "Swim!" just like that?'

'At least the child would have a chance! I am like to have none, the way things have been going thus far. Let me try to swim, Rosslyn!'

'But what if ye ... drowns? Has ye considered that?'

'I'm drowning already! Drowning in words, in doing nothing while time slips away, drowning in my own frustrations. Give me a chance!'

Rosslyn sighed. 'Nay, lad. It is *far* too soon yet.'

Guthrie got down on his knees, hands clasped imploringly. 'Teach me.'

The old Closterer gestured him up irritatedly. 'Ye're being foolish,' she snapped. It was the first sign of anything like ordinary human emotion Guthrie had seen in her.

He stayed on his knees. '*Teach* me!'

Rosslyn only looked at him, long and steady and silent.

Guthrie held himself firm, refusing to flinch from that hard gaze.

'Ye has not the patience to travel the slow path.'

'Then teach me the quick!'

Rosslyn sighed. 'It is not safe, lad.'

'Let me be the judge of that.'

'Ye does not know enough to judge. There is a cost to what ye demands of me.'

'I will pay the cost. Willingly!'

The old Closterer shook her head.

'There is nothing else left me,' Guthrie said. 'You deny me my only hope!'

Rosslyn sighed. She closed her eyes, opened them again. Her gaze slid from Guthrie down to the skull. She crossed her arms, put one hand to her chin, staring at the dead Abbod's bare-bone face. For long moments she was silent. Then she turned from the skull back to Guthrie, sighed again, nodded. 'All right. Perhaps there is more at stake here than just an impatient boy's ambition. Perhaps we are all channelled. But passing the nameless gate is no easy task. And that is what ye must do ... without the preparation most have to support them in that passage.'

Guthrie looked at her, torn between excitement and unease. 'The ... nameless gate?'

He felt the book flutter in his hands.

'Read,' she told him.

He looked down:

> The way is not clear to the ear or the eye,
> Or the mind's agile fingers, so wanting to pry.
>
> Pathless the way, for what ye await.
> Change is the journey, change is yer fate.
> Change is the way through the great nameless gate.

'Is ye ready to *change*?' Rosslyn demanded.

Guthrie swallowed, nodded, his throat suddenly gone tight. He felt the hairs along the back of his neck prickle uncomfortably.

'Come, then.' Rosslyn rose to her feet. She pried the book from his fingers, put it down carefully in its wrapping, then gripped Guthrie's arm, hauled him to his feet, and began to pull him away.

Guthrie held back, his belly knotting up anxiously. He felt abruptly frightened. And foolish, like a small boy being led to some unpleasant chore by his mother. But when he tried to draw back, Rosslyn merely gripped all the harder. There was surprising strength in the old woman's thin frame.

147

Guthrie saw the skull left behind on the ground behind him. He tried to draw away from Rosslyn's grip again, feeling a pang of unease go through his belly as he always did when he got too far from the eerie thing.

But the grip on his arm never faltered.

'Rosslyn! I can't ... I've got to bring the ...'

She said not a word, merely hauled him along.

'Where ... where are you taking me?' he demanded, but received only a harder tug for answer.

Through the screen of pines they went. Guthrie felt the tug of the skull upon him. 'Rosslyn, I have to ...' Dragged along behind her as he was, with only one hand free, he could not effectively fend away the needled boughs as they slapped back into his face from Rosslyn's passing. 'Ross – aieee! Rosslyn!' he complained. But she might have been deaf for all the response he got.

And then they were on the shore of the little rocky-shored lake she had named Mirrormere.

Rosslyn let go his hand. 'Watch,' she said.

Without any further preamble, as if it were the most natural thing in the world, she calmly walked out across the still surface of the lake. The water dimpled under her feet, the way it would under the feet of a water spider, the surface bending inwards slightly but not breaking under her weight. There was no watery splash as her feet lifted up and put down, and the hem of her grey Closterer's robe, where it brushed close to her heels, remained dry.

All thought of the left-behind skull fell away from Guthrie's mind.

Rosslyn turned to him, smiling, and did a little hop-foot dance step. The water moved gently under her as if the surface of it were composed of some translucent, impossible sort of blanket, stretched tight from shore to shore, upon which she bounced.

'Come on in,' she beckoned, grinning her crooked-tooth grin. 'The water's fine!'

Guthrie could only stare, open mouthed, shaken by the utter, unexpected suddenness of it.

She beckoned to him from where she stood upon the water.

Guthrie shook his head. He felt his heart thumping. Simply to look at her, standing there impossibly like that, with such impossible calm, made him feel dizzily sick. The conviction he had once had that what Rosslyn did was only illusion fell from him: his cramping belly told him otherwise.

148

'Confusing in its formless form,' Rosslyn said, 'and silent in its noise. Whirling like a liquid storm, and filled with painful joys.'

Guthrie realized she must be quoting from *The Book*, but the words enlightened him not at all.

'Join me,' Rosslyn called. She had padded out a fair ways from the shore by now.

Guthrie shivered. He eased down to the water's verge, one hand on the rough, lichen-clothed surface of the shoreline rocks for support, and put a finger out, hesitant, not knowing what to expect. He thought, perhaps, that she had put some manner of spell upon the very substance of the water itself, rendering it thus springy and firm underfoot. But no. What he felt was water, ordinary, chill, liquid water.

Rosslyn laughed.

Guthrie stared at her.

She glided back towards him until she stood only a few hand's breadths from the shore. The water lapped against the rocks in little wavelets, moving under Rosslyn's feet in faint, liquid undulations, but she stood calm and solid as if she were on dry land.

Guthrie faltered back from her. He felt as if somebody had just kicked him, hard, in the belly. It was difficult for him to draw a proper breath.

Rosslyn held out a hand, beckoningly. 'Join me.'

Guthrie shook his head.

'Join me.'

Guthrie drew back, his belly clenched painfully upon itself.

'This is what ye demanded of me. Walk with me now through the nameless gate. *Change*.'

Guthrie shook his head. He pointed to the water under Rosslyn's feet. 'It's ... it's *water*!'

Rosslyn smiled. 'The name that can be spoken,' she said softly, 'is but a token. A cloud across a star. A doorway and a bar. A shackle to be broken.'

Guthrie remembered the words from *The Book*.

'Join me,' Rosslyn urged.

'But how can I ...'

Rosslyn backed across the water, away from the shoreline. Her hands came up, beckoning.

Under the old woman's steady gaze, Guthrie put one foot out upon the surface of the water, let his weight down upon it gingerly.

149

With a splash, he went in up to his knee, soaking boot, foot, trousers and all in frigid water.

Rosslyn laughed, the sound clear as a ringing bell across the still surface of the lake.

Guthrie scowled at her. 'Very funny,' he snapped peevishly, shaking his drowned foot. 'I get a soaker in this stupid lake of yours, while you dance upon the water. Very instructive lesson, that!'

'The name is not the name,' she called to him. 'The name of the name is not the name.'

Guthrie stood on the shore, panting, feeling the fool and not knowing what to say.

'Come,' Rosslyn said softly.

'How?' Guthrie demanded. 'What am I supposed to do?'

'It cannot be put into words or a rhyme,' Rosslyn replied. 'And pathless the way, like a long journey's climb, is the route to its wonders, its dazzle and play.' She came close enough to shore so that the hand she reached out to him came within touching distance. 'Pathless the journey, and pathless the way.'

She smiled her crooked-toothed smile. 'Walk the way with me. *Change.*'

Guthrie swallowed. Awkwardly, he lifted a hand to hers.

At the instant of contact, some strange, potent force shivered through him, almost jerking him off his feet with the sudden, painful jolt it gave him. The familiar solidity of the world about him fell away into confusion. He could feel nothing but a terrible, squirming chaos all about. His belly clenched up like a fist, and he shrieked in sudden terror, struggling against what was happening to him.

With an almost audible *snack*, the world came rushing back into shape around him, and he found himself on his knees, sobbing.

Rosslyn looked down at him from where she stood still upon the water's surface. She stood there calmly, as if all that had occurred was perfectly ordinary.

'Wha ...' Guthrie gasped, 'What ha ... happened to me?'

'Ye took the first step, lad,' Rosslyn told him softly. 'And as folk are so fond of saying, the first step is always the hardest.' She reached a hand down to him again, beckoning.

Guthrie stared at the hand. At that moment, he would rather have taken hold of a snake poised to strike at him.

'Take my hand, lad.'

Guthrie shook his head, pulled back. 'No!'

'Ye must, if ye want to learn. Ye *must!*'

150

Guthrie shivered. He did not think he could stand to face again that terrible, paralyzing rush of chaos.

'Guthrie!'

He saw her hand reach out for him and shied instinctively away.

Rosslyn stepped from off the water's surface onto the solid shore, and Guthrie sighed, relieved. But as he watched, stricken, she sank up to her neck into the ground with a kind of earthy splash.

She laughed and raised an arm up out of the earth, spilling little clods of dirt and wriggling earthworms like thick dark water from her finger tips.

She climbed out of the earth, like an ordinary person might climb up out of water to the shore, and stood upon the surface of the water, dripping earth.

The unnatural reversal of it all made Guthrie gag.

Rosslyn laughed and held out her hand.

Guthrie swallowed. He struggled up from his knees. The things he had witnessed here shook him to the marrow of his bones, as if his very body rebelled at what he had seen.

And yet ...

Yet this was what he had demanded of her. She was right. A sickly shiver went through him. Almost, he turned his back and slunk away, unable to continue. But he forced himself onwards, reaching out.

Shaking, he put his hand in hers.

His senses were nearly torn away by the awful rush of it, his eyes blinded in their sockets, his ears shredded to deafness. The ordinary, solid world was gone, and in its place there was only a dark, moving confusion, pulsing sickeningly without and within him. He screamed, or thought to scream, but could feel no mouth to scream with, no ears to hear. He felt himself being torn apart, ruptured into chaos like the very world itself.

In panic, he tried to thrash free of it. But he could do nothing. He could no more resist this dreadful, rushing chaos than a tumbling leaf could resist the autumn gale. It was killing him. Killing him ...

But it did not kill him.

He hung motionless, bodiless, mindless.

From somewhere, he heard words:

Silent and still, 'tween the stars and the seas and the crest of the hill, the Seer sees a motionless motion, a soundless commotion, a greatness receding, a far away seething, returned with his breathing, gone silent and still.

Guthrie shuddered.

Breathe, a voice commanded. *Breathe!*

Guthrie took a great, shuddering breath, distantly feeling his ribs expand, like a pair of multi-fingered hands unclenching.

Breathe.

He breathed, and as he did so, the chaos about him seemed to pulse and flare with the rhythm of his breath.

A motionless motion, a soundless commotion.

He sensed it clear now: a moving, soundless commotion all about him. The familiar world was far gone, a memory, a dream.

His body returned to him like a numbed limb coming back to life, tingling. But it was a queer, flickering sort of body. He felt light as air.

'Look about ye,' the voice directed, Rosslyn's voice he realized. Guthrie could feel her hand now, gripping his still, keeping him steady somehow, like an anchor steadies a drifting ship.

He looked about. It was not sight he used, yet he knew not what else to call it. It was as if his mind, shaken beyond all reason by what had happened to him, fell back instinctively to familiar ways of perceiving.

On the edges, there was movement, like hundreds of knuckly little fingers thrusting upwards, leaping upwards towards a great, throbbing eye above, yet leaping slowly, so slowly ...

He could feel the pulse of that great eye, if eye it was. It seemed fitting to think of it as such, for he seemed to feel it watching him, watching all things, a great, warming eye, pulsing with warm radiance far above.

Guthrie shivered. He felt his body faintly, a glowing shadow, lightly bobbling. Under him he made out a glimmering, pewter-coloured surface. He pushed down and felt the surface give elastically. It glimmered, smooth and fine as a perfect, grey-silver carpet, a mesmerizing, beautiful, glowing thing that pulsed softly with the greater pulsing from the eye above.

A long veil of green light moved like a graceful, glowing serpent across the mirror-calm, pewter surface, shimmered, expanded, disappeared.

The twitching fingers creaked and tittered.

They formed a kind of fringe around him, he now saw, stretched around the edge of the glowing surface. He sensed the yearning in them as they thrust themselves up and up, ever upwards.

The great throbbing eye above, the hundred knobbly fingers

152

leaping their slow leap upwards, the gentle undulation of the shimmering carpet beneath his feet ...

Utterly, utterly *strange*.

Guthrie felt Rosslyn's hand grip his the harder for an instant, and then, to his complete consternation, she released her grip and he fell, fell tumbling through the beauty and the terror of that otherwhere in which he had found himself and out into the ordinary world.

For one stunning instant, he found himself in the middle of little Lake Mirrormere, standing upon the surface of the water as he had seen Rosslyn do, the water firm and elastic under his feet. And for that one instant, he seemed to see two worlds, a fleeting after-image of the strange *other* place where he had been, superimposed upon the ordinary world he knew – above, the sun pulsed like a great, all-seeing eye, the knuckly fingered trees on the lakeshore yearned upwards slowly, and the water under him glowed like a resilient grey-silver mirror.

And then, with a sickening rush, he came fully back to himself and to the world, and to the sinking realization of exactly where he stood.

The water closed over him with a great splash and he found himself gasping and struggling for breath.

Spluttering, he thrashed to the surface, only to see Rosslyn standing upon the water as she had all along. She was laughing.

'Very funny,' he said, outraged and soaked and shivering.

But Rosslyn merely laughed on. 'Yer face ...' she managed after a moment. 'Ye should have seen the look on yer face when ye recognized the water under ye.'

Guthrie frowned, outraged. But then, despite himself, he felt the laughter bubble up through him. Rosslyn's mirth was infectious. 'I ...' he stammered, 'I ... walked on ... water!'

'That ye did,' Rosslyn agreed. 'For a moment.'

Guthrie splashed across to the shore and dragged himself out. He stood on the bank and shook himself like a hound. He could hardly believe.

Hesitantly, he poked a hand at the water. But it was just water now, wet and liquid and cold. He looked up at Rosslyn. 'How did you ...'

But Rosslyn merely smiled and shook her head.

Guthrie blinked, rubbed his eyes, patted the liquid wet surface of the water with the palm of one hand. 'I walked on it,' he murmured, shaken. The world seemed to reel about him drunkenly. He felt an uneasy thrill of exaltation go through him. '*I walked on the water ...*'

X

Guthrie sat alone, back pressed against a pine bole for support. He shook his head, as a man might coming out of a dizzy spell. He felt as if his poor brain were about to fold entire, collapsing in upon itself like a shattered cabin tumbling down.

Too much. Too much ...

The exaltation that had thrilled him as he stood gazing amazedly at the water he had walked upon ... was gone. Every certainty he had once held for true was gone. The world was not as he had thought it to be. He was not as he had thought himself to be.

His past life seemed like a long dream from which he had now awoken.

He looked about at the familiar patterns of earth and rock, at the green-black webbery of the pines, the great, cloud-threaded, blue dome of the sky. He looked at his hand, saw the small veins pulsing with life. He scrunched his eyes shut, opened them again. The world seemed to throb with his own heartbeat. He saw trees, and something other than trees, half glimpsed, a great tracery of hidden ... something.

Tree and rock, blue-veined hand, cloud and sky – all were ... *masks.* And beneath or beyond or under the focus of his ordinary vision, lay some great, mysterious *other*.

Rosslyn had brought him somehow out of the world, or through it, to show him that *other*. And now, he could not forget.

Guthrie blinked, rubbed at his eyes with the heels of his hands. He could feel his pulse hammering through his limbs. He let his head fall back against the rough bole of the pine against which he sat, and looked up at the green-prickled thumb of one of its boughs. He felt himself slipping, no longer able to focus simply on needle-leaf and limb and root, not seeing simply sky and cloud, nor hand nor foot, not perceiving any of the familiar, solid, complete things as he had once supposed them to be. Instead, he *sensed* the swoop and surge of that great, complex *other* that underlay everything. His

155

belly shimmied up into his throat, as if he had just been plummeted off a great height.

Half-glimpsed, seething movement, like dark currents in the dangerous depths of a pool, hidden by the bright sundance of light on the water's surface ...

Guthrie fell out of the ordinary world and all the old, familiar, solid shapes were entirely collapsed, or erased, or simply forgotten. And in their stead, all about him, the *other* surged, shapeless, yet patterned somehow with great, heaving complexities. He felt himself tumbled helplessly like a leaf in a gale, torn from anything familiar, plunged into a depthless, chaotic maelstrom.

Terror gripped him. The trees! The sky! How was he to get back? All he had ever known was gone, whirled away like a cry on the wind.

He felt his heart tremor.

His heart.

His body.

He blinked, gasping air suddenly as if he had come up from a deep dive. Sunlight poured over him like bright water. He felt the brilliance of it through his fingers, heard the heat of it. Against his back, he felt the solid, rough support of the pine. His heart hammered, and his arms and legs shook as if he had taken a deathly chill.

The Pathless Way. He thought he understood now. There were no paths in that *other*. It was a place where all forms dissolved. And the way there was pathless indeed.

He twisted round, pushed his palm gently up against the pine bole, cherishing the simple, reassuring solidity of it. He could feel the rough, tiny valleys of the bark beneath his fingers, could see the paleness of his flesh against the dark bark.

But he could also *sense* something other. His hand seemed an illusionary shape, the rising tree bole no more than a pulsing, translucent column. The double vision made him giddy.

Slowly, he pushed his hand into the tree.

With his ordinary vision he watched his fingers sink into the pine trunk as if they were sliding through nothing more solid than molasses. He wiggled his fingers, feeling the substance of the tree move like warm jelly under his touch.

He pulled his hand out, flexed the fingers, stared at them.

He felt dizzy and slightly sick.

The tree seemed to shimmy, fading in and out of his ordinary vision. He could sense clearly the *otherness* of it that lay beneath the familiar tree-image. He pushed his hand back in, feeling again the warm-jelly texture of the living wood, until his arm was sunk into the wood up to his elbow. He sensed the slow-leaping spirit of the tree, a tide of warmth striving upwards. His own spirit was drawn with it, up and up into white light and dancing greenness.

It felt most strange.

And then, suddenly, Guthrie grew deathly afraid.

What was he *doing*?

He yanked his arm out and sat shaking, terrified, trying to stifle his awareness of the *other*. He did not like this. It was too *strange*. He wanted only the familiar world about him again. Tree and rock and solid, solid earth.

Guthrie shuddered and hung on to himself. He could feel the insistent presence of the *other* like a strong current tugging at him. He felt that if he were to let go and give in to that current, he would be siphoned off, dissolved like a clot of earth in a swift flowing stream, his very self coming apart in a swirling cloud as the form of the ordinary world came apart about him.

Suddenly, it was all he could do just to breathe to be.

Guthrie shivered. He was changed for ever.

For ever.

The utter, unnerving *strangeness* of what the world was become, of what he was become, overwhelmed him. His old self reared itself in instinctual terror. He was Reeve Guthrie Garthson, the Reeve of Reeve Vale. A tree was a tree, a rock a rock. He could reach out with his hand and touch the rough-barked bole of the pine behind him. He could breathe and feel the pine-scented air in his nostrils.

Old Rosslyn must have tricked him somehow, or he had been the victim of some drug-induced vision, or had dreamed the whole thing. The world was what it had always been. He was who he had always been. It was and he was!

But beyond the simple solidity of the pine bole, he *sensed* still the great, moving shadow of that *other*. And beyond his old self, he sensed the shadow of the new being he had become, was becoming.

Guthrie shivered, feeling sick with the very immensity of the change, and tried to draw away from it inside his old self, like a snail slipping back into the safety of its shell. *I am Reeve Guthrie Garthson*, he said to himself. *Reeve Guthrie Garthson* ... over and over like an incantation, asserting his old, simple self, insisting on it.

It helped.

He managed a kind of precarious balance.

But he still felt a threatening shiver at the heart of his very being. And he failed to banish the *other*.

So he hovered between, precariously balanced.

And as he held himself thus, a shuddering thrill began to build in him. He felt like some manner of flying creature, hovering as he had seen gulls do sometimes, unmoving, buoyed up by the wind's hidden hand. He could *sense* the depthless, dark currents of the *other*, but he somehow managed to keep his equilibrium and stay ... above them – though, in fact, there was no clear and simple 'above' or 'below' where that *other* was concerned. Gradually, as he hovered there between, Guthrie was able to re-focus his ordinary vision, seeing the familiar green shapes of tree limbs clearly once again.

And nearly tumbled back into chaos.

He was hovering in the pine-scented air, high enough so that a tall man might just be able to reach up and touch him with an outstretched hand.

At the instant of realization, he felt himself slip. For a terrible few moments he seemed pulled in opposite directions at once, towards the *other*, down towards familiar, solid earth, towards the bird-like sense of hovering between.

It was the *betweenness* that won out, and Guthrie held betwixt the familiar and the *other*, sky and earth, form and chaos.

A breath of air blew him sideways, tumbling him like slow thistledown. He managed to hold himself aloft, balancing on the breeze, balancing between the worlds, learning how as he went, falling and rising jerkily, making clumsy little shifts and starts of correction and overcorrection every other moment, an effort constant as breathing. Below him, the hard ground waited; and beneath (or behind, or beyond) that, the *other*.

It was a purest thrill – a mix of fright and exhilaration in equal parts.

Guthrie did not truly understand what it was he did to keep himself thus impossibly afloat. But in some dim yet absolute way he grasped so much: all his life he had ... *agreed* at the level of will and blood and bone to abide by a man's accepted place in the scheme of the world.

Such *agreements*, however, no longer meant anything to him.

Hovering thus impossibly in the air was enough to give a man ideas about what else he might be capable of.

He had been unable to avert disaster at the Closter, unable to combat the Sea Wolves. He remembered their mocking laughter, and the terrible, nagging sense of his own complete helplessness. But he was helpless no longer. And as long as he could keep himself from being overwhelmed entirely by this strange *other* – surely the strength of its pull upon him would lessen as he grew accustomed to it – and had Rosslyn to teach him eventual mastery of it, there would come a time when he would make the cursed Sea Wolves rue the day they ever heard of Reeve Vale. A revenge far beyond anything he had previously imagined. The very thought of it made him pleasantly dizzy.

The breeze had blown Guthrie almost into one of the pines that rimmed the little clearing where he had been sitting. He righted himself with awkward effort and reached a hand to ward away the prickly green-dark needles of a limb. A sudden chunnering made him start. Above, small hands clasping the end of a branch, a tuft-eared red squirrel hung and scolded him. The bright black eyes were wide with outrage.

Guthrie grinned. Impulsively, he *reached* for the little animal – an instinctive stretching of will rather than body – and eased it out of the tree to hover in the empty air with him.

The squirrel shrieked in terror, spittle flying from its mouth, and flailed madly to regain the safety of the tree.

'Guthrie!' a voice cried.

Guthrie turned in the air and saw Rosslyn come walking into the clearing. 'Look!' he called to her excitedly, gesturing to the struggling squirrel, to himself, to the height at which he hung aloft.

Rosslyn made no move, no sweep of hand or arm, and she spoke not a word, but Guthrie felt a sudden thrust, as if a massive, invisible hand had swatted him, and all his balance disappeared in an instant.

He plummeted abruptly out of the world, smacking into the jarring chaos of the *other*. It was like being suddenly plunged into dark and dangerously surging water, and, like any diver, he fought desperately to struggle free before the maelstrom of it swallowed him entirely.

He came out of it winded and gasping and utterly shaken, lying on his back on the hard ground, with Rosslyn standing near him. A lance of quick pain shot through his shoulder as he pushed himself up, and he winced. Struggling to his knees, he turned on Rosslyn. 'Why did you ...'

Overhead, the squirrel still shrieked. Guthrie craned his neck and saw it guided through the air – none of his doing – and back safely into the tree where it clung, its little russet breast heaving.

Rosslyn glared at him, hands on hips. 'What did ye hope to prove with such ridiculous, childish antics?'

Guthrie shrugged self-consciously. 'I was only ...' He felt suddenly like a small, foolish boy showing off for his mother, only to find her brutally scornful of his best efforts. He felt himself flush with anger.

The old Closterer's expression softened. 'Ah, lad,' she said, shaking her head. She held a hand out to him.

He struggled to his feet on his own, ignoring her proffered help, and stalked off to the edge of the little clearing. The dead Abbod's skull rested on a mossy boulder there. He reached it up impulsively. It had still uttered no word to him, shown him no guidance, but he felt better, somehow – ridiculous or not – with it now in his hands.

Rosslyn looked at him and sighed. She lifted off the ground – rising in one smooth, impossible movement – and coasted over to him, coming to rest cross-legged in mid air, her eyes on a level with his. She smiled her crooked-toothed smile. 'Yer face is like a stormy sky, full of dark clouds and rain squalls.'

Guthrie shrugged.

'Listen to me, lad,' Rosslyn began, and the smile was gone now. 'Ordinary folk see only their own little image of the world, and their world is bounded, full of limits, known, knowable, stable, exact. But a Seer – one who sees what others are blind to – has experienced too much to know such limits. As ye well knows by now. A Seer is no longer ... ordinary.'

Guthrie nodded, his anger washing away. He felt a long shudder go through him.

Rosslyn looked at him pointedly. 'It becomes ye not at all to misuse the little folk.'

'I meant no harm by it!' Guthrie snapped, stung.

Rosslyn nodded back to the pine limb where the stricken squirrel still hung, gasping. 'Tell that to our small friend.'

Guthrie shifted uncomfortably, looked away from her down at the skull in his hands.

'A Seer can accomplish such things as would make ordinary folk cower.' Rosslyn frowned. 'And there are some who *like* the feeling of power over other folk.'

Guthrie glanced quickly up. Rosslyn's gaze was coldly steady, a grim, assessing look. 'I am not ...' he started, but the very grimness of her look silenced him. He had known such power-liking men. His father was one. Even as second son, he had felt the seductive touch of power himself on occasion. But he was not one of those for whom power over others was as meat and drink. Was *not*!

'It has never drawn me,' he insisted in the face of Rosslyn's silence. The steady, weighing look of her unnerved him. 'Never!'

'Perhaps,' Rosslyn replied. 'But can ye tell me that ye has not harboured ... ideas? Ye whose home has been destroyed by outland raiders?'

Guthrie swallowed. 'It would be *justice* to visit retribution upon them!'

'And ye knows what justice is, then?'

Guthrie shrugged sullenly. 'What do you wish me to say?'

'Power,' Rosslyn responded, 'is *dangerous*. It is like a too-bright light, blinding those who wield it. Those who hunger for it are dangerously blind to the secret heart of the *other* and all it means.'

'And that ... is?' Guthrie urged.

Rosslyn floated slowly back down to the ground. 'What has changed for ye, lad, since ye passed the nameless gate?'

Guthrie blinked at the sudden change of topic. He sat with her, placing the skull on the ground by his thigh. 'Why everything! Nothing in the world is left to me as it once was. All ... *all* is changed.'

'The world is different, then?'

Guthrie laughed. 'Different? Aye. Everything I thought I knew about the world has turned out to be wrong. The world is not what I thought it to be.'

'Blind boy.'

Guthrie stared at her.

'The world has not changed.'

Again, Guthrie laughed. But it was a tight, unfunny laughter. 'What, then, has happened to it?'

'Blind boy,' Rosslyn repeated. Before he could remonstrate, she reached into her satchel and brought forth *The Book*. 'Here,' she said. 'Read.'

Guthrie looked to the page at which the book was opened:

> *For passage through the Nameless Gate,*
> *For knowing what it is and not,*
> *Simple words for which we wait:*
> *Change the potter, change the pot.*

Guthrie looked up, puzzled.

'We are all potters, lad, and the world a great pot.'

Guthrie shook his head. 'I don't ...'

'The world has gone different about ye,' Rosslyn said. 'Ye sees that clear. But it is not the world that has changed. It is *ye*. Change the potter, and ye changes the pot.'

'But ...' Guthrie sputtered. 'But ... Do you mean that nothing is real? Is it all just sham and illusion, then?'

Rosslyn shrugged. 'What is *real?*'

Guthrie ran a hand over his eyes. He shivered, glancing at the familiar, solid-seeming things about him that were only masks across the *other*. 'Rosslyn, I don't understand. Is the world all chaos underneath? Tell me the truth about the world.'

Rosslyn shook her head. 'There is no *truth* about the world.'

Guthrie bit his lip. 'You know,' he said accusingly. 'You *must* know. Why do you keep it from me? Am I too stupid to be trusted with the secret?'

Rosslyn laughed. 'Secret?'

'Aye!' Guthrie said, but uneasily. 'Secret knowledge.'

Rosslyn stopped laughing. 'There is no secret knowledge. There is no truth.'

'But you see into the world, *through* the world. You must understand more than ordinary folk. Tell me!'

'It cannot be understood,' Rosslyn said. 'But it can be lived. *Must* be lived.'

Guthrie sighed. 'I understand nothing of this.'

'Good,' Rosslyn responded. 'That is a good beginning.'

Guthrie sighed again.

'Ye is no longer an ordinary man. Ye can no longer act like ordinary men.'

Guthrie looked at her uneasily. 'Meaning?'

'The Seer sees, but does not seize.' Rosslyn reached a hand to him. 'Does ye not sense it in yerself, the *change?* Ye must adapt to it, lad, or perish in the end.'

Guthrie swallowed. 'Perish?'

'Aye. In one way or another. Utterly.'

Before Guthrie could respond to this, Rosslyn reached to him, placing the fingertips of one hand over Guthrie's eyes, closing the lids. 'Be still,' she commanded him when he would have flinched away. Her other hand bracketed his forehead, her fingers cool and dry, and uncannily strong. He felt a tingle seep along his skull.

With a gasp of dizzying amazement, Guthrie felt a sort of knot

162

begin to unwind him, like a tight-tangled spool of yarn letting go, and things became ... *clear*.

Just as the world was not the simple, stable, solid place he had always thought it to be, so no more was he the self he had always thought to be – he was not simply Guthrie Garthson, any more than a tree was simply a tree.

He was not simply a man, either, for that too was a kind of mask.

He was not simply even a human being.

Masks, masks over masks.

He was a ... *being*, a feeling, wondering, alive being, as mysterious and incomprehensible, finally, as the very living world itself. All else was only masking. He was a part of the world's mystery the way an autumn leaf is part of the wind, or the river part of the fish ...

Rosslyn's fingers lifted from his forehead and Guthrie opened his eyes, blinking in the light, stunned.

The old Closterer regarded him with her steady green eyes.

Guthrie felt stricken and dizzy. The vision – if that was the word for it – she had granted him had shaken him to his very core.

'It is all potters' work,' Rosslyn said. 'Our precious selves and all. Only potters' work.'

Guthrie turned away. He did not wish to look at what Rosslyn was trying to show him. It made him sick in his belly to think on it.

But he saw it all too clearly.

All his life had been a response to one ruling passion – to be the Reeve of Reeve Vale. Everything he had done or not done had been in response to that one overweening desire. The disappointment and frustrations of his second-son status had shaped his days.

And then, unlooked for, to be granted his desire: bitter indeed to be Reeve in such a way and at such a cost; but bitter or not, he had felt himself, however briefly, to *be* the Reeve, and to have the right to exact vengeance for what had been done to him and his.

But now, to his dismay, he could not help but see how his self – Guthrie, frustrated second son of Reeve Garth – was indeed a mask as surely as everything else.

He had put together and put on this mask of his self over the years, all unknowing. But now that he had passed the nameless gate and passed beyond the old, familiar world, he had also passed beyond his old, familiar self. Too much had happened to him that was too strange. He had far-travelled beyond the borders of his previous life. And as he continued to far-travel, that old self would become more and more ... irrelevant.

163

It felt to Guthrie as if a great pit had opened before him where he thought to find only solid ground.

All he had ever been, that previous self. What could there be left of him without it? It was a kind of death he looked at, a destruction of all he was, and had been, and thought to be.

He ached to have his old life back, to be that simple self once again.

Too late.

Guthrie shuddered, wrapping his arms about himself.

'Ye is no longer an ordinary man,' Rosslyn said gently, 'and no longer has ordinary choices.'

Guthrie shuddered. 'What if I no longer want this? What if I don't *like* this?'

Rosslyn shrugged. There was the hint of a smile in her eyes, but her words were flat and uncompromising. 'Then ye should have thought more carefully before ye demanded it of me.'

Guthrie bowed his head.

'It is a great gift and a great burden ye has taken upon yerself.'

'Aye,' Guthrie agreed. 'This is not the learning I looked to receive from you.' He laughed hollowly. 'Burden indeed, to be torn from out of the world like a bird from its nest.'

'Perhaps,' Rosslyn said. 'But gift as well.'

Guthrie found nothing to say.

Rosslyn leaned closer. 'I have said there is danger in wielding power over others. But the real danger is not in the wielding of that power in itself. The real danger is in the clinging to one's old self, in the denial of the change the *other* brings about in all of us.'

She reached out to Guthrie, placing her hands on his where he still held *The Book*, for he had not put it down since she had handed it to him. 'Ye must let yer old self drop aside, like a discarded skin.'

Guthrie shuddered. 'How can I? It would be the death of me, Rosslyn.'

'Nay, lad. It would be the life of ye.'

He only looked at her.

'Ye must cease to be an ordinary man.'

Guthrie shuddered. '*How?*'

'Be as a river or a bird.'

He stared at her in dismay. 'I don't understand.'

In Guthrie's hands, *The Book* fluttered and opened to a new page. He looked down and read:

The rivers sing their flowing song,
Towards the sea, where they belong.

There's not a river flowing free
But cries its yearning for the sea.

Guthrie blinked, shook his muddled head.

Rosslyn took *The Book* from him and closed it. 'Ordinary folk are full of beliefs about the world, for they see nothing of what underlies the simple surface of their beliefs. They would scoff at ye if ye told them their solid, stable world was no more than a great pot they turn on their own wheels. But a Seer knows the world is too huge and too strange. He cannot make decisions about the world as ordinary folk do.'

'But how then does he ...'

'A Seer *becomes* the world. As a river becomes the sea.'

Guthrie shook his head. 'I still don't ...'

'Ye must let go and live this new life that has come upon ye, letting the world live through ye.'

'What if I cannot, Rosslyn? It is a sort of death you ask of me. What if I *cannot?*'

'Look at me,' she said then. 'Tell me what ye sees.'

Guthrie hesitated, then said, 'I see a woman, not ... young, grey haired, green eyed, thin, dressed in a Closterer's grey robe.'

Rosslyn nodded. 'Fair enough. Now turn your other-sense upon me.'

'My *other-sense?*'

'Aye. Slide out of the ordinary world and into the *other*, and *sense* me.'

Guthrie swallowed.

'Enter the *other*,' Rosslyn commanded. 'Ye knows how.'

Guthrie hesitated, feeling his heart start to speed nervously. But the look in Rosslyn's eyes gave him no choice.

Though he had gained some experience by now of entering that *other* wilfully, he was still desperately uncertain. And Rosslyn's scrutiny made him self-conscious and clumsy. He began to let himself slip from the world with painful care, like a man lowering himself into deep, dangerous water, ready to leap back at the first sign of disaster. He felt the seethe of it come over him like a great wave, over and under and through him. The swoop and lift and surge of it overwhelmed him, like too-strong currents, and he had to struggle to gather himself.

165

'Grade up,' he heard Rosslyn say. 'But do not draw yerself altogether back into the world. Breathe deep. Breathe slow. Aye ... that's the way.'

In a manner he could not quite grasp, he felt her guiding him until, gradually, he found an equilibrium.

He became aware of Rosslyn near him. But it was not his ordinary bodily senses he used here, and the familiar human shape of her was utterly changed. It was as though she were a complex glowing funnel. He could *sense* the world move through her the way water might flow through an intricate chute, and it was hard to distinguish what was her self and what the flowing movement of the world through her.

Guthrie felt Rosslyn's presence withdraw from him. His balance went, and the seethe of the *other* almost swallowed him. He thrust himself out of it desperately, coming back with a painful snap into the ordinary world, gasping and blinking in the sunlight. His heart thumped painfully, and his belly was cramped with residual fright. For the moment, all his concentration was locked on holding himself in the ordinary.

Rosslyn seemed as calm as ever, yet she too had been there with him in the *other*; he had *sensed* that clear enough. He looked at her enviously. She had a mastery over the chaos of the *other* that he desperately wished for. 'How do you control it?' he demanded of her once he had breath enough. 'Teach me how to master it like you do.'

'Blind boy,' was all the answer she gave him.

He stared at her, utterly confounded.

'What did ye *sense* of me?'

Guthrie hesitated, confused. Rosslyn's insistent gaze, however, left him no option. 'I *sensed* the world ... moving through you.'

Rosslyn nodded. 'Aye. As it must be. The world moves through all of us.'

'The Powers,' Guthrie said.

'Aye. Whatever *they* might be.'

'But the Powers exist. Are real!' By at least so much, Guthrie hoped to salvage some of the stable world he had always known.

Rosslyn shrugged. 'What is *real?*'

To that, Guthrie no longer had any easy answer.

'You were like a – a funnel,' he said after a pause.

Rosslyn smiled. 'I have never heard it put thus, but ... aye, that is not so bad an image for it.'

166

'Are all folk like that, then?'

'No. We are all funnels, as ye puts it. But most have blocked themselves off, sealing themselves with the glue of their own desires and beliefs, their wishing-dreams and fears. With their potter's work.'

'What ...' Guthrie swallowed. 'What do I look like?'

The old Closterer regarded him soberly. 'Ye is sealed, still.'

'How, then, does one *unseal* oneself?'

'There is, finally, only one way,' Rosslyn said. She rose to her feet, a remarkably graceful movement for one of her age, and beckoned to him. 'Come, follow me.'

'Where?'

'Ye will see.' She started off away through the clearing. 'Come.'

Guthrie started to follow after, but at the clearing's verge he skidded to an abrupt halt. Turning, he went back for the skull, then hurried along in Rosslyn's wake. He felt his heart thump with unease, remembering the last time the old Closterer had led him off like this.

Through the pines she took him, along the shore of Mirrormere, and thence onwards still, climbing the slopes of the hills that bordered the little lake's northern shore, up and up, until they were come eventually to grassy meadows above the trees. Through it all, Rosslyn kept her silence, and kept up a brisk pace, too, so that Guthrie had neither time nor breath for questions.

When, finally, she brought them to a halt high on the side of a stony hill, Guthrie was gasping and dizzy-headed. He leaned against a grey-green boulder, head hanging, trying to catch his breath.

Rosslyn grinned at him. For all their exertion, she seemed none the worse for wear. She did a little jig step.

'Very funny,' he wheezed.

She laughed, softly, but the instant after turned sober. 'Come,' she said. 'Follow me.'

She took him to the far brow of the hill, to a stony precipice. 'Go and look,' she said.

Guthrie hesitated for a moment, puzzled, then did as she bade. He edged close to the drop and looked down. It fell away sheer, a dizzying wall of grey rock. At the bottom were dark pines and shadows. He felt his guts lurch, standing there staring down into the nothingness of that drop, and the ordinary world began to slip from him. The seethe of the *other* swept over him and, for an instant, there was no difference between the fall of rock beneath his feet and the fall of chaos that was the *other*. The two merged into one great, terrifying plunge into nothingness that would mean utter destruction for him if he were not able to pull himself back.

He struggled away, gasping, stumbling back from the edge.

Rosslyn looked at him. 'We all must do it.'

'Do what?' he asked, but in his heart he had a stricken certainty as to what her answer would be.

'We all must give ourselves to it, make the plunge.'

Guthrie turned and looked back at the precipice, shuddering. 'Into *that?*'

Rosslyn nodded. 'A leap from all that is familiar into all that is not. No going back. No half measures.'

He stared at her.

'I have done it,' she said soberly.' She nodded at the skull Guthrie still clutched against him. 'He did it, when he was a living man. We all must. Nothing less will suffice,'

Guthrie stared at her.

'And ye must do it alone. Without aid.' Again, she nodded at the skull.

'But ...'

Rosslyn's face was implacable. 'Put him down.'

Her manner left him no choice. Guthrie placed the skull on the ground.

'Go,' Rosslyn said, 'to the edge.'

Guthrie shuffled close to the brink of the precipice once more. 'Just leap out into ... nothing?'

Rosslyn made no reply.

He pointed to the rocks at the bottom, the sharp points of the pines, like so many blue-green lances. 'But it is certain death!'

'Not for a Seer such as ye.'

'You have too much faith in me.'

'Ye has too little.'

Guthrie looked down, imagining himself taking that plunge, the leap into empty air, into seething chaos, the terrible, helpless plunge of it, the shattering impact when he hit the stones, blood and bone and wet-splattered rock. And a no lesser shattering when his self came apart in the *other*, for he had done nothing but dip shallowly into it as of yet, he realized, scrambling quickly back to the familiarity of his ordinary world and self.

He shuddered, backed away. 'I *cannot* ...'

Rosslyn looked at him, stern faced. 'The great world is a mystery far beyond our understanding. Ordinary folk shroud the mystery. It is too terrible for them. But a Seer does not, *must not*. A Seer must face it fully.' She pointed to the brink upon which he had stood. 'One day ye must make the jump. Here, or some place such as this. Ye may turn yer back to it now, but it will always remain. Always. One day ye *must* make that leap.'

Guthrie shuddered, remembering the black drop, the quiver of the two worlds intertwined. 'Not this day.'

Rosslyn regarded him unblinkingly for long moments, then nodded. 'But one day.'

Not knowing how to respond, Guthrie shrugged uneasily. He felt overwhelmed. He felt he would never be ready to take that awful leap.

Rosslyn gestured him away from the brink. He came, bending to retrieve the skull, and followed her. Round the crest of the hill she took him, to a sheltered spot between two upthrust trunks of moss-furred stone. A little breeze riffled gently over them as they sat, silent. The day was beginning to wane. From the height here they could see far across the tree-shrouded slopes of the hills. The sky was laced with slow clouds.

Rosslyn crossed her legs under her where she sat by Guthrie's side, tucking them up with a suppleness Guthrie could not help but envy a little. 'None of this is what ye expected, lad, is it?'

'No,' Guthrie agreed. 'I thought – secret skills, tricks, hidden knowledge. But not the *dying* of everything I was and am.'

'Ye has come far in a very short time, too short a time, perhaps. It is not a light journey, the Pathless Way.'

Guthrie sighed. 'Pathless indeed.'

'There is no turning back, once one has passed the nameless gate. Does ye not feel the pull of the *other* upon ye?'

Guthrie nodded. He had never been entirely free of that nagging pull since Rosslyn had plunged him into the *other* on Mirrormere.

'It will never leave ye.'

'Never?' Guthrie felt sick. 'I had thought it would fade once I grew accustomed to it, that you would teach me how to ...'

'It will never fade,' Rosslyn said with utter certainty. 'Does ye think ye has the strength to resist, to fight it all yer days?' She turned to him, dead serious. 'Ye has a simple choice for how ye will spend the rest of yer life, yer *life*, lad. Ye can attempt to fight the *other*, resist, struggle to keep yer old self intact. Or ye can let go.'

'But –' Guthrie started.

169

'Ye knows the story of Tancred Black Robe, the dark sorcerer behind the Demon War of long ago.'

Guthrie blinked, nodded. 'What does *he* have to do with any of this?'

'Tancred was a Seer. Nothing more. Nothing less. As ye is.'

Suddenly, Guthrie found it hard to get a clear breath. One of the bogies of his childhood. He and Black Tancred? The same? 'But –' he started again.

Rosslyn cut him off. 'Tancred and those like him become bent men. They cling, and their entire lives become a struggle of will to keep the *other* from overwhelming them. They fight to control everything, the world, the folk about them, the *other* itself. An endless struggle ... And that struggle warps them, twists them into bent men, feeding on power and control and fear, and they are unable any more simply to live.'

Rosslyn looked at him, her green eyes implacable as stone. 'Is that how ye wishes to be?'

'No,' Guthrie replied quickly. 'Of course not.'

'Then ye must make the jump. Ye must let go and give yerself entirely to the world. No holding back. No pretending. Ye must jump for the rocks and mean it.'

Guthrie could feel himself going pale. 'But it is death.'

'Nay, lad. It is the *only* way to life. A man who passes the nameless gate and denies the *other*, who clings to his old self, is lost. He fears, and lets that fear rule him, and thus has to rule all about him lest the fear destroy him utterly. Like a fish that dams and drowns the river because it fears the current.'

Guthrie looked at her uncertainly.

'Ye must not let the fear rule ye, lad.'

He thought of the precipice they had left behind, and the terror of it was like an icy blade still in his guts. He felt sick and cold even thinking about taking that leap into destruction.

Silence settled between him and Rosslyn. The bellies of the clouds began to turn slow crimson as the sun set. A distant crow slow-winged its way across their sight, *caw cawing* softly.

'If ye were part of a Closter it would be easier for ye,' Rosslyn said after a while. 'They are peaceful, quiet places. The one in yer wild northern Vale especially so – or it was. In a Closter ye would have companions who follow the same path along with ye, preparing as ye is. What ye needs more than anything now is peace, and the passage of quiet time.' Rosslyn leaned back on the mossy stone outcropping against which they sat. 'The eyes must be closed for the sight to clear.'

Guthrie looked up. 'Something more from *The Book?*'

Rosslyn shook her head. 'Nay. A simple truth. A fasting. The belly must be empty for the body to be clear. The senses must be empty for the heart to clear. Ye needs a fasting of the heart.'

'And that is?'

'The spirit is not limited to any one sense. It must have the emptiness of all the senses, all the faculties before it becomes clear. Think of a window in a house. Nothing but a hole in the wall, perhaps, yet because of it the whole room is filled with light. So when yer senses are empty, yer spirit will be as filled with light. And only then can yer heart be clear.'

Rosslyn gestured to the green expanse of the wild hills before them. 'Ye needs to walk away, lad, to find a place of green silence. Ye needs to sit and do nothing. Ye needs to let yer senses still, let yer mind still. Ye is as a bucket filled with water, shaken until the water sloshes about inside it. Ye needs to let the bucket rest, let the water settle until it is calm enough to reflect the world around it. Ye needs to be long alone in the world.'

Guthrie looked at her, looked to the hills.

'Go,' she said softly.

'What, now? Just like that?'

'Aye.' She nodded towards the wild green. 'Take nothing. Walk. Find a place to sit. Fast. Do nothing. Exist in the world. Farmers let each of their fields lie fallow for a time, do they not? Well, ye too must lie fallow. It is what ye needs more than anything now.'

'Just walk off by myself into the wild and find some place where I can ... sit?'

'Exactly so. A fasting of the body and of the heart.'

'But I don't know enough, Rosslyn! The *other* ... It is all too new. I have no mastery. There is too much more I need to learn from you. What if ... if I make some stupid mistake and end up killing myself through very ignorance? You agreed to teach me. How can you just *abandon* me like this?'

'I have shown ye all ye needs, all I can. What remains, I cannot teach ye. Ye must learn it of yerself.'

'But what if I get lost and cannot find my way back to you?'

'I do not think ye will be returning to me.'

Guthrie only stared.

'Does ye not *feel* this?'

171

'I feel only confused, Rosslyn!'

The old Closterer put one hand lightly on Guthrie's arm. 'I do not feel ye to be drawn back to me. Ye has other paths to walk, where I cannot follow.'

'But there's still so much for me to know! How can you –'

'One does more and more each day in the pursuit of knowing,' Rosslyn said. 'But follow the Pathless Way, the goingless going, and each day one does less, until one reaches fundamentalness.'

'*The Book*,' Guthrie said. 'You quoted that at me the first time we met.'

Rosslyn nodded. 'A clear heart is what ye needs now, not mastery, not knowledge. Go. Allow the world to flow through you. 'Tis the only way.'

'But –'

'Go,' Rosslyn merely repeated. She let go Guthrie's arm and stretched her hand briefly out to the skull which he had kept on his lap throughout their talk. 'Ye is not entirely alone.'

Rising easily to her feet, Rosslyn turned and reached the skull gently from Guthrie's hold, cradling it in her palms so that it faced towards her. To Guthrie's sight, the pale bone seemed to glow, as if the skull were a bowl of bone filled with soft, dancing radiance.

The old Closterer was silent for long moments, gazing down at the dead face. 'Rianna, old friend,' she said softly. She tipped her hands, and the skull slid out of them, hanging in mid-air.

Guthrie stared up at the floating skull from where he sat. The glow about it was fading. He was no longer sure it had not simply been a trick of the light, or his own imagination.

Looking at Guthrie, Rosslyn said, 'Ye has a guide. I had none such when I was yer age.'

'He's done precious little guiding so far,' Guthrie could not refrain from saying. 'And in life, he was a *fool*, Rosslyn. He made a promise to me, and he broke it.' The very remembrance of it made Guthrie shiver with old anger. 'He brought about the death of everybody within the Closter. Innocent folk all. He opened the gates and let the Sea Wolf pack in ... A fool's act if I ever saw one, that!'

'Do you then understand all there is to understand about the world?' Rosslyn asked him.

Guthrie shook his head. 'No. Of course not. But any fool can see –'

'Any fool can see what he wishes to see. Ye must look with better eyes than that. The world is no simple place.'

The skull slid gently through the air, swivelling about until the face turned towards Guthrie. With a start, he realized he could see the glow of eyes now in the empty sockets, dimly radiant, as if they had no physical substance at all but were composed entirely of soft light. They gazed at him unblinkingly, clear as clear.

The anger in him slid away into nothingness. He reached the skull out of the air. The bone felt warm as living flesh in his hands. The eyes gazed at him with the dead Abbod's familiar calm.

In the wonder tales of Guthrie's childhood, there had been no lack of magical talismans and companions – swords, hammers, rings, wise talking salmon, clever crows, the ancient North Wind itself – but all such had conferred understanding, or power, or some wondrous skill upon the tale's hero. Thus far, the dead Abbod's skull had conferred nothing of the sort upon him.

But now, for the first time, Guthrie began – with the little hairs prickling along the nape of his neck – to feel that the shade of the dead Abbod might indeed be able to bring about something truly wondrous.

Breathlessly, Guthrie waited for it to happen, for the skull to speak to him, something.

But nothing of the sort occurred. The skull remained silent in his hand, the eyes gazing at him unblinkingly.

'Speak to me,' he said to it. 'Say something!'

Silence.

Guthrie looked across at Rosslyn imploringly.

She said nothing.

Guthrie sighed, swallowed his disappointment, tried to accept what was: this was no child's wonder tale he lived.

'And now,' said Rosslyn, 'ye must be going.'

'But, Rosslyn! How can I ...'

Standing, the old Closterer looked upon Guthrie in silence for a long few moments, then bent and placed a hand gently on his forehead in blessing. 'Remember, a fasting of the heart. There is no other way. Fare well, Guthrie, lad.'

Guthrie could find nothing to say. It was too sudden. He looked down at the skull, looked up ... And in that instant, Rosslyn had gone. Simply disappeared.

Guthrie scrambled to his feet, his heart beating wildly. 'Rosslyn!' he cried. '*Rosslyn!*' But there was no response, nothing but the empty echoes of his own voice along the empty hilltop where they had been sitting.

For long he stood there, utterly dismayed, staring at the empty space where she had stood. He thought of running after her, of returning to their camp by Mirrormere. But it would be no use, he knew. He would not find her.

And then, as if his acceptance of the situation had somehow opened his eyes, he saw the little bundle sitting on the grass where she had stood. He reached it up, unwrapped it. It was *The Book* she had left him. He hefted it, opened it to the first page that came to hand:

> *A man of the way will follow the way*
> *Beyond what he can see or hear.*
>
> *A man who still fears will hold and stay,*
> *And all his way will be filled with fear.*
>
> *A fearing-man will be hard and cold,*
> *A fearing-man will fear to be bold,*
> *A fearing-man will be desperate to hold.*

Guthrie sighed. *Desperate to hold.* Remembering how he had felt on the edge of the precipice, he understood that sentiment well enough.

He took a breath, feeling the nice weight of *The Book* in his hands. Slowly, he thumbed through the vellum pages, *snick, snick, snick,* until one seemed to come clear:

> *Water, the fish fears not,*
> *Nor air, the bird.*
>
> *Wings, the Seer has not got,*
> *Nor fins, I have heard.*
>
> *Yet fly he must,*
> *And swim,*
> *Or die he must.*
> *'Tis up to him.*

Guthrie shivered. He closed the book, re-wrapped it carefully. But the words stayed clear in his mind: *Fly he must. Or die he must.*

He thought of the precipice, of the leap Rosslyn said he must make one day, and shuddered. To fly without wings, indeed. He gazed at the world around him – tree and rock and far blue sky and silence. Nothing more than reflections on the surface of a deep, deep, down-swirling pool into which, one day, he must plunge.

But not this day.

The very thought made his guts churn.

Guthrie felt filled with a conglomeration of thoughts, like a school of drunken fish darting this way and that through his mind: the pathless path; goingless going; the great, hungering surge of the *other* (which he still felt pulling insistently at him like a tide); his never returning to Rosslyn; his own path; the unexpected warmth of the skull and the dead Abbod's glowing eyes; his own confused and faltering heart ...

He glanced down at the skull, but the mysterious warmth had gone. It seemed inert as any stone.

No way back, now. Rosslyn was right enough: he needed to find a place of silence. If there were any hope for him at all, he needed peace in which to try to gather himself, to find himself, to find the path that was no path.

With a sigh, Guthrie gathered up the skull and the wrapped book – all he had left in the world – turned, and began to tread a slow way across the grassy slope towards the wild green hills.

XI

Alia moved between the trees, coming out through a scree of white birches on to a stony bluff above a valley. Since leaving the Fey in the early morning, she had travelled all day, moving at a determined dogtrot through the pine-strewn slopes. But though she had covered a lot of ground, and had, she was certain, kept to the right direction, there was still no sign of any of the more familiar landmarks that signified she was drawing close to Hunters Vale.

And precious time was passing.

And now here she was, on this stony, birch-tufted bluff, looking down into a valley she recognized not at all. She was utterly weary, and still in unknown territory, and she tried not to give way to despair. The Fey's little glen up in the wild heights had been *much* farther off from familiar land than she had thought.

Alia felt a long shiver go through her. She shied away from thinking on the Fey.

She needed to take a rest before moving on. This place seemed as good as any. The air was cool on the height here. Birds cried from the trees behind her. A small river wound below through the valley floor, a gleaming serpent half hidden by veils of evening mist. The sun crested low across the valley's far slope, a glowing, red-orange orb in salmon pink, hazy sky.

'Globe of fire, globe of light,' Alia began to murmur. 'Brightest yellow, shining bright. Glowing ...' she lost the words momentarily, then recalled them. 'Glowing red at daylight's ending. Glowing red, my sorrows mending. Fire of evening, fire of morn. Fire in which my hopes are born. Light of morning, dawnfire burning. Gone at dusk, but soon returning.'

An old rhyme from her childhood, that. Having it rise up thus unexpectedly in her brought back what life had been for the girl she once was. Painfully clear remembrances: the rough gang of her brothers running the sheep to pasture with kicks and whoops, her mother's thin voice raised in plaint, her father's hard hand. Alia

176

shivered. How many times at day's end like this had her girl-self sneaked off to sit, watching the sun slowly die in the sky, aching for release from the cage that was her home life?

And how many times had she yearned toward the mysterious beauty of the wild lands all about? She could still feel that yearning now, the world bathed in dying sun-glow, all mist and distance, stony height and deep sky. It called to her, like flowers called to the bee, or night-lights the flapping moth. She fought not to think of the Fey, of what the Fey had offered her. Of what she had refused.

There was an ache in her, like hunger, but having nothing to do with food.

Alia sagged against the trunk of one of the birches that rooted here at the edge of the bluff. Unthinkingly, she put her left hand out for support, felt a stab of pain, drew it back hastily. Against the white bark of the birch a little strawberry of blood showed. Examining her palm, Alia saw fresh wet blood trickling from the marks the demon-creature had carved in her skin. Sucking at her palm, she felt a little twinge of worry. By now the scabs ought to have formed fully.

She stared at the intricate little pattern incised into her skin, but could still make no clear sense of it. An ugly face, perhaps? In her mind's eye, she suddenly saw the demon-creature's great, inhuman yellow eyes, the grotesque, tusked face, the hand out to her, beckoning.

Alia shuddered. She was only glad the uncanny creature was gone. Soon enough, no doubt, this little wound would heal – it was on her palm after all, and the scabs kept getting broken as she flexed and bent her hand, and so it would take time – and soon enough it would all fade from her memory.

She leaned tiredly against one of the birches. The white bark of the tree next to hers hung in dangling peels. She reached out and fingered one idly, twisted it loose in a curling strip. Slowly, she tore the thin, papery stuff into pieces, stepped forwards away from the tree, and tossed the torn bits down over the bluff's sheer edge, one by one. They fluttered like small white birds.

It was a mindless act, her fingers tearing and tossing the bark almost of their own accord, a little test of her left hand, a little, instinctive distraction to keep her from brooding.

But the image of the fluttering white bark-birds sent a jolt of unwanted recollection through her, and superimposed over them

177

she saw, or seemed to see, the ivory fey-bird, gracefully gliding on finger-feather wings.

Looking down from the bluff's steep rocky verge, Alia felt her belly lurch suddenly. Below her was a dizzying fall of grey rock plunging to dark pines and shadows. For one terrible instant, it seemed to her that she was staring down at a great, terrifying plunge into surging nothingness that would mean utter destruction for her. She felt herself falling, tumbling, flailing ...

And came back to herself, panting and shaken, still rooted on the bluff's edge. She took a trembling step back, another.

It was as if she had almost fallen *out* of the world somehow. As if the physical plunge of the rock had somehow precipitated in her another sort of plunge entirely.

She did not understand.

The world about her lay still as still.

She tried to let the solid familiarity of it fill her – the dimming glow of the sun, the winding silver shape of the river below, the curl of mist, the long curve of the valley crest, ragged with pines, the swirling black dots of a gang of distant crows. She could just hear, faintly, their cawing to each other.

Day's end. A little death. There had been too much of endings for her of late. The very world seemed seeped in sadness, suddenly.

Alia gazed at the blue-green shoulders of the mountains, forest cloaked, up to the bare, stony crests of them reaching to the sky. She took a breath, another. A long shiver went through her. She felt a strange flutter of fear and expectancy, as if she were balanced on some great height, about to leap into the unknown.

But there was only the world, silent, fading slowing into the night's dimness.

Alia shuddered. It was all so unnerving. Demon-creatures, seductive Fey, the very world itself gone uncertain. What was happening to her?

There seemed no answer.

She shook herself, trying to put it all from her mind. There was Orrin and poor Patch reliant on her. She had stood here long enough.

Through the dimming twilight she moved, bow in hand, arrow knocked – by long habit more than any pressing necessity. There was the possibility of chance encounters with bandits, but it seemed remote. She was still well out of the territory they frequented.

But she trotted along through the trees softly nonetheless, as a hunter ought, disturbing as little as possible, wary and quiet.

Away from the airy openness of the bluff, the slanting, day's-end sunshine seeped through the lacery of the pines in a dancing, half-light. Out of the corner of her eye, Alia caught sudden sight of movement away to her left and downslope. For one frightened instant, her heart shuddered. Then she recognized the shape ahead of her for what it was – a young roebuck.

The animal came stepping delicately along through the trees towards her. Looking up and seeing her for the first time, he froze, staring at her with liquid dark eyes, one foreleg gracefully poised. The antlers above his forehead were like a pair of elegantly posed, bony hands.

It had been long since Alia had last eaten properly, how long, exactly, she could not recall. Here was meat. Gently, so as not to aggravate her tender left hand, she drew back on the bow, anchored her thumb carefully against her still sore cheek, sighted down the length of the arrow.

The buck took a step towards her, slow as a dream. His liquid eyes gazed at her steadily.

He was hers.

It happened at times, this strange, silent intimacy between hunter and hunted. A bond came into existence between them. There was no fear in the buck's eyes. He would give himself to her, so that his death would give her life.

'Freely given, freely taken,' Alia recited in a half-whisper. 'One to sleep, one to waken. For the giving of your life, I thank you, friend.' She took a breath, held it lightly, sighting over the buck's ribs for the heart shot.

But, in the end, she did not release the arrow.

His liquid dark eyes gazed at her calmly. She had killed more than a few bucks in her time, but this moment, somehow, was different. Along the shaft of the drawn arrow, she watched him.

As he watched her, calmly.

A shiver went through her. There was no human wisdom in those dark animal eyes, yet there was something ...

'Go,' she told him softly. 'Go, little brother. Live your life.'

He looked at her, for all the world as if she had disappointed him. Then, with a soft snort, he pivoted and danced away, showing her the white flash of his tail in farewell.

Slowly, Alia lowered her bow. She was not entirely certain what had prompted her to stay her hand. She felt hunger, indeed. But the thought of fresh meat seemed somehow ... unappealing. And, having killed two men already, she did not feel she would ever be able to meet out death with the assurance she once had. The buck had been so *innocent* in his giving of himself to her.

In the dimming light, Alia smiled softly. 'A long life and full,' she wished the vanished animal. Not to kill was the only gift she had left to give in these bad times, and something in her felt the better for having given it.

It was a bittersweet feeling.

Turning, she continued silently on her way into the darkening forest.

It was not long, however, before Alia realized there was something dreadfully wrong.

She stood, heart thumping anxiously, staring eastwards at the purple-black, early night sky. Where was the moon? Her round silver face ought to be visible by now. Full moon had been only yestereve.

But the woods were dark and cold and there was no sign of the moon.

Alia did not want to think on what it might mean.

There were stories of what happened to those who were seduced away by the Fey. Time ran differently where the Fey dwelt, it was said. Ordinary mortal folk aged differently, or not at all.

Alia shuddered. It had seemed only a single night she had been amongst the Fey, only the one night of the dance, then she had come to herself once again the next morning. She had unquestion-ingly accepted that as fact. It would never have occurred to her to question such a thing. But now ...

How long had she been gone out of the ordinary world?

There was no way of knowing.

Alia felt her belly cramp up with panic. What of Orrin and poor hurt Patch? How long had they been stranded alone in the Heights?

How *long*?

She started running, skittering desperately along through the darkness. What if it had been days and days? Or longer? She felt sick at the very thought.

In the dark, she half tripped, smacking an elbow painfully up against a tree trunk and then going stumblingly down on one knee and tearing her sore left palm on some unseen hard thing. She knelt where she had landed, gasping, sucking at her hurt hand, the blood-pulse pounding in her ears. There was no point dashing about blindly like this in the dark. She had to get hold of herself.

Slowly, Alia stood. She tried to calm her breathing, her heart. The world seemed to pulse about her strangely, and for a long, frightening moment, she experienced a recurrence of what had happened to her earlier: the ordinary world seemed only a sham face, a fanciful design laid over something ... *other*.

Alia took a grip upon herself, upon the world, shaking off the shuddering strangeness of it.

She moved off determinedly, but more slowly now, for deep night had taken the wood; all was shrouded in blackness, the air cold and still. She would walk through the night, she told herself, going without sleep, and keep on all through the next day – and the next, if need be. Surely, *surely* she could not be more than a couple of days' travel from Hunters Vale.

Onwards she went, trying to keep hunter-quiet even in the dark, ignoring the weariness that crept over her, forcing her tired legs to take step after step.

Onwards through the endless, tree-filled dark ...

And then, out of nowhere, she smelled woodsmoke, the scent of it clear as clear on the black night air.

It stopped her dead, like a sudden shout echoing down from the unseen heights about her.

Alia's heart tremored. Who could possibly be out here in the wild lands?

XII

Guthrie sat cross-legged in a little glade, staring into the dancing, bright flames of a fire. Dark night lay all about like a cloak. Far above, the stars shone softly in a moonless sky. The air was chill, with the first taste of the coming winter in it, and he savoured the fire's warmth. It was a quiet place, this, a grassy hollow amongst ancient mountain pines, high up a sloping hillside. A murmuring stream rolled through mossy rocks nearby, the water cold as ice and tasting of stone.

Guthrie did not know how many days or nights he had sat here. No food had he taken since parting with Rosslyn, nothing but the icy mountain water. His body felt light as thistledown. The day-time world about him seemed to glow, and stones and trees and occasional slow-flapping crows seemed not much more than hollow illusion. He remembered walking through a high meadow, like a great green wave frozen in the very act of breaking upon the shore of the forest, remembered the stone shoulders of the peaks in the distance, the enclosing dimness of old pines as he trod a winding way amongst them – and that was all the recollection he had of his journey here.

He remembered staring upwards through the ragged, high-slope pines that sheltered this little glade as the sky swirled and filled itself with purple clouds. Thunder rumbled. Cold rain soaked him. He did not know when that had been. He seemed dry enough now, though he had painful shivering fits still.

Guthrie fed wood onto the fire before him, watching the flames yearning upwards, focusing on the leap and play of them with his ordinary vision. Sometimes, without his apparently having slipped from the ordinary world at all, the very trees about him would transmute into an intricate tapestry woven of line and curve, and it was only with effort that he brought them back into focus as separate and recognizable trees once again. And once, he had thought he heard a tree murmur faint words to him.

The border between the worlds was grown uncertain for him, and Guthrie was all too aware of the *other* underlying everything, like a great, moving shadow. The tug of it continued to work at him, unremitting, without and within him, pulling him under, weakening the bonds that held his self together, straining his hold upon the world to the very breaking point at times. His sleep was uneasy at best, filled with dreams of falling. Once, he had awoken to find himself utterly buried in the chaotic seethe of that *other* and had very nearly drowned there for good and all, able only with the greatest of difficulty to recall who he was or where he might belong. It had been long after that before he had been able to let himself sleep again.

'Ye is as a bucket filled with water,' Rosslyn had told him, 'shaken until the water sloshes about inside it. Ye needs to let the bucket rest, let the water settle until it is calm enough to reflect the world around it. Ye needs to be long alone in the world. Ye must learn to be still.' Alone he had been, and for long, long days. But nothing seemed settled within him; old feelings rushed through him like a torrent of white water pouring through a skein of rocks till he felt exhausted, shaken, drained. There were periods when he found himself dwelling compulsively on the past, raging as the remembered frustrations, the unfulfilled hopes, the injuries he had endured as second son rose up inside him. Other times, he could not shake the terrible remembrance of the death and devastation caused by the Sea Wolves, and he felt the revenge-hunger take him, imagining those same Sea Wolves prostrate before him, helpless against his power.

No. Nothing was settled in him. And yet he was changed, nevertheless. There were moments when he felt removed somehow from the disturbing torrent of his feelings, as if it were somebody else experiencing the anger or fear or frustration, and he merely an observer. And sometimes all the old feelings seemed simply irrelevant: how should he worry about being second son, or about revenge, or being or not being Reeve, with the world gone so strange and the *other* pulling, pulling at him like a dark tide?

A man aboard a boat has ties with others aboard – kith or kin, friend or foe – but let him once be plunged far overboard into a seething sea ...

He was still struggling to understand. There did not seem to be any easily apparent, constant rules by which the change in him worked. And he was not *enough* changed. He felt himself to be neither one thing nor the other.

'The world has not changed,' he remembered Rosslyn telling him. And he remembered the extract from *The Book* she had shown him:

> *For passage through the Nameless Gate,*
> *For knowing what it is and not,*
> *Simple words for which we wait:*
> *Change the potter, change the pot.*

He was still not sure what, exactly, had changed: him, or the world, or both somehow?

Guthrie flipped a little more wood onto the fire, listening to the crackle and hiss as the flames fed, stared at the dancing flames themselves. They had no such problems as he. They were pure, yearning purely for their rightful place above. He did not care what Rosslyn might say on the beliefs about the world he had grow up with; he could *sense* the flames' upwards yearning. The explanation he had grown up with was as good a one as any.

He envied those leaping flames their purity of purpose. No confusion. No doubt. Simply the graceful and perfect dance, the pure upwards leap.

Guthrie blinked, shook himself, feeling his grip upon the ordinary world about him loosening. His eyes could see little in the darkness beyond the fire. He gave way and let himself slip ever so slightly into the *other*, careful and tentative as always.

He was beginning to learn, slowly, in fearful little starts. And one of the things he had learned was that the mysterious *other* was not entirely chaotic, and he not entirely blind. Through that *other*, he could become aware of the life of the wood all about him, for all the things in the ordinary world cast their shadows in the *other* (or were cast shadows of that *other*; he did not know which). It was not any familiar sense perception – he neither saw nor heard nor felt in any simple bodily way – yet he was aware all the same, and *sensed* things, oftentimes more clearly than he could ever have sighted them, as if distance did not hold the same meaning in that *other* as it did in the ordinary world.

Like a bird hanging on an unpredictable wind, Guthrie balanced precariously between the worlds, casting his attention outwards until the initial chaos of the *other* began to settle into patterns of meaning.

Nearby he could *sense* the flashing, bright little sparks of wood

184

mice, and over there the nervous flare of a rabbit. The old latticework of the high-slope pines, wise in their slow way, surrounded all, like an intricate basket. With his ears, he heard an owl call and *sensed* the dropping flow of its flight in the near distance.

Guthrie shivered. The world throbbed about him eerily, shifting in and out of the focus of his ordinary senses. He felt the *other* surge, or his senses did, in a great heave that nearly took him, and he jerked himself hastily back into the ordinary world, shaking, panting like a hound.

Despite all the terribleness of the *other*, however, the pull of it was all but irresistible, and once he had got his breath back and his heart calmed, he let himself be drawn into it once more. This time, however, he focused all his will on keeping precisely balanced, trying to hold both his ordinary vision and his *other-sensing* simultaneously clear.

Leaning forwards, he put his hand slowly into the fire's flames. The bright flame-tongues licked eagerly at his flesh, trying unsuccessfully to consume it.

They merely tickled.

Guthrie laughed softly, feeling how it was: he could *reach* with his will, as if that will were a kind of intangible hand which he could use to effect changes in the *other*, which in turn effected change in the ordinary world. He could *sense* an intricacy of deep pattern upon pattern, and use his will to ease change into that patterning, make his hand there and not there, a hand and not a hand, and the flames were powerless over his flesh. For his flesh was not merely flesh, and the flames not merely flames.

He played with the fire, cupping little flowers of flame in his palms, lifting them, flipping the flame-petals off into the dark night air and watching them flutter into nothingness, like golden, exotic little birds.

Self-consciously, he withdrew his hands from the fire, remembering the squirrel he had lifted from out of its tree back by the Mirrormere, and Rosslyn's scorn.

He was able to do *amazing* things. But it was only distraction, only make-work, a filling in of time before he had to face what must be faced.

On the ground at Guthrie's side lay *The Book*. He reached for it, unfolded the wrapping, opened it at random. In the uncertain light of the fire, he had to bend close and peer to make out the text of the page that lay open to him. It contained a single, short verse:

> *Leap, or ye have not got*
> *A word*
> *To be heard.*

Guthrie felt a fit of the shivers come over him.

Leap.

Carefully, he re-wrapped the book and put it down. On the ground next to where *The Book* had been, the dead Abbod's skull rested, facing the fire as if watching the dance of the flames. To Guthrie's ordinary sight, the skull was inert as any stone. But he knew by now that things were not that simple. He slid gingerly over the edge into the shallows of the *other*: the *other*-skull seemed a great glowing torch, a swirling flower of energy in a delicate basket.

'Useless thing,' Guthrie muttered, back in the ordinary world once more. He stared morosely at the hollow, bony face. No ordinary dead man's skull. Like one of the magic talismans in the old tales indeed, come unexpectedly true to life. But this one had provided neither help nor guidance. It was like having a sword that refused to be drawn from the scabbard.

Guthrie sighed, shivered, hugged himself. He felt the pull of the *other* still upon him, insistent, eternal.

He remembered once, as a very young child, he had come upon a huge spider unexpectedly at the edge of the woods one summer's morning. The creature had hung from a shivering web at little Guthrie's eye level. With its disgusting, hairy legs splayed out to balance on the web strands, it was fully as large as his child's outspread hand. He had stared at it, paralyzed with revulsion and fright. But though his heart beat painfully, and though he had to swallow hard to keep from being sick, he did not run. There was something compelling about it.

He felt like that now: simultaneously repelled and attracted, terrified yet compellingly drawn.

He let the *other* take him a little, though he kept a determined grip on the ordinary world at the same time. Hanging there suspended *between*, he felt strange currents wash over and through him. He could *sense* the *other*-patterns of the wood all about him, but beyond those lay an appalling depth and distance of – he knew not what. It was like a great chasm, but not just down – there was neither 'up'

186

nor 'down'. In any direction he faced, there was nothing but the endless, encompassing seethe of it.

Into *that* he must leap.

Guthrie shuddered and focused all his will on keeping his awareness at the shallow level, searching for the reassuring presences of the small things, the close things, the simple flicker of owl and skittering mouse, slow-lifed tree, quick-moving rabbit.

Instead, Guthrie *sensed* something else entirely.

Drawing near from out of the night's dark.

Nothing clear could he make out with his eyes, nor hear anything yet with his ears. His heart beating fast, he reached his awareness out, slipping from the edge a little further into the *other*.

It was no familiar forest creature, this, no deer or rabbit or fox.

A person, then? Who could it possibly be out here in these wild lands?

But Guthrie *sensed* the creature move towards him with delicate grace, and though he could not see it in any normal sense of the word, he grew aware of how it moved, stepping the way a heron might, long limbs lifted and placed as if in a slow, flowing dance.

It was not the motion of any ordinary man or woman.

Guthrie felt fear knot his belly as a sudden surmise struck him. Was this creature coming towards him of the ordinary world at all? Suppose the *other* had its own denizens. It was a completely new notion to him. He shivered in mixed fear and excitement. Was he about to encounter some being so far removed from ordinary human kind that he would be unable to comprehend it?

What did it want of him?

Holding himself precariously balanced *between*, Guthrie caught his first glimpse of the creature with his ordinary vision: a pale, dark-eyed face amongst the trees, faintly illumined by the fire's flickering radiance.

One of the Fey.

Guthrie shivered. In his sole previous glimpse of such a being – the one that had returned him the Abbod's skull at the birch pool – he had found it oddly difficult to focus. Now, despite the uncertain flicker of the fire, he could see this one before him with surprising clarity.

The Fey took a graceful step away from the shadow-dark under the trees.

Guthrie started nervously, lost his balance, and inadvertently fell out of the *other* and into the ordinary world with a thump that jarred his nerves.

The Fey before him was transformed into a wavery, half-guessed shape.

Guthrie shook himself and asserted his will, balancing himself between the worlds once more, using double-vision – his ordinary eyes and his *other*-sense – to focus.

The Fey returned to clarity.

It was just like any ordinary person in many ways, legs and arms and face, though longer and slimmer and inhumanly graceful in its movements.

It came close to him, squatting on the ground, long legs easily folded, knees up near its shoulders. The big dark eyes gazed at him unblinkingly.

Guthrie stayed as he was, frozen.

It reached a hand to his face, softly.

Guthrie forced himself not to flinch at the Fey's touch. The queer, too-long fingers were cool, gentle as a butterfly's wing brushing his skin.

Softly, they withdrew.

The big dark eyes stayed fixed upon him.

'What ... what do you want of me?' Guthrie asked.

He received no reply save for that unblinking, intent gaze.

'What?' he repeated. In an effort to discover what the Fey might be about, Guthrie slid deeper into the *other* and tried to *sense* the being's intentions. There was no distance between them now, and he *sensed* the Fey more clearly than before.

What he perceived, however, was totally unlike anything he had experienced.

As of yet, the only person he had *sensed* was Rosslyn. But this being squatting before him was no glowing funnel such as Rosslyn had been. The Fey was like ... like moving water. Guthrie could feel no clear distinction between it and the wood about them. The *other*-patterns flowed through all. The Fey was ... translucent. Guthrie could think of no other word to properly express it. Rosslyn might be a clear, open funnel, but she was also clearly a vessel through which the world poured. The Fey was so open to, so much a part of, the wood around them that it hardly seemed to exist as a separate vessel at all.

In trying to understand, Guthrie fell back into his old, familiar grasp of the world. The Fey before him was like a human person, but more pure. In the words of his old self, he would have described a person as a mix of the five elementals, as having a soul that held all five in easy or uneasy balance. But this being before him was far purer than that. Its soul was an earth soul, pure and simple. No admixture at all. It was a part of the wood, the rocks, the soil, in a way no human being could ever be.

For all this his mind made explanations. But in some other way, he simply *knew*. It was a perfect, pure being before him, wedded to the earth so intimately that it would die were it to be separated from its home.

Pure in its own way as the flames themselves.

Guthrie came more closely back to the ordinary world, blinking it into focus. The Fey was standing now, gazing at him still with its great dark eyes. There was no telling what thoughts might lie behind those eyes. He could *sense* no clear thing about it save for its purity.

This being suffered none of the uncertainties and confusions that he did. There was no awful leap for it to contemplate. It was wedded to the earthliness of the wood for ever, and nothing could ever shake it loose save the complete destruction of that earthly wood itself. It *belonged*.

Guthrie shivered as the realization came over him, envious in his very bones.

The Fey turned then and, with its strange dancer's grace of limb, walked away from him.

'Wait!' Guthrie cried. 'Don't leave!'

It turned and looked silently back at him for a moment, its dark eyes utterly inscrutable. It lifted one long-fingered hand – in salutation, beckoning, dismissal? Guthrie could not tell – then faded silently away into the trees and was gone.

Guthrie stood staring. With his *other*-sense, he followed its going until it melded into the far underpatterns of the wood and disappeared.

The Fey's departure left him feeling strangely bereft. It had slipped back into the forest like a seal slipping under the waves, leaving him stranded and alone on the barren shore, unable to swim after.

Why had it come to him? He could not understand its motives; perhaps ordinary folk could never understand the motives of such beings.

Sighing, Guthrie turned back to the fire and settled himself down before it. The night air seemed to grip him with cold fingers and he fed the hungry flames with more wood, relishing the warmth they gave off. He hugged himself, feeling abandoned and bleakly alone.

He had no clear sense of what he was doing out here. Why had Rosslyn sent him off so completely unprepared, so totally unguided? He felt pulled in different directions, as by conflicting currents, and felt himself becoming more and more uncertain and confused. And this unexpected visit by the Fey merely added to that confusion.

Guthrie picked up the dead Abbod's skull, needing to do something, and sat with it in his lap. 'You might as well be a stone for all the use you are,' he told it. 'You were a fool as a living man, and you are a fool as ... as whatever you may be now.'

A part of him hoped to chivvy the shade of the dead Abbod into some kind of response with such accusations. But, as usual, the skull remained silent.

Guthrie felt the rounded hardness of the bone in his hands. This hard bowl had once been part of a living, breathing human being. He could feel the intricate lines of the small, perfect joints of the cranium under his fingertips. The back of the skull flared out a little in a ridge of bone. Guthrie ran a finger along it, wondering involuntarily if the dead Abbod himself had run his own living finger along just this same bony ridge – clothed with flesh and scalp and hair as it had been then – and for a sudden, shocking moment, it was as if he were the Abbod, feeling the bone as his own, fleshed and pulsing with life.

With a little bitten-off cry, Guthrie dropped the skull and scrambled to his feet.

There was something almost obscene about this; he did not feel it proper to have such intimacy with the dead. It made him shiver sickly. He stared at the skull lying there next the fire, his teeth chattering as with an ague.

A man died. His spirit went to the Shadowlands, to be reborn again when the time was ripe. That was how things were *supposed* to be. Not this ...

But the skull only lay still and inert as any stone.

Cursed, queer thing.

Guthrie sighed. He felt shivery, light-headed and dizzy and out of breath, as if he had just run a long, long race. He sat down again. The skull had rolled on to its face, and he righted it, brushed dead pine needles out of the empty eye sockets. He fed a little more wood to the flames, tucked the wrapping more securely about *The Book*, trying to occupy himself with such little things.

190

The *other* pulled at him persistently.

As before, he tried to focus on keeping his awareness at the shallow level, searching for the reassuring presences of small, recognizable things.

And then, as he had before, he became aware of some being moving through the forest towards him.

Close now.

He had been too self-absorbed to pay attention to his surroundings. Now he could *sense* something very near.

His first thought was that the Fey was returned.

But this was no Fey. It was far less graceful in its movement and far more defined. Where he had *sensed* the Fey as a watery translucence, this being was far denser, more defined; like the skull in a way; like a moving basket filled with very faint radiance.

It took him a long few moments to realize what it was: an ordinary human person. A stranger.

Guthrie felt a sudden prickle of fear.

His hand went instinctively to his belt, where he used to keep a knife – and in the days of the Sea Wolves, a sword. But no blade hung there now. He sighed. Scant use it would have been anyway, against anybody aggressive enough and properly armed ...

Sitting as he was, still facing the fire, Guthrie closed his eyes and tried to *sense* who or what the intruder might be. Nothing clear came to him, but he could feel a kind of tension, like a net of chords too tightly strung, emanating from whoever it was out there.

The person was afraid. Or nervous. As somebody might be before nerving himself to an attack.

Guthrie shivered. His belly clenched in an anxious knot. The person was creeping closer.

It was happening too suddenly.

He did not know what to do.

XIII

Moving upslope haltingly in the darkness, Alia spied the faint glimmer of a campfire far off through the trees.

Having spotted it, she hid herself behind a crest of stone, silent, uncertain. The night air was chill. She wrapped her arms about herself, shivering. The firelit camp ahead seemed a little enclave of potential warmth and human company.

But the question remained: whose fire was this?

Bandits, it was, most like, around that fire. The very thought made her stomach curdle. Stupid notion to have come even this close. Best to turn tail and flee while she still could, quick as she might.

But what if it were Vale folk out here, with no inkling of how any had survived the terrible disaster of the Sea Wolf raid? She could not just walk off and leave such poor folk to remain here, ignorant of the fate of friend and kin.

After anxious moments of hesitation, Alia laid bow and quiver where she could retrieve them later, knowing she could run that much better through the trees without their encumbrance. She planned on using her wits and feet in case of trouble, and her belt knife, it worst should come to worst.

Her heart thumping, she crept cautiously towards the radiance of the distant fire.

It seemed to take forever, but she refused to let herself be rushed by either fear or hopeful expectation. Slow and careful she went, creeping from one bit of cover to the next, despite the certainty that anybody standing near that fire would be blind to her presence here in the forest dark.

Finally, she came within spying distance of the fire. But though she spent long moments squinting through the intervening, black lacery of the tree limbs, she could make out nobody at all.

Alia shivered and froze, remembering the shock she had felt when the two Militia guards had come at her that first night when she had slipped up on Hunters Camp through the dark. She held her breath, staring about her into the night every which way, suddenly terrified that some stranger would land hard upon her and drag her along into the firelight like so much baggage.

Almost, she turned and fled away.

But there was not the slightest sound of movement about her. The forest lay utterly still. She waited until the beating of her heart grew less harried, then crept closer for a better vantage point.

Edging carefully round the trunk of a mountain pine, careful of her still-sore left hand, she peered into the dim distance, blinking things into focus, and was finally able to make out a lone man sitting by the fire, head bowed, still as stone, little more than a shadow amongst shadows.

Alia stared. One man, totally alone. From what she could see in the uncertain light, he seemed a Vale man from his clothing. He sat hunched up, legs folded beneath him, gazing fixedly at some roundish thing in his lap which reflected the firelight dully.

Who could it be? Some Valer lost and stranded here since the raid? The notion made her shiver. The poor soul, lost and alone, unknowing, thinking friend and kin dead.

Alia's heart went out to him. On impulse, she rose to her feet. But caution stopped her, experience having made her more wary than she once had been. There still might be others about. The man could be dressed in clothes he had taken from some Valer he had murdered.

She settled back down again uneasily, waiting for something to tip the balance one way or another, to tell her if she ought to flee or not.

For long heartbeats nothing happened. Alia squatted there, shivering in little fits from the cold of the night air, silently watching. The man by the fire moved not at all, merely stared down at the thing in his lap.

Then Alia heard him say something.

She glanced round frantically for some newcomer to whom he was talking, but could see nobody. The man's gaze was still fixed on the object he held in his lap. Though Alia strained, his voice was too low for her to make out any of the words. She leaned forward, away from the sheltering shadow of the tree against which she hid.

The man by the fire let out a little, bitten-off cry, dropped what he had been holding, and lurched to his feet.

Alia started, cracking her temple painfully against the trunk of the pine against which she was hid. She half rose, poised to flee, her heart pounding.

But the man merely stood as he was, silent, staring down at the thing he had dropped. In the flickering dance of the flames, it looked like a largish, smooth round stone.

Alia could see him a little better now. He was young, perhaps not much more than a year or so beyond her own age. Long pale hair was knotted loosely at the back of his neck.

He moved, and she hunkered down closer to her tree. But all he did was retrieve the stone – if such it was – and sit down once more.

Alia drew back. What was this young man doing here all alone in the wild? What normal man talked with a stone?

But there seemed nothing especially threatening about him. She could spot no weapon on or near him. Perhaps he was, after all, what she had thought: some poor, stranded Vale man, half mad with grief and loneliness.

He sat, unmoving now.

Alia crept a careful few paces closer so as to be able to see him the better.

'Come out,' the man said.

It took Alia a long moment to realize he was speaking to her.

'Come out and show yourself,' he said, slewing round where he sat and looking exactly in her direction now.

Alia felt her belly cramp up. How could he, with his firelight-dazed eyes, see her crouched out here in the darkness and distance?

'Come out,' he said a third time. His voice was tight. 'Whoever you are, stop skulking about like a bandit in the dark and come out into the firelight!' He had laid the stone on the ground and was on his feet now, his hands clenched before him, staring at where Alia still crouched.

He seemed strangely vulnerable standing there like that, unarmed, silhouetted against the fire. If she'd brought her bow and had a mind to, she could have placed an arrow through his ribs before he knew what had happened.

Alia shuddered. What sort of person was she becoming? She had never used to think thus.

Perhaps it was his using the word 'bandit' (in a way she imagined no true bandit would), or the shock of recognizing the mad violence in her own thoughts, or perhaps it was the man's seeming vulnerability, or all three, but Alia felt galvanized to step forward out of the dark.

194

He said nothing as she walked uncertainly into the fire's radiance, merely stood, stiff with tension, regarding her warily.

Alia felt like a fool, being caught skulking about this man's camp in the darkness and flushed into the open like this, as if her hunter's skills were as nothing. She kept her eyes on him, her right hand on the hilt of the knife in her belt, and walked uneasily on the balls of her feet, ready to strike out if she must, or turn and flee at the slightest hint of trouble. She felt the sweat clammy along her back. The hand resting against the knife's hilt quivered.

But the man remained as he was, silently regarding her. The fire snappled softly, the flames dancing their way upwards towards where they belonged. A puff of shifting air brought the smoky aroma of the burning wood to her. There was no sign of anybody else about.

Alia squatted by the fire, on the other side of it from where the man stood. She held her hands out to the flames, welcoming their heat, keeping a careful eye out. But the man continued to stay as he was. From where she squatted, she could see his face more clearly. A young face it was, as she had thought, shadowed by the flickering firelight, but there was something a little unnerving about it. He looked starved, gaunt cheeked and hollow eyed, and there was something ... haunted – she could think of no other way of describing it – about his expression.

They stared at each other warily across the flames.

'Who are you?' Alia asked after a little, shifting nervously on her haunches.

He said nothing, merely stared at her still.

Alia bit her lip. 'How did you know I was out there in the dark?' she asked instead.

He shrugged stiffly.

Alia felt her heart thumping. She drew her legs in, ready to leap to her feet and away if need be. 'Who *are* you? What are you doing out here all by yourself?'

'Who are *you*?' he demanded in return. His voice was hoarse, as if he had not used it in a long while.

Alia was unsure what to say. He seemed a Vale man, right enough, ragged and young and alone. Perhaps he was indeed the simple, lost refugee she had thought. But she could not dispel the suspiciousness she had learned from hard experience, and there was something unnervingly strange about this man she could not yet put name to.

195

She looked him up and down as he stood there on the far side of the fire from her, his limbs stiff with tension. His gaunt face was turned from her now and she saw his long pale hair knotted in a ragged braid. His tunic looked to be cut in the familiar Vale fashion, but it was much the worse for wear. Now that she could see it more clearly, though, she realized that it was of superior workmanship and cloth, the sort she might expect to see on a member of one of the Vale's ruling Families. His breeches, too, looked to be expensive work.

Alia recoiled instinctively, rising to her feet. Save for Charrer Mysha, she had scant liking for such men. This one might be ragged and gaunt and worn, but she thought she could see in him still the basic look: as if he had never so much as felt snow over his boot-tops before the Sea Wolves' sudden, bloody attack. The thought made her scan his boots, and, sure enough, they were expensive, southern crafted, extravagant things.

By his left foot, she noticed, lay the stone he had put down.

Alia gasped. No stone, this. The blind eye sockets of a fleshless human skull stared up at her!

She scrambled to her feet and backed hurriedly away. The skull seemed to shine softly in the fire's light. For an instant, Alia thought she saw faintly glowing eyes in the dead sockets, gazing at her. Like the other one, the jewelled man's. She stumbled back a step, shook herself, rubbed her eyes, looked again. This time she saw only empty, dead sockets.

The man across the fire started at her abrupt movement, and his eyes seemed to glow suddenly like some night-beast's in the firelight.

A trick of the light and her own imagination, surely, all of it, the glowing skull-eyes, this man's uncanny look. Yet it almost sent her fleeing, nonetheless, heart in her mouth.

But the man raised his hands, palms out, in a disarming gesture. 'Peace. I ...' He lost his voice momentarily, coughed, swallowed. 'I mean you no harm.'

Alia hesitated, her heart still thumping. She would not have been surprised at bullying arrogance from him, scion of some ruling family as he seemed. But he showed none. Yet.

'You ... you are a hunter?' he asked.

Alia realized that in the firelight he could make out the hunter's stag-head crest on her sleeve. 'Aye,' she replied, still poised and uncertain.

The skull seemed to stare at her still. Alia shuddered. Part of her said flee, fast as could be. But this man seemed truly to be a Vale man, and he had none of the aura of menace the jewelled man in the bandits' camp had radiated.

The man stood looking at her from across the fire, silent. The tension that had been in him seemed to loosen a little. He said, 'I had not ... thought of the hunters.' Though his voice was less hoarse now and he hesitated less, he sounded awkward when he talked, as if it were a foreign language he used, yet his accent marked him clearly enough as a Vale man, born and bred. 'You must have escaped the Sea Wolves' slaughter, hidden up in the Heights as you were.'

'You know about the Wolves, then?' Alia asked in return.

He nodded. 'I was at the Closter when folk there were ... massacred.'

Alia blinked. 'Massacred?'

'Surely you have heard, even you hunters. The Sea Wolves came and besieged the Closter. The Closter's Abbod, he ... allowed them in and they killed everyone there. I ... I was lucky enough to escape with my life.'

'But nobody was massacred in the Closter. A few died, aye. But the most came out sound of limb and safe.'

'What?'

'Hone Amis led them into the safety of the hills. Charrer Mysha gave them sanctuary at Hunters Camp. It's the bandits we have to look to now. They ...'

'Hone Amis?' he said, interrupting. If she had just sprouted a second head, he could not have looked at her in any more startled a fashion. 'Hone Amis is alive? The Vale folk are alive?'

Alia nodded. 'Aye. The Vale was trampled right enough, and the Militia fared badly against the Wolves. But most ordinary folk survived in the end.'

'Hone Amis, *alive*?' he repeated.

'Aye,' Alia confirmed. 'You know him, then?'

He nodded. Slowly, like a man struggling for balance, he lowered himself to the ground and sat, staring blindly into the fire's dancing flames.

Alia took a breath. She was not sure what to say or what to think, and stood staring. She found her gaze drawn uneasily, unavoidably to the skull which lay now near his knee. Again, she thought she saw eyes, or the ghost of eyes, in the empty sockets. She felt a cold shiver go up her spine.

197

For long moments, silence held between them. Alia heard an owl hoot in the dark distance. The fire crackled softly.

'I thought them all dead,' he said eventually. 'I thought them massacred.'

'You have been out here in the wilds by yourself since then?' Alia asked, thinking what it must have been like for him, stranded and lonely and believing everything destroyed and gone.

Still staring into the flames, he shrugged.

Silence.

Alia could not suppress her unease. There was indeed something strange about this man. He somehow seemed ... not quite all there, as if he were listening to voices only he could hear. Alia found herself straining to catch any hint of such voices. But there was nothing.

'What ... what is your name?' she asked of him finally, when the continued silence had begun to wear on her nerves.

He looked up at her, startled, as if he had forgotten her very existence. 'My name?'

'Aye,' she snapped, exasperated at his seeming woolly-headed-ness. 'You *do* have a name, don't you?'

'Aye.'

'Well?'

'Guthrie. My name is Guthrie. And you?'

'I am called Alia.'

He smiled then, a strained little grin. 'You bring unexpected news, Alia.'

She tried to smile back, but it was a brittle attempt, for her belly was still curdled with unease.

'Tell me what happened in the Vale,' he said, gesturing for her to sit next to him. 'Tell me all you know.'

She moved closer, but stopped, staring down at the skull that lay on the ground between them. He shifted it hastily aside, placing it near his other knee on the side away from her. He seemed almost embarrassed by the thing, yet at the same time the way he cupped it in his hand was a possessive gesture, as if it were somehow valuable. And he said not a word of explanation about why he kept such a gruesome object.

For an instant, Alia had a sudden conviction that his mind had gone: she imagined him wandering the heights here, stricken with grief and loneliness, perhaps with a wounded kinsman in tow who had later died. She saw him bowed over the corpse, weeping,

198

chasing the carrion birds off as long as he could, but with weakening success, until only the bare, stripped bones had been left. And now he carried the skull of some dead kinsman, perhaps in pathetic, mad hope. The thought of it made her shudder, but grief was something she could understand.

He was looking at her, impatience writ clear on his face. 'Tell me what happened in the Vale,' he repeated, half rising towards her now. 'Tell me!'

Alia skipped backwards nervously.

But instead of coming after her, he sank back down to the ground with a sigh and mumbled something she could not make out.

After a moment, uneasily curious, she asked, 'What did you say?'

'It does not matter,' he replied.

'No,' Alia said. 'Tell me.'

'It does not matter,' was all his response.

All threat had gone out of him entirely. Sitting there, he seemed sad and pensive, and there was this ... something about him still, this listening to far-off voices she had already noticed. He was not like any man she had ever met.

'Your kin are most likely alive,' Alia said, meaning to reassure him. 'You can return to them now.'

He looked at her and slowly shook his head. 'My kin are killed.'

'How can you know that?' she demanded of him, irritated by his glum certainty. 'You thought *everyone* had been killed until I told you otherwise.'

'I know for a certainty my kin are killed,' he said.

'How can you ...'

'Have you heard what happened to the Reeve?' he demanded.

'Aye,' Alia replied after a moment, thrown a little by this seeming sudden change of topic. 'He was killed in battle with the Sea Wolves.'

'And his elder son?'

'Killed also in the fighting.'

'And the Reeve's wife?'

Alia sighed. 'Killed too, as far as anyone knows.'

The man nodded.

Alia took a step nearer to him. 'But surely ... the Reeve's death does not mean your kin are killed too.'

'They *are* my kin.'

Alia blinked. She thought of the obvious, expensive quality of his clothing. 'Who ... are you?'

He shrugged.

'Who *are* you?'

He looked across at her, his gaunt face half shadowed by the firelight. 'I am Reeve Guthrie Garthson.'

It took a long moment for that to sink in. 'The ... the Reeve's son?'

'Second son.'

Alia stared. Reeve's son! She could hardly credit it. 'But how ... Why?' She did not know what to think. 'Everybody thought you killed!'

He shrugged again, uneasily.

'But ...' Alia felt her mind spinning. Reeve's son. Reeve himself now, with the death of his father and elder brother.

Unless he was lying ...

'How do I know you are telling me the truth?' she demanded of him.

He shrugged. 'You do not, I suppose. But it does not matter if you believe me or no. It is too late.'

'Too late? Haven't you been *listening*? Your family is dead, aye, but the Vale folk are survived! How can you just –'

In mid-sentence, she stopped, rendered speechless by the strength of the realization that had just struck her. If this man was indeed Reeve Garth's son, and Reeve in his own right now, then there was a real chance life could go back to what it once had been in the Vale. And that meant Hone Amis and all his lot would be gone out of Hunters Camp and out of the hunters' lives for good, leaving everything to go back to how it had once been. Vale folk, desperately needing something familiar to centre their lives, would rally about the new Reeve. The bandits could be driven off once and for good. If she brought this Reeve's son back with her, she could do far more than just bring help for Orrin and poor hurt Patch. The hunters could recover the peace they had lost, the way of life they looked to have lost ...

Alia squinted at Guthrie, doubt abruptly gnawing at her. She had never seen him before, but she had heard stories about this second son. Along with the other ordinary small folk of the Vale, she had been hearing about the Reeves all her life, about the great and the minor things they did or had done. All the public gossip she could recall about him was trivial stuff, women, and laziness, and a spoiled boy's bad temper.

But looking at him now, she saw none of the natural arrogance of Hone Amis. He did not hold himself with the same purposeful

200

control, and his face had none of the officious stiffness of the Militia Master's. He was gaunt and haggard, and there was this other something about him, too, this ... vagueness, as if he was listening to things unheard.

No, he seemed no new Hone Amis, this one. And no more the spoiled second son either, by appearances.

Alia felt her heart beating fast. She wanted to grab hold of this new Reeve, the way a drowning person might grab at salvation. She wanted to yank him away from his fire and race off through the hills with him, getting him back as quick as could be. Instead, she took a long breath, trying for calm. 'You are the Reeve now,' she said to him. 'You must return and take your rightful place.'

He blinked, shook his head, stared at her.

'Folk survived the Sea Wolves ... but there are bandits come into the hills now, and they threaten everything.'

He stared at her.

'Aye, *bandits*! As if the Wolves were not enough. After them came these bandits – a hundred of them, more maybe. Like nothing we've ever faced before.' Alia leaned towards him. 'It's grim hard times the Vale folk face. They need their Reeve back.'

For an instant, he leaned forwards, his eyes alight, as if he were about to leap to his feet and start off immediately. But then he sagged, shook his head, shrugged. 'You do not understand. It is too late.'

'No it's *not*! There is still much of the Vale left. Folk will work hard to recover what they can for the winter. So long as these cursed bandits are driven off, the Vale can be rebuilt. But folk need somebody to lead them, somebody they can tie their hopes to.'

'You mean well no doubt, Alia, but it's too late,' he repeated.

This was the first time he had used her name. It caused her a little thrill. Folk of her station never expected to see the Reeves except at a distance. And *never* to converse with one face to face like this. Sitting here, talking with him now was like ... like talking to a story-character come to life.

And if she, who had forsaken Vale life for the open, green freedom of the wild, could still feel this thrill in the presence of the Reeve ... then what would ordinary Vale folk feel?

Alia's belly shivered with excitement. Hone Amis was a mere steward. Folk obeyed him because he had the power to enforce his commands, and because behind him stood the shadow of the Reeve. But this man ... The Reeve had more than just power; he had all the long-standing authority that went with his status as ruling head of the family that had founded the very settlement of Reeve Vale itself. He would provide exactly the focus for people's hopes that was needed, a reminder of the organized life they had once lived, of continuity, of future promise.

And Hone Amis would be brought to heel, and Hunters Camp returned to its former silence, and life returned to the way it had once been.

Alia tore herself away of such heady thoughts. 'Come back with me,' she urged. 'All you have to do is return and folk will ...'

He shook his head. 'I am no longer Reeve.'

'But how can you ...' Alia lapsed into silence. He did not seem to be paying her any attention. Once again, he had that listening look, as if he were privy to hidden secrets on the night air. His eyes stared blindly, shining like river stones in the firelight.

'Reeve,' she said. 'Reeve!' Getting no response, she leaned closer and reached her hand to him. He felt hot and fevered. 'Gu ... Guthrie!' She stumbled over calling the Reeve directly by his birth name.

What was *wrong* with him? Alia wondered uneasily. Had his mind indeed come apart under the impact of the terrible things that had happened? She fervently hoped not.

Guthrie looked at her. There was no recognizable expression on his face that she could see. It was as if he were looking right *through* her.

'Guthrie!' she called again.

He blinked then, focusing on her properly.

Alia felt a flush of angry disappointment surge up within her. Here she had found salvation, the solution to every difficulty, the missing Reeve himself. She had walked right up to his fire as if the Powers themselves had guided her. But instead of the leader she ought to expect, she had found this vague, fuzzy-minded, confused and confusing refugee.

'Reeve Guthrie,' she said, trying to catch his attention.

He shook his head. 'I am Reeve no longer.'

Alia took a breath, trying to stifle her irritation, deciding that patience was the best approach. 'Now that your father and brother are ... are killed, you are the Reeve. Who else if not you?'

'You do not understand. I am ... *changed*.' He shrugged uncomfortably. 'You cannot understand.'

'What's *wrong* with you?' she demanded angrily of him. 'How can you just sit here when ...'

Alia stopped, took a breath, began again. 'Are you so sunk in yourself, then, that you will ignore the needs of your own folk? Do you consider yourself so important that you can sit here by your fire alone in the heights and count the suffering of others as nothing?'

That stung him a little, she could see by the way his eyes flinched.

'You *must* take up your rightful position as Reeve! If you don't return to the Vale ...'

Guthrie looked at her, vague as could be.

'Oh, what do *you* care?' Alia snapped.

He was looking through her again now, as he had before. All her arguments were pointless. It was like a fit taking him, though with none of the bodily franticness that would mark any ordinary fit, as if his spirit had somehow fallen silently out of the world.

Black despair overwhelmed her. He was mad, this lost Reeve's son. It grew more and more obvious to her. He sat here alone by his little fire in the wild heights, his mind obviously dazed and shattered and working only in fits, with a dead man's skull by his knee. Mad and fevered, helpless and useless to anyone, even himself.

Alia felt like slapping him, Reeve or no.

But that, too, was useless.

She fed some sticks into the fire, tried to collect herself. She ought simply to leave, abandon him here and now. Each moment more she wasted here meant that much more time lost for Orrin and Patch.

But, mad or not, he was still the Reeve, and still represented the best hope, perhaps the only hope, of restoring life to what it once had been. And back amongst ordinary human company, she tried to convince herself, his loosened mind would right itself, surely. Whatever was wrong with him, at least it did not leave him raving.

There must be some way to reach him, to convince him to follow her back. So much might depend on it. There *must* be a way.

203

XIV

Guthrie shivered. He felt as if a sudden fever had gripped him. The ordinary world flickered in and out of focus. The swirl and seethe of the *other* tugged at him.

It was too much. That he should be Reeve again, that every dream he had ever had was come true ... too late.

Reeve!

He tried to deny the *other* entirely, to push it aside and close it off. But it was useless. Might as well try to push aside the ocean itself. He would never be free of it, as Rosslyn had warned. He could never again be the self he had once been – could never be the Reeve he had once so longed to be.

All the days he had wandered alone and lost and in despair, all the while he had spent with Rosslyn, thinking himself the lone survivor of the Sea Wolves' attack ...

It was so grossly unfair it made him want to spit.

'You cannot simply abandon your own folk!' the hunter girl was saying now.

He did not know how to answer her. How could he return? How could he take up everything that had once been his dream only to have it mean nothing of what it once had?

And suppose he yielded to her urging and did take his old life up, and suppose it ... seduced him. What then? He could feel the temptation of it. He could retreat from the abyss of the *other* that awaited him, fall back into his old life, avoid the leap.

But would he not then become one of the bent persons Rosslyn had talked of?

'Do you not feel anything for them at all?' the hunter girl persisted. 'After all the Vale folk have endured, and with bandits threatening them ... The Reeves were always said to be a responsible family. Folk respected them. What sort of a man are you, that you do nothing ... *nothing*, while the folk your family brought to the Vale suffer?'

He could only stare at her, mute. There was no way for him to explain.

'What's *wrong* with you? You sit here huddled by your little fire in the wilds, a dead man's head at your side. Is life so wonderful up here, then? You look like you haven't had a good meal in weeks! Well ... Guthrie Garthson, we've all suffered, all been hurt, and very few have run away like you. There's no point in turning your back on disaster and hiding like you have. Return with me and *face* it!'

Almost, he laughed. The girl had no notion whatsoever of what he had had to face, was still facing.

She stared at him, distraught. He could feel the desperation in her. 'You can't just abandon your own folk!' she said, her voice hoarse.

He *ached* to do just as she asked. In his mind, he saw himself returning to the Vale folk, them cheering, him the focus of everything, men hanging on his every word, Hone Amis there as always, but deferring to him now as he had once deferred to his father. It was all his boyhood dreams come true at last.

But underlying it all, undercutting everything, lay the *other*. He had learned, was learning, to skate a little across the shallow surface of it, like a water-spider across a deep pool, but the depthless depth of it remained.

What matter any of his former hopes when everything – his self, his position, his dreams, the familiar world of the Vale itself – was naught but ... potters' work, and when the *other* waited for him, implacable, endless, eternal?

So ... But suppose he *did* turn away for ever from his folk and his old life. Would it help bring him any closer to the brink of the leap he must make? He could not see how.

Guthrie shuddered. Back and forth he swayed, yea and nay a half a hundred times. Any way he turned, he was damned.

He dearly wished Rosslyn were here. *The Book* was of no use. He needed a living person to talk with, one who understood his dilemma.

Of a sudden, a desperate thought struck him. He had been able to use the *other* to perceive things at a farther distance than he could see with his ordinary eyes. Might he somehow send his attention through the *other* and contact Rosslyn?

How?

He had no inkling. But the need was surely upon him.

205

Uncertainly, he edged his attention over into the *other*, threading a way into the seethe of it.

Rosslyn.

It was not words Guthrie employed, but he contrived to make it the clearest sort of call he could, shaping the funnel-image of her in his mind, sending his need through the *other* like a little leaping fountain of water in a storm.

Rosslyn!

He *reached* with all his will, keeping a clear sense of her in his mind, attempting to close the world's distance between them and contact her.

Rosslyn!

ROSSLYN!

But it was no use. There was no sign of response.

Guthrie had sunk himself farther and deeper into the *other* than ever he had ever willingly tried before. Now, recognizing the futility of his attempt at reaching Rosslyn, he strove to return to the ordinary once again.

To his horror, he discovered that he could not find the way. There was only seething confusion. Terror filled him. He would have screamed, save he had no mouth to do so. He could no longer feel his bodily self at all. He felt a wave of dissolution sweep through him and struggled desperately to resist it. But he was like a clot of earth flung into a turbulent river, coming apart as the current tumbled it.

And then, in the distance – though 'distance' was not the right word properly to describe what he experienced – he made out something glowing – though 'glowing' was, again, not the right word – like a beacon, a lone *something* that had form and place in the otherwise soul-wrenching chaos. He struggled for it, like a swimmer against a rip-tide, keeping it before him clear as he could, until he drew near to it – or drew it near to him, he knew not which. What he used to perceive it was not sight, but his mind insisted on interpreting things in familiar ways: therefore before him he 'saw' a swirling flower of energy in a delicate basket.

The skull!

He could make out a ghostly outline of bone now, cranium and jaw and eye sockets. And in those sockets, the eyes burned like flames.

Guthrie *reached* his will to it, clutching after it with the terrible desperation of a drowning man, straining, reaching ...

And came out into the ordinary world again sprawled upon the dirt, the skull clenched in his hands.

For long moments it was all he could do just to lie there, his face pushed into the ground, breath coming in great gasping pants. He clung to the skull as to an anchor, till the sickening swirl that tore at him should settle.

The hunter girl stared at him as if he were quite mad. Well she might. What must he have seemed to her while he was torn and swayed by the *other*?

Guthrie drew himself shakily to his knees. He gazed at the skull. It felt comfortingly warm in his hold, but looked no different than usual; the eye sockets were dark and empty. Yet it had guided him. It *had*!

He sat slumped over it, mortally confused. A burden and a broken promise and an embarrassment: that was what he had truly begun to believe the thing was. But now ...

The hunter girl continued to stare at him, her eyes wide and uncertain. Self-consciously, Guthrie tried to straighten himself. He put the skull down, picked it up again with awkward haste, for it anchored him and he felt adrift without it. He did not want this girl about, staring at him so. He wanted to be alone with the skull, to be able to explore this new thing that had happened. He looked down at the skull again, wonderingly.

'Are you all right?' the girl asked.

Guthrie blinked, shook himself. 'Aye,' he murmured. The world stayed blessedly firm about him, but his balance was delicate. The slightest little thing could tip him over.

'Was it some sort of ... fit?'

Guthrie shrugged, not knowing how to explain. He felt awkward, on his knees as he still was, and tried to shift to a more stable sitting position.

The girl moved to help him. He fended her off vaguely, but she brushed aside his hands, bent over him, and shifted him about so that he ended up sitting facing the fire. Her grip was strong and sure, yet gentle enough for all that.

She crouched next to him, one hand still on his shoulder. 'Are you certain sure you're all right?'

'Aye,' he answered self-consciously.

On her face, he could read pity mixed with dismay, but he also saw resolve harden in her, felt it stiffen the hand that continued to rest upon his shoulder. Her gaze upon him grew steady as Rosslyn's own. She was a spirit not easily balked, this girl.

Guthrie blinked, trying to keep her in focus, feeling the ordinary world fade for a moment about him.

'Listen to me,' she said. She shook him. 'Please! You must listen to me.'

'I am listening,' he replied. He concentrated on the feel of her fingers upon his shoulder. It was like an anchor, that grip, as the skull in its way was an anchor.

'What can I say to you? How convince you?' She looked him straight in the eyes, and it seemed to Guthrie as if the world narrowed at that moment to just him and her. Perhaps it was an after-effect somehow of what he had just endured, of her very closeness to him in his shaken state; perhaps it was something else entirely; he did not know. But he felt her gaze upon him as solidly as he felt her hand on his shoulder, the very intensity of that gaze holding him immobile. Guthrie shivered. It was as if a conduit had been opened between the two of them.

'Folk *need* you,' she said.

Gazing at her, he suddenly *sensed* clear the naked need in her, and the need of others echoed strongly in hers, and it was abruptly hard for him to get breath. In all his life, nobody had ever needed him like this.

She stared at him, imploring.

He felt as if a hook had been set in his guts. It was a pull upon him strong as that of the *other*.

Stronger.

'The Vale folk,' Alia was saying, 'need their Reeve returned to them if they are to prosper. They *need* you, Reeve Guthrie Garthson.'

Her using of his full name was somehow like a conjuring. Reeve Guthrie Garthson, the Reeve of Reeve Vale. *Reeve Guthrie Garthson* ...

Guthrie blinked, shook himself, gulped a breath. He was not sure how it had happened. The hook was embedded too quick, too deep. He felt the pull of it too strongly. Whatever the consequences, he could not turn away now.

The moment of choice was suddenly past.

'All right,' he said in a small voice. 'Aye. All right ... I will go with you ...'

XV

So Guthrie found himself following along behind the hunter girl, Alia.

But the travelling was hard. His limbs felt trembly and weak. He was thirsty all the time and prey to fits of wracking shivers. He ached, joint and limb.

And the weather was most foul.

The first of this year's winter storms had come pounding in from the western ocean when the Sea Wolves attacked. Since then, there had been nothing, really. Now, however, the winter storm-time seemed upon them with a vengeance. The west wind howled. Rain fell in furious sheets, freezing cold and driving against one's skin like so many icy nails.

Their journeying had the taste of nightmare for Guthrie. He swung between the ordinary world and the *other* clumsily, unsure where he might be, lifting a foot to place it upon a rain-slicked, mossy ridge of stone, only to find himself tumbling in the *other* as in a strong current, then whirled about and flung out again to find his foot skidding off the rock and him on his knees in cold mud, shaking uncontrollably.

And sometimes he simply fell out of the world entirely, plunging into the depths of the *other* like a heavy stone through swirling, dark water. Only the presence of the skull kept him from falling away entirely on those occasions; the skull was become a beacon of sorts now that he relied on, a stable radiance in the seething dark of the *other* that allowed him to find a way back. But anchor him, it could not.

Onwards he went, following Alia through the pine woods, sheltering with her when the rain became too much to bear, plodding on and on and on. He lost all track of time; it seemed to him his whole life had been one long, painful, endless stumble along rain-slicked, treacherous, sloping ground, which, in turn, was no more than a thin and untrustworthy membrane stretched over the all-devouring seethe of the *other*.

Almost, he had forgotten the point of it all. Only the journey remained clear, and the figure of the girl ahead of him, beckoning when he slowed.

Yet there were moments of odd clarity, too.

Such as now.

They were moving up a rough slope, slabs of mossy stone forming a kind of stepped side-wall past which they worked their way. There was too much stone here for the trees to be very thick, and the way was more open to the eye than was usual in these deeply wooded hills – and more open to the cold rain, too. Rainwater trickled down his back in icy dribbles. The *shruushing* sound of the rain and wind was a sea-sound, constant, rhythmic.

Squinting ahead through the rain, Guthrie could see a long rise leading to a cleft between two slopes. Their route lay up through that cleft and down the other side. The skull hung at his side, along with the carefully wrapped *Book*, in a sturdy, cleverly knotted net-bag that Alia had constructed from tough meadow grass. He shifted the bag to his leeward side, to give it what protection he could, wiped rain away from his eyes, shook himself like a hound, and pushed onwards and upwards at the best pace he could manage.

Despite the driving rain and uncertain footing, the girl in front of him moved as quietly and carefully as any wild creature, with a wild creature's unconscious grace. He envied the ease with which she moved. These rocky slopes beat the breath out of him.

A wilful girl, and strange, as all such hunter-kind were strange. But comely too, for all the boyish way she dressed and moved. From a distance, no one would think her a girl at all. Up close, though, with her long black hair, her big dark eyes ...

Watching her light-foot it ahead of him, Guthrie experienced a sudden flash of the way things had once been, of how *he* had once been, before the Sea Wolves had brought destruction upon everything.

In the old days, whilst his father dickered over finding a proper wife for him, Guthrie had relied on his privileged position to amuse himself. As Reeve Garth's son, he had bedded several young women very much like this one. She had said nothing of her origins, but he knew the type: a fisher's daughter, or a shepherd's, or some such. The families of the women he chose had been both pleased and proud to have a daughter of theirs bedded by one of the Reeves. If any children had resulted from these unions, they would have been outside the line of the Reeve inheritance, but they would still have been provided for, thus guaranteeing the family some degree of prosperity.

This girl's family would have proved no different, he was sure, from the families of his previous girls. A quick chat with her father, and he would have had this one for as long as he liked.

Guthrie found himself wondering what it would be like to take this hunter girl, to open her up and explore the slim comeliness of her. He looked upon her in his old way, as a farmer might regard a young cow, admiring the line of her slender haunch ...

The world about him surged, and he was abruptly plunged into gut-wrenching chaos.

He came out of it quickly, to find himself on his knees, gasping, hands gripping a slab of mossy stone.

Ahead, the girl had stopped to stare back at him. Still on the edge of the *other* as he was, he could *sense* her: a flexing, intricate basket filled with soft radiance. What he saw with his ordinary vision was mere mask, like so much else. Beyond that, she was an incomprehensible, mysterious being in an incomprehensible, mysterious world.

For an instant, Guthrie felt something entirely new, something akin to sudden reverence, steal over him. He near laughed at the preposterousness of who and what he had been, strutting blindly about like some game-cock eyeing the hens. He perceived so much more now than he had ever been able to experience as his old self. He had been so blinded all of his life ...

But this instant of revelation was shattered in a seethe of confusion as he struggled, once again, to keep himself from being swept away from the ordinary. He staggered to his feet, nearly sprawled face first, saved himself only by flinging an arm about a nearby rock. Heart hammering, he resolutely turned his will to the ordinary, to the hard edge of the grey upthrust of rock under his hands, the slim back of the girl up ahead of him.

He felt the *other* ripple about him, through him, as if he were some little bobbing cork upon a great body of heaving water. When he was able to settle the world once again, he looked up wearily and saw Alia staring back at him impatiently. 'Do you need another rest so soon?'

He felt a sharp stab of resentment, but quelled it; she could have

211

no inkling of what he must endure. 'No,' he responded, pulling himself properly to his feet.

'Need help up the slope?'

'No.'

She regarded him for a long moment, uncertain, then shrugged and continued on.

They were halfway up the rocky slope now. The rain made the going trebly hard, obscuring vision, making footing treacherous. Guthrie shivered, hugging himself, pressed on up the slope as best he could.

The view ahead was partially blocked by a great, moss-cloaked stack of white-grey stone. Around this they went, careful, for a single misstep could mean a hard tumble upon the rain-slicked rocks. The corner of the stone stack ahead was like a building, sharp edged. On the other side, they found themselves in a lee, blessedly protected from the force of the rain. They stood there, the stone rise at their back, heads bowed, panting, shaking with fatigue and cold.

The constant *shruushing* of the rain was distanced here. Guthrie shivered in a long fit. Alia looked at him concernedly. 'Perhaps we should find shelter for the rest of the day. You look like you need it. Travelling in this weather is not easy –'

A sudden *crack* made them both start.

Two ragged men appeared upslope, not thirty paces from them, blocking the cleft between the hills towards which they were headed.

'Bandits!' Alia hissed.

Guthrie saw her shudder, felt the sudden fear that had risen in her at sight of these two. Looking at them, Guthrie saw only a pair of ragged, hungry-looking fellows, little more than ordinary beggars by the sight of them.

But ordinary beggars did not arm themselves with crossbows.

'Hoi!' one of the two shouted, levelling his weapon at them. 'Who are ye and what d'ye want here?' He was a thin fellow, not young, with a jagged scar marring the left side of his face from chin to forehead. Guthrie found it strange to hear this man talk with the same southern accent as Rosslyn. The man glared at Guthrie and Alia along the haft of his crossbow, the bolt aimed menacingly at their bellies. 'Ye're trespassing on our lands!'

Guthrie's old self would have bristled at such a claim. It was Reeve land, this, if it was anybody's. But he could not, somehow, summon up anger. He felt the world waver about him and concentrated on holding himself, and thus it, stable.

Alia had carried her bow strung, with an arrow nooked to the string. With forced, slow casualness, she was trying to ease it up to firing position.

'Don't even think about it, boy!' the second bandit cried, bringing his own crossbow to bear on Alia. He was much younger than his companion, his face partially covered with the pale, wispy beginnings of a beard through which a scattering of inflamed adolescent pimples showed. 'Try to use that bow and I'll skewer ye like an autumn pig.'

'Well?' the scarfaced one called out. 'I asked ye a question. Are ye deaf, the two of ye? Answer up! Who are ye and what're ye doing here on our lands?'

'We are ... are strangers here,' Alia began. 'We've been lost in these woods for –'

'Ye're lying, boy,' Scarface cried, interrupting. 'Ye look to me like –'

But he, in his turn, was interrupted by his younger companion. 'That ain't no boy, Barly.'

Scarface squinted at Alia for a long moment. Then he shook his head. 'It can't be ...'

''Tis, though,' the other replied. ''Tis the very same little boy-looking bitch we took up in the Heights that day in the storm-fog, the one who cut Torno's thing off and escaped with it.'

'Unbelievable!' Scarface said, shaking his head.

The younger one smiled through his wispy bard. 'Sethir ain't here to take her from us this time, is he?'

Scarface nodded. 'Drop yer weapon, girl,' he called out. 'Now! Or I'll put a bolt through ye.'

Alia hesitated.

'*Drop it!*'

For an instant, Guthrie thought Alia was going to try to bring the bow up anyhow, crazy as that seemed, and he reached a hand out. There was death in the very air here, he could *sense* it hovering like a dread presence. His heart thudded. 'No!' he hissed, frightened for her. 'You'll only get yourself killed.'

She glared at him. 'What are you suggesting? That we give ourselves meekly to them. Easy for *you* to say!'

'Drop it, girl!' Scarface ordered.

Alia looked around her, as if searching for some desperate, last minute reprieve. But there was nothing. Slowly, her hands shaking, she laid the bow down.

'Good,' the pimple-faced youngster said. Then, without another word, he turned, aimed at Guthrie, and fired.

The crossbow *clakked*.

Alia cried out.

Guthrie *sensed* the bolt streaking towards him, like some vicious small bird of prey, mindlessly intent on death.

The sudden shock of *sensing* the little death hurtling down upon him nearly proved his undoing. He felt what it would be like, the terrible, bursting force of the iron-tipped bolt as it tore through his breast bone, the drowning flood of blood in his lungs and throat, agony ripping through him.

He felt his own death clear as clear, felt the cold wind of the Shadowlands, the place of the dead, upon him. A snatch of old verse went through his mind: *Bitter ash and leaf and thorn, the Darkling Hills lie sere and worn.* He saw the Shadowland dark, the looming humps of the Darkling Hills themselves, felt his spirit pulled away, tumbled out of the world like a leaf in a storm.

All this in an eyeblink.

Guthrie pulled himself back, denying the death.

Reaching his will instinctively through the *other*, he felt after the rushing bolt. Somehow, it was both hurtling towards him still and already embedded in his breast, like a long cord attached to the bandit's crossbow at one end and his stricken heart at the other.

Guthrie *reached* to that cord and broke it, twisting it away from the straight and deadly path to his death. He *reached* it to a standstill, reducing the long, deadly length of it down to the simple bolt itself, a short length of innocent wood and iron and feather.

The bolt hung in space before him. He stretched out a hand and took it, easy as lifting a soup-spoon from a table, and pushed it past him and away. The world seemed to pulse about him, a great *shroosh* of dizzying movement: out, then in, like a single, shuddering breath.

And he found himself standing in the world once more, gasping, his heart pounding. The crossbow bolt splintered harmlessly against the hard stone behind him. He blinked things into focus, took a breath, unsure exactly of what he had done or how he had done it. It felt to him as if he had indeed died and dwindled into the Shadowland dark, then pulled himself back to the world.

The scarfaced bandit muttered a curse and fired, the *clakk* of his crossbow sounding startlingly loud in the silence.

Guthrie *sensed* the bolt's approach, the cord of its flight. He *reached*, shifting that flight-cord, deflecting the mindlessly intent little thing away from himself so that it splintered harmlessly against the hard stone, as the first bolt had.

The two bandits stared at him, open mouthed. Scarface made a warding sign with two fingers. Then both he and his younger companion scrabbled desperately to re-cock their crossbows. They got as far as hauling back the strings to arm the bows, but were not given a chance to slot in new bolts.

'Don't!' Alia cried. She had her own bow in hand again now, arrow drawn and anchored against her cheek. She aimed the razor-headed hunting arrow at Scarface. 'I can drop you before you take a breath.'

The man lowered his weapon.

'And you,' Alia added, gesturing with her chin to the younger one. 'Put your weapons down, the both of you. Now!'

'Don't do it!' Scarface hissed to his younger companion. 'She can't take both of us at once. If she tries, one of us can arm and take her before she can get another arrow nocked and off.'

'What about *him?*' the younger one hissed.

'What's he going to do? He doesn't have no weapon. It's the girl we have to watch out for.'

'Put your weapons down!' Alia ordered.

The two bandits stood sullenly as they were. 'Piss off, bitch!' the younger one said. 'We ain't going to do what ye says.'

Guthrie saw Alia chew on her lower lip anxiously. She might have the upper hand for the moment, but there were still the two of their crossbows against the one longbow of hers. She would not be able to take the both of them. The bandits were beginning to smirk.

Guthrie felt sick in his belly. It was not just the obvious threat the bandits offered; the whole of this situation rocked him badly, in a completely unanticipated way.

He could see in Alia the same sort of revenge hunger that had once burned so hotly in himself. He could recall the yearning for bloody revenge that had filled him at sight of what the Sea Wolves had done. But now, somehow, he could find nothing of the sort in himself any longer. It was as if some other person entirely had felt that burning desire for vengeance.

Instead, he only felt appalled at what was happening here.

215

He was too changed.

These two men and Alia would as soon kill each other as talk. It seemed insane to him.

And he was unarmed, carried nothing, in fact, save for *The Book* and the Abbod's skull in the grass-net shoulder bag; short of hurling the bag at the two bandits – ludicrous thought – there was nothing he could do in any ordinary way to stop what was about to happen here.

But Guthrie was beginning, slowly, to learn more than ordinary ways to deal with the world.

With great care, he *reached* through the shallow edge of the *other* towards the bandits' crossbows, not knowing exactly what he was doing or how, feeling his way through what he needed to do. Ignoring the tidal pull of the *other*, he focused on *sensing* the hard, tight lines of the weapons, the solid spine of each bow's stock, the springy resilience of the bow arms, the curled-up, deadly power each held within itself. The bowstrings were like ligaments, strong and supple, woven of immensely tiny, parallel lines of glowing force. Guthrie *reached*, unravelling them until they flew apart in an abrupt burst of radiance.

He hauled himself back into the ordinary world, weak and shaking.

The two bandits were staring in dismay at their weapons. The bowstrings were useless, snapped, frayed, dangling.

Alia, too, was staring. She cast a quick, sideways glance at Guthrie – a shaken, confused look – then returned her attention to the bandits. 'Drop them!' she ordered, meaning the crossbows.

Having no other option now, the bandits complied.

Alia stood, grimly triumphant. She let out her arrow a little till it was but half drawn, but held the bow steady and dangerous. 'So you were the ones who took me in the Heights, were you?' she said to them. 'The ones who wanted to have me right then and there, like so many blind stags in rut.'

The bandits said nothing.

'Aye, it was you. I recognize you clear enough now.'

Guthrie could see Alia's hands shaking. Her face was gone white with a growing fury. He did not know what incident she might be referring to, but her accusation obviously made sense to the bandits, for they cringed visibly.

'Scum!' Alia spat. She drew the arrow all the way back, anchoring it at her cheek.

Guthrie could *sense* the cold fury that was building in Alia, like a current of black liquid filling her. He could feel the tension in her fingers where they held the arrow anchored, could almost see what she saw, sighting along the straight length of the arrow's shaft at the helpless bandits.

She was going to do it.

Guthrie was appalled. 'Alia, no!' He made no move towards her, afraid he might spook her into acting. 'Don't do it. They're helpless now. Powerless to harm you.'

'What do *you* know of harm?' she snapped at him. 'Reeve's son as you are. You never felt harm in your pampered little life!'

Guthrie blinked. Once, he might have risen angrily to such a barb. Not now. 'Don't do it, Alia,' he repeated.

'They deserve it!' she replied. 'The stinking bastards.'

'Who are you to say who *deserves* death?'

'Listen to the man, girl,' the scarfaced bandit said, his voice little more than a desperate croak.

Alia glared at the man along the shaft of the arrow still anchored at her cheek and laughed an unfunny laugh. 'Shut up, you!'

'Don't do it,' Guthrie said again. 'Let them go.'

Alia flicked a glance at him out the corner of her eye. 'Are you *crazy?*'

'Are you a murderer?' Guthrie responded.

That gave her pause.

Guthrie did not know how properly to explain to Alia what he was feeling. Death was a part of life, aye. No denying that. Death fed life, and life death. But death here fed nothing. It was unnecessary, utterly pointless, appalling.

'What is *wrong* with you,' he demanded of Alia, 'that you would kill so easily? They can do us no harm now. What will their deaths accomplish? Hasn't there been enough already of death?'

'You know nothing!' Alia spat at him.

'Let them go,' he repeated.

'And what happens when they return and put a crossbow bolt through your back?' Alia demanded.

Guthrie shrugged. 'Perhaps they will not.'

'Perhaps they *will!*'

'Let them go, Alia. Their death feeds nothing.'

Alia shook her head. 'You understand *nothing* about this, Reeve's Son. You've been off by yourself all this while, innocent of what the rest of us have had to endure. You don't *know*! You don't know the kind of men these bandits are.'

'And you do? You know *everything* about them?'

'I know *enough*! You saw what they would have done here. They are *scum*!'

Guthrie looked across at them: two ragged, frightened men.

'Talk sense into her, man,' the scarfaced one pleaded.

Guthrie could just catch a hint of the shadow of the two men's *other*-selves: flexible baskets filled with radiance; as complex and fundamentally mysterious under the surface as anything else in the world, as the girl beside him, the very stars themselves. The raggedy-bandit aspect of them was no more than a thin mask. If only Alia were able to perceive them as he could ...

Guthrie turned to her: 'And what is it that makes these men ... "scum"?'

'Are you blind and stupid? They would have killed you, unarmed as you were. *Murdered* you outright as you stood there, helpless to ...'

He saw the realization come to her. She half lowered her bow, her face puckered in consternation. 'Damn you!' she hissed at him. 'Why couldn't you just let be? Now I don't ...'

The two bandits, seeing Alia's hesitation, whirled and fled, scrambling desperately upslope for cover. Instinctively, she raised the bow and sighted at the nearer man.

'Don't,' Guthrie said.

Alia's hands shook. He saw her jaw working. She lowered the bow, looked at him, disgusted. 'Only pray you don't live to regret what you've done here today,' she snapped, glaring at him accusingly.

He felt as if a chasm had opened up between them. He could think of nothing sensible to say.

She shook her head. 'Come on. Let's get *out* of here. There could be more of them about.' With that, she turned and stalked off.

Guthrie took a ragged breath. A fit of the shivers took him. He swallowed, his mouth parched. Now that it was over, he felt self-conscious, foolish, confused. His old self would not have scrupled at the execution of a pair of ragged bandits. It was only common sense – and indeed stupid to let such men go free and unharmed.

But he was no longer that old self, and no longer in the grip of such simple, brutal certainties. At the moment of *sensing* the two

218

men as he had, it had not felt either stupid or foolish to prevent their destruction.

Sighing, he turned and stumbled along the way Alia had gone. The world shuddered momentarily, and he paused, fighting it. From ahead, Alia gestured to him impatiently. He looked at her, held her gaze a moment. He wanted to explain, to tell her what he experienced, to talk with her. But he felt the distance between them too keenly, an unbridgeable distance she was entirely blind to, and there were no words he could use.

Turning her back on him, she strode away.

He took hold of himself and hurried as best he could to keep pace.

XVI

'Down this way,' Alia said. She and Guthrie stood atop the crest of a rocky bluff, looking down at the forested dell below. A view of the wild hills lay beyond, the ranks of their stony shoulders clearly seen from this vantage point, green, blue-green, blue-purple as they receded into the distance. Wisps of dawn mist clung to the dell's lower slopes. The air was chill and crisp. Alia gestured towards the long, wooded slope that lay ahead. 'Over through the hills there on the far side, and we are nearly arrived.'

Guthrie nodded, silent.

'Well, come on, then,' Alia urged, after the silence between them had dragged on for a good few moments. 'Let's be off!' The chill air felt good in her lungs. This was the first fine day they had had, and she felt thrilled with the stunning clear blue of the early sky and the bright, new-morning sunlight. She itched to be moving. Four days now, they had been travelling. The Powers alone knew how long it had been since she had last seen Orrin and poor Patch. She felt a prickle of helpless panic in her belly just thinking on it. Now, back once again in familiar territory, she wanted only to make speed.

Before setting off, though, she took a careful look about, using the vantage of their high position to scan the surroundings – a caution that had grown instinctive.

All seemed undisturbed. She led the way. It was a steepish descent, ridged with crumbling upthrusts of old stone. Morning sunlight slanted through the pines. She skipped down the rough slope with the agility of long practice, taking pleasure in the play of her limbs, the good stretch of the movement that began to take the travel-aches out, until she had got well ahead of Guthrie, who moved with none of her agility. Part way down, she had to pause, waiting for him to catch her up.

She scratched gingerly at her left palm, which still had not scabbed over properly. The scratching brought on a little spasm of pain, and she stopped, wincing. Listening to the noise of Guthrie's slow approach above her, Alia felt a rush of irritation. He moved like an old man. Without him to worry about, she would have been back at Hunters Camp by the second day of their travelling, and here they were, twice that time gone, and still with a full day's hard trek ahead of them.

Alia sighed, shook her head, reined her impatience in as best she could. She only hoped she had not made a fatal mistake in choosing to shepherd this Reeve's son home.

His face was gaunt and white, and he moved with the weak-limbed awkwardness of a man who had not eaten properly in a long while. And he was fevered, plainly enough, and their forced travel through this rough country, and in bad weather, had done little to help that fever. But there was something about him that neither hardship nor simple fever could explain. Each morning, it seemed as if there was less and less of him there, as if he were slowly slipping away from the world in some manner she could not quite grasp. It unnerved her.

And there was that fit, or whatever it was, he had thrown the night she had first discovered him. And those ... blank periods of his when he would simply stop walking, when he seemed to be seeing things none other could see, or listening to voices only he could hear. The idea of a mad Reeve who heard private voices made her queasy. What might such voices urge him to do?

Perhaps it was just such mad voices that had prompted him to manoeuvre her into letting those two bandits go free and unharmed. Of all the stupid things to do ... What sort of Reeve was the man going to make?

It had been altogether too queer, that meeting with the two bandits. How had they managed to miss their mark so completely when shooting at him? And the miraculous snapping of their crossbow strings. How had *that* come about? Thinking on it made her strangely uncomfortable.

And there was the mysterious wrapped package, and that repulsive skull he insisted on carrying about with him. He even slept with the thing. Having been forced at the beginning to accept that he refused to give it the decent burial it deserved, Alia had woven the grass-net shoulder bag in which he now kept both it and the package. By so much had common sense been able to prevail, so that at least he need not carry the gruesome object out in the open, like an offering, and she did not have to look at it.

Alia sighed, shook her head. What might he do, this uncanny

221

Reeve-to-be, when he found himself amongst people once again? How would he react to the power they would hand him? There were moments she felt fully convinced he was quite mad, others when she thought him merely a man shaken out of balance by events, and others when darker explanations occurred to her.

What if he had been ... possessed by something? What if this were not the real Reeve Guthrie Garthson at all, but something else entirely that had taken him over, body and spirit? Such things, she had heard, were possible. Perhaps she was leading something quite deadly into Hunters Camp.

Such uncomfortable thoughts had kept Alia awake nights during this trek. The idea of running off and stranding him tempted her. She could simply slip away and leave him, lost in the hills.

But that meant abandoning what might prove a last hope without even giving it a chance.

Probably he would come round all right once he was returned to the company of ordinary folk and took on the role he had been born to.

She most profoundly hoped so.

Immersed in her own troubled thoughts, Alia had let her attention lapse. Now, with a sudden twist of her heart, she realized that there was no sound of movement from the slope above.

What had happened to him?

Quietly, Alia drew an arrow from her quiver and nocked it. Her heart was thumping in earnest now.

Not a sound from above.

She padded upslope, alert as a hunting hound, listening, sniffing. They had seen no sign of bandits since that one meeting two days back. But now ...

Round a mossy ridge of stone she crept, half on her knees.

Silence still.

Half crouched, she peered round the stone.

What she saw made her gasp. Guthrie was there on the slope above her, unharmed, alone. But ...

But he seemed to be floating half a man's height above the ground!

Alia blinked, shook herself. The mere sight of him floating so impossibly there made her feel strangely sick, and she had to look away, shuddering.

When she turned back, he was collapsed in a heap on the ground, like a child's abandoned rag doll.

Alia rushed to him, confused, outraged, worried, frightened. She let her bow drop – it and the nocked arrow landing with a clatter – and knelt by him. His face was white as new bone, and his breathing came in shallow gasps. He lay curled in upon himself, his eyes staring sightlessly, and he seemed not to see her at all. 'Reeve Guthrie!' she hissed, his given name still awkward on her lips. 'Guthrie!'

He groaned. A long, febrile shudder went through him. Under her hands, he was hot with fever.

She attempted to turn him, and found his hands were locked about the skull. He had ripped the grass bag with the intensity of his grip upon the thing, ruining much of her knotting-work. She tried to pry his fingers away from the skull, to shift him to a more comfortable position, but he resisted all her efforts. Alia felt him twist under her, as if some powerful, invisible thing were tugging at him.

She thought of him floating in mid air so impossibly, and her mind recoiled. She must have imagined it. A trick of the upslope perspective. Something of that sort. He lay in her grasp, shivering and moaning. He must have had another of those debilitating fits like the one she had seen come upon him that first night. She pushed his long, tangled hair away from his face. He was wet with fever-sweat. He moaned, shuddering. She stroked his hot forehead in sudden pity. The poor soul. What terrible things had he undergone to unmake him so?

Looking down at his face, she could see the sufferings of his spirit mirrored in it. His lips were thin and white, and there were lines etched about his mouth. His eyes were clenched up with agony, or despair. It was a broken face, somehow, as if in the process of being remade. She continued stroking his hot forehead, trying to smooth the furrowed lines there.

Perhaps they should lay up for the remainder of the day, she thought. The travel was hard on him, and a rest might make all the difference. A man could travel with a fever if he had to, but Guthrie seemed no longer to have the reserves needed. And as for Orrin and Patch ... she was already so delayed that another day could not make all that much difference.

As she gazed down concernedly at him, Guthrie started to come back. He blinked, his eyes focusing on her.

Alia lifted her hand from his brow, a quick, self-conscious movement.

He started confusedly.

'Easy,' she said soothingly to him. 'Rest easy.'

She reached to lift the skull from his hold so as to put it down and help him to a more comfortable position, but he snatched the thing up, gouging her in the pit of her stomach with a sharp elbow, and turned his back on her, cradling the skull to himself.

Alia gasped, winded by the force of the blow he had given her, and the sympathy she had felt for him evaporated in an instant. Ingrate. She was only trying to help. She felt like slapping him.

Instead, she took a ragged few breaths, reached up her dropped bow, replaced the loose arrow in her quiver, and went to sit on the nearby upthrust of stone. She regarded him from that distance with distaste. He stayed hunched over like a cripple, the skull still clutched to him, mumbling incoherently to himself, or to the skull, or the trees, to the very sun himself for all she knew. Guthrie Garthson, Reeve-to-be of Reeve Vale and all its folk. It was an unfunny joke the Powers had played upon her. He was naught but a hopeless witling. All the more fool, she, to have pinned any hopes upon him.

Once more, she felt the temptation simply to turn away and strand him here. She even got so far, this time, as to rise quietly to her feet and begin to walk off. But she could not do it. The way he was now, it would surely mean his death. She was out of easy choices.

'Come along,' she said to him after a time, sighing. 'Can you walk? We still have a fairish ways to go.'

He swivelled round at the sound of her voice.

'We have to *go*,' she said.

'Aye.' Guthrie nodded, rising shakily to his feet. He gazed at her, shook his head groggily. 'I ... I ... '

Despite herself, Alia's heart went out to him again. He seemed so weak and alone and desperately uncertain, like a lost little boy. She slipped from her stone perch and went to him, putting a hand out to him supportingly.

But he brushed past her, hardly looking at her, as if she were naught but a nuisance. He took a few steps, turned, stood there shakily, clutching the skull still as if it were a vital anchor of some sort. His mouth opened, closed, opened again.

Stung by his rejection of her help, Alia stayed where she was, arms folded, and waited none too sympathetically for what explanation he might give. But no words came. His face went vague. What sympathy she had left evaporated completely as he just continued to stand there, mouth half open, looking stupid.

She turned on her heel and began to head off downslope. 'Come on,' she called over her shoulder. 'Guthrie, come *on*!'

Her using his name seemed to call him back. He looked at her with ordinary recognition in his eyes, shook himself, took two following steps, and fell sprawling on his face with a groan.

Alia turned back, feeling the impatience and irritation in her turning to naked anger. 'If you can't –' she started.

But the sight of him emptied all the anger from her abruptly. He lay like a dead man.

It was a long moment before Alia could move.

She rushed to him then, heart thumping, flung her bow down once again, gathered him in her arms.

Guthrie moaned, a sound soft and piteous as any sick babe's choked little cry. Alia breathed a long sigh of relief. He lived. But his brow burned white-hot now with the fever, and he was soaked with dank sweat and racked by shivering.

She got a shoulder under his arm and levered him to his feet. He was not a large man, but the weight of him was more than she had expected. 'Come on,' she urged. 'We must get you to a stream. Cool water's what you need.' As they moved haltingly off, she bent to retrieve her bow where it lay on the ground. The movement overtipped their balance, and Guthrie tumbled over her shoulder before she could prevent it. He landed hard, sprawling awkwardly on his belly.

Alia lifted him again, more carefully, and they staggered off.

At the edge of a little mossy brook she managed to find, Alia bathed his face and hands and wrists, carried him handfuls of the cold water to drink. It seemed to soothe him, enough at least so that he fell eventually into a kind of troubled sleep in her arms. She half sat there, supporting him, worried. It was no use. The only way they were going to make Hunters Camp this day would be if she carried him. And that she could not. And it might be days before he was recovered sufficiently to travel again without help.

Which meant she either spent the days waiting here, doing what little comforting tasks she could for him. Or she left him and made the quickest way she could down to Hunters Camp and returned with help.

It was a good enough little spot, this. The ground was a soft carpet of brown pine needles. Sunlight filtered through the pines, scintillating on the bubbling water of the brook, warming her back and Guthrie's haggard face. The fact that he could sleep was good. A few days of it would work wonders.

There were worse places to be left behind ...

By mid-day, Alia sat taking a breather upon the rocky outcropping of a ridgetop, gazing downwards into one of the vales between the hills. She had made good time. Hunters Camp was close enough now for her to reach easily before day's end. She only hoped Reeve Guthrie stayed put as she had asked him to. He seemed to understand what she had intended well enough, but fevered as he was, and with whatever else was the matter with him, she was not altogether certain of what he might or might not clearly understand. She had done her best ...

In the wooded vale below her, a lone crow circled the air, flapping slowly. As Alia watched, another joined the first. She heard the *caw caw* of their talk. Then both birds veered, a sudden oaring of wings, and slid off and away.

What had startled them?

Alia leaned forward, peering.

It took her long moments, but eventually she was able to make out the shape of a man working his way through the trees along the vale's far slope. She slid quietly from the rock she had been sitting atop and flattened herself behind it. Chance had given her the perfect vantage spot up here, with the rocky outcrop to hide her and distance and height to give her a view. From her hidden position, she scrutinized the man as he slipped from cover to cover along the vale's further slope.

Raggedy clothing, unkempt, armed with a crossbow.

A bandit scout.

The man's progress was slow and careful, as if he were expecting trouble. Taking a position next an ancient, lightning split pine part way up the slope, he crouched down and gazed about him, near and far, intent, methodical. Alia slipped unobtrusively down behind her rock. No hunter, perhaps, but he had the moves of a man who knew what he was about.

After a little, she chanced another glance at him. He was still crouched as he had been, still patiently scrutinizing what lay before him.

And then, along the way he had just come, she saw another man move through the trees, and another, of the same ragged sort. These two joined the first next the old pine, and the three of them conferred, a whispered conversation she could hear nothing of. After a little, one of them turned and headed back whence they had come, but the other two fanned out and continued on, working their way past Alia's vantage point.

Headed in the direction of Hunters Camp.

Alia stayed as she was, frozen. Her heart thumped in painful anxiety. Perhaps it was just chance. Perhaps this was merely a hunting party. Bandits needed meat, like everybody else. Her sore left hand began to throb. She massaged it gingerly with her right, trying to think what she ought to do. Return to Guthrie? If she had only been able to overhear the men's whispered conference ...

Motion below caught her eye.

A group of ragged men moved past through the trees on the vale's far slope. More followed. She counted as best she could, five, seven ... no, nine in all. Then more movement. Suddenly, the little vale below her was filled with moving men, pouring through the trees like so much dark water, too many to count. It looked like the whole of the bandit horde was on the move.

Headed towards Hunters Camp. Alia's heart clenched. There was no doubt left in her now.

She crawled away from her rock and headed off along the ridgetop. Her nerves told her to run, hard, but she moved slowly and carefully instead, for there was no knowing how far out the bandits might have their scouts. Padding along near the top edge of the ridge, she parallelled the bandits' route.

After a little, she made out the sounds of their passage in the vale below, though she could not see them from here. There were too many of them to be able to move in silence. She pushed on, alert, until she had safely distanced them and the sound of their passage dwindled away behind.

Then she ran for all she was worth.

Alia came down across Sundog Ridge in the late afternoon, making a hasty way through the pines. There was one particular tree she knew from which she could see the clearing of Hunters Camp from afar. She *had* to see.

Reaching the tree, she hung her bow and quiver from a branch, then scrambled upwards. She was clumsy, her limbs stiff with fatigue, for she had maintained a hard pace getting here. But the old pine was mercifully easy to climb, with thick branches like an irregular ladder. High above the ground she hung, panting, and peered out through the pine's limbs at Hunters Camp off in the distance below.

Everything appeared normal, though the camp clearing seemed somewhat less crowded than it had been. Folk strolled about from campfire to campfire, chatting with each other. Alia felt a quick stab of panic. She was ahead of the bandit horde, but she did not know by how much. And those below seemed fatally innocent.

She shimmied downwards as fast as she could, barking her shin painfully on a branch in the process. Grabbing up her bow and quiver, she sprinted off towards the camp.

Across a long, stone-veined slope she raced, leaped a little brook, and thence onwards through the trees, panting, her thighs burning with the effort, her side beginning to be stitched with running-pain now.

In front of her, a man suddenly reared up out of cover. Alia nearly shrieked with the shock of it. But it was one of Hone Amis's Militia, and no bandit. The man called something to her, but in her haste she could not make it out. He tried to stop her, barring her way with outheld spear, but she thrust it and him aside, moving too quick for him to stop her. 'I must warn the camp!' she gasped, dashing on.

She came hurtling into the camp clearing, gasping. Faces turned, shocked at her sudden appearance.

'Where's Charrer Mysha?' she demanded of the man nearest her, a Vale man.

He only stared at her.

'Are you deaf?' Alia demanded. She stood, hands on her knees, her chest heaving. 'Where ... where's Mysha? I have to talk with him. Or Hone Amis. *Now!*'

'Alia!' she heard a voice call.

It was Orrin.

'*Orrin!* How did you ...' Alia stared about her, confused. 'But if you're back, then ... everybody knows. The bandits, Orrin! Why haven't you moved camp? What's *wrong* with you all?'

Folk were beginning to gather about her now, their faces uncertain.

'Where's Patch?' Alia continued. 'What *happened*, Orrin?' She reached out to him, but he stood stiffly off from her, arms crossed, his expression stony.

It was like a slap in her face.

'Get that wretched girl away from here!' Alia heard a familiar voice call out in command. Hone Amis himself came striding towards them. 'Get her away, I say! She'll spoil everything with this commotion.'

At the sight of the Militia Master, Alia froze. The camp seemed totally unprepared, yet here he was, arrogant as always, giving his orders. Surely he could not be blind enough still to deny the truth of the bandit threat? Not now, with Orrin's testimony to support her story.

Orrin ... She looked at him, and her heart clenched. What had happened that he was back here now, and so cold towards her? How long had it been since she had left him and poor Patch?

A Militiaman strode up and grabbed her suddenly by the arm. 'Come along, you,' he said.

Alia yanked herself from his hold.

He grabbed for her a second time. 'Come *on*, girl. Do as Master Amis orders!'

Alia skittered away from him.

Orrin beckoning to her impatiently. 'Do as the man *says*, Alia.' And then, to the Militia: 'Bring her here.'

Uncertain, Alia let the Militiaman drag her over. 'Has everyone gone mad, Orrin? The bandits are on their way. I saw them! And folk are just strolling about here as if all is fine with the world. It's Hone Amis, isn't it? He *still* doesn't believe there's bandits out there that will –'

'Oh, do shut up!' Orrin snapped.

Alia stared at him, shocked.

He turned to the Militiaman. 'I'll take charge of her.'

The man looked uncertain and glanced back over his shoulder to where Hone Amis still stood a little ways away. The Militia Master waved them off irritatedly.

'She won't cause any more fuss,' Orrin said. 'You have my word.' The Militia man stared at him. 'It had best be as you say, hunter.' Orrin nodded. 'It will be.'

'Take her, then. But keep her quiet and out of trouble. Clear?'

Alia expected Orrin to explode with temper at being addressed so by a Militiaman, but he did not. 'Clear,' was all he said. Then he grabbed Alia by the arm and led her away, none too gently.

'Orrin!' Alia started. 'You've got to make folk listen. I saw the bandits. I *saw* them! They were on the move, coming here! Oh, Orrin! We've got to ...'

Orrin hauled her hastily along. 'Just shut *up*, girl! Or you'll ruin it.'

'Ruin *what?* And stop telling me to ...'

He yanked at her roughly. 'Come *on* or you'll ruin the plan.'

Alia tried to yank herself out of his grip, but he held on tight and continued to haul her along. 'What *plan?*' she demanded. 'What's wrong with you, Orrin? And where's Mysha?'

'Gone.'

'*Gone?* Gone where?'

'He went with the others. Master Amis assigned him to –'

'Orrin! What's been *happening* here? *Tell* me!'

'Come *on*, girl,' was all the reply she got, along with a hard yank on her arm. 'Don't be stupid!'

Alia managed to twist away from him, shaken. 'I'm not being stupid! What's *wrong* with you? And where's Patch?'

'Patch died,' Orrin said flatly.

Alia stared. 'No!'

Orrin glared at her. 'Aye. Patch *died*. And where were *you*, girl, when we needed you? I worried over you. I thought you had died, too.' He shook his head. 'But you look well enough to me.'

'Orrin!' Alia said desperately. 'Did you think I'd just ... *desert* you?'

He shrugged. 'I don't know what to think.' He shook his head once again. 'Doesn't matter any more.'

Alia only stared at him.

'We've other things to think on, more important things.' With this, he grabbed her again and hauled her onwards.

Alia was too numbed and confused to try to resist.

'You can play a part in Master Amis's plan, if you just quit your –'

'*Master* Amis?' Alia enquired icily, but the ice seemed lost on Orrin.

'The man gets things *done*, Alia. He's brilliant!'

'The man's an arrogant arsehole,' Alia snapped.

'He's a bit brusque at times, I'll grant you that.'

'*Brusque!*' Alia said unbelievingly. 'How can you possibly –'

Orrin cut her off. 'You haven't *been* here, Alia. You have no right to criticize. Once he understood what was happening ...'

'He accepts that there *are* bandits out there now, does he?' Alia said coldly.

Orrin nodded. 'He gets things *done*, does Master Amis. We've ... misjudged him.' Orrin ran a hand through his red hair, looked about. 'We spend most of our time arguing. Do you realize that? We hunters can't do the slightest little thing without turning it into a lengthy discussion. And Mysha's no help at all. But Master Amis ...'

Orrin gestured at the camp. 'You should have seen the confusion when we got back here, Patch and I.'

'You carried Patch here by yourself?'

'What else was I going to do? With you not –'

'Orrin,' she interrupted. 'How long has it been since that day in the hills?'

Orrin looked at her, brows knitted. 'What sort of a question is that?'

'How *long*?'

He shrugged. 'A double handful of days, at least.'

Alia felt her guts heave. 'No! It can't be more than ... five at most!'

'A double handful,' he replied coldly. 'I should know. It took me three days to carry Patch here. He died on the fourth. Where *were* you?'

'I ...' Alia did not know where to begin.

'Doesn't matter,' Orrin said. 'Not now. Come on.'

They had reached the camp's verge. He pulled her through into the cover of the trees and kept right on going.

'Where are you taking me?' Alia demanded.

'With Mysha, it used to be that we took forever to decide anything,' Orrin said. 'But with Master Amis ...'

'Where are you *taking* me?' Alia demanded again.

'I'm trying to tell you, if you'll just listen! Once Master Amis makes up his mind, he takes complete charge. When he says a thing is to be done, it gets done! Once he recognized the bandit threat, he had folk organized and out of here and packed off to safety in no time at all. And then he presented us with the plan.'

'The *plan*?'

Orrin nodded eagerly. 'He kept most of the Militia back, and those of us hunters who could fight. There's hidden scouts strung out all along the hills to give us warning. The plan is for us to pretend we don't suspect anything. When the bandits come, they'll think we know nothing. But instead of them ambushing us, we'll be the ones ambushing them! It's beautifully simple.'

'And what was Mysha doing all this time while Hone Amis was concocting this *plan*?'

'Mysha?' Orrin frowned. 'Mysha was ... no use at all. He doesn't have Master Amis's command of things. When Master Amis gives an order, folk had best do as he says. With Mysha ... well, you know.

Mysha's never there when you need him. And he could never tell anybody to do anything, anyway.'

'Where *is* Mysha?'

'Master Amis assigned him to the folk that left here, as a guide.'

'*Assigned?*'

Orrin nodded. 'He'd be no use here. He's not a fighter. Best to get him safely away where he can't interfere.'

Alia stared at Orrin, her mouth open. She could not believe she was hearing such things from him.

'Don't look at me like that, girl,' Orrin said irritably. 'Time you woke up like the rest of us have. You haven't *been* here. You don't understand. You didn't see Mysha dithering about like an old woman. And you didn't see the way Master Amis took charge and ordered things. Without him ...' Orrin shrugged. 'Without him we would have never organized anything, and would have been sitting here, still arguing, when the bandits came down upon us. Master Amis has his men under control. He took the situation under control. He even assigned temporary ranks to the likeliest ones amongst us hunters.' He produced a brimless leather cap from a pocket somewhere and put it on. The cap's front bore a small metal badge: crossed spears above a sword blade, with a single star above. 'I'm a Squad Chief,' Orrin said proudly. 'With twenty men under me.'

Alia burst into stuttering laughter.

'This is no funny matter,' Orrin snapped angrily. 'That's exactly our problem. Don't you see it? It's as Master Amis says – we hunters can't do anything without arguing. You won't even come with me without making trouble over it!'

'I'm not making trouble!' Alia managed to twist out of Orrin's grip momentarily, but he grabbed her again, by her sore left hand this time. 'Let go my hand. You're *hurting!*'

Orrin stopped, let her hand go. He glared at her, his face was gone hard and set and as wrinkle-browed serious as that of Hone Amis himself. 'I've got things to do, girl. We all have. There's no time to argue. I'm going to hand you over to a Militia Chief-Major. Then I've got to get back to my own squad.'

Alia started to reply, but he cut her off with an impatient gesture.

'Just do as you're *told*. Otherwise, you'll ruin everything. You very nearly did that already with the scene you made back in camp! What do you think would have happened if a bandit scout

232

witnessed that? Bang goes the deception of innocence we were working so hard to keep up.'

Alia did not know how to respond. She let Orrin lead her further along through the trees in silence. The late afternoon sunlight cast long shadows where it was able to break through into the pines. The air was cooler here, amongst the trees.

In a little, they came upon a group of men, armed with bows, strung out in concealment behind a stony ridge. A Militiaman with a cap badge like Orrin's but with three stars rose at their approach.

'Here's another archer for you, Chief-Major,' Orrin said.

The Militiaman looked Alia over. 'She's a girl.'

'She's a hunter, and a better shot than most of your lot.'

The Chief-Major scowled.

'You know Master Amis's standing order,' Orrin told him. 'Hunters are to be accepted wherever they prove useful. This girl will prove useful with her bow.'

'Very well,' the Chief-Major agreed after a pause, though scowling still. 'But I don't like having *girls* in on the fighting.'

'She's already taken out two bandits on her own,' Orrin responded. 'With her bow.'

The Chief-Major shrugged. 'Will she take orders?'

'I vouch for her.'

Alia felt her face flush with irritation at the way they talked over her. 'I don't see why I —' she began.

Orrin cut her off, took her by the arm and led her away a few paces. 'It's all part of Master Amis's plan,' he told her. 'We'll rid ourselves of these cursed bandits once and for all! Just do as the Chief-Major says. I've vouched for you. It's *my* reputation that suffers now if you cause trouble.'

Before Alia could think of anything appropriate in the way of an answer, he had handed her over to the Militia Chief and was gone, trotting off back towards the camp.

'Take a spot at the far end of the line,' the Chief-Major ordered her. 'And keep your head down and keep quiet.'

Alia nodded, biting back her irritation.

'And don't do anything unless I tell you to. That *clear*? You hunters are far too unruly for my liking.'

Alia kept her peace, and took up the position he had directed her to, hunkering down behind the stony ridge next to the last man in the line.

'Welcome to the war,' the man said softly. He was a Vale man, neither hunter nor Militia. He seemed none too enthusiastic.

Alia merely grunted. She tried to settle herself more comfortably. She felt as if somebody had worked on her insides with a trowel. Everything had happened with such confusing speed. This was not the camp she had left. Hone Amis in total command. Mysha sent off. Orrin singing the Militia Master's praises. It was betrayal.

A sudden noise made Alia whirl. She saw a runner come panting up to the Chief-Major. 'They've been spotted,' the man said. 'Master Amis says be ready.' With that, he dashed off.

'All right,' the Chief-Major said to the line of waiting archers. 'Be prepared. But no shooting till *I* give the order. Is that *clear?*'

A murmur of acknowledgement ran along the line. Men turned to little necessary things with nervous care, adjusting an arm-guard, smoothing an arrow's fletching, setting out lines of arrows point first in the ground for easy reach. Alia did the same, emptying half her quiver. She crouched behind the stony ridge, feeling her pulse begin to speed, wondering uneasily what was going to happen here and just how much of it was really accounted for in Hone Amis's wonderful, all-encompassing *plan*.

Only then, as the long moments dragged by, did she realize that in all the hubbub and confusion and upset of her arrival, she had said not a single word to anyone about Reeve Guthrie Garthson.

XVII

The first indication they had of the fighting was distant cries and shouts. Alia heard somebody scream – a wailing squeal like she had heard pigs make sometimes in the autumn butchering. She shuddered, not wanting to think on what might make a man cry out like that.

The line of archers fidgeted nervously, waiting. There was a long slope of open area immediately before the stony ridge behind which they crouched, but beyond that the screening tapestry of the pines made it impossible to see anything.

'Keep steady, you lot,' the Chief-Major said, his voice a harsh whisper. 'Wait for my order.'

The shouting went on, distant, yet unnervingly clear for all that. Alia leaned an elbow on the ridge's stone crest, scanned the trees, looking for shape, movement, anything. But there was still nothing. She felt her pulse hammering in her throat. Her palms were slick with sweat, and she wiped them across her thighs. The sore left one began to sting suddenly, fiercely. She shook the hand gently, blew on it. The stinging only grew worse, as if somebody had spritzed hot acid over her skin.

'Here they come!' said the man next to Alia. He half rose, drew his arrow, let fly hastily, ducked back for cover.

'*Fool!*' the Chief-Major hissed. 'That's *our* men!'

The man's arrow had gone wide, doing nothing more than send a brace of pine cones clattering to the ground. He ducked his head sheepishly, and Alia heard him cursing under his breath in a steady stream.

'Nobody, *nobody* shoot until I say so!' the Chief-Major ordered. 'Next man who does, I'll personally put a blade through his guts!'

Nobody said a word.

More men were showing through the trees ahead of them now. Peering over the top of the stony ridge, Alia could make out a uneven line of them, falling back at a dogtrot.

Then she heard Hone Amis's familiar voice giving orders, subdued yet near enough to carry. 'Spread out. Keep them from bunching up.'

She saw him come trotting out through the trees. 'Send the whole of the squad up that slope,' he ordered a Militia under-officer who came panting up. 'And hurry them up, or the cursed bandits will see them before they're in position!'

More men were coming out of the trees now, Militia, ordinary Vale men, hunters. It looked like a full scale retreat. Alia swallowed and hoped that Hone Amis did indeed know what he was about.

The Militia Master fell back to the stone ridge behind which the archers crouched. 'Ready?' he asked the Chief-Major.

'Ready, Master Amis.'

'So we wait, then. Adelbard ought to be giving the order just about ...'

In the distance, they heard sudden, excited shouting.

Hone Amis nodded. 'That ought to be it. Think they've got us on the run, do they? Well, let's see how they like our little surprise.'

Alia could make out nothing of what was happening yet, but the distant shouting was clearly coming nearer. Militiamen came pelting out through the trees suddenly. No ordered retreat, this. Men leaped like terrified rabbits, some tumbling heels over head in their haste, picking themselves up, fleeing onwards. From the thick of the trees at their backs came a wild and triumphant howling.

'Something's *wrong*!' Alia heard somebody say.

'Ready yourselves,' the Chief-Major commanded.

Alia half rose, bow up, her heart thumping painfully. Her left hand was throbbing now, each beat of her pulse sending a stab of pain from her hand up through her arm and into her shoulder. It was hard for her to hold the bow properly. She tried simply to ignore the pain.

Ragged bandit figures began to appear now, haring after the retreating Militia, howling in triumph.

'Hold steady,' the Chief-Major said, his eye on Hone Amis. 'Hold ...'

Alia felt a stab of agony go through her left hand, sudden and brutal as a knife thrust. It all but blinded her. Her bow and fallen arrow clattered noisily across the stone ridge.

Hone Amis whirled, glaring at her.

At the same instant, a leaping figure appeared from amongst the trees, howling demonically.

236

Alia stared.

The figure wore a glittering scale-mail byrnie, brandished a long blade that glimmered queerly in the low-slanting forest light. Its face was grotesque: long ivory tusks, great, yellow, inhuman eyes.

The demon-creature that had delivered her from the bandits!

Alia's hand was on fire now, shooting agony up through her arm. She could hardly breathe. Everything seemed to fall away into insignificance, Hone Amis, Militia, bandits, all ... There seemed only her and the creature. It stared at her, great, inhuman yellow eyes unblinking, and it was as if a hook were set in her guts. She fell backwards awkwardly, overwhelmed.

'What *is* it?' she heard somebody ask in a shaken voice.

'Demon!' some one else cried.

A man came flying over the stone ridge, nearly landing knees first on Alia's belly. He scrambled up, cast one terrified look behind him, and raced off. Others followed.

'No!' she heard Hone Amis shout. 'Fools! *Cowards!*'

Alia struggled to her knees, staring about. Militia were fleeing haphazardly towards the ridge. Half the archers had turned and fled already. The demon-creature was howling and whirling the long, glimmering blade over its head in a eerie, luminous arc.

'Hold your ground!' Hone Amis was shouting. He used the flat of his blade upon several men attempting to flee past him. 'There aren't enough of the bastards to overwhelm us if we stand firm. Hold your ground!' The tide of fleeing men slowed, but that was all.

The Militia Master threw his head back and shouted, 'HOLD YOUR GROUND!' His voice cut through the confusion like a knife through jelly.

Men slowed, turned back from their flight.

'Archers,' Hone Amis ordered, 'Shoot! *Shoot!*'

What men were left behind the ridge sent off a ragged volley. Several bandits went down, caught unawares.

A little shout went up from the Militia, but the volley barely slowed the bandits.

'A demon! A *demon* has come upon us!' somebody was still wailing in a broken voice.

'Shut that man up!' the Militia Master ordered. 'Demon or not, he's doing precious little down there other than wave that blade of his about.' He gestured at the demon-creature. 'Look, you fools!'

The creature howled like a lost soul, leaped about in great,

237

inhuman bounds, brandished the glimmering blade. But it came no nearer to the Militia than the edge of the trees.

'Give me your bow,' Hone Amis ordered a man near him. He took aim and let fly at the demon-creature. The arrow splintered harmlessly against the scale-mail, but the creature jumped noticeably. 'Ha!' Hone Amis said in satisfaction. '*That* upset him. He's mortal enough to feel the thump of a good arrow shot.'

Men were beginning to take heart now. More arrows flew, at the demon-creature and the bandits in general. Those bandits armed with crossbows tried to shoot back, but they could not cock their weapons fast enough. A deadly crossfire began to take effect, with arrows coming both from the archers along the stone ridge with Alia and from some hidden group across the clearing she had not known existed.

Suddenly, the demon-creature had disappeared, and the bandits began fleeing away as fast as they could.

'Stop shooting!' Hone Amis shouted to the archers. He raised both his arms in a great, sweeping command to somebody off in the distance. 'After them!'

A swarm of Militia came pouring suddenly from out of the trees above the clearing where they had been hidden. Crying out triumphantly, they raced off in pursuit of the fleeing bandits.

Alia knelt against the stony ridge, her hand throbbing, though more bearably now. She stared about. Dead and dying lay amongst the trees. She heard groans. In the distance, the shouts and cries dwindled.

It was over.

Hunters Camp was filled with jubilant men.

And those in pain, too.

Alia stumbled under the weight of a Militiaman she had half carried out of the forest. He had taken a crossbow bolt through the leg, the bolt skewering the long muscles of his thigh. He was moaning and delirious, and kept trying to wrench the wooden shaft free, but had succeeded only in making matters worse. Blood welled up in a steady flow down his and Alia's legs.

In the camp clearing now, she laid him gently on the ground. Her back was one long burning ache from the weight of him, and she breathed in gasping heaves. 'Sit back,' she told him. And then, 'Leave the leg *be*!' as he worried at it again, like a dog gnawing blindly at a hurt. Blood pooled wetly about him. Alia felt her belly heave.

She tore a long strip from his trousers and used it to re-bind his thigh, trying to staunch the blood flow. But it was hard to find the right placing; the bolt itself got in the way, and he kept pushing her hands clumsily away and trying to tear the bolt out. In a fit of worried exasperation, she had to shove him onto his back, hard, so that he smacked his head. He groaned, shivered, then went limp.

For a terrible instant, she thought she had killed him. But no. He still breathed. She tied and tightened the trouser-binding, feeling little lances of pain shoot through her sore left hand, then stood up, panting, both hands wet and crimsoned. That bolt had to come out, and quick. She looked for help, but there was altogether too much confusion and commotion, with men laughing and weeping and rushing about in the camp clearing. The infirmary was on the far side of the camp from her, she realized, beginning to orient herself now. She whirled, leaving the wounded man behind, and scurried away.

She held her sore hand to her as she went, to protect it from chance bumps in the chaotic surge of men in the camp, and tried to ignore the pain that still throbbed through it. The image of the demon-creature filled her mind. She tried to ignore that, too, focusing on the ground underfoot, the grey wall of the infirmary tent as she drew near to it.

'I left a wounded Militiaman back there,' she said to the first person she encountered, an elderly Vale man with a haggard face.

'D'you expect *me* to fetch him, then?'

'He's a bolt through his thigh. If it isn't –'

'Him and twenty others!'

'He's *bleeding* to death!' Alia cried.

The man put a hand on her arm. 'We'll get to him fast as we can, girl.' He sighed wearily. 'Sorry. Didn't mean to be so brusque. It's just that we're ... so overwhelmed.' The man ran a hand over his eyes, took a breath. 'Where is he, this hurt man of yours?'

Alia pointed. 'Over there by the far verge, next the two big pines.'

'Right. I'll send a couple of lads over in a moment. They'll fetch him back.' Looking at Alia's bloodied hands, he raised an eyebrow. 'And you? Any of that blood yours?'

Alia shook her head.

'Let me see.'

He took her hands too quickly for her to pull away. She winced as he spread the fingers of her left hand apart.

'Nasty little wound you have here. Not healing well, is it?'

Alia shrugged.

'Where'd you get it?'

Again, Alia shrugged.

The man shook his head. 'All right, play coy if you like. But you come back later, you hear? When we're not so damned over-whelmed. It needs dressing properly, this wound of yours.'

Alia nodded agreement, backed away. She did not understand why, but she felt herself cringe suddenly at the very thought of him, or anyone, ministering to her hurt hand. She tucked it away protectively against her breast, curled up like a little embryo, and hurried off.

In her mind, still, she saw the uncanny demon-creature, the great inhuman eyes staring at her. *Inviting* her. She felt completely certain of that, somehow. But inviting her to what? Why? How?

Alia shook her head, trying to clear herself of such troublous notions. She walked to the camp stream, washed her bloodied hands, swilled her face, drank. Her left hand seemed the better for the coolth of the water. She sighed a long sigh, sitting on her heels at the little stream's verge. Evening was coming on now, the western horizon beginning to crimson. It seemed only moments ago that she had come dashing into camp. And now ... Things had happened altogether too fast. She had to find Mysha. There was Reeve Guthrie to be dealt with. She felt a little stab of panic. Too late now to be able to fetch him back before the morrow. And what if some calamity should befall him before then?

Alia stood up, feeling sore muscles complain all along her back and thighs. Her vision went blurry and a wave of dizziness swept through her. In her mind, she saw the demon-creature again, beckoning as he had in the dreams that had haunted her the first days after her escape from the bandit camp. She had forgot those dreams somehow.

She saw him beckoning her now. And then it was as if all that had happened to her in past days came in a great wave to overwhelm her: the Fey; the demon; Reeve Guthrie; the utter strangeness of the world that she had glimpsed under its ordinary face. She felt like a cork bobbing on some great, heaving sea-wave.

Alia shook herself, brought herself out of it like a swimmer struggling out of a rip tide. She shivered, blinked the world into focus about her, stretched sore muscles. She had to find a way to Mysha. That before anything. Time enough later to try to make sense of things.

But looking about, trying to figure the best way to get to Mysha, Alia felt at a sudden loss. From here on the edge, the camp clearing seemed fairly to seethe. Like an ants' nest, it was, full of shouting. A prospect of daunting confusion. She could only look on for the moment, balked by the semi-chaos of it all.

She saw two men – a hunter and one of the Militia – carry in a wounded comrade who could not walk. They bore him carefully out of the trees near her, then lowered him to the ground. Wearily, the hunter and the Militiaman leaned against each other. Alia expected the same haggard expression on their faces as she had seen on the man at the infirmary tent. But these two were ... grinning. Their faces showed an identical, grim look of strange exaltation.

A sudden, louder shouting went up from the camp's verge. Alia whirled and saw a clump of Militia come surging out of the trees. In their midst stumbled a captive. The man's hands had been bound behind him. Alia saw one of the Militia shove him as they entered the camp clearing proper, and the man went down heavily, unable to break his fall.

'They got one of the bastards alive!' Alia heard somebody say nearby.

'What's the point of bringing him in alive?' somebody demanded near her. 'Kill 'em all, that's what I say. Every last mother's son of them!'

Alia looked at the man uneasily, a Vale man and a stranger to her. He had that same fell look of exaltation on his face as the others.

'Gave them something to remember us by good and proper,' someone else said. Alia turned and recognized the speaker, an older hunter, Varry by name. A quiet, sober man, as she remembered, who kept to himself mostly. 'Those villains won't be coming back in a hurry!' he said to her.

'I bet they're still running,' another hunter said, coming to stand at Varry's side.

The two laughed. Both were filthy, their clothes ripped. Both grinned identical, fierce, wolfish grins at her.

A Militiaman who had been within earshot came up to them. 'Laugh all you like,' he said, 'but too many got away. If you hunters hadn't been so slow off the mark up that slope to cut off their retreat –'

'It's you Militia that were the problem,' returned Varry. 'You move through the trees like a herd of milk cows.'

Alia stepped towards the three men uneasily. She had had more than enough experience of the uneasy tension between Militia and hunter, and feared a fight might break out here under her very eyes.

But, to her confusion, the men were grinning at each other, Militia and hunters both. The Militiaman slapped Varry on the back companionably. 'Let's see what Master Amis wants to do with this captive of his.' Both hunters nodded, and the three men strode off, leaving Alia behind, forgotten.

The captive bandit squatted near one of the fire hearths, bruised and battered. A shallow slash marred his forehead, oozing blood into his eyes. He shook his head, trying to blink the blood away, unable to use his bound hands, and looked about him, ashen faced.

An angry murmur went through those gathered round. 'Do for him!' somebody yelled.

'Kill him now and be done with it!'

'Creeping bastard!' somebody cursed.

The crowd edged closer and the man cringed instinctively.

'Kill him!'

'No!' It was Hone Amis. 'This man has information we need. He knows where their camp is up in the Heights. We keep him alive so that he can talk.'

'And what if he don't *want* to talk?' a hunter demanded.

'There are ways to ... persuade him,' said Hone Amis.

A hush settled upon the camp then, but none spoke out against what the Militia Master appeared to be suggesting.

The bandit shivered.

Alia felt a similar shiver run through her. She remembered her own fury at the two bandits up in the Heights, recalled clearly enough how much she had wished to destroy them. But this was different. This bandit captive was helpless. She could not feel the same burning hate she had before. He seemed just an ordinary enough man, vulnerable and shivering with fright.

She did not want to believe she had understood Hone Amis properly. The very thought of it filled her with horror. Had they all gone mad here? She saw the same look still on each face about her, grim and exalted. But there was a new shade to it now; it was the intent look of a cat facing a mouse held helpless between its paws.

Alia shuddered. Was she the only sane one left here? She tried to step forward to where the captive bandit squatted, but the surrounding men formed an instinctive fence against her. There were too many of them. It felt like facing a wolf pack. She backed a few steps away, feeling helpless. Desperately, she stared about in the forlorn hope that somebody, somehow, would come and stop things here. The evening light was dimming quickly now, the forest beginning to turn into a solid, dark wall about the camp clearing. The sun was gone, leaving only a backwash of dying radiance across the horizon.

Through the twilight, Alia saw a figure appear from out of the trees and come padding into the clearing. To her amazement and relief, she saw it was Charrer Mysha, just as if some Power had discerned her need and sent Mysha to her aid.

She dashed over to him. 'Mysha!' she gasped. 'You've got to *stop* them!'

Mysha regarded her with his far-seeing eyes. With a start, Alia recognized something familiar in his gaze she had never seen before; the unblinking look of the Fey, the deep gaze of a man who saw through the ordinary face of the world. She stopped, staring at him, overwhelmed momentarily.

'What is it, girl?' Mysha asked. 'Stop who?'

Alia shook herself. 'Hone Amis and the rest. They're talking torture.'

Charrer Mysha started. 'What?'

'*Torture*,' Alia repeated. 'You must stop them.'

Mysha took a breath, stared at the crowd gathered about the bandit captive, and hurried off towards it.

He pushed through the clustered men, and almost before they knew he had come amongst them, Mysha was standing at Hone Amis's side, next to the bandit.

'You!' Hone Amis said in irritation, seeing him.

'Me,' Mysha replied.

'What are *you* doing here? I gave you orders.'

Mysha shrugged. 'I am not yours to order about, Amis.'

Hone Amis stabbed a finger at Mysha angrily. 'Can you not even carry off the simplest of missions? All you had to do was guide those folk to safety. Instead, you come wandering back here. I suppose you've left them stranded somewheres? No wonder these hunters of

243

yours were such a hopeless lot. With you to look to as an example, how could they –'

Mysha cut him off. 'What is this man doing here?' he demanded, gesturing to the squatting bandit.

Hone Amis blinked. Visibly, he swallowed his anger at Mysha's interruption. 'This,' he said, jerking his thumb at the bandit, 'is a prisoner of war. We captured him in the fight that drove the bandits off. Thanks to me, we have –'

'And what,' Mysha said, interrupting again, 'do you intend to do with this *prisoner*?'

Hone Amis crossed his arms over his mailed chest. 'He has information we need.'

'And so?'

'So we intend to question him.'

'And if he does not wish to answer your questions, what then?'

Hone Amis shrugged. 'We shall have to ... persuade him.'

'Make yourself plain, Amis,' Charrer Mysha said, his voice uncharacteristically hard. 'Just *how* do you propose to *persuade* this man to talk?'

Hone Amis shrugged again. 'That need be no concern of yours, Ser Charrer.'

Charrer Mysha regarded the Militia Master with his steady, far-seeing eyes. 'I would have an answer to my question, Amis.'

Hone Amis looked away uneasily, jerked a thumb towards where the bandit sat. 'That man has information we need.' Mysha made to interrupt, but Hone Amis waved him to silence. 'Information we *need*, Ser Charrer. He knows the location of the bandit camp. He must! Once we know that, we can wipe out these vermin once and for good! Too many of them got away alive and unharmed today. Our very lives, the very existence of Reeve Vale itself depends on our knowing what this man knows. We must get information. By any means, we must.'

'You can not –'

'I can and will do whatever is necessary for the good of the community!'

'But what you suggest here is ... monstrous. You cannot just ... *torture* this man before our very eyes.'

Hone Amis laughed an unfunny laugh. 'If you are weak-stomached about it, I can always see that the ... questioning takes place out of your sight.'

'No,' Charrer Mysha said. 'No!'

Hone Amis made a gesture, and a row of Militia stepped before Mysha, blades drawn, halting him.

Alia tried to push a way through the ranks of the gathered men but they refused to budge for her. Then, craning her neck, she saw Orrin come up to where Mysha stood. She felt a surge of relief to see that Orrin was alive and seemingly unharmed. Surely he would stand by Mysha in this. He must see the insanity of what Hone Amis was suggesting. Surely ...

But Orrin stepped up to Mysha, put a hand on the older man's shoulder, and urged him away. 'Come along,' he said. 'There's nothing for you to do here, Mysha. Let Master Amis handle things. He knows what he's about.'

Mysha pulled back from Orrin in shocked dismay. 'He intends to torture the poor soul!'

Orrin spat. 'Poor soul, my arse! They have already used torture on our folk.'

Mysha stared: 'How do you know this?'

Orrin glanced at Hone Amis, who made a small, encouraging motion with one hand. 'One of our scouts saw them.'

An angry murmur went up from the gathered crowd.

'They have forfeited fair treatment by their own actions,' Orrin went on. 'Let the consequences be upon their own heads!' With this, Orrin grasped Charrer Mysha by the arm. 'Now come *on*,' he ordered, beginning to haul Mysha along as he had hauled Alia earlier.

This was too much for some of the hunters gathered here. A grumble of unease went through them. Several of the older hunters slipped out from amongst the press of men and came to stand at Mysha's side, facing Orrin.

'Leave him be, boy,' one of them said, no one too gently.

After an uneasy moment, Orrin grudgingly released his hold on Mysha's arm.

Alia breathed a sigh of relief.

But then a group of younger hunters appeared suddenly at Orrin's back, supporting him.

For tense moments, the two groups eyed each other, Mysha in the middle between. In the dimming evening, the firelight began to take on prominence, staining and shadowing the men's faces, giving them a strange, savage look.

One of the young hunters behind Orrin drew a knife.

'No!' Mysha cried. 'Put it away. No shedding of blood.'

245

'Then back off!' the young man with the knife snapped. 'Leave Master Amis to do as he needs to do.'

Mysha stood, uncertain. He stared about him. 'What has *happened* here?' he asked lamely.

'We have brought some order to this bedraggled, chaotic camp of yours,' Hone Amis said with satisfaction. And then: 'Now leave us. We have matters to attend to.'

An angry mutter came from those hunters who had gone to Mysha's aid, but he waved them to quiet.

The rank of Militia that Hone Amis had ordered to bar Mysha's way still stood before him, blades still drawn. Short of precipitating bloodshed, Mysha had no option left. Like Alia, he could only stare, along with the rest, as Hone Amis approached the captive bandit.

'You have information we need, fellow,' Hone Amis began. 'I am Master of Militia, and acting Reeve of the Vale. You *will* tell me what I need to know.'

The squatting bandit looked away, saying nothing, refusing even to look at Hone Amis.

Hone Amis back handed him, hard, across the face. It was a sudden, vicious blow, and the man yelped.

'Look at me when I am talking to you!'

The bandit spat blood. He stood up. A fit of shivering went through him, but he glared at Hone Amis defiantly. 'Do your worst, you pig. You won't make me tell you anything. I *know* your sort.'

Hone Amis laughed. '*My* sort? What about *your* sort. Vicious, stupid, lawless fools, trespassing on the land of others. You've no more morals to you than a pack of weasels! You *deserve* whatever you get here this day.'

'And *you* are different?' the bandit demanded.

'Yes!' Hone Amis snapped. 'We are defending our lives.'

'And we have no right to defend *our* lives?'

Hone Amis glared. 'You are no better than beasts! We defend our families, our homes and our property. You *prey* on other people like a pack of vicious wolves gone mad.'

'We defend our lives! Just as you do. No more and no less. Winter will be upon us soon. We need –'

'You need to be driven out of these lands once and for good!' Hone Amis interrupted angrily. 'Your sort makes me sick! You come here, preying on others. Why don't you stay home like decent men ought to?'

'Home?' The bandit spat. '*Home?* Easy enough for you to say. But

246

my home is long gone. Swallowed up by men just such as you, high born men full of their own selfish importance!' The bandit glared at Hone Amis. 'Do you think I am what I am through *choice?*'

'I do not *care* why you are what you are, fellow. What I want from you is information, not whining excuses.'

The bandit looked at the Militia Master in silence for a long moment. Then, slowly, he sat back down. 'Piss off,' he said. 'I shall tell you nothing.'

'Very well,' Hone Amis said. 'So be it.' He turned and spoke to a Militia under-officer nearby. 'Build up the fire. We will need it to be nice and hot.'

But before the under-officer could move, a voice called, 'Enough!' Charrer Mysha pushed against the hedge of blades that barred his way. 'I am coming through,' he told the Militia facing him. 'You will either let me through or spit me on those blades of yours. But I *am* coming through. This has gone far enough!'

The Militia backed a pace, uncertain.

The little group of hunters that had supported Mysha tried to move with him, but he waved them back, pushing towards the weapons held against him alone.

A young Militia man placed the tip of his blade against Mysha's chest. 'Pass no further, hunter,' he commanded.

Mysha did not slow. 'Kill me then, boy, and have done with it.'

The two looked at each other over the length of the blade.

Mysha stepped forward, leaning his chest against the blade's tip.

The young Militia man could not do it. He let his weapon drop, abashed. Mysha strode through the rest of them and came to stand beside Hone Amis and the bandit.

'I will *not* allow you to do this thing,' Mysha said levelly.

Hone Amis laughed. 'Your days of "allowing" things are over, Ser Charrer. *I* command here now. Not you. And what *I* say has to be done *will* be done.'

'No,' Mysha repeated.

'Look about you, you fool,' Hone Amis said. 'How are you going to stop me?'

Mysha faltered. He turned as Hone Amis had directed.

'How many of you stand with Ser Charrer here?' the Militia Master demanded.

The small group that had already come to Mysha's support shuffled forwards – but they had dwindled in the past few moments, and were only the merest handful now. Other than Alia in the back,

247

and she doubted Mysha could see her, there was no one else to support him.

He blinked, took a ragged breath, opened his mouth, closed it again in silence.

'Well,' Hone Amis said, satisfied. 'Now that we have got *that* out of the way, we can get on to what needs doing here.' He turned and pointed to the rank of Militia he had ordered to block Mysha's way in the first place. 'You lot! Now's your chance to redeem yourselves. See that Ser Charrer and his ... friends are escorted away from here. And *keep* them away. Clear?'

'Clear, Master Amis,' one of them replied. Then, 'Come along, you,' he ordered Mysha. 'You heard Master Amis's orders.'

Mysha stared at the blades raised against him. For an instant he stood, firm and defiant, his far-seeing eyes fierce as any hawk's. But there was too much arrayed against him. He let himself be forced away into the gathering dark outside the firelight, his few supporters along with him, defeated.

Alia turned her back on the gathered men, furious, disheartened, livid with outrage. She hurried to catch up with Mysha and his party. Seeing her approach, Mysha nodded to her in silent welcome.

Behind them, they heard the bandit cry out. They halted, staring. It was almost night now, the sky blue-black, the first stars shining delicately. The group gathered about the fire the hunters had just left stood out in dark silhouette, an anonymous mass. It seemed to Alia as if they were no longer men at all, but had been transformed somehow into a single, predatory, dark beast. Her left hand throbbed painfully. She hugged it to her breast and tried to banish the image of the demon-thing that seemed still to cling to her mind.

The bandit cried out again, a long, whimpering wail. Alia shuddered. Beside her, she heard Mysha muttering a curse under his breath.

'Come on, come on,' one of the Militiamen who had been detailed by Hone Amis to run them off complained. 'Master Amis said for you to get away from the vicinity. So get a move on, the lot of you!'

The little group of hunters began to shuffle away. The Militia formed into a fan at their rear a little distance off, herding them.

'Gone,' one of their little group said in a hoarse, shocked voice. 'Everything we had is *gone*! And there's not a single solitary thing we can do about it.'

'No!' Alia responded. 'There is something.'

Everyone looked to her.

248

'Mysha,' she said, lowering her voice so that their Militia guard could not overhear. 'I've ... I've found the Reeve!'

'The Reeve?' said someone.

'Where?' demanded another.

'How?' said a third.

'Hush!' Alia cautioned. 'Not so loud. He's up in the wild hills. I'll explain it all later. We've got to fetch him! With him brought back, Hone Amis will be checked. The Vale folk will return to their homesteads. Everything can go back to the way it *was*.'

Mysha gazed off into the darkness, his far-seeing eyes softly glimmering, like a cat's. He sighed. 'It's too late for that, girl.'

'No!' Alia replied. 'How can you *say* that? With Reeve Guthrie returned, everything can go back to normal again. It *can*!'

'Aye,' one of the others put in. 'Get somebody else around here to give orders other than that cursed Militia Master. Heartless bastard that he is!'

'Can't make things any worse,' another added.

'We've got to fetch him back, Mysha,' Alia insisted. 'It's our only hope!'

Charrer Mysha kept silent.

Alia smiled a desperate little smile. 'Things will be all right, Mysha, you'll see.'

Mysha still said nothing.

'We can fetch him back first thing tomorrow. Everything will be all right then.' She reached out to him. 'Mysha?'

Mysha sighed. 'Aye, perhaps. All right, then. Tomorrow.'

'Hurry it up!' one of the Militia guard called suddenly from behind. 'Over there by the camp's verge. That's where we'll set you for the night.'

The hunters moved as they were directed, but slowly. It was all the resistance they felt able for, given the circumstances.

XVIII

'Here, lad,' Hone Amis said. 'Get some of this down you.'

Guthrie sat up, took the wooden bowl of broth Hone Amis offered him and sipped at it. His hands shook and he spilled the first swallow all down his front, but after that it went more easily. He looked around him, uncertain, wondering why the Militia Master was feeding him instead of Julianna, his father's regular cook. And was he in a tent? Guthrie shook his head, took another swallow of the broth. He had had a dream, a terrible dream filled with death and strange enchantment. A fever dream perhaps.

Guthrie let out a long sigh of heartfelt relief. It felt good to wake once again to his own normal mind, his own normal world, to feel the wholesomeness of the broth seep into him.

Only a dream ...

He blinked, slurped more broth. The light about him was wavery and dim and ochre tinged. He could smell canvas. He definitely was in a tent, then. From outside, he could hear the comings and goings of folk, but in here all was quiet and subdued.

'A hard time of it, you've had indeed, lad,' Hone Amis was saying. He stood watching as Guthrie sipped at the broth. 'You're thin as a rake.'

Guthrie said nothing, concentrating instead on the broth's soothing warmth and rich flavour. He shivered, and the world seemed to shiver a little uncertainly around him.

'But now that's all over,' Hone Amis went on. 'You're returned to us.' He shook his head. 'I could hardly believe it. Didn't even recognize you at first.'

Guthrie smiled weakly over the bowl, confused still. Tipping back, he swallowed the last of the broth and put the empty bowl on the ground at his side. A grass-net carrying bag lay there. There was a rectangular something in the bag, and, on top of that, something round. He reached his hand out, slid his fingertips between the grass knot-work, felt the solid curve of bone ...

250

And everything came back to him with a sickening rush.

The skull.

The Book.

Rosslyn.

The *other!*

Guthrie shuddered. He felt the ordinary world begin to dissolve as the *other* surged up all about him. He clung to the skull with everything he had, feeling it round and solid and sure in his hands' hold, perceiving it as an equally sure, anchoring radiance in the *other* itself.

With an effort, he brought himself back, shaking.

Though still no easy task, it seemed not so hard as it once had been for him to regain the ordinary world. He felt himself beginning to find the first glimmerings of – balance.

Guthrie held the skull close and concentrated on bringing his awareness into order. The utter, depthless maw of the *other* still remained. He *sensed* it, and tried to focus away from it for his own safety's sake. He looked at the tent, at the familiar, bearded face of Hone Amis. He tried to remember how he had come here ...

Bit by small bit, like the pieces of a puzzle, his past came back to him. He remembered the struggle through the wild hills with the hunter girl, Alia. He remembered fever, and awful dreams. He remembered being alone for a time, and then Alia coming again, and other hunters who carried him away through the trees.

He remembered standing unsteadily at the verge of Hunters Camp, Alia next to him, facing a Militia guard, and the guard raising his pike, blocking their way, demanding, 'Who is this ragamuffin?' Meaning him, Guthrie.

'Out of our way,' one of the hunters had said by way of reply. 'It's none of your business who he might be.'

'Don't mess me about,' the guard returned. 'You know what Master Amis's standing orders are. Any strangers brought back to camp are supposed to be ...'

Alia tried to push past, bringing Guthrie with her. The Militiaman lifted a carved wooden whistle that dangled on a lanyard from his neck and blew three loud, shrill notes.

Other Militia came running.

Amongst them, Hone Amis himself.

'You lot!' the Militia Master spat, seeing the group of hunters. 'What are you up to now?' He pointed an accusing finger at Alia, who had an arm about Guthrie in support. 'And who is this scarecrow you have with you? You have another think coming, girl, if you imagine you can just ignore my orders and sneak anybody you wish into –'

'Amis,' Guthrie had said in a hoarse, quiet voice.

The Militia Master stopped dead in his tracks, staring. 'Guthrie?' he said. '*Guthrie?*'

Guthrie smiled awkwardly, nodding. 'None other.'

'I thought ...' Hone Amis came stumbling forwards, flung his arms about Guthrie, and lifted him off his feet in an exuberant bear-hug. He did a little dance, Guthrie in his arms, twirling about. Then he dropped him to the ground again, puffing self-consciously, and stood staring at Guthrie as if he expected him to disappear the instant he took his eyes off him. 'I thought you *dead*!'

Guthrie shrugged. 'I thought *you* dead. All of you.'

'But what happened to you? Where have you *been*?' Hone Amis frowned. 'You look thin, lad. Thin and worn.'

'And you,' Guthrie returned. 'Where is your belly gone to?'

Hone Amis looked down at his stomach, surprised. 'I had no idea,' he said softly.

'Hard times,' Guthrie said.

'Aye, lad,' Hone Amis agreed. 'Hard times indeed.' For a moment he stood as he was, sober and serious and worried. Then he laughed. ''Tis *good* to see you hale and well and alive, lad.'

Guthrie blinked, shook himself, coming back to the present.

Hone Amis was watching him uneasily.

'How ... how long have I been here?' Guthrie asked.

'Two days. You've been fevered. Not yourself.'

Hone Amis offered him a flask of cool water. Guthrie put it to his mouth and took a long drink.

'I had the healers here, bathing you and such, brewing herbs. How do you feel now?'

Guthrie shrugged. 'Better.'

'You had me worried, lad. Raving, you were. I've never seen anything like it. You're yourself again now, though, aren't you?'

'Aye,' Guthrie agreed.

The light in the tent was beginning to dim. Hone Amis lit a little lantern and hung it from one of the tent poles, cleared his throat. 'I ... I've been sitting here, waiting, hoping ...' He stopped, ran a hand over his face, started again. 'There's bad news, lad. Your father's killed. And your brother Garrett. No possibility of doubt.'

Guthrie nodded soberly.

'And your mother, too, is gone.'

Guthrie nodded again.

'You are the lone surviving Reeve.' Hone Amis shook a clenched fist at the tent walls, at the world itself. His shadow, made big by the lantern light, danced on the canvas wall behind him. 'What did we ever do to deserve such a catastrophe as was visited upon us? I tell you, lad, the world is a terrible hard place.' He paused, looked at Guthrie. 'But now ... Now the Powers move with us in this. It must be so! How else should you be returned to us just at the moment when the need is greatest.'

Guthrie took a breath. 'How ... greatest?'

'If we are to survive, we must bind the folk together once more. And as for this cursed bandit scum ... They must be dealt with before the season turns or they'll be like a pack of mountain wolves plaguing us all winter.'

'And so?'

'And *so?*' Hone Amis scowled. 'If we are ever going to bring back the days that were, folk need their Reeve. With you standing before them, they can see everything that was, and everything that will be again. With you to lead them, we cannot fail.'

'Lead them in ... what?'

'First, to wipe out these bandits. Then we can build again. We can ...'

Guthrie stared at Hone Amis, dismayed. There was a blind fierceness now about the Militia Master that he did not remember. It reminded him suddenly, uncomfortably, of the violence he had witnessed in the confrontation between him and Alia and the pair of bandits up in the wild hills. He could not grasp it, this blind will to bring immediate and utter destruction upon others. It made him shudder. 'These bandits ...'

'Must be destroyed.'

'It was always enough, for my father, simply to drive off any bandits that might wander into our hills. A few, perhaps, might have been killed, aye. But never ...'

Hone Amis came closer to Guthrie and squatted down. 'Times have *changed*, lad. We don't have the luxury any more of chastising them like wayward children and driving them away. For one thing, there's too many of them this time. And this lot's different.'

'Different how?'

Hone Amis rose to his feet once more, his knees popping. 'Things

253

have changed, lad. They mean to destroy us, these bandits. It's them or us.'

'But how do you ...'

'Don't be naive. It's the dark workings of the world.'

'But what you are speaking of is war, Amis.'

Hone Amis snorted. 'Call it what you wish, lad. But the fact remains that we must eliminate these scum as quick as may be. Or they will eliminate us.'

'But surely there is some other ...'

'You don't know,' Hone Amis said quickly, 'what they have done. Lost and alone in the wild hills as you were, you can't know. They're no better than beasts. If we don't –'

Behind the Militia Master, the tent's doorway flapped open and a young man in green hunter's dress slipped abruptly in. 'Master Amis,' he said.

'I'm busy here with the Reeve. Can't you see that? I gave orders not to be ...'

'I'm sorry to intrude.' The hunter nodded respectfully at Guthrie. He doffed a brimless leather cap on which a Militia badge gleamed, revealing a mass of carroty red hair. 'It's just that there's a problem developing that you should know about.'

The Militia Master faced about. 'This had better be important, Orrin.'

'It's about the hunters that brought the Reeve in.'

'So?' Hone Amis demanded.

'They don't like it that you've ordered them off to the other camp with the women and children.'

'So?' Hone Amis repeated.

'They're spreading talk, saying you and the Militia and all ought to go back down to the Vale and leave things be here. They're angry, Master Amis. We've about got the most of the hunters here to come around to our side in things now. Such talk as they're spreading about undercuts all we've gained. Charrer Mysha is not a man you ought to ignore. Perhaps you could speak with him. He and the rest are –'

'Bah!' Hone Amis spat. 'You hunters have got to learn to take orders like everybody else.'

'There are those who disagree.'

'Like Mysha? Do you expect me to coddle him and his little coterie of followers? Would you have me ask their opinion before I issue an order?'

'No,' the other responded. 'Not that.'

'What, then?'

'Is it necessary to be so ... unbending?'

Hone Amis scowled. 'You saw where my ... *unbending* got us during the bandit attack. What would have happened if I had "bent" when that ... that sham demon appeared?'

The young hunter shrugged unhappily. 'But –'

'But me no buts! Go back and make sure Ser Mysha and his crew do as they've ordered, and quell these discontented hunters of yours.'

'And how do you expect me to –'

'Just do it!' The Militia Master stabbed a finger at the young hunter. 'You made a commitment, boy, when you joined with me and mine, a commitment to work for a better future. Did you imagine it would be *easy*? You must learn to manage men. Or have I made a mistake in raising you to the rank I have?'

'No,' the hunter said quickly. 'You have made no mistake.'

'Then go back and do what needs to be done!'

'Easy for *you* to say, Master Amis. But how do you ...'

Looking on, Guthrie began to feel more and more dismayed. He saw what these men did, heard what they said, understood their words and movements. But it all felt senseless, somehow. It seemed to him that the substance of their discussion was really only a veil over something else entirely – the push-pull of personalities, the bullying tone of Hone Amis's voice, the sullen face of the young hunter ...

The men's shadows hovered behind them, wavering, distorted shapes thrown by the lantern light upon the tent wall, like two ogres, knob-limbed and angry, long-fingered, unhuman hands raised in queer shadow-gestures. It was like watching a strange kind of theatre.

With his ordinary vision, Guthrie could see the two in front of him, shadow and shadow, man and man, hands and legs and faces. But he had lived with the *other* long enough now to also be able to *sense* what they were. Keeping one hand on the skull as an anchor, he moved on purpose a little out of the ordinary world, using the sense of balance he was beginning to feel to hang *between*. His mind transformed the unsensory knowledge of the *other* into visual image.

The young hunter was all expansion. Like a sapling yearning upward, the woven 'branches' of him all thrust outwards, a growing screen within which hot radiance pulsed.

255

And Hone Amis ...

The Militia Master was a complex, shifting latticework, like a flexible shell. And inside this shell, showing now and then like a little lamp behind protective bars, was a small and vulnerable being, wrapped protectively inside like some strange, ethereal snail in a convoluted shell. The small, glowing being quivered frightenedly at every move of the wider world about it, and the shell twisted and flexed to cover it defensively.

It was an uncomfortable revelation for Guthrie, this half-vision. The Hone Amis he had always known was a tough, skilled, intimidating man. Guthrie remembered feeling small and incompetent beside him. To see how terribly vulnerable the man actually was at his core came as a shock. For an instant, Guthrie seemed to feel things as Hone Amis might: the world was a threatening, frightening, dangerous place where terrible things leaped upon one unawares, against which one had to be perpetually on guard; a place that had to be constantly controlled and contained else it would break out destructively.

And more than this, Guthrie understood how Hone Amis's sense of his self was intertwined with his fear of the world's unpredictable disasters: Amis saw himself as a saviour, as the one clear-sighted man who struggled to protect the rest from the threats they were blind to. Without himself, Amis believed, Reeve Vale would crumble into chaos and disaster.

And anything anybody might say to dissuade Amis from his fear of the unpredictable would simply, for him, be another example of the blindness of others. Every disaster confirmed Amis's beliefs, and confirmed the structure of the self he had constructed.

Guthrie tried not to let the dismay he felt overwhelm him. He could hear the sound of continued debate between Hone Amis and the young hunter, but the words meant nothing to him. He only saw the flex and thrust and parry of the intricate webwork that was each of the men before him. The hunter pushed, expanded, thrusting himself upon Hone Amis. The Militia Master pushed back, his own webbed shell growing harder and darker and more solid as he did so, constraining, controlling, subduing and ordering the younger man. It was like a kind of dance, almost, the two intricate shapes ducking and weaving about each other, or like the way sparring mountain rams might fence.

Beyond the canvas confines of the tent, Guthrie could *sense* the rest of the folk of the camp as they went about. The same, all the same, each an intricate latticework woven over the radiance underneath, containing it, barring it in, each struggling to maintain or increase or diminish, to help or hinder, to create or destroy.

And all of it potter's work.

Folk here had walled themselves off from the moving current of the world, blinding themselves to the great mystery of it. They built these intricate baskets of personality about themselves, and all their energies went into defending these baskets, and everything they did, they did as sustenance for what they had created out of themselves.

Guthrie shuddered. Had he been like this?

They were like folk skittering blindly along on thin ice, totally unaware of the enormous depth of dark water underneath their feet.

Guthrie felt as if he had suddenly been dropped amongst the strangest *creatures*. These were his folk, the folk he had grown up amongst, yet he now felt no common bond with them whatsoever.

He was come here too late.

Once again, he felt the bitter irony of this Reeveship of his.

Almost, he wept.

He was as different from these folk now as a bird was from schooling fish, or a sighted man amongst the blind. He had experienced the *other* and knew all too clearly the depthless depth that underlay all.

'Guthrie,' he heard a voice calling, insistent, worried. '*Guthrie!* Are you all right, lad? Are you *all right?*'

Guthrie blinked, shook his head. He realized he was lying supine on the tent floor with Hone Amis hovering above him.

'What's *happened* to you?' Hone Amis asked anxiously. 'You were always so healthy. Never a sick day in your life. Just like your father in that.'

Guthrie could think of nothing to say. How could he explain anything of what had happened to him?

After the half-vision he had just experienced, he looked at the familiar features of Amis's face and felt he was looking at a stranger. Yet there was no mistaking the genuine concern writ clear in that face, nor the relief as Guthrie levered himself up on one elbow.

'Never mind,' the Militia Master said softly. 'It's exhaustion, is all. It'll all come right no doubt when you've had a few days with good rest and proper food.' He gestured to the young hunter, who hovered nearby concernedly. 'Fetch me that waterskin over there.' With the waterskin passed to him, Amis knelt at Guthrie's side. 'Here, drink some of this.'

257

Guthrie drank, relishing the soothing, liquid coolth of the water.

'Bring a couple of those blanket rolls over,' Hone Amis ordered the hunter, pointing to where several blankets lay piled in the tent's far corner. He bent and lifted up the grass-net bag in which lay the dead Abbod's skull. Instinctively, Guthrie made to snatch it out of his grasp. Hone Amis gave a sudden tug, and the skull spilled out unexpectedly onto the tent floor. Guthrie grabbed at it in a quick, awkward lunge, but only sent it skittering.

In shocked silence Hone Amis and the younger man, furled blankets tucked under one arm, stared at the skull as it rocked to a stop near Guthrie's foot. Guthrie snatched it up.

For long moments, silence held between the three men.

Hone Amis scowled, glanced quickly at the hunter. He ran a hand over his face, uncertain. Then he shook himself and beckoned the hunter over. 'Give them here,' he said, meaning the blanket rolls. With those in his hands, he bent and began to make Guthrie more comfortable. No word did he say about the skull still in Guthrie's hold, nor even glance at it as he packed one of the blankets behind Guthrie's head and shoulders then draped the other over him for warmth.

'Sleep, lad,' was all he said. 'You're back where you belong again. Sleep now.'

Guthrie did not know how to respond. He was *not* back where he belonged. Too clearly, the half-vision he had experienced filled his mind. How could he possibly play the Reeve that Hone Amis and the rest wanted him to be?

The Militia Master stood staring down at him concernedly. It was the same sort of look Guthrie had seen in Alia, and he sensed clearly the need in it.

They *needed* him, these folk.

Or believed they did ...

Guthrie swallowed, sighed. 'Tha ... thank you,' he said, his voice hoarse.

Hone Amis nodded. 'Rest yourself, lad. We'll leave you now. Unless there's anything you need?'

'No,' Guthrie replied.

Hone Amis waved the hunter out, then followed behind, leaving Guthrie alone in the tent.

From outside, Guthrie heard the hunter say, 'Did you see that? He had a *skull* in that tatty bag of his!'

'Hush!' Hone Amis said.

'A dead man's skull! There's something *wrong* with this Reeve of yours, Master Amis. I'll wager he's –'

'I said *hush*, boy! You go and deal with this matter of Mysha and his troublesome little crew, hear? Deal with it quickly and quietly. And you will not breathe a word of what you have just seen to a living soul. Not a *word*. Understood?'

'But what if he –'

'*Understood?*'

'Aye,' the other said after a long moment. 'Understood.'

'I do not know what may have happened to him,' Hone Amis went on. 'Who knows what terrible things he has had to endure? He was always a quick-tempered lad, not steady like his father or brother, and with a wayward spirit. Perhaps he's a little unhinged at the moment. Perhaps ... But he is still the Reeve. And you *know* what the situation is! He is still the only hope we have for stability. And I will *not* have you or anybody else under my command spreading damaging rumours. There's already enough of those about as it is. If I hear that you ...'

The rest of the conversation was lost to Guthrie as the two men walked off away from the tent and their voices dwindled.

Guthrie lay where he was, propped on the blankets Amis had arranged for him. He shifted position, sighed. He wanted to hear Rosslyn's wise voice. He wanted the skull to speak to him, just once, finally. He wanted to be away from this whole bizarre situation, away from folk's hopes and expectations. He did not *belong* here ...

The temptation to run away from it all was almost irresistible. All he need do was slip back into the wild land, find Rosslyn, walk off with her. There was a whole wide world waiting for him; all he had to do was go to it. He could leave everything behind and make a break with his old life and old self that was total, clean, irrevocable.

He would be free, able to make what peace he could with the *other* in his own time and in his own way.

He only need wait for nightfall, then slip away.

In his mind's eye he saw himself doing it, padding through the night-dark camp and away through the trees, looking back from the heights and seeing the camp below, small and far away and no longer of any consequence.

But he remembered the need he had seen on Alia's face, and on Hone Amis's.

Again, Guthrie sighed. He shifted position, rolling onto his side, unable to settle. He closed his eyes, trying not to think of either past or future, wanting only the peace of a little normal, healthy sleep.

The sound of rasping canvas made him start. Rolling over, he saw Hone Amis come ducking in. The Militia Master closed the door flap and moved to stand at Guthrie's feet, hands on hips, glowering, silent.

Guthrie gazed up at him, uncertain.

'You!' Hone Amis said finally, pointing a stiff finger accusingly. 'You were always an impatient, wayward lad. Many's the time your father and I talked long into the night, worried about your flightiness and blessing our luck it was Garrett who was the elder. He, now, was *always* stable. Never gave way to a moment's weakness in his life.'

Guthrie lifted himself up on his elbows, shifting the blanket from his shoulders, shocked at this sudden, unexpected tirade.

Hone Amis pointed at the skull which Guthrie, through unconscious habit, still held and which lay half revealed as the blankets had slipped away. 'I don't know what mad things you may have got up to out there in the wild hills. But you are the Reeve now, and I will not – *will not* – have you acting the fool!'

Guthrie felt a spasm of anger. 'You can't –'

'Don't interrupt me!' Amis snapped. 'With that hunter here, I couldn't speak my mind – can't have the likes of him seeing dispute between us. But now ... now you'll listen to me, Guthrie, and listen well! You have a *duty*. Folk look to you. And the situation here is *far* from settled.'

The Militia Master began to pace, short steps that took him side to side in the confines of the tent. 'There's Obart Pettir for starters. The man's trying to have his idiot nephew Malone declared Reeve. Think on that! With Obart Pettir whispering instructions in Malone's ear all the while! Family Obart were always a niggardly, jealous bunch, and always overly ambitious. Old grey-beard Pettir is sly as any fox. Now he sees their chance. And Merith Roul – the fat upstart – is backing Pettir in this ploy. After the disaster of the Sea Wolves, those two have emerged as a power to be reckoned with. There's no knowing what deal they've cooked up together! I've been playing a hard game, trying to keep them from usurping your family's rights, all the while struggling to instill some order into things here, and trying to deal with this bandit scum in the Heights.

'And then, against all hope, you return to us. And what are folk saying? Obart has his rumour mongers out, putting it about that you've lost your mind, that you're unfit to take up your father's office.' Hone Amis turned and stabbed a finger towards the skull. 'What do you imagine would happen if it became common knowledge that you carried around a dead man's skull? It'd play right into Obart's hands, that.'

The Militia Master reached out for the skull. 'Give it to me! I'll see he gets a decent burial, whoever he is.'

'It's the Abbod,' Guthrie said.

'From the Closter?'

Guthrie nodded. 'Aye.'

'So?' Hone Amis plucked at his beard. 'And why is it you end up with the Abbod's skull in your lap?'

Guthrie looked away. He was sorry he had let even so much information slip out.

'Give it over to me,' Hone Amis said, holding out his hand again.

Guthrie shook his head, not trusting himself to say anything.

The Militia Master scowled. 'Now don't give me any of your boy's foolishness. This is no adolescent game we play! When you were second son you could indulge yourself as much as you liked. But *not* now! Now, you must take up your responsibilities like a grown man. Give it to me!'

'No,' Guthrie said.

'*No?* Think, Guthrie. *Think!* We can return life to what it once was in the Vale, you and I. We can bring back the old stability and order. But *not* if you act like a crazy person. You are duty bound!' Hone Amis gestured impatiently for the skull. 'What possible use is the gruesome thing to you? Give it over, I say!'

'No.' Guthrie struggled to his feet. He could *sense* the fear buried in Hone Amis. The vision he had earlier had returned, and Guthrie perceived the Militia Master as a small, frightened being trying desperately to control all that was threatening. But Guthrie also felt anger kindling in himself. It was an odd, almost welcome feeling, the first ordinary, recognizable human response he had felt in what seemed a very long time. He glared at Amis, remembering how, as a boy, he had felt himself bullied in just such a manner as this: 'Go here! Go there! Do this! Don't do that!' For a moment it seemed as if all the ensuing years and events had never happened, and he was a boy again being chastised for waywardness, on the receiving end of Amis's unwavering convictions about how disaster was to be averted.

But he was no boy now.

261

'I will not give the skull up, Amis.'

The Militia Master stared at him. 'Why, in the name of sanity, *not*?'

'You would not understand.'

'That's right, boy. I *don't* understand. You jeopardize all our futures for the sake of this mad fancy for a dead man's skull. What is *wrong* with you?'

Guthrie shrugged. 'I will keep it well hid.'

'How can you ...' The Militia Master shook his head. 'Have you no sense of duty left *at all*, then? Your father would never have done something like this. Garret neither. Why, if they were alive today ...'

'But they're not, are they?'

Hone Amis scowled. 'And a black day it was for the Vale when they were killed. Decent men, the two of them, ready to shoulder hard responsibilities.'

'As opposed to me?' Guthrie snapped.

Hone Amis took a sudden breath. 'No. Of course not, lad. You're ... different is all. You just don't have the experience you need yet. And you never had the –' The Militia Master halted, swallowed, went on quickly. 'Never mind. With me at your side to keep you from making mistakes, you'll do fine. Listen to me! I know I can be brusque at times, but I know what's best. You must listen to me! Together we can return life in the Vale to what it once was, to the way it's supposed to be. We can even bring these damnable wayward hunters back into the fold. Just do as I say and ...'

'Be quiet!' Guthrie said abruptly.

Hone Amis stared at Guthrie, mouth open in mid-word, shocked.

Too many times had Guthrie stood like this, berated by the Militia Master. The novelty of it had worn thin years since. He had had enough. 'Am I the Reeve or am I not?' he demanded.

'Of course you are.'

'Do I command in Reeve Vale?'

'Of course!'

'Then I command you to leave me, Militia Master.'

Hone Amis merely stood.

'Did you hear me?'

Hone Amis ran a hand across his face, took a shaky breath. He looked as if somebody had just kicked him in the belly, hard. 'What has *happened* to you, lad? You were never like this.'

Guthrie shrugged self-consciously. He had already begun to regret having taken refuge in giving commands. But it was too late now.

The two men stood staring at each other in troubled silence.

Hone Amis opened his mouth, paused, closed it again. He cast one quick, accusing glance at the skull, then, without a further word, turned and ducked out through the tent's doorway.

Guthrie sighed and, sighing, sat down and wrapped himself in the blanket. He ran a hand over the skull's dome of smooth bone. 'Much help *you* are,' he muttered. Then he sighed again. He felt his stomach churning with the remnants of the old anger Amis had brought out in him. But he felt a seductive sort of elation, too, at having forced the Militia Master out. It was the first, the very first, time he had ever ordered Amis about. He felt some part of him swell with satisfaction.

But he felt a little sickened, too.

He shook his head. All about him, at the uncertain edge of perception, he could still feel the inexorable pulse of the *other*, and the echo of it inside his self, and that *other* made all such victories as he had just experienced seem of no real consequence whatsoever. What mattered it who commanded whom when that great, enigmatic *otherness* underlay all?

Once again, the thought of running came to Guthrie. He only need slip away through the night into the wild lands ...

But it was too late now. Like it or not, he knew that for the truth. For better or worse, good or ill, he had become the Reeve.

But he felt like a stranded fish, forced to take charge of a flock of fowl. He only hoped it did not end in utter disaster for all concerned.

XIX

They were met together in council the next morning in the ochre-dim interior of the big pavilion-tent Hone Amis used as a sometime headquarters.

Guthrie sat cross-legged at the tent's far end, facing them all. At Hone Amis's unbending insistence, he had left the skull behind in its net-bag in his own tent. It felt strange to be without the thing, but he seemed able to cope, aside from the occasional sharp pang of unease. He kept his *other*-sense repressed. It was a sort of relief to do so, and necessary here in his role as Reeve. He was weary and still a touch fevered, and things about him seemed insubstantial, a little transparent at the edges. But he was beginning to find it less difficult to keep himself solidly in the ordinary world, as if his self-conscious awareness of his position and the presence of all the folk so close about him acted as a ballast of sorts, to keep him stable. He concentrated on being entirely ordinary, until the *other* and the strange *sensing* that went along with it were only faint, underlying shadows to solid ordinarity. There were moments, indeed, when he felt almost entirely his old self again, and the *other* only a fading memory.

Despite Rosslyn's dire warnings, he did not know whether such a development was truly good or bad; he did not know how to judge. He felt himself two people now, the old and the new, and it was far from certain which, if either, would dominate.

The immediate space in front of Guthrie remained clear, but the rest of the tent was packed, with men pressed elbow to elbow. He focused on the faces gathered before him.

It was a mixed group, with representatives here from the different walks of Vale life. They had separated themselves, staking out their territory by both affiliation and status, physical proximity to the Reeve being the measure. Those connected with or related to any of the Vale's five ruling Families sat closest, those of the seven craft families next, then Militia officers, behind which were packed what

264

ordinary Vale folk were included here, with the hunters relegated to the back, up against the sloping canvas walls. Guthrie was re-remembering the importance of such unspoken niceties; it gave him a shiver of unease to see the geography of power so clearly outlined before him.

Hone Amis sat at Guthrie's right hand, as was befitting his position as Militia Master. At Amis's elbow sat a Militia Chief-Major and a pair of Captains. Several lesser Militia officers – amongst whom Guthrie recognized the young hunter he had met the day before in his own tent – sat together in a closed rank against the angle of the right-hand tent wall, and more occupied the left, forming a thin human fence screening the Reeve. Amis's doing, that, Guthrie thought. Just like the man to anticipate trouble and try to block it in advance.

On the other side of the Militia barrier, closest to Guthrie, Grey-bearded Obart Pettir sat. Next to him was his nephew Malone, about Guthrie's own age, with thin black hair and a face sharp and cunning as any weasel's: he who was being put forward as claimant to the Reeveship, according to Amis. Pettir had a ring of armed men close about him. Nearby sat bald and pudgy Merith Roul. Obarts and Meriths: the first and the last of the Five ruling Families. An unlikely alliance, Guthrie thought.

Representatives from almost all the twelve Families Major were here, though the only established family Heads of the Five to have survived were Pettir and Roul, it seemed.

The group murmur of subdued voices filled the tent.

Hone Amis lifted a hand, calling them to order. 'We are met,' he began, 'to settle our future.' He paused, looking at them all. 'For we now have a future once again, clear and promising and sure. Life will again be what it once was for us. We will endure. We will recover. We will *prosper*!'

Once more he paused, both hands out dramatically now. 'We have a centre upon which to balance the life of the Vale once again.' He gestured to Guthrie with his outstretched arms. 'Reeve Guthrie Garthson is returned to us. Let there be an end to confusion!'

Guthrie nodded to the assemblage, hiding his self-consciousness, keeping his demeanour as commandingly calm as possible. He could see Obart Pettir regarding him with cold assessment.

'We had a good life in Reeve Vale,' Amis went on, 'and we shall have so again. But before we can take up this future that is ours, we must first rid the Vale of this cursed bandit scum that has come to plague us.' He looked at the gathered men once again. 'They must be killed.'

'Every last mother's son of them,' one of the Militiamen agreed, and a general chorus of muttered agreement followed from the Militia ranks.

'And how do you propose doing this?' one of the hunters demanded from the back of the tent. 'How do you expect to find them in the maze of the wild hills?'

Hone Amis snorted. 'You hunters are always putting up objections to everything. We *will* find a way. There's always a way if one works hard enough at things. Look at what we've accomplished here in the past days. And there were plenty who raised their voices against what we did here, too.'

Hone Amis raised his clenched right fist, brought it down with a *smack* against his open left palm. 'We will rid the land of these cursed bandits for good and all.'

'But what of this sorcerer that it is said travels with them?' one of the ordinary Vale men asked.

'Sorcerer ... Hah! A charlatan and a fool, I doubt not. And more fool you and all the rest to believe in him. We have only that – what's her name? that *girl* – to vouch for this deadly "sorcerer".'

'What of that demon-thing, then?' somebody else demanded. 'We don't need to rely on anybody's word for that. We saw it clear enough. What of *it*?'

The Militia Master shrugged. 'If you saw this "demon", you saw what happened. It ran like any coward once I put an arrow to it. You can suit yourselves. Believe whatever you like. But I, I believe in cold iron and my own good right arm. Any fool can style himself a sorcerer or put on a demon suit and try his ploys on the gullible. But a blade in his guts will stop him as easy as any other man.'

Charrer Mysha stood at the back, his head pressed close to the tent's slanting canvas ceiling. 'It is war you are speaking of, Amis.'

'And if it is?' the Militia Master returned. 'Do you think we have a choice?'

Mysha was silent for a long moment, then, in a quiet voice, he replied, 'There is always a choice.'

'Hah!' the Militia Master snorted. 'Fine words, no doubt, but in the real world events do not work in such a way. Do you think these bandits will give us any choice? You can't run away from *this*, Mysha, as you have from everything else. If it wasn't for the stout-hearted lads in my Militia, you and yours would all have had your throats cut long before now.'

Mysha did not rise to the Militia Master's barb. He merely shrugged. 'Perhaps you undervalue our abilities, Amis.'

The Militia Master eyed Charrer Mysha. 'Do you have an alternative to offer? Or are you questioning my right to hold this meeting?'

Mysha shook his head. 'No. But I would like to know what the Reeve thinks on such a grave matter.'

All eyes turned.

Guthrie swallowed uneasily. They had argued this, Hone Amis and he. The naked violence Amis advocated made him queasy; Guthrie could find no fire in himself any more for such violent remedies. But Amis had been obstinate as any rock, insisting on his own measures as the only ones that would bring back the security of Vale life as it had been. Amis had maintained that Guthrie had been gone too long properly to understand the way things were now. Public disagreement between the Militia Master and the Reeve might start a rift that could fragment the whole community, Amis had persisted. Which would do nobody any good, he had added, except perhaps Obart Pettir and his scheming.

There was no way of changing Amis's views, and no way that Guthrie could imagine to manage without him, so he had been forced to agree – temporarily, he told himself. He took comfort from the fact that not even Hone Amis could push things through so easily as all that. Mysha's query was but the beginning, surely. There were too many level-headed men and women here.

Guthrie was uncomfortably aware that all eyes were upon him. He took a breath, felt a little fever-shiver quiver through him. Holding himself steadily in the ordinary world, he gazed at the gathering with as much quiet assurance as he could muster. 'The Militia Master speaks for me in this matter,' he said, repeating the words he and Amis had agreed upon. But he added, 'However, I would not wish to see such a decision made without healthy debate.'

Hone Amis took a sharp breath, shot a quick, hard glance at Guthrie, then recovered himself. 'Which debate we are engaged in,' he said. 'Are you content now?' he demanded of Charrer Mysha and the hunters in general. 'I speak for the Reeve in this matter.' He nodded in satisfaction. 'We shall rid ourselves of this bandit scum.'

'Easily said, Militia Master,' one of the hunters piped up, a slim, grey-haired woman who half rose on her knees. 'But you are talking death here, death and pain and blood, for us as well as them.'

'Are you frightened, then?' Hone Amis countered.

The woman shrugged. 'Aye, I am frightened. As any sane person would be by what you are proposing.'

Hone Amis snorted disgustedly, shook his head, glared at Charrer Mysha, who was still standing. 'I told you not to bring any of these women here.'

Mysha shrugged.

'Women are no use to a council such as this. They will always plead for caution rather than bravery. They think with their wombs, that's the problem. Men think with their balls.'

It was the hunter woman's turn to snort derisively. 'That is *exactly* the problem!'

'Enough!' Hone Amis snapped. 'Think, the lot of you. *Think!* What other option have you to offer me? Will these bandit invaders just walk away on their own? Would you have me offer them our lands for the taking? Or do you suggest *we* retreat and give them free rein with the land that is ours?

'Can we not try talking with them?' one of the hunters suggested.

Hone Amis laughed. 'Talk? *Talk?* Do you suppose they will just leave because you ask them to?'

'But surely,' the same hunter went on, '*surely* there's some way we could ... could negotiate.'

'Negotiate *what?*' Hone Amis demanded. 'This is *our* land! They are nothing but scavengers. Do you really think that such as they will sit quietly by and listen to you *talk?* They'd as soon slit your belly open!'

The Militia Master glared at the gathered assembly. 'Think *sensibly*, the lot of you! These bandits must be routed. What alternatives can any of you offer me to accomplish that other than the use of the blade? *What?*'

Silence.

'There are times,' Hone Amis continued, 'when nothing save the sword will supply the answer.' He struck his right fist into his open left palm once more, a sharp *clupp*. 'We will cut these rag-tag bandits *down!* With Reeve Guthrie returned to us, we have the spirit to do it.'

The Militia Master paused, leaned forward. 'We who meet here are more than the common herd. For every one of you here, there's twenty more outside waiting to hear what we decide. *We* are the

268

decision makers, the leaders. And I speak now to you as leaders, all. It is spirit that counts in any contest of arms. I'll take a dozen men with spirit against half a hundred whey-faced grovellers any day. With a Reeve to inspire them once more, to remind them of all that once was here in the Vale, and what could be again, the common folk will fight like wild cats. And so shall we all! None can stand against such a force as we will make.'

An excited murmur came from the Militia ranks, spreading to some of the Vale folk and even a few hunters.

'There's nothing especially inspiring about your Reeve at the moment,' Obart Pettir's nephew Malone said, putting an end to the murmuring.

Hone Amis glared. 'Mind your tongue, boy. The Reeve has been through hard times. Anybody with half an eye can see that.'

'Mind your own tongue, Ser Amis,' grey-bearded Obart Pettir warned. His voice was soft, but sharp and cold as a blade of hard ice. 'My nephew is no homeless witling, to be chivvied so.'

Guthrie leaned forward, but Hone Amis made a surreptitious hand motion Guthrie remembered all too well: *leave off*, it meant. Guthrie kept his silence, not nearly sure enough of himself yet in such a public setting.

'Neither is the Reeve one to be publicly belittled in the manner your nephew just attempted, Ser Obart,' Hone Amis said. 'I trust you will warn him to keep a more civil tongue in future. He's only a foolish boy, and obviously knows no better yet.'

Malone half rose, his weasel's face darkened with sudden anger.

'We wouldn't want,' Hone Amis continued calmly, 'for him to set a bad example to other foolish boys, now would we?'

Obart Pettir said nothing. He motioned for Malone to sit, a quick peremptory gesture that the younger man obeyed after a moment's hesitation. Then Obart Pettir sat quiet, regarding Hone Amis with narrowed eyes, combing his fingers slowly through his grey beard, his expression inscrutable.

'If you have *quite* finished,' Charrer Mysha spoke up, 'I would like to ask a question.'

'Go ahead,' Hone Amis responded.

Mysha spread his arms in a gesture that took in all of the close-packed seated gathering. 'You insist we must all go to war with these bandits. But what if some of us do not wish to do so?'

'They are either with us or against us. And will be treated accordingly. Simple as that.'

269

Mysha stared. 'Meaning what, exactly?'

'All will fight, no exceptions.'

Mysha shook his head. 'You would force men to fight against their own judgement, against their own will? That's *madness*! The only fair course is to –'

Hone Amis laughed. 'Fair? Where have you been living, Mysha? Was it *fair* what the Sea Wolves did? Or these bandits? Was it *fair* that we should have our fields and homes destroyed?'

'But you cannot simply –' the hunter woman who had spoken earlier began.

Hone Amis cut her off. 'The world is a dangerous place, woman. An *unfair* place. I do what I must to make it safe as I can for me and mine.'

At Hone Amis's side, the young hunter/Militiaman Guthrie recognized said, 'Master Amis I don't think you should –'

'Are you presuming to give me *advice*, boy?' the Militia Master snapped at him.

The other's face flushed.

'Do you think you know better than I what needs to be done here?'

He shook his head.

'Do you question my judgement?'

'No.'

'Or my motives?'

'No,' again.

'Good.' Hone Amis smiled. 'That matter is settled, then.'

The younger man subsided, scarlet faced, breathing hard.

Guthrie looked on with growing unease. Amis was bullying his way through this council far too roughly.

'Does anybody else,' the Militia Master demanded, 'wish to question my judgement on this issue? Does any of you have a workable alternative to what I am suggesting? Some way of ridding ourselves of this bandit threat without resorting to the blade?'

Charrer Mysha started to say something, but Hone Amis cut him short. 'A *workable* alternative, I said. Not some half-baked, idealist's dream.' He glared at Mysha, then regarded the rest of the gathering enquiringly.

There was some shuffling, a few coughs, an unintelligible murmuring. Mysha looked grieved but kept his peace.

'No? Nothing, then?' Home Amis demanded.

Silence now.

Hone Amis nodded, satisfied. 'Good. Now, if there are no further unnecessary interruptions ...' He gestured to the rank of the hunters. 'None? Good. If you would care to sit down, Ser Charrer, we can begin to lay our plans.'

'But surely ...' Mysha began. He scanned the gathered company, a desperate, imploring stare. Save for the few hunters at his side, there was no support for him. Slowly, he sank back down.

'If we do this right,' Hone Amis continued, 'we'll have these bandits eliminated before the snows come, and then we can get back to our proper lives again. Now, we know where their base camp is. The captive we took told us. This is how I've planned it ...'

Guthrie felt his heart sink. War. Hone Amis had somehow accomplished it before any of them had had time to comprehend its full meaning. Guthrie leaned forward, hands out.

But nobody was paying him any mind.

The Militia Master had turned to the Militia Captain who sat near him. 'Captain Loew here has a chart we have prepared. We will divide men into units, each under the command of an experienced Militia officer. It is imperative – *imperative* that all commands be obeyed.' He looked at the hunters again. 'Do you understand that, you lot? A combat unit must act as a single entity, the commander the head, the men-at-arms the limbs. The head commands. *Only* the head. And as long as ...'

Guthrie felt himself begin to drift. He felt dismayed, weary and sore still, and the fever-shivers were coming upon him again. But there was naught to do save sit as he was, keeping himself as composed as might be, keeping up appearances; having committed himself to being Reeve, Reeve he must be. He felt eyes upon him: the assessing, cold regard of Obard Pettir; Malone's predatory stare; the ambivalent glances of the hunters; the Militiamen's possessive gaze; the seeking stare of the ordinary Vale men, looking to him for reassurance. And every now and then Hone Amis would look at him, no more than a quick flick of the eyes, a complex look composed of unease, shared purpose, halting suspicion.

Guthrie swallowed, keeping himself firm. He could half *sense* the dynamics of what was happening around him, the give and take of the intricate baskets of energy that defined each man or woman in the tent. It was like some incredible, complicated dance, or the boiling of a complex mix of currents in deep water.

'And so, if we keep to our original intent ...' Hone Amis was explaining.

271

Guthrie tried to concentrate, to keep from slipping away.

Eventually, it was decided.

They would carry the fight into the hills, make war upon the bandits in their own wild territory until there were none left.

Guthrie watched the most of the men and women file out of the tent, some of the hunters still muttering their dissatisfaction. He sympathized with their discontent. Hone Amis had pushed through this war of his, letting nobody gainsay his plans, and now they were committed. Blood and dying and destruction would come of it. He tried to feel Amis's righteous anger at the bandits, but could not. Though he was almost his old self again, some parts of him seemed unable to come back. He could ignore the *other*, but never quite enough to forget entirely. And that trace of reluctant memory kept him from sinking entirely into his previous self.

The last of the hunters were gone. Guthrie could not help but wonder if they would indeed obey Hone Amis's instructions. Guthrie sighed. They were a wild-hearted, unpredictable lot. Not a one of them but looked a man in the eye straight. He thought, suddenly, of Alia. With so much happening to him since his return, he had all but forgot her till now. She was of that same mould, possessed of a real will. Rosslyn would have liked both her and her kind; they had the same straightforwardness as she.

The thought of the old Closterer made Guthrie pause. What would she think of the goings on here? She would laugh at his Reevely pretensions, no doubt, quote something from her precious *Book* at him.

For a moment, then, it was as if he heard her voice, reciting:

> Nothing's what it seems to be,
> Neither you and neither me.
> There's not a river flowing free
> But cries its yearning for the sea.

Guthrie shook his head, chuckled thinly. He had spent too long under her influence, and was become infected with her penchant for quoting obscure verse.

Cries its yearning for the sea ... The line echoed in his mind, and for a moment he was completely overwhelmed by a bitter envy for all such rivers, beasts, beings as could live out their days in simplicity, carried to fulfilment by the great, hidden currents of the world.

He was neither fish nor fowl, as the old saying had it. He might yearn for the sea ... but what sea was it? He had undergone such experiences as had changed him for ever, yet at the same time had not changed him enough. Caterpillar, or moth? He did not know which he was to be, or what manner of resolution was possible.

He felt the world tremble, and set himself to deny it, to remain in the ordinary, stable. He must maintain his self as Reeve, nothing more. He had managed well enough all through the lengthy council session and was not about to let himself lapse now.

'Reeve?' he heard a respectful voice ask.

Looking up, he saw the men that had remained behind, mostly Militia, were staring, waiting soundlessly on him.

'Are you ... all right, Reeve?'

Guthrie nodded. 'Aye, I was just lost in reverie is all.'

'Planning,' Hone Amis put in quickly.

'*Planning?*' bald Merith Roul snorted in disgust. 'The boy's a witling, Amis! It's time you conceded it.'

A shocked silence greeted this.

'Well, don't all stare like stupid, shocked geese. It's about time *somebody* said it!' This from Obart Pettir, the first words he had spoken since his initial exchange with the Militia Master.

'Now you listen, Ser Pettir,' Hone Amis started, moving in on the other man.

'No!' Obart Pettir replied. '*You* listen! It's all very well to put up this boy as a figurehead. The ordinary folk need such a one. But here, amongst us who make the decisions that *matter*, let there be no more pretence. The boy's a witling, as Ser Roul so aptly puts it.' He gestured disgustedly at Guthrie. 'Just look at him. Skinny as any scarecrow, blinking stupidly like a mole caught in sudden daylight.'

Guthrie swallowed, not knowing how to respond.

Obart Pettir went on quickly. 'I say, let him stand before the ordinary folk as Reeve, but amongst us, let him have no say in our council. His brain's been addled. Such as he had in the first place. He was never the man either his father or brother were.'

Guthrie felt the sting of that. It evoked old memories, painful memories. Always, it seemed, he had lived in the shadow of his father and his brother.

'And when we have matters with these hill bandits well enough in hand,' Obart Pettir continued, 'we can discuss more ... permanent arrangements for the Reeveship.'

'This has gone *quite* far enough,' Hone Amis snapped. 'If you don't stop this foolishness, I'll –'

'You'll *what?*' young Malone demanded. He made a quick, slight motion with one hand and a gleaming blade appeared. Obart Pettir motioned to the little group of armed men about him and they rose as one, hands on the hilts of their sheathed, short-bladed swords.

Hone Amis's face crimsoned. 'What is *this?*' He glared at Malone. 'Have you gone *completely* mad? And you accuse the Reeve of being the witling!'

'These are hard times, Amis,' Obart Pettir said. 'I mean you personally no especial ill will, but if we are to survive here we must make hard decisions. And I will *not* stand by while this witless boy of yours –'

'Enough!' Guthrie said. Under the pressure of the moment, he had inadvertently slipped a little into the *other*. Obart Pettir shone like a blazing torch to Guthrie's *other*-sense, and he perceived in a sudden rush how it was with Obart Pettir: the man was getting on in years, and in some ways, like Amis himself, convinced the world was a dangerous, untrustworthy place, and unconvinced that others could take care of matters as well as he; and he was, even more than Amis, a man used to having his own way in things. Guthrie could *sense* how it had been for the man, the terrible unexpectedness of the Sea Wolves' raid, followed by the bandit threat, Pettir's family scattered, his property razed, the whole of his world toppling. In his own mind, Pettir had put up with enough shilly-shallying. It was time to put things in order. And if his own family benefited more than others, so much the better.

Guthrie glanced across at Hone Amis, who stood impotently, on his face a expression of shocked anger. The Militia Master returned his glance, but it was an empty look, as if he had already decided there would be no help to be found.

For a moment, Guthrie felt overwhelmed by the futility of it all. He was not, could never be, the Reeve. Almost, he gave in to it with relief. Let them squabble amongst themselves like cats. All the easier, then, for him to slip away.

But it was not that simple. Too late, already, for him to take that easy way out: he had committed himself too far, was too much his old self again, was become Reeve for better or worse.

Malone glared at Hone Amis and started to say something.

'You will be *quiet*, Malone,' Guthrie commanded.

Malone started. He stared at Guthrie. His eyes went wide with surprise, then narrowed sharply.

Hone Amis tried to intervene, but Guthrie waved him off.

274

Levering himself to his feet, Guthrie focused his gaze levelly on Obart Pettir. He had witnessed his father do this many a time, drawing out the silence, glaring at some man or other who had offended him. Guthrie had himself been the recipient of such hard, silent stares and recalled clearly what it felt like to be on the receiving end.

For long heartbeats, Pettir returned the stare, steady and unblinking. But Guthrie's gaze was implacable, and eventually the older man faltered, let his eyes drop uncertainly.

'Did you,' Guthrie began then, 'or did you not swear your loyalty to my father, Ser Pettir?'

Obart Pettir shrugged, muttered something too low for any to hear.

'I did not hear you, Ser Pettir,' Guthrie said.

'Aye,' Obart Pettir snapped. 'I did.'

'Did what, exactly?'

'Swore ... loyalty to Reeve Garth.'

'And ...' Guthrie prompted.

'And to his sons and his sons' sons.'

'And is this how you abide by your oath, Ser Pettir? Your *oath?*'

The older man flushed.

Guthrie kept his gaze fixed on Pettir, letting the silence stretch once again. Somebody coughed, softly. One of Pettir's men shifted uneasily, clunking his half-sheathed blade inadvertently against a tent pole.

Guthrie remembered his father and Garrett, his brother, discussing the Obarts once. 'A hard-hearted lot,' his brother had said. 'They'd burn their own mother at the stake if they thought they could gain from it.'

His father had laughed – he had always laughed easily around Garrett – and replied, 'Aye, a hard lot indeed. And far too ambitious. And far from stupid. But the Obarts have one virtue. They stand by their word. That is their pride. Remember that.'

Guthrie stared at grey-bearded Obart Pettir, remembering his father's assessment. 'Witling, you called me,' he said eventually. 'In what manner are you competent to judge me, Ser Pettir?'

Obart Pettir eyed Guthrie uncertainly. He said nothing.

'Did you, then, follow me into the wilds and witness all I have undergone? Did you talk with me, then? Spend time in conversation with me in order to understand what I have experienced?'

To this, Obart Pettir gave no answer.

'Then it occurs to me that you might have had some especial

275

reason for such a hurried judgement of me. Such a *convenient* judgement of me. Here you stand, ringed round by your own private guard, making threats at me and mine. I have to ask myself why, Ser Pettir. And the answer that occurs to me is far from pleasant.' Guthrie lifted his chin, gesturing at the armed men who still stood protectively about Pettir. 'You look to me like a man with ambitions. Like a man who fancies he sees a chance to advance the fortunes of his family at the expense of others. Is it *this* that the much vaunted Obart oath my father valued so much has come to? Is your word worth no more than this, then, to be dispensed with when it suits you for convenience's sake?'

The barb went home. Guthrie could see it in the flush that coloured the older man's face. 'My father always rated the honour of your family highly, Ser Obart. Am I, then, going to have to change his assessment of you?'

Obart Pettir ran his fingers through his beard in a little nervous gesture. 'I ... I do not know what to say, boy. You ...'

'Reeve,' Guthrie said evenly. 'You will address me as "Reeve". Unless you have reasons to do otherwise.'

Obart Pettir hesitated, glanced quickly about him. Bald Merith Roul had backed away suddenly. Pettir's own men were looking uneasy and confused, and, surrounding them now, were Militia, a ring of sheathed but ready blades. Pettir fingered his beard, swallowed. 'I have no such reasons ... Reeve.'

Guthrie nodded. 'I thought you would not. I am Reeve, Ser Pettir. Make no mistake about that. I *will* take up my father's stewardship.' He looked around at the company gathered in the tent. 'I think it time for a renewing of oaths.' He smiled at Obart Pettir. 'And to you, Ser Pettir, as Head of Family Obart, and to your nephew Malone, I give the privilege of being first to do so.'

Obart Pettir hesitated, glanced about him, then marched forward and bent himself stiffly on one knee before Guthrie. 'By my red blood and ... and white bone,' he began, the words coming only haltingly, 'I swear to be ... to be true to you and yours, to your sons and sons's sons, while ... breath ... remains in me.'

It had begun as a grudging move on Obart Pettir's part, but the intrinsic power of the words, and of the ritual itself, somehow began to work its magic upon them all: this was the bond that held the Families together, held the very Vale itself together, renewed each spring and with each new generation, a mutual swearing of allegiance and support and responsibility.

276

From his half-kneeling position, Obart Pettir held out his two hands, clasped together, and Guthrie took them both in his, enfolding them.

'I am your man, Reeve Guthrie Garthson,' Pettir said, his voice hoarse. 'I and mine.'

'By blood and bone and breath,' Guthrie responded, 'I give my oath in return: to never misuse you or yours, to never lose sight of the good of the whole, to never forget my position.'

Guthrie bowed his head. 'By the great Powers that flow through the world, let it be so.'

'By the Powers,' the rest repeated. 'Let it be so.'

Guthrie released Obart Pettir's hands and the older man raised up, looking more than a little dazed, staring at Guthrie as if he had become something entirely other than what Pettir had expected.

Hone Amis was quick to step into Pettir's place. 'By my blood and bone, I swear ...' he said, repeating the words.

'By the Powers ...' they all ended.

And so it went, Malone next, stiff and angry but of necessity compliant. Each of the men there swore their allegiance, the simple Militiamen swearing for themselves, those, like Obart Pettir and Hone Amis who were Family Heads, swearing for themselves and all that was theirs. And word went out, quietly; others arrived, coming into the tent in ones and twos and threes, half kneeling, renewing the oath they had given Guthrie's father, renewing the oath they had given to their community and to their future together. The air in the tent came alive. Men wept, softly. Men might at such a moment.

Guthrie felt his own eyes wet with tears.

When it was finished, he stood in the the silent tent, shaken, surrounded by those men that still remained – Obart Pettir and his crew not among them. Guthrie's heart was filled to bursting, as were the hearts of all the rest still here, if their glowing faces were anything to go by. But, looking at those shining, too-open faces, Guthrie shivered. He felt a sudden disquiet, like a splash of ice-water through his guts. He had not intended any such occurrence as this. His demand for oath taking had been out his mouth before he had thought.

No way back, absolutely no way back now.

He was caught as surely as any beast in a hunter's snare. And a part of him despaired, knowing all too well how precarious his self was at the moment, feeling in his belly that everything would come to terrible grief. But another part of him exalted – he could not help it – for this was every wish of his come true, and he was become Reeve indeed.

A man came backing in suddenly through the tent's doorway, trundling a small barrel.

'Ah, good!' Hone Amis exclaimed. 'Broach it.'

The man tipped the barrel over and drove a spigot into it. Around his waist a string of little wooden cups dangled.

'Something we managed to save,' Hone Amis explained to the company in the tent. 'I think the occasion calls for it.'

With a little *gloop galloop* the first of the liquor spurted out into a cup.

'Yours, Reeve,' the barrel-man said, offering the cup.

Guthrie sipped the fiery stuff, gagging. It brought tears to his eyes.

The company laughed together at the sight and turned to the barrel.

Guthrie sipped gingerly at his cup. But those about him showed no such reticence. Toasts were begun, men sharing cups, lifting them to the bright future they all envisioned together here.

'Death to all bandits!' somebody proposed.

'And a long life to our Reeve.'

And then somebody said, 'What about the hunters, then? Are they to deny our Reeve his rightful due? None of *them* have taken their proper oath.'

'Not so!' answered one or two.

'*You* lot don't count!' came the reply. 'You're with us now. It's the others, like those who skulk about with Charrer Mysha.'

'Aye,' a Militia under-officer said. 'Where *is* Ser Charrer Mysha?' He emptied the cup in his hands, held it out for more. His cheeks were flushed. 'Why has he not taken his oath? He is become Head of Family Charrer now, what with the Sea Wolf killings. Curse them! Mysha should be forced to take his proper oath like all the rest.'

'Aye! Bring the hunters here and make them take the oath.'

'At bladepoint, if need be! And if they refuse ... why then we'll –'

'Enough!' Guthrie cried, appalled at the sudden turn things had taken.

Men stared at him.

'There will be,' he said slowly, '*no* forcing of *anything* upon *anybody*.'

'But ...' a dozen voices began. Men began calling out all at once in a confused hubbub.

278

'Be *quiet*!' Guthrie snapped. 'All of you.'

Men stared at him, abashed.

'What good is an oath,' Guthrie demanded, 'if it is forced from a man at bladepoint? Has this liquor addled your wits entirely?'

'They're a surly, rude lot, those hunters,' somebody called from the back of the tent. 'Think they're so high and mighty. They deserve being taken down a bit, they do!'

'Aye!' others joined in.

'Take them down!'

Guthrie held up his arms. '*Enough*, I say!'

Silence.

'Get out,' Guthrie said, suddenly sickened by it all, by the stinging taste of the liquor on his tongue and the uncomfortable fire it had lit in his belly, by the pettiness of the emotions the liquor had roused in those about him, by the whole messy, confused business of men's hearts entirely. He felt a great surge of dizzy nausea stab through him, felt the implacable, dread tug of the *other*.

'Get *out*,' he said, his voice hoarse. He clutched his head in his hands, the tent about him pulsing in and out of focus.

Men stared.

'You heard the Reeve,' Hone Amis called. 'Clear the tent. Now. *Now*! Clear the tent, I say!'

Guthrie sank to his haunches, ignoring the confusion about him, intent purely on holding himself together in the ordinary world. He felt a momentary, panicky pang of regret at having left the skull behind in his own tent ...

But it was only a shallow slip, this one. He was grown familiar with the process.

When it had passed, he looked around to find the tent empty save for Hone Amis, who stood gazing down at him uneasily. 'You all right, lad?'

'Aye,' Guthrie responded, levering himself back onto his feet. 'Just the remnants of the fever. And the liquor.'

'You sure?'

Guthrie nodded.

The Militia Master crossed his arms over his barrel chest and regarded Guthrie thoughtfully. 'You handled yourself well here this day.'

Guthrie shrugged, smiled weakly. 'The send-off I gave them was nothing to boast of.'

Hone Amis waved that aside. 'Unsheathe the blade, your father

279

used to say. Show them a little iron now and again. You did that. Gives men something to think about when they get out of hand like that.' Hone Amis shook his head. 'My fault, I'm afraid. I should never have given orders for the liquor to be broached.' He slapped Guthrie on the back. 'You handled it well, lad. Better than I could have hoped.'

Guthrie shrugged again, self-consciously.

'But something has to be done about these hunters. The men were right enough about that. And Charrer Mysha must be brought into line. They're naught but a cursed nuisance. Won't obey instructions. Something *must* be done about them.'

'It was a hunter who found me, who led me back here.'

Hone Amis snorted. 'So? Chance! Nothing more. And that one ... I *remember* her. She's as much nuisance as any three men.' Back and forth, Amis began to pace. 'Perhaps there's something in the idea of forcing these hunters to take the oath. Make them face a choice, join with us or go against us once and for all.'

'And give us *two* sets of enemies if they don't accept?' Guthrie put in.

Hone Amis frowned. 'Aye. There's always that. But there aren't very many of them, and ...'

'Leave them be, Amis. You can't control everything.'

'I can at least *try*. You mark my words, lad. They're just trouble waiting to happen, that lot. The only way to deal with their sort is to stop them before they can get properly started. I've known Mysha since he was a lad. He could never put his mind to anything that counted. Ran off into the wild lands like a silly boy. He refuses to fit in. It's like a sickness with him. As long as he's about, the rest will continue to be trouble. Perhaps we should – *deal* with him on the quiet. If we could get him out of the way ...'

'Leave the hunters *be*!' Guthrie said quickly, not at all liking the direction of Amis's thought. 'And leave Mysha be.'

Hone Amis looked at Guthrie narrowly. 'Have you made some ... private arrangement with him, then?'

Guthrie shook his head in irritation. 'Of course not. I leave such plotting to the likes of Pettir.'

'Then why –'

'Enough,' Guthrie interrupted. He could try to explain it all day, he knew, and never manage to make Amis see the dangerous consequences of his compulsion to control. He felt abruptly, numbingly weary. 'The issue is closed.'

280

Hone Amis bristled. He was a man, Guthrie knew, who coped ill with having his will baulked, in little things as well as large. Still, there was nothing for it. 'I am weary,' Guthrie said. 'I will return to my own tent.'

'Aye,' Hone Amis agreed after a moment. 'You look like you need the rest. But consider, lad. If you let Mysha wander about loose and uncontrolled, and his hunters the same, who knows what damage they might —'

'Amis!'

The Militia Master sighed. 'Aye. All right.'

To Guthrie's surprise, Amis smiled at him. 'You have more of your father's iron in you than I ever thought, Guthrie lad. 'Tis good to see it in you.'

Guthrie was not sure what to say to that.

'Just make sure to use judgement along with it, is all.' Hone Amis smiled. 'Come, I'll walk with you to your tent.'

Guthrie smiled back, tiredly. He gathered himself together and followed the Militia Master slowly out of the tent and into the outside air.

XX

'War,' a woman said, her voice bleak. 'Powers preserve us!'

'Aye,' somebody agreed.

Alia squatted quietly a little distance from the fire, away from the flickering radiance of the flames, listening. The night was chill and she hugged herself. An old crescent of waning moon ghosted along in the star-lit sky atop the cliffs that overhung one side of the camp clearing. All around were unfamiliar faces, unfamiliar hills, unfamiliar trees. Alia shivered. It had no feeling of home, this camp.

'Well, *my* old man's not goin' to no *war*. And that's *that!*' a portly, middle-aged woman said vehemently.

'Neither he nor you got any choice in the matter, woman,' responded an older, balding man with a lined face. 'Master Amis's orders are that every able-bodied man report.'

'Well, *Master* Amis can go lick a dog's arse for all I care!' the portly woman said tartly. 'We never had to fight no *wars* with bandits before. Why start now? My old man ain't going, I say!'

'Your old man'll be in serious trouble if he don't,' the balding man said. 'It's the lash for anybody who shirks, I've heard. And full outlawry.'

'But that's *mad!*' somebody exclaimed. 'They declare a war against bandits, and threaten to make bandits out of anybody who doesn't want to fight the war.'

'Folk were saying that now we had a proper Reeve again, things would be getting back to normal,' someone put in wistfully.

'He's a witling, this young Reeve. Everybody's sayin' it. Can't tell a hawk from a handsaw.'

'That's not true! I saw him before they made me leave Hunters Camp. He looked poorly, but that was all. Any of us might look like that if ...'

Alia got up quietly and padded off. There were at least a dozen and a half fires here in this camp, each with its circle of folk, women

282

and old men mostly, all engaged in the same discussion now that the children were abed.

War.

Alia shivered, half with the night's chill, half with the very thought of the word.

War.

So much for her hope that the return of the rightful Reeve would be a return to the way things had been. It had only made everything far worse. No Vale folk had left for their farms in the lower valleys. And instead of the hunters being allowed to take up their former lives, they were now forcibly conscripted into this mad war. 'Witling', somebody at the fire had called Guthrie. Witling indeed, it seemed. And, worse than that, pawn to Hone Amis. She cursed her ill judgement in bringing him in.

Alia clenched her fists in frustration. She had had no say in any decision making. She had not even been permitted to attend the council session in Hunters Camp. Not *permitted*! How dare they? Like all the rest hidden away here in this 'safe' camp Hone Amis had instituted, with a circle of Militia in place to 'protect' them, Alia had had to wait to hear the results of the meeting second-hand from those who had eventually trickled in with the news of war.

Some few of the hunters were showing up here now – to avoid contact as much as possible with the Militia, Alia figured. But there were many missing who ought to be here.

Like Orrin.

How had Hone Amis managed to take a lad like Orrin and turn him so completely around? And the others like him? How could the free hunter community they had once all shared so easily come to an end so terribly quickly?

It hurt.

She felt lost and abandoned. Everything had been taken from her. Was it for *this* that poor Tym and Patch had died? That she had denied the Fey's invitation? That she had struggled to return Reeve Guthrie to his people? Was it for *this* she had fought and killed and striven?

Her left hand hurt still, a throb of dull pain. And just as the pain nagged at her, so the image of the demon-creature did too. Her dreams were haunted still by its beckoning. And now, in the fire-lit uncertainty of the night, she seemed to see the glowing yellow eyes of that tusked and unhuman face everywhere.

The world was come apart, and there was nothing to be done to put it back together again. There was nobody she could even talk to about what had happened to her – Fey and demons and all. Nobody would understand.

Except perhaps Mysha.

But there had been no time to talk with him before, and nobody had seen him after, the 'war' council. Where was he? How could he have let things come apart like this?

With a shiver, Alia remembered Orrin saying, 'Mysha ... well, you know, Mysha's never there when you need him.'

Alia cupped her face in her hands, ran her fingers over eyes that smarted with tears. The demon-face loomed in her mind's eye and she struggled to dismiss it. Where *was* Mysha? Why had he disappeared on them all?

Or had he been disappeared?

The thought made her a little sick. Could Hone Amis – and the new Reeve? – be *that* ruthless?

But then Alia suddenly recalled a place Mysha might be.

Once, within the first few weeks of her arrival in Hunters Camp, she had taken a stroll through the forest. It had been all too easy to get lost, innocent as she had been of woodcraft in those early days. For the better part of a day, she had wandered, utterly lost, terrified, tearful and desperate, convinced that she would die alone amongst the endless trees, food for the worms and crows.

But she had come upon a little dell in a sloping beechwood, with a small stream frothing up out of the ground. And seated by the banks of that stream had been a man and some other thing. She remembered well the fear and confusion she had felt, thinking that it was not, indeed, a man she had found at all.

But man it had been, and none other than Charrer Mysha himself, in converse with one of the Fey, though Alia had been able to see nothing more than the faintest of moving, pale shadow-shapes. She remembered vividly the special feel of that little dell: singing water, beech trees bowed in elegant, still gestures, green calm.

Perhaps, just perhaps, Mysha had returned there in this time of hurt and unrest. It seemed the likeliest place – presuming he had not fallen victim to some skulduggery of the Militia Master's.

Alia recalled the spot well enough to find it again, she thought, though it had been years since that day. But whether she found Mysha or not, searching for him would, at the very least, get her out of this camp, and she felt a sudden, desperate need of doing just that. She was a refugee here, more so than any Valer, she felt.

Squatting against a tree bole at the verge of the camp, her heart thumping, Alia stared about her. She had waited till well into the night to try this. The moon was westering now, folk abed and long asleep, the air chill and damp. There was no sign that anybody had noticed her disappearance into the black shadows under the trees.

She stood up, settled her bow and quiver more comfortably, then moved off, careful as though she were on a hunt, slipping away from the last of the dim firelight and into the trees' inky black maze.

The rearing shape of the cliffs that walled in one side of this camp rose like a huge wall to her left, casting a shadow-cloak of utter darkness on all beneath them. Alia had to feel every step, her hands out before her lest the sharp tip of some unseen branch stab her in the eye. Only when she was out of the cliff's shadow did the faint radiance of the waning crescent moon help reveal her path, and she began to be able to make her way with a little more surety. She had no notion of where exactly the Militia perimeter might be, but she could guess. She had no intention of trying to explain to them what she was doing out like this alone in the black of night.

Still moving almost as much by feel as by sight, she crept onward, alert as could be.

And then, in the distance ahead and to her right, she caught the murmur of hushed voices.

With that as a guide, she crept along, keeping her distance from the source of the voices, hoping to slip between two points on the ring of guards set about the camp. As she drew closer, she began to be able to make out words.

'... cursed villainous bandits!' a voice muttered. 'Until we can rid ourselves of them, we're *stranded* out here in this stupid wilderness.'

'We'll get rid of them, right enough,' a second voice responded.

'Better be soon,' the first voice said petulantly. 'I don't even know if the farm is still there. And what about my father's sheep? Thanks to these thrice-damned hill ruffians, I haven't been able to get down to the Vale yet to see what the cursed Sea Wolves left behind. If they left *anything* behind.'

Alia heard a long sigh.

'Bandits, Sea Wolves ... what is the world coming to?'

'Stinking bad times indeed,' the second voice said. 'Thank the Powers we have Hone Amis to steer us through.'

'Aye,' the first one agreed. ''Tis true, that. Without him to guide the young Reeve ...'

'I hear he's addled, that one. My cousin, Bart, told me that ...'

'Hissst,' the other interrupted. 'Did you hear anything just now?'

Alia froze.

'You're imagining things,' the first voice said after a long, silent moment. 'Black of night like this, and after all that's happened ... well, 'tisn't surprising.'

'Most like you're right,' the other agreed. 'Who could be out there? Apart from the Fey.'

'Let us hope *they* leave us well alone, the fearsome things.'

'Aye ...'

'My grandfather claimed he once saw ...'

Alia crept away, clambering carefully up a long, gradual, tree-filled slope until she was safely beyond the Militia cordon. In a little clear spot, she looked back and could just see the vermilion twinkle of the camp's low-burning fires within the cliffs' black shadow. She took a long breath of the chill night air, like liquid ice in her nostrils. The crescent of the moon hovered low over the cliffs. It seemed to her, suddenly, to be a lopsided grin. She grinned back at it, and standing here, safely away from the camp, she felt as though a weight had been lifted from her. With a little laugh, she turned and continued on.

It proved a wearisome, finicky journey, however, through forest she did not know well. Twice, she nearly lost herself completely. It was mid-day before she finally reached her destination. She found the beechwood: wetter, more fertile soil than in the rocky high country she was used to. It smelled richer here, moist and earthy and green. But it took a wearisomely long time, matching memory with her surroundings, before she was able to stand against a sun-dappled beech trunk within earshot of the soft burble of the stream for which she searched.

She stood where she was for a long few moments. Her sore left hand ached, and she rubbed it gently. The forest stood utterly quiet save for the soft singing of the unseen water and an almost inaudible sighing of breeze.

And what if Mysha were not here after all? Suppose she had been wrong in her guess he would come here. Suppose he had indeed fallen victim to some treachery or other. All the effort the journey had cost her. For nothing. And what would she do next?

286

Alia sighed. Whatever the case might be, she had to go and see. Carefully, she padded onwards.

The little dell was as she remembered, lit now by golden shafts of soft sunlight falling through the entwined limbs of the enclosing beeches. It took a little time in the dim, dappled light to see him, but a figure did indeed sit at the burbling stream's side, quiet, legs folded.

Mysha, right enough. Alia let out a long, relieved breath.

But he was not alone.

Alia felt the hairs along her scalp rise in a shiver, seeing what kept Mysha company: a wavering, ghost like Fey-form, pale and transparent. She remembered her own Fey's feather touch upon her, remembered the clarity with which she had seen him then. There was no such clarity now.

'Alia,' Mysha said softly, turning to her without surprise. He patted the ground at his side. 'Come. Sit by me.'

Slowly, an eye to what hovered near Mysha, Alia walked over and sat, shrugging off her quiver and setting it and her bow beside her.

'You see my ... companions,' Mysha said softly.

Alia blinked. 'There are more than one?'

Mysha nodded.

'I can only catch glimpses.'

Mysha regarded her with his strange, far-seeing eyes. 'You see clearer than you once did.'

Alia shrugged uncomfortably.

'You are changed, girl.' Mysha sighed. 'It is the times.'

'Aye!' Alia agreed with sudden vehemence. 'And bitter times they are indeed! Though *you* seem calm enough off here away from it all with your ... friends.' She stopped, embarrassed. She had intended no such outburst, but the sight of Mysha sitting calmly here had somehow upset her. He seemed so ... unaffected by everything. She looked at him uncertainly.

Mysha only shook his head gently. 'You will disturb my companions. They do not feel comfortable around most human folk at the best of times. They say human folk are like ... like little rivers in spring flood, full of noise and rubbish.' Mysha laughed, a soft sound. He turned from her and addressed the fleeting presences about him. Alia could not catch the words. They were spoken too softly and too quickly. And they came from Mysha's lips strangely.

After he had done speaking, Alia saw the luminous shadow-shapes of the Fey move nearer to him. He sat still, as if listening, though Alia could hear nothing save the stream, and the breeze whispering softly through the beeches that leaned over them. She blinked and squinted, stared, crossed her eyes, but nothing seemed to bring the faint shapes of the Fey into sharper focus for her. She felt a shiver go through her, feeling the strangeness of this place and the half-seen beings about her. She yearned for the clearer vision that had once been hers.

After a while, she could not even catch the faint, shifting quiver of them. 'Are they ... gone?' she asked.

Mysha shrugged. 'Yes and no.' He smiled a tired smile, stretched, reached a hand gently to her. 'What brings you out here, girl?'

Alia let out a long breath. She did not know where to begin.

Mysha gazed quietly at her. In the sun-dappled light his far-seeing eyes seemed to shine softly. But she noticed now that they were bruised with a too-human weariness, bracketed by haggard lines. His long, grey-streaked hair hung in an untidy mass. Ragged stubble shadowed his chin and cheeks.

But it was a kind face still, for all the weariness plain to be read in it, and Mysha smiled softly, keeping his silence, waiting for her to say something.

For a moment, Alia felt overcome with misgiving: too kind, that face. Mysha was too gentle a man, perhaps, to deal with what had come amongst them now. He seemed a sad, withdrawn figure, no longer young, bowed with weariness.

Yet it was he and none other that had drawn them all here to Hunters Camp originally.

'You've got to *do* something, Mysha!' she said.

'About what?' he returned softly.

'About *what*? Are you blind? About what has been happening. About these cursed bandits. About Hone Amis and his Militia. About the war he's declared! About what Hone Amis has done to us. About Orrin, who's become one of them. About ... about ...' Alia bit her lip, tears filling her eyes. 'Make everything *right* again, Mysha!'

Mysha shrugged unhappily. 'I cannot, Alia.'

She stared at him, blinking the tears off.

'It isn't mine to put right.'

Alia felt like slapping him. 'What's *wrong* with you? Everything we've ever had is being stolen from us, and what are you doing to prevent it? Nothing! You ought to be back at the camp trying to deflect the course of Hone Amis's interference, not sitting out here with ... with *them* ...' she gestured to where the Fey had been, 'far away from ... from those who *need* you! Don't you *care*?'

'You misjudge me if you think that,' Mysha replied sadly.

'Then *do* something!'

'There is nothing for me to do.'

'No! I don't believe that. How can you be so defeatist? You're our leader. You've *got* to do something to save us all.'

Mysha shook his head. 'I was never your leader, Alia.'

Alia did not know what to say to that. It was like a blow. She turned from him, the tears coming back.

'Alia,' he said, 'look at me.' Gently, he reached his hand to her chin and swivelled her round. 'What do you expect of me? That I march into camp and start shouting orders like Hone Amis himself?'

'No. Of course not. Just ...'

'Just what?'

'I ... I don't know. *Something!*'

'There is nothing I can do. I am a man folk follow, Alia. Not a man who leads.'

Hearing this, Alia felt suddenly hollow.

Since her thirteenth summer, she had accepted Mysha as one of her world's givens, wise and gentle and watching over all of them in his quiet way, the centre of all they did in Hunters Vale. Mysha had always held the answers.

But now ...

She remembered Orrin saying: 'Mysha's never there when you need him. And he could never tell anybody to do anything, anyway.'

She thought of who and what Mysha was: eldest son to the Charrer family, one of the ruling Five Families. But Mysha had forsaken that birthright and fled into the wild lands while still a lad. There were all manner of stories about him: how, at his birth, unearthly music had been heard in the Hills; or how his mother had seen an eerie pale face at the window on the night of his conception and lapsed into a deep faint for three days. A strange child, he had been, and a strangely gifted man, able to converse with the Fey like few others, at home in the hills like a wild creature.

Mysha's family disinherited him. But as word spread about the Charrer's strayaway, a few folk began secretly to desert Reeve Vale, searching after something better with Mysha. And so, over the years, the Hunters had come into existence as a community.

289

Alia had fled to Mysha like others, in a desperate attempt to escape the smothering constraints of her life. Like them all, she had looked to Mysha as the leader, the focus, the wise man who had led them all to freedom ...

But now she began to wonder suddenly if she and all the rest might not simply have been blinded by their own dreams.

As if privy to her thoughts, Mysha said, 'I was never the man you all thought. I never set out to create a community. It just happened, forming around me like ... like leaves blown by the wind into a drift. I had never intended any such thing.'

Alia looked at him accusingly. 'If we were such a *burden* to you, why did you let it happen?'

'It was not mine to prevent.'

Alia swallowed. She felt as if the world had just been turned upside-down on her. 'You never wanted us? You never –'

'No, Alia,' he interrupted. 'You were ... are my family.'

'Family! Is this how you treat family, deserting us all in our moment of need, just like ... *that?*' She snapped her fingers bitterly.

Mysha sighed. 'Of course not.'

'Then *do* something!'

'You do not understand, Alia. I never held any of you to me. You were never mine to command. You say young Orrin has become one of them. What am I supposed to do? *Order* him to change his ways? The world is not patterned in that way, Alia. I am not.'

Alia blinked, tongue-tied for a moment, caught up in misgiving and anger. 'So you intend to just give in, then? You'll just let Hone Amis trample everything that was ours under his foot. He's a right bastard. All he cares about is power and ruling others. He *likes* making others jump to his command. I've *known* men like that! My father was one such.'

But Mysha shook his head. 'You're wrong about him, Alia.'

Alia clenched her fists in frustration. 'How would you know?'

'I knew him as a boy. We're almost of an age, Amis and I. He's only a few years younger. We were friends once, as lads.'

Alia blinked in surprise.

'Not so strange, really,' Mysha said. 'The Hones and the Charrers always had close ties. I was engaged to Amis's sister before I ... before I left.'

Alia stared. She had never heard Mysha talk about his life before Hunters Vale.

'Amis was always the one who made up the rules of the games

we played,' Mysha went on. 'And he made sure the rest of us abided by those rules.' Mysha laughed softly. 'I remember well how angry he could get when one of us broke those precious rules of his.'

The laughter died, and Mysha grew suddenly serious. 'Amis sees himself as a kind of champion, fighting against chaos. And the world constantly upsets the order he tries to bring to it. Taming the wild lands, taming the hunters ... it's all the same to him. It's all chaos trying to break out, disorder that must be subdued.'

Alia shook her head. 'But that's a sort of craziness.'

Mysha nodded. 'Undoubtedly. But it's the sort of craziness that flourishes in a settlement like Reeve Vale. Amis is far from unique. The settlement was *carved* out of the wild, Alia, like one carves a chop from a deer's haunch. The Reeve Vale settlers never tried to fit themselves into the wild land here. They fit the land to them. But the land never quite obeyed their commands.' Mysha shrugged. 'One does not trust a servant that doesn't obey commands.'

'But the land is no *servant*.'

Mysha nodded. 'If you thought of it as such, you wouldn't be a hunter. No, *we* see the land very differently. To us, it is mysterious and wonderful and even a little dreadful perhaps at times. We fear it and love it, admire it, even dislike it, by turns. We have a *relationship* with it. We give to it. It gives to us. But Vale folk – have you so easily forgotten, Alia? – see the land only as a means to an end, something they must control, else it will control them.'

'And Hone Amis?'

'Amis will fight to control all about him, not because he loves control for its own sake – you are quite wrong about that – but because he fears chaos. For all our sakes.'

'*Our* sakes?'

Mysha nodded. 'Amis is a good man, Alia. He has the best interests of the entire Vale at heart.'

Alia snorted. 'His "best interests" are like to be the end of us.'

Mysha shrugged. 'Perhaps.'

'Then we must stop him!'

'How?'

Alia paused, uncertain.

'Would you have me try to gather hunters about me and force him off by threat of violence?'

Alia shook her head unhappily.

'What then? Plant a knife between his ribs?'

'No!'

'Do you wish me to talk to him? Do you think I can change the convictions of a man like him?'

'No,' Alia repeated glumly.

'Then what?'

'I don't *know*!'

'Neither do I,' Mysha said sadly. 'Don't you think it breaks my heart to see what has become of us, who were once a free community? But things change, Alia. The world goes on.'

'And you will just – *let* it all happen?'

'It isn't mine to control.'

Alia swallowed. There was such utter, sad certainty in his voice that, suddenly, she found herself believing everything he had said. A great wave of despair washed through her. 'Will you just leave us, then?'

Mysha smiled. 'No. Not that. But there is no simple thing for me to do, no simple poultice I can apply.'

To this, Alia said nothing. She hugged herself, shivering in the cooling air. 'It is over, then,' she said in a small voice.

Mysha nodded.

'The community of hunters ceases to exist. Just like ...' she snapped her fingers as she had before, 'that!'

Mysha said nothing.

Alia stared blindly at the little sun-dappled dell. She felt empty inside.

'What will you *do*?' she asked Mysha hesitantly.

He shrugged, a weary motion of shoulders and arms. 'What I have always done. And you?'

Alia did not know what to say.

'You are changed,' Mysha said softly. 'The past days have been hard on you.' He lifted a hand and ran gentle fingers over the remnants of the bruises on her face. She had all but forgotten them. 'Changed outwardly and inwardly. You have a Fey glamour about you.'

Alia shivered.

'No need to talk of it. I can see you have met with one of them.'

Alia nodded.

'But you came back.'

'I felt ...'

'The call of your own folk was too strong upon you.'

Again, she nodded. 'Have you ...'

Mysha shook his head. 'No. None ever offered me such an invitation. But then, it never seemed needed.'

'Do you think ... Will he ... will he ever come to me again?'

Mysha ran a hand through his tousled hair. 'I do not know. The Fey are like us in some ways, but they are not human folk. They are more complex and yet simpler. They do not offer anything lightly. I have never known them repeat an offer to somebody who denied them.'

Alia felt a sudden wave of such despair that it took her breath away. What had she given up when she refused the Fey's offer? Why had she been such a fool? Patch had died. Orrin was gone from her. The hunters were. Young Reeve Guthrie was simply making everything worse. Nobody needed her. Nobody wanted her. There was nowhere for her to go, and nothing left for her, anywhere.

'I'm *lost*,' she said, her voice breaking.

Charrer Mysha leaned close and put his arm about her shoulders in comfort. For a long few moments he simply held her. Then he said, 'I met a Closterer in the Heights, once.'

Alia sniffled and lifted her head, unsure.

'Years ago it was,' Mysha went on, 'when I was still hardly more than a boy. He came walking down a long slope towards me one foggy morning. Gave me quite a start. I remember him well. He came from foreign parts southwards, a tall thin man, dressed in that grey robe they all wear, with a satchel slung over one shoulder.' Mysha looked up, as if the Closterer he recalled had come to stand there before them. 'I asked him where he was from. He shrugged, pointed behind him, and said, "From back there." I asked him where he was going. He shrugged again, pointed ahead, and said, "Over there."'

Mysha laughed softly. 'Crazy as a loon, that one, or so I thought at the time. We talked a little, he and I. Then he went along on his way, lost and alone in the wild. Didn't even ask for directions. Last I saw of him, he turned to me and waved. He had a smile like a lantern in the dark.'

Alia regarded Mysha uncertainly.

Again, Mysha laughed his soft laugh. 'He was lost, Alia. Totally and completely lost.'

'And?' Alia said, when Mysha paused.

'And he didn't mind.'

Alia shook her head. 'I don't −'

'I thought about that Closterer for days afterwards. I went

293

searching for him, but I never found him, never discovered if he walked out of the forest and made it to the Closter up on the River Esk's shores, or left his bones to feed the trees.'

'Mysha, I don't –'

'No, no. Listen to me for a moment. I learned something most important from that lone, smiling man.' Mysha took his arm away from Alia and gestured to the trees, the sky, the sun. 'It is a big world in which we live, Alia. We are all lost. All of us. All of the time. Just like that lone Closterer.'

Mysha smiled. 'Most of us just don't know it.'

Alia rubbed the tears away from her eyes. She was not sure quite what to make of all of this.

'We are like little animals that build elaborate nests for ourselves,' Mysha was saying. 'We build and build and build. And what happens? We have very nice little lairs. Oh, aye. But we are also very blind to what there is outside of those lairs. Look at Hone Amis! He has spent his entire life building a secure lair for us all, only to have that security torn apart in one black instant of bloody chaos. And now he is busy rebuilding.'

Mysha laughed his soft laugh once more. 'Master Amis does not like being lost.'

Alia was growing more confused. 'Mysha, what are you trying to say?'

'Being lost is not so very terrible, Alia. You were lost before. You just didn't know it. Now you do.'

Alia turned from him. Words were scant comfort for what she felt. Might as well say everything that had happened to her was for the best because it made her life more *simple*.

All the words in the world would not fill the empty place she felt inside her.

'Alia,' Mysha said. 'Listen to me! Your world has come apart. But *the* world has not.'

'Scant comfort that is!' she snapped back at him. 'I have nowhere to go and nobody to go to.'

'You can go anywhere you wish.'

'I'm not going back to that camp,' she returned with a sudden, impetuous certainty. 'I tell you that!'

'Then do not.'

'But where would I –'

'Endings *hurt*, Alia. Don't you think I know that? But every ending is also a beginning, whether we will it so or no. The world is still *there*, Alia. Go out into it. Become entirely lost. I did so once, and it has been the salvation of me.'

Alia rubbed at her eyes. She could not make any real sense of what Mysha was saying. 'You mean just ... just walk off?'

Mysha nodded.

'But that's plain crazy!'

'It is all the advice I can give you.'

Alia stared at him. Was this really the man she and the rest had looked up to all these years? He was thin and scruffy, his hair greying, his face pathetically lined and haggard. She felt overwhelmed by a sudden terrible bitterness. Her life was ripped apart, everything she ever valued lay shattered, friends lay dead, war loomed, and all the wisdom Mysha had to offer was high-sounding rhetoric that amounted, finally, to nothing more than telling her to run away.

As before, Alia felt like slapping him. 'You're a *quitter!*' she said. 'A spineless quitter.'

Mysha said nothing.

Alia stood up abruptly, grabbed her bow and quiver. 'I wouldn't be like you for *anything*! You can quit if you like, but I'm going to do something.'

'Such as?' he asked mildly.

His very mildness enraged her. 'I don't *know*. But I'll think of something. Anything's better than becoming a useless, pathetic little quitter like you!'

As soon as the words were out, Alia regretted them. They were both unfair and untrue. But it was too late. They were said. She glared at him, defying him to argue.

But he did not, merely gazed at her.

She could not bear that quiet, penetrating gaze of his, and turned and rushed off, saying no goodbyes.

'I hate him, hate him, *hate* him,' she muttered to herself, storming off through the beeches. Even as she said the words, she knew them to be untrue. But she was filled with an incoherent, hopeless rage. The very thought of him sitting calmly back there made her tremble. He was so ... *useless*! And to think that she had been worried that Hone Amis might have done something to him. Little need of that!

Alia stormed blindly on, lit like a torch, blazing with the anger in her. Her sore left hand sizzled with pain. She ignored it. She did not know where she could go or what she could do, but she was going *somewhere*, and would do *something*! Better to die than lie down like some stupid, whining little puppy dog and let the likes of Hone Amis trample her. She could have walked *that* path easily enough just by staying home all these years and letting her father have his bullying way with her.

The pain in her left hand was growing worse. She stopped for a moment, propped her bow against a tree, and stood to massage the hand. The inscrutable design carved into her flesh still oozed rose-red droplets of blood, like little liquid jewels glinting softly in the sunlight. She put the hand to her mouth and sucked gently, tasting the salt-iron flavour of blood. What was wrong with her that she was taking so long to heal? It was not natural.

Alia let out a long, weary sigh. Nothing was right in the world any more.

She really ought to go back to Mysha and apologize. She had behaved badly.

But what point was there in apologizing?

Nothing would return life to the way it had been. And she could still feel the anger at him ... sitting there so calmly, as if nothing mattered to him.

Her sore hand throbbed, sending stutters of sharp pain up her arm now all the way to the shoulder. She tried to flex the fingers gently, but it did not help.

What was wrong with her?

Leaning back on the tree she had propped her bow against, Alia slowly sank to the ground. Everything that had ever mattered to her was gone. She felt like a little boat cast adrift upon some great, heaving body of water, tossed aimlessly, helplessly, at the mercy of whatever current might take her. She could drift aimlessly or founder and sink for ever beneath the waves. Those seemed her only choices.

In her mind, she saw the demon-creature. Clear as clear, he seemed. Clear as if he stood before her in the flesh. The great, unhuman yellow eyes gazed at her steadily. With one hand, he beckoned to her. 'Come,' she seemed to hear him say. 'Come to me now.'

Alia shook herself. A long shiver went through her. The hairs on her scalp prickled uncomfortably.

'Come to me,' the echoes of the voice sounded in her mind. 'Come to me now.'

'No!' she all but shouted into the forest quiet, not understanding her own vehemence.

But the words echoed still: 'Come to me. Come to me.'

Why not? a part of her asked. What else was there left for her to do now?

No telling what this creature might want with her, another part of herself cautioned. His unblinking gaze was all together too possessive.

But there was also no telling what he might have to offer her.

At the thought of that, she felt her pulse suddenly quicken. She had rejected the Fey's offer, closed that door for ever it seemed. Should she reject another such offer now? She did not understand how she was suddenly so certain that this demon-creature was, in fact, offering her anything. But, somehow, the certainty was in her that he *was* making an offer.

'Come to me now,' the words echoed again in her mind. 'It is your future. You cannot refuse. Come to me now. You have nothing to lose.'

That last seemed true enough. She had indeed nothing left to lose. 'Come to me now.'

Alia took a long breath. Why not?

She levered herself back to her feet, lifted up her bow. Her hand now throbbed with a kind of pleasant ache rather than true pain. She started off upslope, jogging along at a steady, ground-eating pace, the voice in her mind calling her on softly.

It was long moments before she managed to halt herself.

What was happening to her? She seemed to know exactly in which direction to go. She hesitated, shivering and uncertain. What was she letting herself in for?

But then Alia shook herself. She had had enough of despair and confusion. Let the voice lead her on, then. Let this demon-creature, whatever he might be, offer her what he would. It was, at least, *something*.

With the soft voice in her head as a guide, Alia went onwards.

XXI

He stood waiting for her on a low rise, his unhuman face backlit by the dying light of sunset.

It had taken Alia the better part of two days to come here, toiling upslope through the trees, following the insistent voice in her mind. Now, looking at him, she did not know what to do.

'Come to me,' he said, repeating the words which had drawn her. He held out a hand, beckoning. 'Come to me now.' The voice was guttural and deep, and echoed somehow like a voice in a cave.

Alia shuffled forwards a few steps uncertainly, then stopped, staring at the tusked mouth, the great, unblinking yellow eyes. She shuddered. 'Wha ... what manner of creature are you?' she asked.

'I am unlike any person ye has ever met.' He grinned, or, at least, she hoped it a grin. 'Come to me.'

'What do you ... wish of me?'

The great, unhuman eyes gazed at her, unblinking. 'Ye is a rare find ... one who sees into the dim edges of the world, who sees what others cannot.'

Alia hesitated, uncertain. His words seemed oddly familiar somehow. 'What do you *wish* of me?'

He bowed to her, a surprisingly elegant motion, and swept his arm out in invitation. 'I offer ye that for which ye has yearned. I offer ye a new life. A new world!'

Alia took a sharp breath.

'Come to me. I will lead ye.'

'To ... where?'

'To where ye has always yearned to be.'

Alia shivered. 'How do *you* know what I might or might not yearn for?'

'I know ye well enough, girl. Does the hawk yearn for the wind? Does the young salmon yearn for the open sea? I can see ye clear.' His hand was still out, beckoning. 'Come to me.'

Alia still hesitated.

298

'Yer life has swamped ye, and ye is drowning.'

'How dare you –' Alia began irately.

'Ye knows I speak the truth,' he said, interrupting. He smiled again, a lifting of thin lips over ivory tusks. 'Come to me now. There is nothing else left ye to do.'

Alia hung back, wanting in some desperate way to resist him.

But she *did* feel swamped by the disasters of her old life, as he had said. And if she refused him here, what other choice did she have left, save to ... drown? With an uncertain sigh, Alia moved tentatively towards him, one step, another. He stood still as a carving, hand out to her, palm upwards, in invitation. She reached her own hand to his. It was her sore left hand with which she reached, but that seemed fitting somehow.

She laid her throbbing palm upon his. He closed his fingers, and she felt a pulse of something, like a sudden rushing current.

Alia did not know what she had expected: to be thrust into a strange confusion, as had happened with the Fey's first touch; to feel a rise of fear, or of demon-knowledge; to put on the demon-creature's strength with his knowledge in some magical manner; to see the world transformed; to find herself transformed.

Nothing of the sort occurred.

He laughed, gripping her. Alia's left hand throbbed uncomfortably, as if the very life of him was so strong it sent out a pulsing current of energy. But she felt herself changed not at all.

Then the demon-creature picked her quickly up, as if she weighed next to nothing, and wedged her sideways under his arm. The arrows tumbled from Alia's quiver with a clatter. She dropped her bow, trying desperately to pry loose his hold on her. He whirled and bounded off through the trees into the gathering dusk of evening.

'Wait!' she cried. 'No!'

But he leaped onwards, silent.

Through the growing dark the demon-creature rushed. He vaulted across a stream, startling some forest creature – only a half-guessed, dim shape as they hurtled past. Alia did not understand how he could see in the growing dark well enough to keep the leaping pace he kept.

Her heart raced like a mad thing. She found it difficult to get breath, his hold upon her was so tight and unyielding. Wriggle and pry and shout as she might, there seemed nothing she could do to escape. He leaped onwards into the dark, and she, like so much hapless baggage, could only submit.

For what seemed like a long time, he kept up his impossible, rushing pace. Night fell, drowning the forest in darkness. It slowed him not at all.

And then, for no reason Alia could discern, he did slow.

Somebody called from out of the night-dark: 'Who goes there?'

'Leave well enough alone, man,' the demon-creature replied in his resonant, guttural voice. ''Tis I.'

There was silence, then. The demon-creature strode confidently forwards.

Alia saw nothing, but she caught a little crackling of branches as somebody moved, heard a man's subdued and nervous breathing.

The demon-creature passed by through the night-shrouded trees, silent, moving more at an ordinary man's pace now. After a little, Alia saw the flicker of fire light ahead. 'Where are you taking me?' she demanded anxiously.

He gave her no answer, merely kept his steady pace towards the firelight.

There were figures gathered about the fires. Dim, moving shapes in the firelit dark they were at first, and for a frightened moment Alia took this to be a whole camp of such fearsome creatures as the one that had her in his grip. But as her captor came striding further into the camp, the dim figures resolved themselves into raggedy, gauntfaced men, hungry eyes glinting in the firelight. Ordinary mortal men right enough. Bandits. It was all sickeningly familiar.

The demon-creature strode through the crowd, talking to none. Alia saw men point, heard their grumblings, but no one tried to impede the demon's progress. They melted aside as he approached, giving him a clear path, then closed ranks again behind.

Into a tent he took her, black as any cavern, and dropped her on the ground.

Alia heard a quick scratch and *spuut*. A little shower of sparks lit the blackness, and then the dancing flame of a lantern. She scrambled to her feet, terrified and furious.

'Stay quiet!' he snapped before she could open her mouth. His great unhuman eyes glared at her balefully, glowing in the lanternlight like a wild thing's. She felt her throat constrict. He motioned to the back corner of the tent. 'Over there. Sit.'

Alia stayed where she was, fists clenched, panting.

'Do it!' he commanded.

She glanced desperately at the tent's doorway. If she moved quick enough, she just might be able to ... But no. Stupid thought. There was the bandit crowd out there to greet her. And this demon-creature could catch her up quick enough in any case.

The demon gestured impatiently to the rear of the tent. 'Sit down!'

Alia did as he bid. There seemed no other option. She sat, glaring at him, shaking. 'What do you –'

He cut her off. 'Quiet, girl. I shall not harm ye.'

She was not sure how to read such a face as his. His features were only superficially human, nose, eyes, mouth. But the look he gave her made her shudder. It was a covetous look. No other way to describe it.

At that moment, the tent's doorflap was flung open and a man came barging in, short, thickset, with a black spade of a beard above which were dark, calculating eyes. He stood, blinking in the lanternlight. His gaze flicked from the demon, to Alia, to the demon again.

'Sethir,' the demon said by way of greeting.

Alia recalled the name, recognized the man: he who had killed Torno, the brute bandit leader, with her help. And who had betrayed her afterwards for whatever twisted, scheming reasons he had concocted.

Sethir stepped further into the tent, stabbed an accusing finger at the demon. 'What do you think you're doing?'

The demon merely regarded him silently.

'Answer me!' Sethir snapped. 'Have you gone quite mad? Striding in here with a girl – a *girl*! – tucked under your arm like a haunch of venison. How did you think the men would react to something like that?'

'I care not at all how the men react,' the demon replied.

'You don't *care*?' the other said furiously. 'These men are all you have to make your precious ambitions come true. And you treat them like shite!'

'And ye is a paragon of compassion, then?'

'I use common sense at least. I know better than to flaunt the unreachable before men's noses unnecessarily.'

The demon shrugged. 'It is no concern of theirs. And none of *yers*, either.'

'You have made it my concern by your own stupidity. Striding into camp like that!'

'Mind yer tongue, man,' the demon warned. He took a menacing step forwards.

But bearded Sethir stood his ground. 'Save your posturing for others. You need me, and you know it. I know this land. I know the enemy we face. Without me, where would your precious ambitions be?'

'What does ye know of my ambitions?'

'Enough,' Sethir said sharply. 'Do you think me stupid?'

There was silence between the two for long moments.

'Let me have the girl,' Sethir said eventually. 'Let the men have her. Do that, and we can turn this thing around, make it work to our advantage.'

'No,' the demon replied.

Sethir flung up his arms. 'It is useless talking with you when you're like this. Take it off!'

'No.'

'You threaten all we are striving for. Think, man! What can one lone girl matter? *Think*! Take off the helm and listen to me.'

The demon said nothing.

Sethir turned and regarded Alia where she still sat crouched at the tent's rear. 'What can be so special about ...' His eyes grew suddenly wide, and he whirled about to face the demon. 'It's the same one. It's *her*! You *are* mad, bringing her back here after everything we contrived. Where did you *find* her? How do you —'

'Go away.' There was a irate snarl in the demon's voice now.

'Tasamin! Listen to me.'

'She is more than the likes of ye can possibly understand. I know what I am doing. Now go *away*.'

'This could ruin everything!' Sethir stared at Alia, at the demon. He raised a clenched fist. 'Be warned. I have too much at stake to let you wreck it all for some silly girl. This is not over yet.'

'I grow tired of this,' the demon replied. 'Go!'

His face clenched in anger, Sethir backed slowly out. 'This is *not* finished between us,' he repeated, and then was gone.

The demon's face was contorted into an ugly mask of rage, lips pulled back from the great fangs in a menacing rictus. He took a step towards the tent's doorway, hands out like talons. But he stopped himself, turned, stood there panting, growling deep in his throat like a beast.

Alia faltered back uneasily against the tent's far wall.

The demon took a long, shuddering breath, another. Then he

302

reached both hands to his head. He seemed to grip himself just above the neck, thumbs at his own throat, fingers laced around the back of his skull.

As Alia watched in shocked, uncomprehending horror, he tore his own head off.

She stayed where she was, trying to get breath, staring at him as he stood there with his head held in his hands. The great yellow eyes in that head flared, glimmered, went dead.

Alia blinked, shook herself. She rubbed at her eyes. In the flicker of the lamplight, she seemed to see a decapitated body, gruesome head dangling from limp hands. But then, in some manner she could not quite fathom, as the yellow eyes died in the separated head, the image wavered, changed.

An ordinary man stood before her, head perfectly intact upon his shoulders, his hands holding a roundish, complex object of some sort.

With a gasp, Alia recognized him.

He bowed to her, an elegant, half-mocking gesture. 'I am Tasamin,' he said. His face was almost impossibly handsome, with high, wellformed cheek bones, eyes blue as spring ice. When he smiled, he showed perfect white teeth. His ears were studded with gold plugs in which crimson rubies sparkled in the lamplight. He was dressed in nondescript, rugged forester clothing, but his fingers were sheathed with rings, his arms with bracelets, all set with gems, glimmering and glittering and winking.

'The jewelled man ...' Alia gasped.

He laughed softly. 'As good a name as any, I suppose.'

Alia stared. 'But how ... What did you ...'

He held out the object in his hands for her to see. 'An ancient thing, this. An object of *power*.'

What he held seemed to be war-helm of queer design, constructed from a combination of materials: bone and bronze, iron and wood, and other, less recognizable substances. It did indeed seem an ancient thing, cracked and stained, held together by a threadwork of glinting gold wire into which little gemstones had been woven. Under the golden wire spiderweb, Alia could make out features. Bone tusks protruded from an iron 'mouth', and bone and iron bands crossed the vaulted skull of it. Membranes of cloudy ochre stuff stretched between bronze sockets where the eyes would be. Here was the demon face she had seen, or at least a sort of bare, lifeless skeleton of it.

'I ... I do not understand,' she said to him.

He smiled. 'No. I imagine ye does not.' He lifted the helm and placed it upon his head.

For an instant Alia experienced a sickening confusion of her senses, seeing his human features and the demon ones superimposed. Then it was the demon she saw, clear as clear. He grinned at her, his thin lips curling back from the great ivory tusks in his mouth. The unhuman yellow eyes seemed to glow. Alia shuddered. It was living features she saw, the nostrils flaring slightly at each breath, the lips moving. A glistening red tongue came out to lick at the great tusks.

Then, as before, he reached up and seemed to tear the very head off himself.

Alia felt her belly cramp up.

He came closer to her, altogether a man again, the helm tucked under his arm. 'The world,' he said, 'is not what most think it to be. Most see only the illusionary surface shimmer of it, unaware of the depths over which they move. But some, a few, can perceive more. The shifting heart of the world lies open to them, the hidden secrets.'

Alia stared at him.

'Ye is such. One of the few. That is why I could not let Sethir get ye killed when ye first were brought into camp. Ye were convenient to plans that Sethir and I had been concocting. We removed Torno, set Sethir in his place as leader, and had ye to use as a scapegoat. It suited Sethir, and it suited me. But having ye dead was another matter entirely. Ye is *special*.'

Alia did not know what to say.

'Ordinary folk go along in their little lives, ignorant as wood lice, blind to the great truth of the world,' Tasamin continued. 'But I ... *I* am not blind. And ye needs not be blind either.'

Tasamin's ice-blue eyes gazed intently at her. There was a power to this man, an almost palpable aura of strength. This close to him, she could see that he was, in fact, far older than first appearances made plain. His eyes were set in a network of fine wrinkles. But, aged or not, she sensed the naked power of him as if it were heat he radiated, and flinched away.

'I shall not harm ye,' he said. Backing away a little, he turned and laid the uncanny helm carefully on the ground. Then he straightened and reached out his hands towards the tent's far, dark corner. His fingers curled in a beckoning motion. Out of the corner something moved, rolling up from the ground and sliding through the empty air.

Alia shivered, witnessing such impossible motion. She leaned forwards, repelled and fascinated at once, trying to make out what it was he had called forth. With a gasp, she recognized it for a dead man's skull, dark with age, the same she had seen the jewelled man, Tasamin, with before. Against the peat brown bone, gold filigree work glinted. A myriad of little jewels beaded that filigree, like sparkling, rainbow water droplets in the lamplight. Seeing this skull sparked a flash of recollection – Guthrie Garthson, of the skull he carried. She shivered.

Alia found it suddenly hard to breathe. The skull continued to float impossibly in the air before her. She seemed to see ghostly eyes in the dead sockets, regarding her coldly. She understood none of this. Her belly was twisted up in a painful knot. She could not seem to get her thoughts straight.

Tasamin lifted a hand, palm up, and the skull settled upon it like some impossible, wingless bird settling on a perch. Holding the skull in the one hand, he reached out to Alia with the other.

Before she could think, Alia found herself holding out her scarred left hand.

He took it in his, his grip strong and sure.

Her hand flared in sudden agony, as if liquid fire were running up her arm, her shoulder, through into the base of her skull. She felt a thrust of nausea. Her heart beat wildly.

Then the world seemed to shatter apart all around her and she to plummet through it like a stone shot through dark water. She felt a terrifying sense of dissolution overwhelm her. All was terrible, churning chaos, without and within her. She felt torn apart, bone and flesh and mind.

It would kill her, this! Shred her apart like so much leaf mould in a storm. She tried to scream, to struggle, to tear herself away. But it was no use. She had no mouth left with which to scream. Her very self was gone. She was shattered, dismembered, destroyed ...

With a sickening rush, the world came suddenly back to her, or she to the world.

Feeling her hand released, Alia collapsed weakly. She doubled over, vomiting in a painful spasm.

'That,' Tasamin said over her, '*that* is the underlying truth of the world.'

305

She stared at him, shaken to her very marrow, uncomprehending.

Tasamin stood looking down at her, cradling the dead man's uncanny skull in one hand still. Alia shuddered, retched helplessly one last time. Curling his lip in distaste, Tasamin reached into a pocket and retrieved a little scented bag which he held to his nostrils. He gestured to the back wall of the tent. 'Ye will find a washcloth there. Use it to clean up.'

Alia struggled over, found the cloth where he had indicated. There was a little bucket of water with it. She soaked the cloth, rubbed herself at least partially clean, swabbed up the mess she had made on the tent floor.

When it was done, she looked up at him, still standing there. 'Wha ... what did you *do* to me?'

Tasamin took away the hand that had been holding the little bag to his nostrils, shook his head. 'What did I do? I showed ye the world's *truth*. The world ordinary folk perceive is nothing but a *mask*, girl. Underneath that mask, lies what ye has just experienced ... the Nether Place. The Place of Great Chaos.'

'But how did you ...'

'Underneath all the fine show of the world,' Tasamin went on, 'lies only chaos and destruction. Most live in complete ignorance, never knowing, never caring. But it is the great truth of the world nevertheless.'

'What are you saying?' Alia asked hesitantly. 'That all the world is only a sham?'

Tasamin nodded. 'Exactly.'

'No!' Alia cried.

'Yes!' he responded. 'Only a sham. Unreal as any dream. Ye knows it, girl, in yer heart. Ye has seen glimpses of it, seen into the hidden hollows of the world.'

'Aye,' Alia agreed hesitantly. 'I have caught glimpses of ... something. The world has its hidden aspects. But ... chaos. No. I do not believe it. The Powers ... What of the Powers?'

Tasamin laughed. 'The Powers? Silly children's imaginings to cloak the great, terrible emptiness at the world's heart. There are no Powers, no more than anything else. All sham. *All!*'

'No,' Alia insisted. 'It cannot be!'

'Can ye ignore the evidence of yer own experience so easily, then?' Tasamin demanded. 'Ye has felt first hand the naked truth that underlies the world.'

Alia took an uneasy breath. 'It cannot be,' she insisted.

'It *is*,' he returned.

She did not know what to say.

'Accept it, girl. Ye knows in yer heart it is so.'

'But ...' If he had kicked her in the belly, Alia could not have felt more stricken. 'But the world is *true*!'

'No. What ye has just experienced is *true*.' He lifted the skull, running his fingers along the glinting golden webwork that clothed the thing. The gems of his finger rings scintillated hypnotically in the lanternlight. The skull's uncanny eyes seemed to brighten.

Alia felt a rush of uncertainty, as if the very world were shivering about her. She felt her heart kick in her breast. It was beginning again!

But no. Tasamin lifted his hand from the skull, smoothed the air, as if smoothing the world back into solidity. '*Accept it*, girl!' he commanded. 'For by accepting it, ye gains the only true freedom there is.' He smiled a thin smile. 'And the only true power!'

Alia stared at him, open mouthed.

'Aye, girl. *Power*.'

'It is not power that interests me,' she replied after a little.

Tasamin laughed. 'Power interests *everyone*. Those who claim it does not are liars. Do not lie to me, girl!'

Alia shuddered. 'I want none of this. None of your ... your place of chaos, your power, your uncanny skulls and demon helms and ... and ...'

Again, Tasamin laughed. 'It is too late for that now.'

Alia felt her stomach clench. 'What do you mean?'

'Ye has experienced it. Once a one such as ye has done so, there is no going back. Can ye not feel it calling to ye still?'

Indeed, Alia could. It was like a thin, insistent voice, nagging at her. The unquestioned solidity of the world was undermined. She had experienced this same thing before, she realized: after meeting the Fey, while standing on the birch bluff, gazing down the cliff face into the valley below. But those had been only faint glimpses. It was far, far stronger now.

'It will never leave ye,' Tasamin said.

As if on cue, Alia felt a sudden sickening surge go through her. The world seemed to dissolve. 'No!' she cried. 'I want none of this. *None!*'

She felt a hand upon her, drawing her back. The world steadied. Her belly spasmed in a dry heave.

307

'Here,' Tasamin said. He let go of the skull, which settled slowly to the ground, and produced from somewhere a thick golden chain laced with small, winking blue stones. 'Put it on. It will help anchor ye.'

Alia knelt where she was, heart pounding, staring at the shining necklace. She tried to bat it aside. 'I want *none* of this!'

'Too late now,' he said, and his voice had a ring of triumphant satisfaction. He slipped the necklace neatly over her head.

It settled upon her like a great weight, nearly toppling her sideways. But it did seem to anchor her somehow. The world solidified. Her vision cleared. Her racing heart settled.

'That is better,' Tasamin said, satisfied. 'Now ye will be all right. Now ye is protected from the undertow of the Nether Place.'

Alia glared at him. 'You tricked me! Pushed me over the edge. Made me ...'

'I merely took ye to where ye was always headed. No ordinary person could perceive the Nether Place as quick as ye. Ye did *well*, girl. All my hopes for ye are vindicated.'

'What hopes?'

'Think,' he said, ignoring her question. '*Think!* This is what ye has been searching for all yer life. Did ye not sit, as a girl, *yearning* for something *other*? Has ye not always yearned? Did ye not always feel separate, different, as if ye did not belong where others did? Did ye not feel the call of the world's great mysteries? Now ye has experienced the greatest mystery of all!'

Alia wanted to deny all he said. It was not, could not be, truth. It was not chaos and nothingness that had always called to her. Her hand slipped uncertainly to the heavy golden necklace he had placed around her throat, fingering the links of it, the little rounded forms of the gems. He *had* caught the measure of her all too exactly. There was no denying that. And what he said had a certain ring to it.

She stared at him. 'Why have you done this to me?'

'I have merely begun ye on the path that ye was destined for.'

'Out of selfless generosity, no doubt?' she prodded.

Tasamin laughed. 'Ye has spirit, girl. That is good.' He gestured about him to the tent's walls. 'Does ye think I like living in such scant comfort as this? Does ye think I have no more purpose than to aid some ridiculous hedge bandit such as Sethir No-Name in his blind quest for revenge? I am more than that, girl. I have *ambitions*!

Why does ye think I came north to this comfortless wilderness in the first place?'

Alia shrugged.

'Once, there were great Seers. From the far southern lands. Ye has heard tell of the Demon War, as men call it?'

Alia nodded.

'The ones who led that war held such power as to make the mind reel. Think of the helm ye saw me use. It took me years excavating the remains of an ancient Keep in far Harbour Bay to the south to discover such. And it required every last bit of my skill to resurrect the helm once I had found it. The helm is only the smallest example of what the Old Ones could do. We are ignorant dwarfs compared to them! I unearthed ancient scrolls, artifacts. They could transform the very flesh of living creatures into any shape that pleased them. They could be in different places at the same time.'

Tasamin stood, face flushed, arms out as if he held in his hands some heavy, invisible object. 'They held such *power*.'

Alia shook her head. 'Why are you telling me all this? I don't understand! What does any of it have to do with what I ... what *you* made me experience?'

'Do not act stupid, girl.'

'I am *not* acting stupid!'

Tasamin laughed. 'Then *think!* What does ye suppose was the source of the Old Ones' power?'

Alia shrugged. 'Some, some hidden knowledge. Secret lore.'

'*Wrong!* They were as ye and I, girl. They had seen into the great truth of the world. That, and nothing else.'

'But how ...?'

'*Think!* The world is all a great sham. The only great truth is that nothing is true. And if nothing is true, then *everything* is true.'

Alia must have looked her confusion, for Tasamin laughed once more. 'Ordinary folk are full of ignorant convictions. They *know* how the world works. But their *knowing* is ludicrously shallow. Like seeing their reflection in a pool's clear surface and believing they have seen into everything! The world is like this, they say: the five elements make it up. Or like that: each thing in its proper place. Flames leap upwards, solid objects leap down, each to where it belongs.' Tasamin laughed again, gestured to the skull which floated lightly up from the ground and into the air. 'Oh, ordinary folk *know* what is possible and what is not, all right. But once one sees through the illusion and into the truth of the world, then *anything* is possible.

'The world is a great nothing, girl, which we can shape to our own ends. It is a blank slate upon which we can write whatever we wish. The Old Ones knew this, and raised their art to the highest possible level.'

Tasamin held his arms out in a dramatic, encompassing gesture. 'The world is mine to do with as I will. Here in this wild and empty northern land of yers, undisturbed, I will revive the Old Ones' arts, and revive their age of glory!'

He stopped, stood silent for long moments, regarding her. Alia felt the world shudder ever so slightly about her and fingered the necklace with her left hand for reassurance. It seemed, somehow, that the hand ached hardly at all when she did so. Tasamin frightened her. He repelled her. Her fingers slid along the golden links, across the smooth, rounded belly of one of the gems. But there was something eerily attractive about him as well, somehow. She had to admit it to herself.

'Such as ye and I, girl, are no part of the common herd,' he was saying. 'We have a special destiny. Come with me. I will be yer guide. I had no such living aid for myself, and very nearly came to grief, for the way is perilous in the extreme. The Nether Place is always there, waiting like a great pit for ye to fall into. Ye must learn to control it, and control yerself. If ye fails, 'twill be the end of ye for certain. No one can survive the terrible chaos of it. But learn to keep yer balance, to see through the world's sham appearances, to control them, and ye will live long and prosper as few other mortal folk can.'

He reached forwards, slipped a pair of shining bracelets from his forearms. 'Here. Hold out your arms.'

Alia did so, unthinking.

In one quick, sure motion, he slid the bracelets upon her. 'A gift for ye, and an aid.'

Alia looked at them. Red gold, they were, each an elegant coil of braided metal, rich and shimmering in the tent's lamplight. They were heavy upon her wrists, and felt strangely warm. For a sudden, uncomfortable instant, they seemed to her as manacles, the heaviness of them pulling her spirit down. But the instant quickly went. Silly thought. They were beautiful things. More beautiful than anything she had ever seen, never mind had for her own.

She felt a strange, possessive thrill go through her.

'This is virgin land, this northern wilderness of yers,' Tasamin said. 'Bandit Sethir thinks he is using me, but in fact it is *I* that am using *him*! I play his game, pretend to be his creature, keep myself in check. But once he and his rabble have cleared the way, I shall claim this land for myself. There is none here who can contend against me. And ye can join me, girl. *Will* join me. Think on it! What can we two not accomplish together?'

Alia felt a prickle of unease. 'And the folk already settled here? What of them?'

'Their way of living is already over, girl. Sethir and his rabble will destroy them.'

'Then stop him!'

'I will. But not yet. The world is not such a simple place. I need Sethir still. I must let him have his head yet for a while.'

'He will destroy everything,' Alia lamented.

'Not everything, no. I will not allow it. This is *my* land, or will be. And its inhabitants are *my* folk. I will not allow them to be destroyed so easily. And *ye* must not allow it. Help me, girl. The very survival of yer folk depends upon it. Together we can save them!'

Alia ran a hand over her eyes. The bracelets on her wrists were a warm, solid weight. She felt strangely woozy, and fingered the necklace for comfort. She tried to organize her thoughts. What Tasamin said ... the gemstones were cool and soothing under her touch ... Tasamin was so ...

'I and ye, girl,' he said, smiling.

He was a handsome man, no denying that, Alia thought. And he was offering her a place in the world. Something no other had ever done. He valued her. And he had never threatened or forced her in any way. Like the Fey, that. Tasamin only offered her, leaving the choice to her alone. She admired the red-gold gleam of her bracelets. He was a generous man, too. And only urged her only with words when, perhaps, he could have used less gentle methods. She felt along the links of the necklace. Each link fitted perfectly into the next ... like Tasamin's words, notions she should have seen long ago. A place for her in the world. He and she together. The Vale folk saved. The hunters saved.

It was everything for which she had ever yearned. She saw that clear now. She and Tasamin, together. They would be the salvation of Reeve Vale, of the hunters. Everything that had been shattered in recent times would be put back together again. She and Tasamin together, healing old wounds, restoring old ways.

It was her destiny, this. As he had said, she was not like others. He was so perceptive ... She felt the world shiver uncertainly about her and gripped the necklace for stability. Her heart fluttered a little, but not much. She had his support now, and the help of his wisdom. And now that she understood the truth of the world, she would learn from him the control he promised. And then she would be able to *do* things, set things right. And then ... What could they *not* do, they two together?

Tasamin smiled at her, his striking blue eyes glinting as brightly as any gems. 'I have shown ye the world's hidden truth, girl,' he said. 'And that truth shall set ye free to do great things.'

Alia felt the comforting weight of the necklace upon her throat, the bracelets binding her wrists. She gazed at his handsome face and returned his smile. 'Aye,' she agreed. 'You and I together.'

'Together.' Tasamin nodded. 'Always.' He took both her hands in his. His grip was strong, fatherly, comforting. He had all the strength of her father, Alia realized, but with the wisdom her father had so glaringly lacked.

'Together,' she repeated. 'Always.'

XXII

Guthrie moved along with the others, slowly. The trees were old and thick here, a long, upward-sloping rill choked with mountain oaks, limbs twisted into improbable shapes. The air was chill, the season turning quickly now, the afternoon beginning to dim already. Heavy clouds, pregnant with rain, showed beyond through the naked limbs of the oaks. The ground lay covered in brown, soggy oak leaves. They crept through as quiet as could be, every nerve strung tight.

The little guard-squad Hone Amis had assigned to Guthrie stuck close to him, a moving circle. Like the rest, Guthrie had been keyed up all day, scanning trees, slopes, the distant, glimpsed outlines of hills for any possible sign of bandits. But no sign of anything untoward had there been so far.

Guthrie ached from this, their second long day's upslope, careful plodding.

As they moved, word came down the strung-out line, passed from one to the next. They would soon draw near to the place Hone Amis expected they would take shelter for the night – a cavern of sorts, word had it.

'Hope it's something decent,' Guthrie heard a man near him say. 'Nights get *cold* up here, this time of the year.'

'It's shelter enough, the Mouth is.' It was one of the hunters who had spoken. Mostly, they had stayed to themselves on this march, keeping the rear-guard except for a few who acted as guides of a sort, as this one was doing.

'The Mouth?' a Militiaman asked.

'A big half-cavern,' the hunter replied. 'I've been there. Good enough for the likes of us this night, I reckon.'

'How close?'

'A ways yet, but not too far.'

'All I want,' put in a Militiaman, 'is a chance to sit by a fire, get some food and a hot drink in me. Some sleep ...'

313

Guthrie sighed inwardly, hearing this. He knew how that last man felt. He only hoped the hunter was right about this Mouth being not too far off. His limbs still felt the debilitating effects of the fever, and he did not know how much more he could endure. He felt the world shiver a little about him, thrust that uncertainty away, denied it, concentrated on keeping himself firmly himself in the simple, ordinary world of tree root and stone and sweat and tricky uphill footing.

But, clambering over the tangled roots of an old oak, Guthrie stumbled, slipped ... and slipped inadvertently out of the world through very weariness.

It took him by surprise.

Despite all Rosslyn's old warnings, he had started believing that, indeed, the *other* was fading from his life. He had begun to claim his old self back, like a man building a home, restructuring himself, denying the *other*, renewing his former personality. He was Reeve Guthrie Garthson, the Reeve of Reeve Vale. That, and entirely that, and nothing else. And the more solid his sense of self grew, the more the intensity of the *other* seemed to fade. Soon, he had almost convinced himself, the insistent tug of the *other* upon him would grow to be no more than a dwindling memory. He would be free of it, finally, free to live his life as he had dreamed for so many years.

But no.

The *other* encompassed him, depthless as ever, churning like a great, sucking tide. He floundered in it, desperately reaching for stability. He felt himself whirled helplessly along, plunging, struggling ... Then, before him, suddenly, he *sensed* a ... presence. Stealthy, predatory movement.

He shuddered away, skittering like a terrified silverfish in a riptide. And perceived the distant beacon of the dead Abbod's skull, shining softly, blessedly, for him in the void. He had not lost that, thank the Powers.

The ordinary world coalesced about him, and Guthrie found himself splayed out his back on soggy leaves, his hands clutching at the satchel in which he carried the skull.

'Reeve?' somebody was saying. 'Reeve? Are you ...'

'I am all right,' Guthrie said, sitting up, panting. His head throbbed and he seemed to have smacked his elbow against something. He took a long, shuddering breath.

The men of his little guard-squad were gathered about him anxiously.

314

'Reeve, can you get up? We must keep on. The night's camp can't be far now.'

Guthrie nodded, levered himself to his feet, settled the satchel more comfortably. He tried to brush himself off a little, mortified, silently cursing the *other* and the misery it had brought upon him.

An arm came out to him, steadying. 'Can you walk?'

He nodded, disengaged the arm, started off.

'Can't be too far now,' one of the men repeated reassuringly.

He nodded silently and walked, focusing on putting one foot before the other, trying to throw off the enervating after-effect of his inadvertent plunge into the *other*. The men talked around him in subdued voices.

'This cave or whatever we're headed for can't come soon enough, if you ask me,' one of them said. 'I don't like it amongst all these damnable trees. A man can't see more than a score of paces at the best of times. Too many places we could be taken unawares. At least in a cave we'll have something solid at our backs.'

'Aye,' another agreed. 'Too many places for ambush. Bandit territory indeed, this wilderness. Enough to make a man nervous.'

Ambush, Guthrie thought idly.

Ambush.

Suddenly, he halted. The stealthy movement he had *sensed* ahead in the *other*. Could it be?

His heart beat suddenly fast. He was still so unsure of himself when it came to that *other*. Could anything he perceived there be reliable? And how could he confirm or deny anything?

'Reeve?' one of the men queried uncertainly.

Guthrie realized he had stopped dead. 'I'm fine,' he said. 'A bit weary is all. As you all must be. Why don't we take a short break?'

The men hovered uneasily. ''Tisn't far to go, now. And Master Amis's orders were to ...'

Guthrie waved them to sit. 'Only for a few moments.'

They looked at each other, uncertain, then obeyed.

Settling himself on a knobbly oak-root, Guthrie tried to think. All he need do to test what he might or might not have perceived was to slide a little out of the world, balance himself at the very shallowest verge of the *other*, feel carefully about him. But his belly knotted up and he shrank from the very idea.

He felt fragile now, all the effort of days to reassert his old self undermined, all his hardwon certainties crumbled, by a few short moments in the *other*. He did not wish to acknowledge the fragility of his personality, the artificiality of it. But the experience forced it upon him, for knowledge of the *other* made all else mere surface illusion, world and self alike. Potter's work.

Guthrie shuddered. He wanted to deny it all, to return to his older, simpler self. And he could do it, he felt. If only he could stay entirely clear of the *other* long enough to reassert his old self solidly enough ...

But what if that which he had *sensed* was, indeed, the presence of bandits ahead?

Ambush.

The word made him shiver.

He was Reeve, he told himself, Reeve and nothing else. Nothing else mattered! Yet he had already, once, felt what it was to be Reeve of the dead. And if it *were* bandits ahead ... How could he live with himself if, afterwards, he knew that he had known, and could have prevented disaster, and did not?

Heart thumping, Guthrie let himself slide out of the world, holding on as best he could, like a man dangling over the edge of a great precipice by his fingertips, staring down, shaking but determined.

He felt the great, seething confusion of the *other* overwhelm him, but kept a precarious balance, remembering how he had done this before, balancing between the worlds, balancing between his new and old selves, trying not to lose anything, not be swept away, not blinded. Slowly, he found himself able to hold. And ahead (though 'ahead' was not the right word to describe what his *other*-sense revealed) he perceived stealthy movement. As always, it was not visual, this *sensing*, but his mind made images for him: glowing eggs creeping along on snake-like tendrils, filing along a long slope, settling, waiting. All this, and something more, too, not quite like anything he had yet experienced, a man, and yet more – or perhaps less – than any ordinary man. In the further distance, this somebody lurked, far off; only a kind of dim glimpse did Guthrie catch, and what remained in his mind's eye afterwards was an image like that of a great fruit, hard skinned, wrinkled, solid, a dark, pitted sphere. He knew not at all what to make of such an image, but it was enough to somehow unsettle his guts.

He came back into the world with a start, feeling his body jump as if somebody had given him a hard shove. He blinked, looked about, squinting to focus. The members of the guard-squad were staring at him uneasily.

316

'Reeve,' one of the men said, 'we must keep moving along. Can you walk again? The shelter ahead isn't far now. Master Amis said ...'

Guthrie waved the man to silence. 'There are bandits ahead. If we continue on like this, Amis will lead us direct into a trap.'

The guards stared at him.

'Fetch him,' Guthrie said to one of them.

'But ...' They stared at him as if he had gone quite mad.

'Fetch him. Now!'

'Aye, Reeve,' one man replied, then scurried off.

Guthrie looked about, saw the line of Militia trailing carefully along in the near distance through the trees and delegated another of his guard-squad to go off and halt them. He could still faintly *sense* the presence ahead. Those glowing, snake-tendrilled eggs ... He did not know how he could feel so certain, but he did feel so. Bandits, settling in to ambush ahead.

The men of his guard-squad stood about uneasily, looking at the ground, at each other, anywhere but at him. They said not a word until Hone Amis arrived. The Militia Master's face was clouded and he yanked Guthrie up, hustling him off a little distance so they could talk in private.

'Listen, lad,' he began. 'You can't just call me over like this whenever you've a mind to. We've got to keep *order*! Isn't it bad enough that the hunters still wilfully ignore my instructions? Against my express *command* they allowed women to come on this expedition. Encouraged it, no doubt, as a wilful sign of disrespect. And you, all you did was shrug the news off when you heard. And now, on some *whim* you call me away from where I ought to be. This isn't the way to do things, lad. You've got to *learn*.

'This is your first punitive expedition. I remember well how it feels, remember my own. Why, when your brother Garrett went on his first, he —'

'Amis! Be *quiet* a moment.'

The Militia Master blinked, closed his mouth in surprise.

'You're leading us into a trap.'

The older man shook his head and sighed. 'As I was about to say, before you interrupted me. Your brother did exactly this same thing. He saw bandits behind every bush on that first expedition of his. We teased him about it for months afterwards. Now just you never mind, lad. I've been leading expeditions like this for longer than

317

you've been alive. I know what I'm about. You've a lot to learn yet. Why don't you begin by –'

'There are bandits ahead of us, Amis. I know it.'

'Oh aye? And just how do you *know*?'

'I just know is all.'

Hone Amis snorted. 'Did you develop magic eyes while you were lost and alone in the wilds, then?'

Guthrie shrugged uncomfortably. 'All you need do to see if I'm right is send a man or two off ahead, quietly, with instructions to scout carefully about.'

'And meanwhile, the rest of us just sit around here twiddling our thumbs? Night will be upon us all too soon, and we need to get along or we'll end up spending a hard night here. Or haven't you noticed those clouds overhead? There's shelter up ahead we can use.'

'The bandits know that, perhaps. They're waiting to take us.'

Hone Amis eyed Guthrie. 'Says you.'

Guthrie said nothing.

The Militia Master sighed. He ran a hand wearily across his eyes. 'What am I to make of you, lad. You're changed. You were never like this before. You say crazy things.'

'We're all changed, Amis.'

'Aye. True enough.' Another sigh followed the first. 'But surely you don't expect me to take you seriously on this? How could these bandits know we are coming? Oh, aye, I grant you there's a chance some scout might have spotted us. But they'd never have the time to organize an ambush. That's the very reason we need to keep as much speed as possible. Camp tonight, leave before dawn. Keep surprise on our side. We know where their camp is. We *have* them!'

Hone Amis shook his head. 'Besides, how could *you* know *anything* about *anything* that's taking place well up ahead of us? My scouts have reported back nothing unusual. Why ought I to listen to you?'

Guthrie looked away uneasily. 'Just send a man ahead, Amis. What have you got to lose? If I'm proved wrong, the worst that can happen is that we spend a night's hard sleep here. And if I'm right ...'

'Is something gone amiss, then?' a new voice suddenly asked.

Turning, Guthrie saw Charrer Mysha come striding along in his silent manner, bow in hand.

'This is none of your affair, Mysha,' Amis snapped at him. 'Go back to your hunters and *try* to keep them in some sort of order. They've been all over the place this march, like a pack of straggling children.'

Charrer Mysha ignored the Militia Master and turned, instead, to Guthrie. He looked at Guthrie, one eyebrow raise in silent query.

'There are bandits ahead,' Guthrie said.

Charrer Mysha nodded. 'So we hope.'

'These lie in wait for us,' Guthrie continued.

'Is that so?' Charrer Mysha raised an eyebrow in surprise.

'Enough, Guthrie!' Hone Amis snapped. 'This is *not* the sort of conversation we should be having here.' Turning to Charrer Mysha, he said, 'Return to your own, Mysha. Now! None of this involves you.'

Mysha remained unmoved. 'I'm inclined to disagree, Amis.'

Guthrie turned to Mysha. The older hunter had a quiet, watchful way about him, like a wild thing, wide-eyed, alert. And those eyes of his ... far-seeing indeed did they seem, or perhaps deep-seeing was a better way to put it. Hone Amis, of course, was a watchful man in his way, too. But Amis judged, weighed, assessed, seeing threat and non-threat, good and bad, in everything he surveyed. Mysha, on the other hand, seemed merely watchful, neither judging nor not judging. Might he even see through the world and into the *other*? Guthrie did not know, did not know how to ask, but Mysha had the feel of a man who saw beyond what ordinary men might. Guthrie felt a sudden sense of kinship with him.

'Please,' Guthrie said to the old hunter. 'It would be best if you did leave us. The matter is ...' he flicked his glance in a quick indication of Hone Amis, who stood scowling, 'delicate.'

Charrer Mysha continued to regard Guthrie intently for a long moment longer. 'There is something in you that disturbs me, young Reeve, disturbs *and* reassures me. It is most strange. I do not understand it.' Mysha paused, shrugged. 'But, all right. Let it be as you say, since you ask it.'

'I do ask, Ser Charrer,' Guthrie said.

Mysha paused, nodded. 'Very well.' He turned to Hone Amis. 'A pleasure to deal with somebody with manners, Amis.' Then, grinning, he padded off.

'What was *that* all about?' Hone Amis demanded suspiciously. 'Are you certain you two have no manner of – arrangement between you?'

Guthrie shook his head. 'Of course not.'

319

The Militia Master looked uneasy. 'I do not –'

'Amis! Enough about Mysha. What of the bandits ahead of us? You must call off the advance and send scouts ahead.'

Hone Amis ran a hand over his beard, rubbed his eyes, shook his head. 'It's ... What you're asking is *crazy*.'

'Do it, Amis. *Please!*'

Hone Amis sighed, shook his head. 'No. You're bone crazy, lad, and demanding of me to go along with your craziness. Why ... What if word of this – of the Reeve having craven delusions – gets around? What if word of that ... *thing* ...' he gestured to the skull hidden in the satchel hung over Guthrie's shoulder, 'gets out? Folk won't cope, lad. A mad Reeve. You almost had Charrer Mysha included in our talk here. What would he have thought if he'd heard about this mad notion of yours? Get a *hold* on yourself, can't you? You've got a responsibility. How do you expect ordinary folk to ...'

'Amis. *Amis!* Listen to me. Do I sound mad? Am I wild eyed and raving?'

The Militia Master shook his head reluctantly.

'Then do as I ask.'

'No. I cannot. What you ask is mad.'

Guthrie clenched his fists in frustration. He took the only option that seemed left him. 'You will do as I *command*, Militia Master.'

Hone Amis stared.

'I am Reeve. You are mine to command. I *command* you to send out a scout.'

'Now listen, lad. You can't expect me just to –'

'Enough! Are you my Militia Master or not?'

'Aye, that I am.'

'Then you shall do as I say.'

'And how do you think the men will react when it's found out that you've given such a ... *craven* order, that you're seeing things ahead of us, imaginary things, that make you take a coward's options, imaginary enemies behind every bush. *Think*, lad! What will folk say?'

'And what will folk say if they see the Reeve and his Militia Master in public argument? Take fair warning: I will not back down on this. Are you so eager to air our private disputes?'

The Militia Master's face flushed with anger. 'You would threaten the public good for your own selfish ends? Have you no conscience? What will happen when my scouts come back with nothing to report?'

'They will have something to report. I guarantee it.'

'And if they do not?'

'Send them. Then we shall see.'

Hone Amis hesitated.

'Send them!'

Hone Amis regarded Guthrie, a hard, long look. Guthrie looked him back, unflinching.

'All right, then,' the Militia Master agreed finally, reluctantly.

'And tell them to be careful.'

Hone Amis bristled. 'You think my scouts don't know their business? Or that I don't know mine?'

Guthrie shook his head. 'Not that.' He thought of the queer thing he had *sensed* in the background distance. He did not know who or what it might be, but the afterimage of that *sensation* still lingered uneasily within him. 'Just tell them to be especially careful. They must look for men well hid.'

Hone Amis turned, gestured a nearby Militia under-officer over. 'Where's Boll and Termigen?'

'Back with the rearguard again, Master Amis. Powly and Jont have just taken up the van, as you ordered, and Boll and Termigen switched to the rear, watching our tail.' The man looked concerned. 'Is something wrong?'

Hone Amis shook his head. 'No. But fetch them up. I need their good eyes and light feet. And make sure you set Senn and his partner to replace them. Don't leave us eyeless in the rear.'

The man nodded. 'Aye, Militia Master,' he said, then turned and trotted off.

'If you're wrong about this ...' Hone Amis said, turning back to Guthrie.

'If I'm wrong, you can do as you like. But wait and see. Just wait and see.'

Hone Amis crossed his arms over his barrel chest, lifted one hand and scratched at his grey beard. He shook his head, muttered something too faint for Guthrie to make out, then swivelled on his heel and stalked off a few paces to where an old oak trunk lay across the ground. Calling another of his Militia over, he gave instructions to bring the march to a halt. Then he lowered himself down on the tree trunk, elbows on knees, and prepared to wait. He looked over at Guthrie, snorted, shook his head. He did not invite Guthrie to sit next to him.

The two scouts, when eventually they returned, had news.

One, Boll, was a conspicuously tall, lanky man. The other, Termigen, was shorter but with the same bony lankiness. This one wore a little leather cap, brimless and tight fitting, with the Militia symbol embroidered on the front. A pair of weasel tails dangled from behind. The two of them walked with the light-limbed quickness of a pair of hunting hounds.

'Spread out across both sides of the slope leading up to the Mouth, they were,' tall Boll was saying. 'Don't know how many. Hard to count 'em.'

'At least five dozens of 'em, I'd say,' the other put in. 'Perhaps more.'

'Clever, too,' Boll went on, 'in where they hid themselves. We'd never have spotted them at all if'n we weren't especially looking for something of the sort. And the general company here'd never have seen them till it was too late.'

'How'd they know we would come along this way?' Termigen wondered.

'How'd *you* know they'd be there waiting for us, Master Amis?' Boll asked.

Hone Amis shrugged. He flicked a quick, sideways glance at Guthrie, a complex, uncertain look of veiled unease.

The two scouts looked at each other.

'It was the Reeve,' Hone Amis said. 'He surmised that, given the past actions of these bandits, they'd probably expect us to come after them and would have laid out spotters along the likely trails.'

'Then our march up here was a ploy to draw them into setting up such an ambush?' Boll said. 'You had it already worked out between you, you two?'

Guthrie watched Amis hesitate momentarily, then grab the chance. 'Exactly. It was just a question of when and where.'

The two scouts nodded, accepting Hone Amis's word, looking at Guthrie with a sudden, greater respect.

'And now?' Termigen said. He took his leather cap off and stood there, smoothing the weasel tails methodically.

Hone Amis smiled. 'Now we ambush the ambushers. Spread the word. I want all Company Captains here as quick as can be.'

The scouts nodded and loped off.

'Good to have a Reeve with some smarts,' Guthrie overheard one say to the other as they disappeared through the cover of the trees.

He did not know quite how it made him feel. Turning, he grew aware of Hone Amis's eyes upon him.

'Did you truly know?' the Militia Master asked.

Guthrie shrugged, not knowing how to answer.

Amis eyed him with uncertain appraisal. 'This is either the damnedest piece of luck, lad, or ...'

The first of the Militia Captains began to arrive, and Amis bit off what he had been about to say. Nothing was breathed of the dispute that had been between the Militia Master and the Reeve – Hone Amis valued public unity far too highly for anything of that nature – but throughout the talk that followed as they began to lay out their counter-ambush plans, Guthrie kept feeling Amis's uncertain, assessing gaze upon him.

They filed along on hands and knees, moving with painful care. Guthrie could see men along to his left, could vaguely *sense* more in the near distance.

Holding himself precariously balanced between the worlds, he could construct a sort of lay-out in his mind: the long, winding, slow upslope trail, hardly more than a scuffing of the leaf mould underfoot, along which he and the rest would have been blindly coming, the rocky bluff at the top of the rise, the recessed half-cavern there which Hone Amis had been planning to use for this night's shelter, the pincers of the bandit trap ahead, men strung out along either side of the upslope trail.

But trying to keep such double-vision steady was exhausting, and not a little dangerous. It was such a strange dance he danced, needing the insights that experience of the *other* could give, yet needing just as much – more perhaps – to keep as far from the *other* as he could for his self's sake. And he must needs keep his wits about him and stay firmly anchored to the ordinary, both for the threat that lay lurking ahead, and for the sake of those about him.

Men looked to him.

Hone Amis had tried to argue Guthrie out of coming, claiming it to be too dangerous, arguing that, as Reeve, Guthrie had to keep out of such life-threatening circumstances. But Guthrie had begun to see that folk indeed needed a figurehead, a focus, a fulcrum upon which to balance their hopes. He had become that fulcrum – will he or nil he – and upon him lay the weight of their collective intent. If he were to falter, so would they all. So he kept himself anchored, nodded encouragingly to those who looked his way, and kept his private misgivings private.

A man came along towards him through the cover of the trees, bent double, moving with careful quickness. 'Everything's set ahead,' he whispered, coming up to Guthrie. He was an older man, his face lined like worn leather, dour-faced and sober. 'Master Amis asks for you and yours to hold back, just in case.'

The men – both his assigned guard-squad and the others nearby – halted their upwards progress, waiting for Guthrie's response.

'Tell Master Amis,' Guthrie said, 'that I'll join him in the vanguard.'

'Is that ... wise?' the dour-faced messenger responded.

'Wise?' Guthrie replied. 'Perhaps, perhaps not. But it is necessary.'

The messenger opened his mouth, closed it, smiled thinly, revealing small, jagged ivory teeth. He nodded his head in slow satisfaction. 'Aye, Reeve.'

A general nodding of heads and satisfied murmuring greeted Guthrie's statement. This was the sort of Reeve the men had hoped for.

Guthrie felt a rush of exhilaration. This was the sort of Reeve *he* had hoped to be, had wished to be ever since he had been a lad.

But a part of him was still naggingly discontent, still felt his Reeveship to be only a sham, a role he must play. That part of him remembered the *other* too clearly to take Reeve Guthrie seriously. He fingered the unaccustomed blade that hung from his belt, felt his heart beginning to thump. He was, perhaps, likely to die, playing out this sham existence.

The thought of the violence ahead made him queasy. He was frightened, yes. But, more than that, some part of him was appalled at the sheer, awful brutality of it. He still seemed incapable of recovering the kind of fierce, bloody revenge hunger that had once filled him so. It was just more potter's work.

He wished there were some other way of resolving this than through blood.

Amis's messenger was still standing, waiting to be dismissed, Guthrie's guard-squad beginning to fidget uneasily. Guthrie motioned the messenger away. 'Go. Tell him I shall be right behind.'

'Aye, Reeve,' the man said. And then, as he was turning to go: 'May the Powers be with you.'

'And you,' Guthrie returned. Turning to the guards about him, he said, 'Let's be off, then,' and led the way upslope to where Hone Amis would be.

It was no easy route, and Guthrie was panting by the time he drew alongside the Militia Master. The ordinary world about him began to pulse erratically and he had to grip hard to keep it in focus. Hone Amis said something to him but, in his struggle for balance, he missed it.

'Listen to me, fool boy!'

Guthrie blinked the Militia Master into focus.

'What good will you be down there in the midst of things? You'll just get yourself killed is all.'

Guthrie shrugged.

'Listen to me! What do you know of fighting such as this? Do you think you'll make a hero of yourself, then? Is that it? Have the men tell stories of the young Reeve's prowess in battle, and the women swoon into your arms when we return? Well, let me tell you, there's nothing glamorous about fighting. It's blood and sweat and fear cramping your guts and you wishing you were *anywhere* else. You never were all that much good with a blade, for all the times we spent in practice, you and I. Never had the patience or the interest. If you'd only –'

'Amis!' Guthrie interrupted irritably. 'Enough! I am Reeve. I must do this. I have to go down there. You, of all folk, should know that.'

The Militia Master opened his mouth, closed it. For a long moment he looked at Guthrie, silent, then shrugged resignedly. 'Aye, lad. 'Tis as you say.' He bit his lip, shook his head. 'I've been harsh with you at times, lad. Needs must, at times. We've had words, lately. There's been ... anger between us. Who knows what may happen down there. If it should be the case that one of us doesn't ... come back from it ...'

Guthrie put a hand on Amis's shoulder. 'Aye, Amis, I understand. You do what you do because it needs doing. I understand.'

'Do you? *Do* you? Not as much as you will, one day, if you truly live to be the Reeve your father was.' Amis sighed. 'It is no easy occupation, being a leader of men.'

'As I am beginning to learn.'

Hone Amis smiled. 'Aye, lad. As you are beginning to learn.'

Guthrie felt a surge of sudden feeling. It was so easy to hold grudges against this man, strong willed and oh so certain of the absolute rightness of all he did. So easy to forget the man's soul ...

'This is the way of it ...' Amis was saying. 'The bandits are strung

325

along on either side of the trailway down there, waiting for us to walk up blindly into their trap. Thus far, they haven't spotted us. We've been *careful* in our advance up here. If we continue to be just as careful, we can take them from above. So ...'

XXIII

Guthrie crawled along on his belly with the others, a slow, laborious creeping across cold, damp ground. His mouth was full of the inadvertent taste of leaf and earth. And fear. He could feel his heart banging against his ribs. The long blade was out and ready in his hand, leaf strewn like the rest of him.

The light had begun to go now. Below, he could make out nothing in the dimness save trees and jagged rocks. Were the bandits indeed still there? Or had they given it up as a waste of time and left? He lay still for an instant, let himself slip ever so lightly into the *other*.

They were still there.

The first of the rain began, the droplets making soft *tlat tlat tlat* sounds all about on the fallen leaves. The rain water seemed cold as ice. Guthrie gathered himself altogether into the ordinary world and crawled on, shivering.

Word went along the line, a silent ripple of hand-sign: *be ready*.

Guthrie swallowed. His hand, clutching the hilt of the blade, was slippery with mingled clammy sweat and cold rainwater. Letting the blade loose for a moment, he wiped his palm across his sleeve, then re-gripped the hilt again more securely. He blinked water from his eyes, tugged stray hair away from his face. His mouth was dry as a stone.

Ka-TLAA Kaa-TLAAAAAAAAA.

It was the signal: the blare of Hone Amis's Sounding Horn.

Guthrie leaped to his feet and flung himself downslope with the rest, his guard-squad catching him up quickly, formed up in a close, moving wedge.

Below, all he could see of the bandits through the rain was moving, blurred dark shapes, and the white blobs of their astonished faces as they looked up in horror to discover themselves caught fatally unawares. They had time to let out a single, joint cry of shock, and then their attackers crashed down upon them in a rough wave.

Skidding precipitously along the rain-slicked slope, Guthrie missed his footing and went down on both knees, hard. The painful jolt of the landing went through him up to his spine, jarring him part way out of the world. The disorienting pulse of the *other* swept about him. But more than that, all about, he *sensed* the overwhelming and dreadful chaos of the fighting. It was as if he were tumbled in some violent river current, this way and that. He heard howls and shrieks, rage and agony, *sensed* a great flaring burst as some poor man had his life torn from him – bandit or Militiaman, Guthrie could not tell.

Stricken, Guthrie tried to bring himself back, to shake loose the *other* and bring himself altogether into the world. Things swirled into focus, fell away again. Then he *sensed* something from far off, like a long tentacle of force, or an uncoiling serpent, a *something* reaching into the confusion of fighting all about. Guthrie did not understand what it might be, but he felt it somehow connected with the unknown something he had *sensed* earlier.

The reaching thing threaded itself through the fighting, bolstering the bandits in some strange manner, weaving them together in a pattern and flinging them against their attackers as a furious, organized wave.

The Militia faltered back.

Guthrie *reached*, shuddering. It was like groping after a huge, slimy worm, or a clutch of them, for this was somehow a many-bodied, slippery thing that slid every which way as he tried to contain it.

Focused though he was on the *other*, his ears heard his name cried in a sudden warning shout, hauling him back partway into the ordinary world.

Squinting through the rain, his heart thumping painfully, Guthrie saw a ragged bandit charging down upon him, swinging a big, narrow-bladed woods-axe double-handed, his face contorted with fury. One of Guthrie's guard-squad tried to fend him away, but the bandit hacked him down and kept coming.

'Reeve!' somebody shouted to Guthrie once more.

And another: '*Beware for the Reeve!*'

Guthrie realized he was still on his knees, that the Militia about him must consider him fallen into one of his fits, helpless.

The bandit reared above Guthrie. The axe blade glistened in the rain with watery blood. Wet blood stained the sleeves and front of the man's jerkin. A long shiver went through Guthrie, as if the cold iron of axe itself had already sheered through him. The world seemed to hang frozen for a long moment, the axe wielder poised on one foot, the blade lifted high, his guard-squad locked in awkward mid-stride. In his ears, Guthrie hear a roaring, as of some great beast.

He continued to inadvertently half *sense* the tendrilled something twined through the bandits from a distance, weaving them into action. And the axe wielder charging upon him ... a tentacle of force moved him, like a pulsing wire thrust up the man's spine, slinging him blindly towards Guthrie.

Then the world sprang into motion once more, the axe coming down in a vicious arc aimed at the crown of Guthrie's head, the roar in Guthrie's ears resolving itself into the shrieks and cries of men.

Guthrie came up off his knees in a surge, rearing at once into the world and out of it, part of him *reaching* into the *other* instinctively in a thrust of will that was shadowed by – or was a shadow of – the upward, two-handed thrust he made with the blade in his hands.

The hilt twisted in his grip, the slipperiness of his palms almost betraying him, but the blade pierced upwards through the bandit's ribs nonetheless, catching against bone for an instant, then shuddering free to rip through and out the other side of the man's torso.

The axe stroke the bandit had aimed at Guthrie's skull cut only empty air. The man howled, his face a white mask of horror as he realized he had been taken too quick, and his weapon tumbled from his stricken hold.

Guthrie felt the man's weight upon him, felt the man's thumbs gouging into his throat and face in a last, vindictive spasm of attack. He thrust desperately upwards, using the blade as a lever, and heaved. Shrieking, the bandit tumbled sideways, taking the blade with him, buried in his body as it was, wrenching the hilt from Guthrie's weakening grasp.

Guthrie dropped to his knees, panting, soaked all across one side of his face and shoulder with the man's lifeblood.

'Reeve!' somebody cried. '*Reeve!*'

Hands reached for him, but he fended them away. 'I am all right. 'Tis not my blood. I'm all right, I say!' He shook himself like a hound, gasping, sending droplets of dark blood flying, blinking against the driving rain. He was still not altogether in the world, despite everything, and could still half *sense* the *other*. The desperate thrust he had made – iron blade and will combined – had not only skewered the axe wielder who had intended his death, but also somehow unravelled the serpentine coils that had been weaving the bandits together as a group.

The fighting was drawing to a close.

At his side, Guthrie saw the man he had mortally stabbed try weakly to heave himself up, saw the last, desperate look – a wide-eyed stare of intermingled rage and utter terror – and then one of Guthrie's guard-squad put the point of his Militia spear under the man's chin and thrust quickly, iron grating against bone. The bandit lifted from the ground, thrashing like a hooked fish, then collapsed.

Guthrie shuddered. He could *sense* the raging, destitute wail of the poor man's soul as it was tumbled, like a lone leaf in the wind, inexorably towards the void of the Shadowland dark.

'Reeve!' somebody demanded. Guthrie felt hands upon his shoulders. 'Reeve, are you hurt?'

'I am all right.'

'But the blood!'

'Not mine. I am all right, I say.'

'The Reeve is unharmed!' somebody shouted.

Guthrie shook himself free of the hands holding him, stood up. Only with difficulty did he hold himself steady in the world. He felt dizzy and sick. The ground underfoot seemed a fragile film stretched over a moving void. Everywhere he looked, he saw dead and dying and hurt men, rain drenched and chilled, moaning in their own blood – bandit and Militia alike.

Somebody proffered Guthrie back his own bloodied blade. He wanted to sling the thing away, to have done with it for good. But, as Reeve, he knew himself denied any such indulgence. He took the bloodied thing up, looking at it, unsure what to do now that it was in his grasp.

Night had fallen in earnest now, and several of the Militia had lit sputtering torches, sending an uncertain, dancing radiance across everything through the rain that continued to fall. Seeing him standing like that, weary, blood soaked, the bloody blade in hand glistening in the torchlight and the rain, the company – Militia, ordinary Vale men, hunters, all – let out a cheer, a ragged, inarticulate, triumphal roar.

Guthrie did not know what to do. He raised a hand, the one holding the blade, trying to signal them to silence. But the gesture only brought further cheering, and they began to chant: 'The Reeve! The Reeve! The Reeve!'

Into the midst of this, Hone Amis came striding. His blade too was out, and bloodied as Guthrie's was, and in his other hand he held a spitting pine torch. Smiling fiercely through his beard, he held his blade and the torch aloft, wafting both in intersecting arcs in time with the chanting, the torch making luminous, sparky trails through the dark, rain-streaked air.

'The Reeve! The Reeve! The Reeve!'

'Do you see?' the Militia Master shouted at them once the cheering had subsided a little. 'Do you *see* what we can do when we all act together? When each man does his part? With Reeve Guthrie here at our head, nobody, *nobody* can stand against us!'

The cheering began again.

'Soon now,' Hone Amis began, shouting above the jubilant voices, 'soon we shall have our lands back safe and sound. Soon we shall have our revenge. Soon we shall wipe away entirely that which threatens us!'

Guthrie looked on at all of this bemusedly. He could not help but feel the thrill of it, like a current in the very air that made his hair stand on end and his limbs shiver. But, also, he could still feel the *other* underlying all, implacable as ever, like a layer of black ice underneath all the warmth. And there was that ... something he had *sensed*, that tentacle of strange will-force animating the bandits. He could still feel the shadow of it on the horizon of his senses, like a watchful presence keeping out of direct sight.

It was disquieting, like gazing into the blank green wall of a wood, yet knowing some great beast lay hid there, watching with unblinking predator's eyes.

The cheering had subsided now. Hone Amis was organizing a clean-up detail.

Guthrie stood gazing uncertainly about, still a little sick-feeling in his belly and only part-way solid in the world.

'Look to the Reeve,' he heard the Militia Master order, and several of his guard-squad closed in. One took the blade that still dangled from Guthrie's hand. Another brought a flask of water and a rag and swabbed at what remained of the sticky blood that spread across Guthrie's face and shoulder. The man offered the water flask. Only after the first gulp did Guthrie realize how dry his mouth was.

331

Despite all the soaking rain, he felt parched, and took another swallow and another, thankfully.

The water seemed to settle his belly, to bring him more fully into the ordinary world, and Guthrie looked around him with clearer attention. The rain was beginning to slacken, he saw. Militiamen were dragging the corpses of slain bandits to a central point. Those bandits not killed were rounded up, a small, moaning group, heads hanging dejectedly. More torches had been lit, some set into the ground. Those of their own force who had been wounded were gathered together to be treated. More than a few had lost their lives here. They had won all right, but at a cost. Guthrie was too dazed to count heads, but he reckoned the bandits had made them pay dearly enough for victory here this night.

Guthrie moved across the way and lowered himself wearily against a tree bole. His left arm was beginning to ache sorely; he must have somehow pulled a muscle in his fight with the axe-wielding bandit. He sat, rubbing it. He could feel the remnants of the washed-off blood drying on the edge of his forehead at his hairline. He rubbed gently at it. His hand, when he looked, was stained, the finger tips darkened, as they had been when he was a boy returned from berry picking. It made him feel a little sick again, knowing that this was no berry stain but a man's life-blood – a man whom he had sent to the Shadowlands.

What hopes, what fears had the poor soul had? What ambitions had compelled him to march the long, weary way here from the south only to end his life spitted like any pig ready for the roast?

Guthrie looked away from his stained fingers, sobered and profoundly uneasy. But what he saw about him was a mood of jubilant success. Wounded men made light of their wounds, laughed even as the stitches were placed. Those of the Militia doing clean-up re-lived the fighting with each other – 'Did you see how Pawlly took that big fellow in the throat?' – and chuckled amongst themselves in satisfaction.

After the fear and the pain and the dying ... it seemed unnatural to Guthrie that these men should be so untouched by the horror of it.

Or was this how men were after such fighting? Guthrie did not know, having never been in such a fight before.

But this jubilant mood, he began to see, was not universal. The Hunters stood gathered together on their own, tending their own injured, a sober-looking group. Guthrie felt a sense of kinship with them, feeling their mood an echo of his own.

Guthrie saw Charrer Mysha, exchanged a glance with him. Mysha's eyes seemed to shine in the torchlight like a cat's, but it was an uneasy shine.

Guthrie felt his heart kick in his chest. Something was amiss.

But what?

He looked around. Hone Amis was gone about some business. The area of the fighting was all but cleared now. The bandit dead had been placed in a pile of sorts, their weapons and accoutrements taken and stacked a little ways off. Their wounded had been all but seen to, those that could be easily helped. Everything seemed to be moving on apace.

And then, with a start, Guthrie realized what was missing.

Not a single live bandit anywhere. Where had the group of captured bandits gone to?

Guthrie felt his belly do a little flop. What was happening?

Again, he caught Mysha's glance directed at him. The older hunter tipped his head over towards the right, away from where the Militia were gathering themselves together now, towards the black shadows beyond the torchlight.

Guthrie pried himself up from the tree where he still sat, and hurried over, passing through from torchlight into the wet forest darkness beyond. The rain had stopped altogether now. In amongst the trees, it was very black, the air filled with the *tlipp tlipp tlipp* of water dropping from the intricate, braided canopy of the woody limbs overhead. Disoriented, he stood as he was for long moments until finally catching the sound of quiet voices in the distance. He stumbled uncertainly onwards, using the sounds as a guide, and eventually saw the glimmer of torchlight ahead.

The captured bandits were there – a dozen of them, perhaps fewer – and Hone Amis and a Militia Captain, and a couple dozen or more Militia, blades drawn and out. They had driven several torches into the ground, forming a circle of sputtering radiance. In the midst of the lit area one of the captured bandits knelt, separated out from the group, his hands lashed tight behind him. The man moaned, lifted his head upon seeing Guthrie come up. His eyes flashed white in the torchlight.

One of the Militia stood over him, a naked long sword raised two-handed.

It was all too plain what was going on.

'Amis!' Guthrie shouted.

The Militia Master waved him off. 'Quiet!'

'What are you *doing?*'

'This need be none of your affair, lad. We do what we must for the good of the Vale.'

'But ...'

The Militia Master took Guthrie by the elbow. 'The Reeve need know nothing of this. Walk away. We do what must be done to ensure the safety of the Vale. That's all you need to know. Walk away, now. Leave us to our work here.'

Guthrie stared at him. 'No ... You cannot!'

'I can and I will,' Hone Amis replied. 'For the good of the Vale. Don't go soft on me now. You've acted well thus far. Don't ruin it now with idealistic squeamishness. We came here to eliminate these scum. Whether we do it in open battle or here in this glade matters not a jot. We have a job to do. That is all.'

Guthrie shuddered. He felt the tightness of the blood still across his forehead, remembered his stained fingers. 'What you do here is ... *murder*.'

The Militia Master shook him. '*Guthrie!* Listen to me. Turn around. Walk away. None of this need concern you. Leave it to me.'

'You did this ... this sort of thing for my father?'

Hone Amis nodded. 'Aye. When it was required. Some duties one completes, pleasant or no, because they must be done. This is such a one.'

Guthrie stared at the torch-lit tableau before him. It seemed some scene out of a nightmare, the torches dancing and spitting like live things, the Militiaman with the sword, faceless in the uncertain light, standing astride the kneeling bandit, his blade half raised and glinting coldly in the whirl of the torchlight.

The bandit hunched close to the ground. Twisting himself about, he looked up at Guthrie. 'Sto ... stop them,' he begged, his voice hoarse as a crow's croak. The man's eyes, in the flickering torchlight, shone white and blank with terror. 'For pity's sake, *stop* this!'

Hone Amis hurried Guthrie away, dragging him along by the arm until they were a little distance off at the edge of the dark.

'Listen to me, Guthrie,' he said. 'I will say this one last time. These bandit scum would have killed us if they could. Can't you see what sort of men they are? We have our *future* to ensure here. You are Reeve now. Act like a Reeve!'

334

Guthrie stared uncertainly at the bandits, a small huddled, silent group.

Seeing the direction of Guthrie's gaze, Hone Amis snorted. 'A good hound is worth three of these scum. Just *look* at them!'

Guthrie looked, seeing the ragged shapes of the bandits in the torchlight, haggard faces, staring eyes.

In looking, he felt himself swaying on the edge of the ordinary world, seeing with double vision, partly with his ordinary eyes, partly with his *other*-sense.

They posed a threat right enough, just as Amis insisted. But in Guthrie's double-visioned sight they were no different from anything else: they coasted over the depths of the *other*, like everything, mysterious as moon or stars, as the little ants that walked in columns for leagues, as the boiling march of a thunder cloud or the singing of the wind, as the very Fey themselves.

Guthrie looked across at Hone Amis. 'Lift the cloth,' he found himself saying, 'the threads unwind.'

Hone Amis stared at him. '*What?*'

'Endless mystery will you find.' Guthrie blinked self-consciously. It was part of a verse out of *The Book* which had come to him. He remembered it clearly:

> *Tree and rock and cloud and stream,*
> *Are never what they look to seem.*
> *Mind nor self nor hand nor star,*
> *Nothing's what we say they are.*
>
> *Face and fingers, legs and arms,*
> *Fears and joys and spells and charms,*
> *Warp and woof and nothing more,*
> *Threads to clothe us, nothing more.*
>
> *Lift the cloth, the threads unwind,*
> *And endless mystery will you find.*

Guthrie could not think how properly to communicate what he was feeling, for Hone Amis was entirely blind and deaf to what underlay the appearances of the world.

But he tried: 'There has been enough death, Amis. Let be. These men are no better and no worse than any others, than anything. You cannot control the world by killing. There will always more killing to do. It's all a mystery, Amis. Underneath, it's all a great mystery. You can't —'

The Militia Master yanked at him fiercely. 'What's *wrong* with you, lad? You're raving. Get a *hold* on yourself!'

Guthrie did not know how to answer.

'No more of this, then!' Hone Amis snapped. 'What will the men think? Do you wish to appear as a weakling in their eyes? Or a raving fool? *They* know what must be done here.' Amis put a hand on Guthrie's shoulder, pushing him away. 'Go. Leave this to us.'

Guthrie took a step, another, feeling Amis's wide hand push against his back.

'Go and let us get on with things here. *Go!*'

Another few steps Guthrie took. Then he turned, twisting away from the Militia Master's hand and strode back to the torch-lit circle.

'Guthrie!' Hone Amis called after him.

Striding up to the Militiaman astride the kneeling bandit, Guthrie said, 'Put the blade away.'

The man stared at Guthrie, hesitant.

'Put it away, I said!' Guthrie moved to reach for the blade.

But Hone Amis intervened. 'No! Continue as you were. It was the Reeve's first fight today. He is ... shaken, not himself.' The Militia Master took Guthrie by the shoulders and turned him forcefully about, trying to manoeuvre him away.

Guthrie twisted free, straight-armed the Militiaman in the sternum, sending him stumbling backwards, then stood over the kneeling bandit himself, straddling the man protectively.

For long moments, nobody moved. Except for the soft spluttering of the torches, there was utter silence. The Militia stood about uncomfortably, tense, staring.

'Get away from him, Guthrie,' Hone Amis said, half command, half request. He bent closer, his face livid. 'Where is your dignity? Your common sense? Have you forgotten Obart Pettir and his ambitions? We are still too far from being secure yet. You threaten everything with this craziness of yours. These bandit scum are worthless. Get *away* from him, I say, and let us do what must be done!'

'Or what?' Guthrie prompted. 'Will you have *me* killed, too?'

The Militia Master jerked back, as if Guthrie had kicked him. He leaned in closer again and hissed, 'Don't be *stupid! Think!* Think what you do. Think how this *looks.*'

'Back away, Militia Master,' Guthrie ordered. He was panting and his vision kept slipping off into blackness.

Hone Amis glared, opened his mouth, closed it again. He ran a hand over his face, shook his head, looked about, then seemed to come to an abrupt decision. 'You lot,' he said, gesturing at a portion of his gathered Militiamen, 'circle round behind him. We'll take him all together.'

The men shuffled over as directed, but slowly, showing little enthusiasm for the task of tackling their Reeve.

'Do it!' Hone Amis snapped. 'The Reeve is not himself, I say. Can't you see that?'

'Is this what your oath comes to, then, Amis?' Guthrie demanded. 'Is this what your being *true* to me and mine amounts to?'

The Militia Master shook his head. 'I *am* being true. What we do here *has* to be done, now, quickly, with no debate. For the good of the Vale. You're not thinking straight, or you'd see it yourself. Tomorrow you'll thank me. All the men here will be sworn to secrecy. No one else shall ever know anything of what happened here. It's for your own good that I do this!'

'Not for *my* good, Amis, but for your own.'

'No! What I do is for the good of the Vale as whole. I've *always* put that first!'

'The good of the Vale as *you* see it. The good as it suits *you*!'

'No!'

'Aye!' Guthrie gestured about him at the closing Militiamen. 'Is this what you call the good of the Vale? Ordering your men to bring me down like a beast at bay because I *disagree* with you?'

'This is no simple ... *disagreement*!'

'What, then?'

'You ...' Hone Amis shook himself. 'I will not argue this with you.'

'Oh no? And why not?'

'If you haven't the common sense to accept my judgement in this matter ...'

'If I haven't the sense to accept your judgement you'll have me dragged off and beaten until I do? Is that right?'

The Militia Master stiffened. 'No. *No!* Of course not.'

'What, then?'

Hone Amis hesitated, he and Guthrie glaring at each other. The Militiamen gathered about stood stiff with tension, unmoving, uncertain.

'Guthrie, lad,' Hone Amis started, '*listen* to me ...'

'No! *You* listen to *me*! You swore an oath to my father, *and* to me, an oath of loyalty.'

'How *dare* you question my ...'

337

'Shut your face and *listen!*' Guthrie shouted.

Hone Amis shut up, staring.

Guthrie took a breath, panting trying to focus. 'You push too much, Amis. You strangle things.'

The Militia Master started to reply but Guthrie cut him short with an impatient gesture. 'Look at what you are doing here. If I disagree with you, it must be that I am not in my right mind. Simple as that. And the answer? Have me carted bodily away.' Guthrie paused, looking Hone Amis straight. 'Are you so sure you're right, Amis? Are you *so* sure of it that you will sacrifice *me?*'

'What are you talking about?' the Militia Master asked uneasily.

Guthrie knelt down next to the captive bandit, who had remained a silent, shivering witness to all that was happening. 'If you kill these captives, you must kill me too.'

Hone Amis snorted. 'Don't be an *idiot!*'

Guthrie laughed, a choked, hoarse sound. 'Is everybody who goes contrary to your wishes an idiot, then?'

Hone Amis paled.

'I am the Reeve of Reeve Vale, and I say these captives will *not* be put to the sword here like this. Such ... brutality is *not* what life in Reeve Vale is all about.'

'These are hard times. Hard times require hard decisions.'

'Not *this* decision, Militia Master,' Guthrie replied. 'Not what you intended to do here. Now, will you or will you not honour the oath you swore?'

Hone Amis hesitated.

'The choice is a simple one, Militia Master. Abide by your oath or not. Abide by my judgement or have your own way.'

'You give me no choice!'

'Oh, but I do. Abide by your oath or destroy it.'

Hone Amis shifted uncomfortably, tugged at his beard, looked about him at the gathered Militiamen, the bandits. He took a step towards Guthrie, undid it, backed away.

'Well?' Guthrie demanded.

'You are making a mistake.'

'Then it is *my* mistake and I shall live with it.'

'But what if –'

'*Decide*, Militia Master!'

Hone Amis ran a hand over his eyes, shook himself. Slowly, he nodded. 'I am your man, Reeve,' he said in a soft, hoarse voice. 'I will abide by my oath.'

The knot of gathered Militiamen let out a collective sigh.

Guthrie nodded. 'Good.' He could feel his limbs shaking, from tension and very weariness. Almost, he slipped from the world entirely, catching himself only by an abrupt effort of will, like yanking himself back from a precipice. He stood away from the bandit captive.

The man looked up at him, white faced.

'What are you called?' Guthrie asked him.

The man coughed, swallowed. 'Oss ... Ossbert.' He continued to stare up at Guthrie, a pleading, uncertain look. 'Spare us, Lord.'

Guthrie regarded the man in silence a long moment. He could sense the residual tension in Hone Amis still, and in the Militia. They too were staring at him, wondering what he was about.

'Ossbert,' he said after a little, 'what brought you here to our lands?'

The bandit glanced about, nervous as a hen, his eyes flitting from one man to another. He shivered. 'He said we ... we would have lands of our own.'

'He? Who is *he*?'

'Sethir.'

'This Sethir is your ... leader?'

'Aye, Lord. He is now. He knows this land. He said there was easy pickings. He said we would live like lords. Him and that Tasamin.'

'Tasamin?'

The bandit shivered. 'Makes a man's skin crawl, that one. Never liked him, meself.'

'Who is he?' Guthrie prompted.

'He's a ... he's some sort of sorcerer, Lord. I ... I don't know how else to describe him to ye. He dresses in these fancy clothes, and jewels, and has a ... a magic skull that does his bidding.'

'A *what*?' Guthrie demanded.

Hone Amis leaned closer.

'A dead man's skull, Lord. But he ain't properly dead, if ye knows what I mean.' Seeing the perplexed looks of the men gathered about him, the bandit shrugged. 'It's not so easy to explain, Lord. Ye needs must see a thing like that.'

Guthrie shivered. This was altogether too strange. He stood gazing down at the bandit, lost in uneasy thought for a moment.

'Lord,' the bandit said in a small voice, after a little. 'Lord? What will ye do with me? With us?'

Guthrie flexed his arms, took a long breath, trying to keep himself focused. 'You came here for lands, you say?'

The bandit nodded.

'You had none in the south?'

'I had *nothing* in the south, Lord. None of us did. That's why we came here, on Sethir's promises, him and Tasamin's and old Torno's, too, though *he's* well gone to the Shadowlands now.'

'What if I were to make you a promise?'

'What kind of promise, Lord?'

'If I promised you your life and your freedom, would you swear your oath to me and abide by it, Ossbert?'

The man nodded eagerly. 'Aye, Lord, that I would!'

'Guthrie,' Hone Amis put in. 'This is madness. The man will swear to anything. And once he's free he'll put a knife in your back as soon as look at you.'

'I'd gladly put a knife in *yer* back,' one of the other bandit captives muttered.

A Militiaman smacked the man sharply in the face, silencing him.

Though still kneeling before Guthrie, Ossbert raised himself as best he could. 'I have been a desperate man, Lord, aye. But I am not an honourless man. Sethir was too ruthless, too filled with anger for my liking. And Tasamin ... too uncanny altogether. Ye ... ye seems more an ordinary man, a Lord to follow. And no tyrant like *him* ...' he gestured with his chin at Hone Amis, who bristled.

Straightening himself as best he could, Ossbert looked Guthrie in the eye. 'Lord, give me yer trust and I will not fail ye. Ye will have my oath on that.'

Guthrie regarded the man in silence for long moments, then nodded. 'Cut him loose.'

'Guthrie!' Hone Amis protested.

Guthrie silenced him with a look.

'And you others?' Guthrie asked, turning to the huddled group of captives.

'What other choice does ye give us?' one of them demanded sullenly.

'I will offer you your freedom.'

They stared at him suspiciously.

'Cut their bonds,' Guthrie ordered the Militiamen nearest.

They looked to Hone Amis, uneasy.

'Do it!' Guthrie snapped.

'Aye, Reeve,' one of them said and turned to with a little blade.

340

Two others followed suit, and the bandits were quickly released. They stood in a little bemused group, rubbing at their wrists, staring about uncertainly.

'You are free to go,' Guthrie told them.

'Oh, aye? With no weapons or nothing?' one said.

'Take whatever was yours,' Guthrie replied.

The men stared at him, still deeply suspicious.

'For true?'

Guthrie nodded. 'For true. Take what is yours and go. Or stay and swear your oath to me.'

'And if we do?'

'There is more free land than there once was in Reeve Vale,' Guthrie said.

Ossbert came to stand before Guthrie. He was no young man, close to Hone Amis's own age by the looks of him. His clothing was ragged and he had a long, dark bruise across the whole left half of his face. 'I came northwards to find a life for myself, Lord. If yer offer still holds, I am yers.'

'It still holds. And holds for all of you,' Guthrie said to the group at large.

'Tell me the words of it,' Ossbert said.

Guthrie looked across at Hone Amis. The Militia Master shook his head. 'Guthrie, lad, listen ...'

'Tell him the oath, Militia Master.'

Hone Amis sighed. He turned. 'Listen well, then, Ossbert the Bandit. If the Reeve wishes you to take the oath, then take it you shall.'

Ossbert nodded, silent.

'Down on one knee,' Hone Amis commanded.

Ossbert lowered himself.

'And the rest of you, too,' Hone Amis ordered.

There was considerable shuffling about and hasty, whispered consultation amongst the little group of bandits, but, in the end, not a single one of them refused.

'Know what's good for 'em, this lot,' Guthrie overheard one of the Militia whisper.

'By my red blood and white bone,' Hone Amis began, 'I swear to be true ...'

One by one, the bandits took their oath, bending on one knee before Guthrie and repeating it as Hone Amis gave it to them.

'By blood and bone and breath,' Guthrie responded to them all, 'I

341

give my oath in return: to never misuse you or yours, to never lose sight of the good of the whole, to never forget my position.'

'By the great Powers that flow through the world,' Hone Amis said, 'let it be so.'

'By the Powers,' the company murmured generally, and it was done.

Guthrie felt a great wave of weariness come over him then. Too much had happened. He needed rest, desperately.

Things were far from finished yet. There were more bandits still to be dealt with. And there was this Sethir. And Tasamin, with the dead man's skull.

But first, rest.

Guthrie blinked, shook himself. He felt barely able to place one foot before another. He could feel his balance in the world faltering.

He felt hands under his armpit, supporting him.

'Let me help ye, Lord,' a voice said.

Blinking, Guthrie saw it was Ossbert holding him up.

'Back away!' somebody cried.

Guthrie saw Hone Amis draw his blade. 'No,' he said. 'I am all right.'

The Militia Master shook his head suspiciously.

Guthrie levered Ossbert gently away. 'I am all right. Leave me. Rest is all I need. I will rest for a little.'

Hone Amis elbowed Ossbert to the side and replaced him. 'Lean on me, Guthrie, lad.'

Guthrie did, and with the Militia Master's help began to walk the path back to the main encampment, where there was food to be had, and drink, and blessed rest.

XXIV

Angry voices roused Alia from a pleasant sleep. Her limbs felt sluggish, her mind also, and it took a long few moments for her to be able to make proper sense of things.

'You said ...' somebody was shouting, 'You *said* you knew where they were and what would happen. You *said* t'would be all right!'

An angry, muttering chorus of men's voices greeted this.

'It *would* have been all right,' responded a second voice, controlled and quiet. 'Save that something's amiss down there. I cannot see it clear, but something's amiss, I tell ye. Something's displaced the intended result.'

The world seemed to pulse in and out of focus for Alia. And underneath that pulsing, a dark, formless current flowed. She remembered the terrible chaos of that dark current, how it had almost taken her, and shuddered. Her hands stroked the heavy chain at her throat, anchoring herself with the comforting feel of the warm golden links, until the world began to settle.

Alia looked about, blinking. It was night time. In the faint light of a small, dimly burning lantern, she saw that the tent in which she lay was empty. The shouting that had roused her seemed to be coming from outside.

'That's bloody wonderful,' the first voice she had heard was saying now. 'Something's *amiss* you say! You weren't there. You didn't see! Only a bare handful of us escaped, curse you! And the rest – killed or taken, the lot!'

Alia rolled herself to her knees. She tried to rise further, but felt too dizzy. She was vaguely thirsty, and sleepy. It was *so* tempting just to curl up and go back to sleeping. She seemed to have been having such lovely dreams ...

But the shouting continued, insistent, intrusive.

She crawled across the tent, the bracelets on her wrists tinkling musically as she moved. For a moment, she stopped, shaking her wrists just to hear the golden tinkling of that music, to look at them scintillate so beautifully in the dim lanternlight. What lovely bracelets. What a lovely gift Tasamin had made her.

They were still shouting ...

She got to the tent's doorflap, lifted it a little, squinted out into the night. Fires burned in the near distance, and in front of her tent sputtering torches lit the scene. Two men faced each other, surrounded by the entire camp.

Tasamin. And the bearded one named Sethir.

Sethir stood, feet braced wide, hands slicing through the air as he shouted. His dark eyes, above the black spade of a beard that hid much of his face, were blazing with fury. 'You said there was no need to use more men for such an ambush. You said the enemy would come walking blindly into the trap, never suspecting. You said we couldn't fail. Well we *did* fail. Miserably! And now they are all too close by. Do you hear?

'All the years I worked towards this, all the planning ... and you've ruined everything, you stupid, dandified *idiot*! You with your jewels, your private girls, your fancy clothes and fancy plans. *Ruined everything!*' Sethir half drew the long knife that hung on his belt. 'I will not, will *not* stand by and watch everything for which I have worked for all these years collapse into nothing!'

Alia felt a prickle of outrage. How *dare* the man speak like this to Tasamin?

But Tasamin only smiled thinly. He was dressed in a tunic of shining sienna-brown, crimson trousers tucked into high leather boots, with a charcoal black cloak about his shoulders that clung to him like a great shadow. His jewellery glittered in the dancing torchlight. To Alia's eyes, he had a dignity that Sethir entirely lacked: the bandit leader seemed little more than a draggly rat squeaking impotently at some great bird of prey. Tasamin's eyes seemed bright as any of his gems, and his gaze as fierce and steady as any hawk's. He held the skull, fixed atop a staff now, in his hand. He raised it, his jewellery softly tinkling, and aimed the staff at Sethir, as if it were a weapon.

Alia felt a little rush of excitement. Aye! Let this Sethir see what it was to speak to a man like Tasamin so!

Sethir faltered back a double step.

'Do not insult me, little man,' Tasamin said, his voice coldly quiet. 'There is something amiss down there, I tell ye. I *will* find it out. And when I do –'

'You'll *what?*' Sethir demanded angrily. He gripped the hilt of half-drawn knife still. 'You've ruined me, you and your intrigues! Twice now, you've failed me. The great Tasamin. Ha! You were full of confident predictions about how we were going to take their camp, but you fled like any craven when the fighting turned against us!'

Tasamin merely shrugged. 'I have certain ... limitations, man. Does ye expect me to behave like some some dream-blinded adolescent, flinging my life away uselessly?'

'You ran, Tasamin. Like any frightened boy.'

'Not at all. They were too many of them for us, and too well led. I ran like any sensible man who sees it is time to retreat. Ye did the same. Elementary tactics. By running then, we lived to fight again later.'

'And be miserably defeated!' Sethir spat disgustedly, wiped his mouth with the back of the hand not gripping the knife. 'Bah! Years of struggle it cost me to get back to this land. And now what? I should *never* have listened to you when you first came to me. Look about you. Look! How many of us are there left now?'

'Enough,' Tasamin replied calmly.

'Enough for what?'

'For what I have in mind.'

'More *plans*?'

Tasamin nodded equitably enough. 'More plans indeed. Does ye think I would allow myself to be panicked into defeat the way ye allows yerself to be?'

Sethir took a startled breath.

Tasamin stood, one hand stroking the curved brown dome of the skull, fingers stroking in long, fluid movements. The skull's jewellery winked hypnotically between his fingers, like little lights flashing in an intricate, mazy pattern. Tasamin's eyes seemed almost to glow. Alia felt a surge in her belly, watching him. 'We may have lost a battle or two,' he said to Sethir, 'but the war will yet be ours.'

The bandit leader stared at him. 'You're either bone crazy, or ...'

'Or?' Tasamin asked, smiling a thin smile, stroking the skull still.

'Or a man whose counsel may still be worth following after all,' Sethir conceded after a moment. He blinked, shook his head, thrust his knife back into its sheath, let the hilt go.

Tasamin nodded. 'Now, indeed, ye is beginning to show sense.' He stopped stroking the skull. 'There are things I must needs find out. And that will take a little time.'

Sethir nodded reluctantly. 'How much time?'

Tasamin shrugged. 'Give me until the morning. Perhaps a little longer. Ye must make sure I am not disturbed.'

The bandit leader nodded.

'Soon enough, I will find the answers I seek.'

'And then?' Sethir prodded.

'Then we will move against these enemies of yers one final time. They are close by, as ye says. We will deal them the final blow.'

'Good!' Sethir nodded in satisfaction. 'It is settled, then.' He gestured to the men who still stood gathered about. 'Go prepare yourselves, your weapons. Sleep if you can. We will move against them soon enough.'

The men began to scatter, talking amongst themselves, uneasy but excited, their voices rising in a collective hum, like so many hive insects on the swarm.

'And this other matter,' Sethir began. He and Tasamin stood alone in deeper darkness, only a single torch left now lighting their talk. 'This *girl* ...'

'That matter is settled,' Tasamin replied curtly. 'There is nothing to discuss.'

'Tasamin, listen!' Sethir hissed. 'The men remember. They talk of what you have been doing to her in that tent of yours these past days.'

Tasamin laughed, 'They have no inkling of what I do.'

'It doesn't matter *what* you do! It's what they *think* you're doing with her that counts. Get rid of her. Give her to the men as I first suggested. Do it. Now! Before some fool comes along and –'

'The matter is settled, I have said. Speak to me of it no more! She is mine to do with as I wish.'

Alia, witnessing all this, felt a little shiver of unease. She fingered the necklace at her throat.

And then Tasamin was striding back towards the tent, and she scuttled away from the entrance instinctively.

He flung the doorflap aside, pushed in, saw her crouched on the ground, and halted. A spasm of irritation passed across his face. Alia felt her heart suddenly begin to thump. She faltered away from him.

But his face cleared. He smiled at her, his white teeth flashing in the tent's dim lanternlight. Lifting the jewelled skull-staff, he passed it over her as in a blessing, murmuring all the while softly under his breath. Alia's heart eased, and she felt her limbs loosen comfortably. 'Come, my girl,' he said. 'We have things to do.' He motioned for her to shift herself to the tent's back corner. 'Sit there. I will have need of yer help in a little.'

Alia did not know what he had in mind, but, somehow, it did not matter. She felt content enough just to watch him as he moved about the tent. As she sat quietly, fingering the bracelets binding her wrists, it seemed to her that he moved with a lovely kind of grace. He lit a second lamp, a brighter one, then brought out an ornate little wooden chest from a back corner of the tent. Unlocking the chest, he lifted out a double handful of jewellery, a gold and silver cascade of brilliance. He began laying items out, glinting golden necklaces, shining rings and brooches, a braid of bronze and silver bracelets that glowed with a soft lustre, a slim little length of ruby-studded gold chain.

The rubies gleamed like bright little eyes. Alia moved, drawn irresistibly. Half on her knees, she reached a hand out towards the little red gems.

'No!' he hissed, slapping her hand away, hard enough to sting painfully. His face seemed suddenly a hard mask, his shining blue eyes like cold bits of lifeless ice.

Alia fell back, her heart hammering. She cowered, feeling her belly twist up.

But his smile came back quickly. He reached a hand to her, smoothing her hair, murmuring hidden words. Like music almost, what he murmured in her ear, soothing. 'That's a good girl,' he said softly. 'Stay here now. I didn't mean to startle ye. Only stay here. Stay as ye are. Stay ...'

Alia looked up at him and nodded her compliance. She felt a soothing warmth coming into her.

'Stay as ye are,' he repeated. 'Stay.'

He turned, then, and went back to his jewellery. With slow care, he laid out a circle about three paces in diameter, first marking the tent's dirt floor with the base of the skull-staff, then laying a ring of jewellery, necklace to bracelet to brooch to necklace and so on, until he had completed the circle, leaving only a little gap by which to enter.

He turned and looked at Alia, made a sweeping motion with his hand taking in the jewelled circle. 'A haven,' he said. 'A protection for where we go.'

Alia blinked, uncertain.

'Come,' he said to her, beckoning. She rose and came to him. He took her by the hand and sat her in the midst of the circle. Carefully, he closed the gap with a length of glinting, thick copper chain so that the two of them were entirely enclosed inside by the interconnected ring of jewellery. He stuck the base of the skull-staff into the ground next to him, twisting it until it stood stable, the jewel-glinting brown skull gazing blindly forwards into nothing.

He gazed into her face, his startling blue eyes shining like warm jewels. 'I must needs go exploring. This wild land of yers is full of surprises, and there is something that has arisen about which I am ... uncertain. A problem I must solve, one way or another. And ye must help me.' He reached to her then, took both her hands together, and held them in one of his.

Alia felt a warm tingle go through her arms from the bracelets, where his hand held her, up through her arms into her skull. She shivered at the sudden, unexpected pleasure of it.

'Ye must help me,' he repeated.

Alia nodded, eyes half closed.

The world suddenly shattered apart without warning.

Alia screamed and tried to pull away. 'Do not fight with me,' she heard Tasamin say. '*Help* me.'

Alia felt something flush through her, a sudden eagerness to do as he asked. She felt suddenly needed in a way she had never been before. She was *important* to him ...

'Aye,' he murmured. 'I *need* ye. Help me now.'

All about them, great chaos thundered. Alia felt its shattering impact within her and without her, a huge, violent current that seethed through all. But though the destructive surge of it heaved and tore at her terribly, the fundamental fabric of her self held.

It was disorienting and terrifying, this place of chaos. And she had no ordinary way to make sense of what she experienced. There was no vision, no sound, no feel. She had no body left with which to feel. Yet, even so, she could still somehow dimly *sense* some aspect of what was occurring about her.

There seemed to be some manner of shimmering globe encompassing her. Though she could not literally see, her mind insisted on the visual image: a great interlaced globe, shining and secure. She felt like a chick in an egg, safely secure inside, protected against the outside chaos.

'Aye, safe enough,' she seemed to hear Tasamin say. 'The circle will protect us.'

Alia felt the egg solidify, felt the surge of the dark chaos recede. She could still feel his grip upon her, though here it was not hand to hand. More like two connected coils of radiance. She felt his grip tighten, felt a pull upon her. And then it was as if he had opened some stopper in her she had never known was there. Something began to seep out of her, energy, life, sense ... she knew not what to call it. Instinctively, she tried to fight, to draw back. It was the stuff of her very soul that was leaking out.

'Do not fight me, girl,' she seemed to hear him say. 'Help me. Come with me. Give to me.'

The drain upon her grew stronger. It was hard to keep her mind clear.

'Help me, girl. Give to me.'

Alia struggled, tried to pull free, fighting. It was as if he had opened a vein in her and her life was bleeding out. But his hold was too strong. He was too strong. He absorbed what bled from her, growing stronger still.

'Trust me, girl.'

He was *so* strong, Alia found herself thinking vaguely. How could any harm come to her while she was under his protection?

'Aye, trust me now.'

She felt herself letting go, giving to him entirely. His was the will. His the strength. His the guidance.

She felt him begin to move them then as into the Nether Place they fully plunged, the golden egg submerged like a small bubble in the rolling, dangerous currents of chaos, she submerged in Tasamin, darkness everywhere, and dim motion all about, and great, great nothingness ...

XXV

Guthrie had walked through the night, alone.

Leaning against the knotty bole of a high-mountain pine for support, he shivered, soaked and chilled and bone weary, holding his balance in his self and the ordinary world through an effort of will. At the base of a steep, rocky slope before him lay what had to be the bandit camp, the details of it emerging before his eyes as the night's dark was flooded with cold dawn light.

Something had compelled him here.

Lying back in his makeshift tent after preventing Hone Amis's execution squad from doing its nasty work, exhausted though he had been, Guthrie had been totally unable to sleep. The memory of everything that had happened was too strong. And the thought of what lay ahead had given him no chance at rest.

And there was the strangeness, the queer *thing* he had *sensed* at the beginning of yestereve's fighting. The man with the skull that Ossbert the bandit had talked about. Must be.

Guthrie had not been able to get the thought of that 'skull-man' out of his head. He had tossed and turned in his tent, sleep ruined. The idea of entering the *other* had come to him. But he had shied away from such a course, feeling acutely uncomfortable with the thought. 'Enter the *other*,' a persistent voice had seemed to say to him. He had done no such thing, not trusting the voice, not understanding, but feeling in his gut that safety somehow lay in staying firmly anchored to the ordinary world.

But he was here now, high in the hills, come to the bandit camp all alone, led by he knew not quite what. A series of small steps it had been: unable to sleep, he had risen; feeling confined in his small tent, he had taken up *The Book* and the dead Abbod's skull, both in their satchel together, and gone outside; wanting solitude, he had slipped from the camp, begun walking ... And so it had been, each step innocent enough in itself, yet each one contributing inevitably to this long, lone march of his.

350

To accomplish what, exactly?

He knew not. And standing here, peering down towards the bandit camp, he had absolutely no notion of what to do next.

Movement showed down there now, men beginning to stir the fires up. The dawn air was chill and damp, with everything still wet from yesterday's rain. Guthrie envied these men the simple warmth they coaxed into life.

A soft, unexpected *crackle* from behind made Guthrie turn. A ragged man stood there, an armed crossbow in his hands aimed at Guthrie's middle. 'And just *who* might ye be, then?' the man demanded.

Guthrie shrugged, not knowing how to respond.

'Turn about,' the man ordered. 'Hands up against that tree yonder.'

Guthrie obeyed, felt a hand searching him for weapons. He had brought none, had somehow never even thought to do so.

'What's in yer bag?' the bandit sentinel demanded.

'A book,' Guthrie replied.

The man felt at Guthrie's satchel. 'There's somethin' else here, too. What is it?'

Guthrie was not sure what to answer.

'Never mind,' the man said. 'There's others who'll look into that. Ye ain't armed. That's all I needs to make sure of. Turn around.'

Guthrie did.

The man gestured down to the camp with his chin. 'Start marching.'

The men in the camp muttered in shocked surprise, then stared silently as Guthrie and his captor came skidding down the slope. He was brought to stand by one of the fires. Men gathered, until a fair-sized group stood in a semicircle around him. Nobody spoke. Only the crackling of the fires broke the silence of the cold morning air.

Then a thick-set man appeared. Those gathered about Guthrie made way as he strode through them. He had long arms, this man, and a black spade of a beard. And dark, calculating eyes.

The sentinel who had taken Guthrie said, 'Found him up on the rim, Seth. Just standin' there, he was, lookin' us over. He ain't armed or anything. I checked him good and proper. Just this little bag of his is all, with a book and something else in it.'

The bearded man nodded. He stood, long arms crossed, regarding Guthrie in silent appraisal.

Guthrie stood his ground, though his heart was beating painfully hard. He was beginning to think he had acted with terminal foolishness, walking blindly along into their hands like this.

There was movement amongst the gathered crowd. Men parted, and a new person appeared at the bearded man's side.

Guthrie blinked.

He was utterly unlike the rest of the men here, this one. Where they stood ragged and dirty, looking as if life had used them hard, he was all casual, clean elegance. He wore fine, high-topped sheepskin boots, thick breeches with the sheen of satin about them, a tunic of scintillating sky blue. A long traveller's cloak of black, fur lined, hung from his shoulders in perfect, symmetrical folds.

Guthrie stared, unable to comprehend what such a man might be doing here in a bandit camp in the wild heights.

For the man was not only dressed in impossible elegance, he veritably dripped with jewels: necklaces, bracelets, rings; his sheepskin boot-tops were filigreed with gold, his black cloak veined with strings of shining, tiny precious stones. He took a step towards Guthrie, and Guthrie heard the bracelets and such tinkling softly.

The man's face was well formed, with high cheek bones, his perfect white teeth bared in a half-smile. But his eyes ... his eyes held the blue of mountain ice, and seemed equally as cold. The man was staring at Guthrie, an unblinking gaze, almost reptilian in its intensity.

It made Guthrie shudder.

For long moments silence continued to hold the camp.

Then the bearded man smiled, a flash of feral teeth through the beard. 'I think I recognize you, boy.'

Guthrie kept silent.

The bearded man made a little half bow. 'My name is Sethir. I lead this little band here. And you ... you are the Reeve's younger son, are you not? Though you've grown since last I saw you.'

Guthrie eyed the man uneasily. 'I am,' he agreed after a moment's pause. There seemed no point in denying it. He had no idea when he and this man might have met.

'Ah ...' Sethir crossed his long arms and regarded Guthrie, head tilted to one side. 'What in the world did you think to accomplish by walking in here alone like this then?'

Guthrie shrugged, not knowing himself. He felt ridiculous.

'He *is* alone?' Sethir demanded of the sentinel who had brought Guthrie in.

'I think so, Seth,' the man replied.

'You *think* so? Go make certain. Do you want another repeat of yesterday's nasty surprise, fool?'

The man rushed off, calling to several others.

'The rest of you,' Sethir called, 'get prepared. No knowing what may be out there. Remember, they're close, these enemies of ours.'

Men scurried around, arming themselves, looking nervously about into the thick forest that surrounded this camp. But in a little, the scouts that had gone out came filtering back, reporting nothing to be seen.

'So you *are* alone,' Sethir said to Guthrie then.

Guthrie kept his silence, cursing himself now for a consummate fool to have walked here so blindly, so unthinkingly. What could have been wrong with him?

'Well ...' Sethir began.

'Kill him,' the jewelled man said.

The bandit leader whirled. '*Kill him?* Are you mad? I recognize this young fool only too well. The dead Reeve's son, he is. Reeve himself now, unless I miss my guess. The Vale folk *value* him. With him in our hands we have a bargaining chip worth something. And you say kill him. What would his death give us?'

'Kill him, I say. Ye does not know what ye has here.'

'Oh yes I do, Tasamin.'

'Ye does *not*! He is not what he appears to ye.'

Sethir faced the jewelled man, his hands fisted angrily. 'And just what *is* he, then, oh Tasamin of the infallible insight?'

The jewelled man's face did not change, but his voice dripped sudden acid. 'Do not *play* with me, little man.'

'It's you who are playing with me!' Sethir replied. 'Tell me what he is, then, if I am so ignorant as to not know. Or shut your face.'

'Ye would not understand what he is.'

Sethir looked at him for a moment, then shrugged. 'Fine. Have it your way. But I *do* know he is the Reeve. And he is far more valuable to us alive than dead.'

'Ye is making a mistake.'

Guthrie lost the thread of their dispute. There was something about this jewelled man, this Tasamin, that he found profoundly disturbing. The very look of him, the hypnotic flashing of the gems that adorned him, his hard, penetrating glance, quick and disturbing in some deep way. Guthrie felt his balance going, his hold on the ordinary slipping ...

What he *sensed* made him gasp. The jewelled man radiated in the uncertain surge of the *other* like a great torch. He had the same brilliance that Rosslyn did. Yet he was not at all like Rosslyn. She was a funnel through which the world poured. This man was a ... it took Guthrie some moments to understand what he was *sensing*. This man was a solid, opaque, scintillating sphere, impregnable, from out of which snaked long, mobile tentacles of faintly pulsing radiance.

Guthrie *sensed* one of these tentacles reaching for him now. Using his will like a hand, he batted the slimy thing away with instinctive revulsion.

Guthrie shuddered. This was no *ordinary* man.

Coming back to the mundane world, Guthrie found himself panting like a hound. His back was slicked with cold sweat under his jerkin. His knees quivered.

The jewelled man grinned a secret, malicious grin at him. 'Ye thinks ye knows me now, does ye, boy?'

Guthrie said nothing.

'Ye has much to learn yet.'

Sethir looked at the two of them, puzzled. 'What are you talking about?'

The jewelled man shrugged, his fine cloak lifting and falling in graceful folds. 'Nothing ye would understand.'

Sethir eyed him, uncertain, clearly irritated.

Tasamin crossed his arms elegantly: 'I say kill him, Sethir. He is too dangerous. Or give him to me.'

'To *you?*' the bandit leader said.

'Aye. I know well enough how to handle the likes of him.'

'And what *likes* is he, then?'

'I have already told ye. Ye could not understand.'

Sethir plucked at his dark beard. 'You try my patience to the breaking point!' he snapped. 'Tell me what it is that makes this lad here so dangerous, or have done and leave me be.'

Tasamin shrugged. 'Don't say I didn't warn ye.' With that, he turned and strode off.

'Wait!' Sethir called. 'Wait, damn you. Explain!'

But the jewelled man merely kept walking.

Sethir stood, twisting his beard, glaring uncertainly at where Tasamin had disappeared into a tent at the verge of the camp. He looked at Guthrie, back at the tent, back to Guthrie again.

Guthrie stood his ground. But for all his outward calm, he knew not at all what he could do next. He shivered, half expecting this Sethir to give a curt command and follow the jewelled man's advice – there were ample enough weapons here to end Guthrie's life quick enough.

But no.

Instead, Sethir strode towards him, glowering, until he stood face to face. He made a shallow, mocking bow. 'Welcome to my camp, Reeve Guthrie Garthson.'

Guthrie blinked.

'Reeve indeed are you now, then, after the Sea Wolves?'

Guthrie nodded.

'And Reeve Garth is killed?'

'Aye.'

Sethir smiled. 'Good.'

Guthrie did not know at all what to make of this man. 'How do you know me?'

'Oh I know you well enough. Come. Come into my humble camp.' Sethir motioned him on towards the centre of the camp clearing.

There were armed bandits all about. Guthrie had little choice except to do as he was bid.

'Sit,' Sethir said, gesturing to a spot near one of the fires.

Guthrie sat. He put his satchel next to his foot. Nobody had so much as mentioned it so far, as if they had simply accepted it as a natural part of him.

A little group of the men stood guard tensely, obviously watching Sethir for a cue as to what they ought to do.

Sethir let himself down across the fire from Guthrie, saying nothing.

Guthrie hesitated, glanced about him, took a breath. They were a ragged, hungry, desperate-looking group indeed, these men. And the hunger in them was more than just a belly-hunger. Like the ones he had already met with, they were men with little if anything left to lose, come here to the north in quest of a life.

'I know why you and yours have come here,' Guthrie said after a little. 'I think I can offer you –'

'You know *nothing*!' Sethir spat, cutting him short.

Guthrie recoiled, shocked by the man's sudden vehemence.

'Oh, I know you all right,' Sethir went on. 'You and your kind. Don't think you can turn me with words.'

'I don't ...' Guthrie started.

But Sethir gave him no chance. 'I *know* your sort. Lived a

pampered life, like some southern lady's lap dog. What do *you* know of ordinary folk's pains? Oh, I *know* all right. I grew up in Reeve Vale.'

Guthrie stared.

'Aye. That surprises you, does it?' Sethir said with satisfaction. 'Well it might.' He paused, his eyes closed, looking inward into memory. 'Aye. I grew up in the Vale. But I was banished by your father and the rest of them. Banished without any chance to defend myself. They treated me as if I were one of their sheep.'

Above the black spade of his beard, Sethir's face was gone white with the fury of remembrance. 'I stood there in front of you all – you were there, a snotty-nosed little boy; I remember it well enough – and you all passed judgment upon me. And not once ... *not once* did any of you ask to know *my* side of the story. You all listened to Merith Roul all right – that fat, sweetmeat-guzzling old bastard! Anything *he* said you believed completely.'

Sethir stabbed a finger out accusingly. 'I never killed anybody, boy! I was hardly older than you are now. It was all Merith Roul's scheming!

'But I was a mere fieldhand, a nobody, a nothing as far as you lot were concerned. You passed sentence upon me and laughed, and patted each other upon the back, and felt *so* satisfied with yourselves.'

Guthrie did not know what to say.

'Hone Amis's boot up my arse was the last I knew of Reeve Vale,' Sethir continued. 'He and his bedamned Militia drove me off into the wild lands. They sent me off barefoot, with nothing save a pair of breeches and a ripped shirt. They laughed at me. And I an *innocent* man!'

Sethir shook his head. 'I nearly died a dozen times, boy. I was nothing but skin and bone when I finally made it out to one of the southern settlements.' Again, Sethir stabbed a finger at Guthrie. It was a mannerism that reminded Guthrie of Hone Amis. 'And do you know what kept me alive, boy?'

Guthrie shrugged, shook his head.

'Hate. I *hated* you and yours. It was like food and drink to me, warming my poor soul when there was nothing else. In those long, bleak, cold days, there was only that to keep me going. That and the thought of revenge.'

'I have felt the same,' Guthrie said, remembering how it had been, the lost days of hunger and grief and the ache in him to be revenged.

Sethir paused uncertainly for a moment, looking at Guthrie, then shook his head and laughed. 'Well, I'm having my revenge now, boy,' he went on, not bothering to respond to what Guthrie had said. 'How do you think the Sea Wolves came to know about Reeve Vale? *I* told them. It filled me with joy to stand upon Seaview Ridge and see Riverside in ruins. Justice at last!'

'Revenge, perhaps,' Guthrie said softly. 'But justice?'

'What do *you* know of justice? Blind and stupid, that's what your sort is. But you're not so high and mighty now, are you, boy?'

Guthrie took a breath. 'Sethir, listen to me. I want to –'

Sethir leaped abruptly to his feet. 'No. No more talk!' He made a slashing motion with his hand, gesturing to somebody behind Guthrie.

Guthrie had one instant to turn, see the wooden handle of an axe arcing down at the back of his head ...

And then a sudden, smashing flare of painful light blanked out everything.

XXVI

Guthrie came to slowly, like a man dragging himself out of a dark hole.

His head throbbed from where he had been hit and his mouth tasted foul. He tried to sit up. But the movement sent a stab of sudden nausea through him so that he doubled over and was painfully sick.

When the spasm ended, he sat up weakly. Vomit was spattered all down his front. The odour of it made him gag. As best he could he wiped it away with his bare hands, wiping his hands in turn on the dirt where he lay.

Blearily, he looked about to see where he might be. He held his head with one hand, feeling the pain throb with his pulse in the back of his head, where they had hit him.

He lay in a tent, apparently – a floor of raw dirt, canvas walls, slanting canvas ceiling. The light was dim and ochre, like sunshine filtered through murky water. Guthrie struggled to his knees. The tent seemed empty save for a dim bulk in one corner that, as he stared at it, slowly took on the shape of a wooden stave bucket.

He got one foot under him, then the other, and tottered to his feet, swallowing back the nausea when it threatened to return on him. He moved towards the bucket, hoping it might contain water.

One step, another he took. But that was all he managed. The bucket sat there, not three paces from him, but try as he might he could not reach it. His limbs quivered into helpless weakness and he barely managed to keep his feet.

Stepping backwards was altogether different, he discovered. After two steps back he felt strength again in his legs. But more than three or four steps further in that direction and the same debilitating weakness attacked him.

He did not understand.

After a stumbling while testing this direction and that, he realized

358

he stood in the middle of a circumscribed area, outside of which he simply could not step, no matter how hard he might try.

In a kind of instinctive move for escape, he sank into the *other*. Encircling him, he *sensed* a kind of veil or net, pulsing with cold radiance. It was like a weir, and he a trapped fish.

Guthrie reached his will against the strands of this net, pushing, trying to test, to part, to weaken.

But he could achieve nothing.

It was as if, to his will, the enclosing veil was simply not there. He could *sense* it clear enough, but when he attempted to place his will against it, in the manner he had haltingly learned how to use his will in the past as a kind of *other*-hand, he could not find anything against which to push or pull. It was like trying to crack a wall of water; his will went right through, ineffectual.

He came back out of the *other* gasping and confused. His eyes could detect nothing of the veil here in the ordinary world. Yet there must be something ...

He tried to push against it, forcing himself as close to the bucket, and its promise of water, as he might. And there, at the very limit of what he was capable, he caught a glimpse of something bright and shining in the dirt. A little ruby gleam. And running from it, the soft gold twinkle of a slim chain.

Knowing what to look for now, Guthrie soon saw what it was that hemmed him in. He stood trapped in the middle of a circle woven from jewellery – golden chains, pendants, clasps – all linked together.

And somehow he could not come close to them. Guthrie shuddered. This must be the work of that elegant, cloaked man. Tasamin. Who else? But how?

Guthrie settled down where he was, in the middle of the jewelled circle, helpless to do otherwise. His mouth was raw with thirst and the bitter aftertaste of vomit. His head throbbed painfully. He felt weak as any small kitten. In a daze, he sat slumped over, focusing all his flagging energy on coping with his bodily misery. Water was what he needed more than anything now. Water.

Time crawled by. The light in the tent grew dimmer.

And then the tent's front flap was thrown open momentarily and somebody came striding in.

'Phaugh!' Tasamin said, holding his nose. He stood just inside the tent. Guthrie's satchel hung from one of his hands. He glared at Guthrie. 'Did ye have to foul the tent so, lout?'

Guthrie felt a stab of anger, but he kept his mouth shut.

Tasamin put the satchel down and went to the bucket at the side of the tent. He lifted the bucket over the jewelled circle, placing it on the ground inside. He was careful, Guthrie noted, not to disturb any part of the jewellery. Next, he flung Guthrie a piece of rag. 'Clean yourself up,' he ordered.

With that, he stood back and drew from a pocket somewhere a silken cloth which he held to his nose.

Guthrie barely managed to make it to the bucket, so close as it was to the jewelled circle's edge. But manage it he did, just, after several panting attempts. He dragged the bucket laboriously back to the centre, slopping water as he went.

Finally, he was able to kneel over and drunk his head, feeling the lovely coolth of the water soothe his aching skull. The taste of it in his mouth almost made him swoon, so wonderful did it seem. When he had got his fill of water, he soaked the rag and swabbed at the vomit with it till he was relatively clean.

All the while, Tasamin watched him, his eyes were cold and intent as any serpent's.

'Well, boy,' Tasamin said, 'there is more to ye than one might think.' With a kind of theatrical gesture, he lifted the Abbod's skull from Guthrie's pack and held it aloft.

Guthrie squirmed. The man's touch upon the dead Abbod's skull was painful to him.

Tasamin put the skull on the ground and lifted *The Book* next. 'And a lovely little book, too. A work of art, nearly. Let us see what it contains.' Tasamin's voice dripped with a fake pleasantry. He thumbed through the book, chuckling here and there. 'Quaint,' he said after a little. Then, with one thumb pressed to a page, he began to read: 'Nothing is clear to the ear or the eye, or the mind's agile fingers, so wanting to pry ...' He laughed, flipped a few more pages, read again: 'One does more and more each day in the pursuit of knowing. But follow the Pathless Way, the goingless going, and each day one does less, until one reaches fundamentalness. Trading all for none leaves nothing undone.'

He let the book drop, laughing again. 'Ye reads such rubbish then, boy? Does ye cherish it, thinking it holds hidden secrets, hidden knowledge?' Tasamin shook his head. 'It's complete rubbish. Doing nothing means precisely that: doing nothing! Pap for weak minds to keep themselves occupied, that's all yer precious verses are. To keep from seeing the *truth* of things!'

Guthrie felt a surge of anger at the man's arrogant condescension. 'And just what,' he asked, 'is this *truth?*'

Tasamin shrugged. 'Ye knows as well as I.' He gestured to the Abbod's skull where it rested on the ground. 'Obviously, ye knows.'

Guthrie glanced at the skull, back at Tasamin, shook his head.

Tasamin lifted the skull aloft, balanced on one palm, and looked it over admiringly. 'Quite recently dead, I see.' He glanced at Guthrie. 'How did ye kill him?'

Guthrie stared, shocked.

Tasamin laughed. 'Do not pretend innocence to me.' As he held the skull in one hand, he passed the other, palm down, across the ivory cranium, as a man might pass his hands across a fire feeling for the heat. 'An old master, this one was. Did he meet with an ... *accident* then?'

Guthrie did not understand. 'Why should ...'

Tasamin waved him impatiently to silence. 'Do not insult my intelligence, boy!' He whirled suddenly, jewels and silver tinkling, and snapped the fingers of his free hand in a complicated, twirling pattern. He held out that free hand, palm up. Out of nowhere, silent as a thought, a jewelled skull abruptly appeared in his hold.

Guthrie felt every hair on his body shiver erect.

It was dark with age, this other skull, and against the peat brown bone, gold filigree work glinted. A myriad of little jewels beaded that filigree, like water droplets – shining, rainbow-tinted water droplets – sparkling on a gilded spider's web laid across the dead bone.

The very sight of the uncanny, bejewelled thing was so shocking somehow that it knocked Guthrie momentarily out of the world. In the *other*, the two skulls in Tasamin's hands shone like a brace of torches. The Abbod's familiar radiance pulsed within its basket of bone. But the other one ... That radiance squirmed and writhed painfully, imprisoned somehow. With a shock, Guthrie realized that the jewellery on that other skull was more than simple adornment; in some manner, it acted as a net, imprisoning the life-force of whatever poor, living soul the skull had once helped house.

The very *sensing* of it hurt Guthrie, like a kick in the belly. He shied away, thrusting himself back into the ordinary. The deliberate imprisoning of another's spirit like that ... The sheer, callous ruthlessness of what Tasamin had done nauseated him.

'See?' Tasamin said casually, hefting the jewelled skull aloft. 'I know too much for ye to be able to fool me.' He laughed and shook his head. 'But ye plays a dangerous game, boy, and ye is ignorant as any stupid country lout.'

The old skull Tasamin held up glinted hypnotically in the tent's dim ochre light. The rim of each eye socket was inset with intricate ovals of thin gold wire, laid out in spirals and loops and elaborate curls, with tiny rubies glimmering throughout. From the dark midst of shining complexity that rimmed each empty socket, Guthrie could just make out the faintest glimmer of ghostly eyes, shimmering like the Abbod's sometimes did, or seemed to do.

Guthrie shuddered.

'Ye must needs be far more careful about such things than ye has been. I can detect only the weakest of bindings upon this ... ally of yers. He could break free at any moment.' Tasamin grinned, a one-sided, mocking stretch of his lips. 'And *then* where would ye and all yer great plans be, eh, boy?'

Guthrie did not understand. 'What ... plans might you mean?'

Tasamin sneered at him. 'I've told ye not to try playing the innocent with me. I know yer sort. I *am* yer sort, boy. Only *I* am further along the path than ye.' Tasamin laughed once more. 'And *that* makes all the difference.'

Laying down both skulls, Tasamin stepped towards Guthrie. 'I was younger than ye. Not much more than a little lad, really.' He blinked his ice-blue eyes. 'Askin was an old man. He might have been a Closterer once, I believe. But, if so, he had left them and taken his own path years before I met him.'

Tasamin laughed coldly. 'I was a farm lad with big dreams, and was just beginning to see that the world was not about to grant me those dreams when Askin came pilgrimming through our village. I saw him cure a man who had been suffering from lung fever for a month. Everybody thought the man would die. But after Askin treated him, he was up and walking within two days.

'I remember thinking that anybody who could do what Askin had done must have power. *Power*, boy. That was what I lacked, and I knew it all too painfully.'

Tasamin played with one of the slim gold bangles on his wrist, twisting it round and round. 'So I wooed the old man, toted and carried for him, did his chores. And in return, after he had made me wait a good long time, and after I had done more than my share of humiliating service, he began to teach me.'

Tasamin smiled. 'And ye knows what *that* means, does ye not, boy? There came the day when he led me into the Nether Place.'

362

Guthrie looked his confusion. 'The ... "Nether Place"?'

'This pretence of ignorance on yer part is wearing *thin*, boy,' Tasamin said waspishly. 'The Nether Place. That was Askin's name for it. Call it what ye will. The Between Place. The Hidden Place. The Place of no Paths. The Other Place. What ye will. Ye knows well enough of what I speak.'

Guthrie nodded.

'And once he showed me *that*,' Tasamin went on, 'I realized I no longer needed him. Or, rather, I no longer needed him as he was.'

Guthrie stared at the jewelled skull. 'You ... killed him?'

'Aye. As ye killed yers.'

'No!'

Tasamin made a slashing motion with one hand. 'Don't lie to me, boy. I know better.'

Guthrie did not know what to say.

Tasamin grinned at Guthrie. 'Sethir wants ye for his own, boy. He has plans for ye, thinks he can use ye as a bargaining chip. But *I* have plans as well. And *this* ...' he pointed to the dead Abbod's skull, 'will be *most* useful to me.'

Guthrie said nothing, but his stricken look was plain enough.

Tasamin laughed. 'And so all yer plans tumble into nothing. What was it ye was about, eh? Setting up yer own little empire out here in the wilderness. Well, boy, 'tis too late for ye to attempt that.'

Tasamin flipped his wrist, jewellery tinkling softly, ran a hand through his long black hair to smooth it. 'I never thought to find one of *our* sort here in this wilderness. Ye nearly upset all my plans, boy. I was blind to ye, not expecting what ye were. Ye has upset my plans, aye. But not fatally. This northern land will be mine, to have and to hold. And with this ally ye brings me ...' Again Tasamin laughed. 'Well, what can I say? A fine and selfless act of generosity for ye to bring it to me like this. With only a little prompting needed on my part.'

'On *your* part?' Guthrie said.

'My part, aye. Ye didn't think ye came here all on yer own, did ye? Such touching naiveté.'

Guthrie blinked confusedly. His head ached, a sullen throbbing, and he found it hard to think clearly. Had he indeed walked here blindly at the man's hidden urgings? Was such a thing possible? He felt like a stupid, helpless boy before this Tasamin. The man was clothed in power and assurance as surely as he was in jewels and silks.

Guthrie felt himself fall a little way into the *other*. As he had earlier before the campfire, he *sensed* Tasamin: a solid, opaque sphere, impregnable. Guthrie had experienced nothing like it. Such unbelievable solidity. Neither seam nor crack nor opening of any sort. Perfect, in its way. And even, in its way, with a kind of elegant attractiveness, the mobile tentacles of Tasamin's will faintly pulsing with something like soft radiance.

But it was, finally, a repellent attractiveness, like the elaborate patterns of a serpent's skin.

Tasamin's laughter brought Guthrie back.

'Ye are not far enough along the path yet, boy. I can *feel* how unsteady ye is. Ye does not know the rules yet, falling in and out like a babe. Ye has not woven enough protection for yerself yet. What a pity. A little push is all it will take, just the smallest of pushes, and ye will tumble away forever into the black chaos of the Nether Place. And I will be rid of ye for good.'

Guthrie tried to hurl himself at Tasamin. But it was hopeless. He ran up against the invisible barrier of the woven jewels and stumbled to a painful halt. Tasamin only laughed. Guthrie felt a long, sickly shudder go through him, helplessness before this man's power.

Tasamin turned, weaving one of those complicated little series of hand gestures Guthrie had seen him make already, intoning a muttering little hum as he did so. A few moments later, the tent's doorflap opened and somebody came in.

Guthrie gasped, recognizing her. 'Alia!'

But it was a changed Alia. A heavy golden necklace hung about her throat. Gold chains laced her feet, waist, arms. Two large gold bracelets hung like shackles on her wrists.

'Alia,' Guthrie called. 'Alia!'

All she did was look at him with calm, indifferent eyes.

Tasamin smiled. 'My helpmate,' he said, gesturing to her. 'She too is one of our sort, boy. Though more pliable than ye, being less experienced.'

Taken aback, Guthrie did not know what to think.

'Alia,' Tasamin said, 'come to me.'

Alia came like a pet dog.

Tasamin nodded his satisfaction. 'Good girl.' He stroked her face, her arms, his hands coming to rest upon the manacle-bracelets. 'Ye must help me again now, for we must deal with this awkward boy here. He has caused me trouble, Alia. He would cause ye trouble, too, if he could. He is not a *nice* boy. Ye *knows* that, doesn't ye?'

Alia looked at Guthrie. Her eyes narrowed in dislike. 'Aye,' she agreed. 'He's not *nice*. I can see that about him clear as clear.'

'Alia!' Guthrie protested. He did not understand how Tasamin could be exerting such impossible, complete control over her. She had always seemed so independent willed. 'Alia, it's *me*!' he said. 'Guthrie!'

'I know who you are,' she replied. 'Do you think me stupid?'

'No! Of course not.'

Tasamin leaned forward, his face intent. 'Enough! Let us end this quickly. Ye is too troublesome to let live, boy. I shall have to drown ye.' He shrugged. 'Sethir loses his bargaining chip. What a pity ...' He held out his bejewelled hands, palms down, and pushed, as if submerging something.

Guthrie felt the *other* surge up all about.

'Think on it!' Tasamin cried. 'Down ye will go into the Nether Place. Down down down ... alone, all alone, where darkness and chaos rule, where the dark forces will tear ye apart like so much paper-bark. No protection, no hope. Destitute. Abandoned. Alone. And as ye struggles to reach the surface of the ordinary world, there will I be, me and my ally and my helpmate, pushing, pushing ye down again. Until ye has ceased to be.'

Guthrie felt his heart thump. The *other* seethed all about him, hungry.

The jewelled skull rose from the ground by itself and came to hover next to Tasamin. It seemed to glow eerily. Tasamin let go of Alia with one hand, stroked the skull, then executed a series of intricate finger motions in mid-air, jewellery scintillating and tinkling rhythmically. 'Down, boy. Down into the hungering dark. Alone. Swallowed by the great mouth of darkness.'

Guthrie felt a terrible pressure upon him, pushing him out of the ordinary world and into the *other*.

He struggled in desperation, as terrified as he had ever been by the dissolution the *other* threatened. Down, down, down he was plunged, thrashing and fighting. Drowning indeed. And worse. Drowning in a current that tore him apart, tore through him, inside and out, shredding him.

Somehow, through it all, he heard the echoes of Tasamin's distant, gloating laughter.

A surge of hot rage went through him. It was like a spine of fire, and he clung to it, nursed it, bound his self to it, feeling the rage, feeling his own self ...

At the edge of his perception, Guthrie *sensed* the Abbod's skull, shining like a beacon. An empty ally the queer thing might have been, more burden than help, but it shone clear and strong for him now, and he was utterly grateful.

The pressure Tasamin somehow generated kept pushing at him, and the *other* tore mercilessly at his self, but with the skull's glowing beacon to call him, Guthrie found himself somehow able to rebound back out of the dangerous seethe of the depths, like a cork in an ocean storm, torn and tossed and sunken, but bobbing back.

Guthrie struggled upwards – as if he were indeed submerged deep in turbulent water and were yearning upwards towards the surface where daylight glimmered like pearl – and *sensed* where Tasamin hovered at the boundary between the ordinary and the *other*, he and his allies, waiting to thrust Guthrie back.

He was so strong, this Tasamin, and all will. Iron-hard, implacable, incontestable will.

Guthrie struggled to keep himself from sinking away.

Tasamin's jewelled skull glowed as the Abbod's did, but less brightly. It was like a lantern half covered, shining only spottily. Guthrie *sensed* how Tasamin had bound the spirit of the dead man, using that implacable will of his, binding both spirit and bone, the interlacing jewellery acting as a focus for his iron will, channelling and embodying it. Making a slave of the poor soul, locked in a bone prison. A cruel and unnatural act.

Guthrie *sensed* how Tasamin drew on Alia as a kind of power source, like a creature sucking blood. But it was his captive skull that he relied on more, drawing from it, forcing the unquiet spirit of the dead man to aid him in pushing, pushing at Guthrie, weaving a bejewelled, twinkling pattern with his hands through the air, chanting guttural, rhythmic verse, focusing his iron will, pushing, pushing ...

Guthrie could *sense* him growing impatient now, wanting to submerge Guthrie for ever. Growing irritated. He, Guthrie, should have dissolved away into gibbering bits long before this.

But the radiance of the Abbod's skull remained firm, a glad beacon Guthrie hung all his precarious safety on. The *other* tore and tossed him, Tasamin pushed, hard, harder, trying to drown him. Guthrie battled up. It was like some kind of agonized, slow dance between the two of them, push and twist and struggle, push and pull, down and up, push and push and push.

And then Guthrie *sensed* something new. A subtle connection was beginning to grow between the two dead spirits in the skulls. Tasamin drew on his, as one might suck liquid from a waterskin, drawing power greedily, ruthlessly, paying no more attention to its being than a thirsty man might to the waterskin from which he drank. But though Tasamin had bound the skull tight, there were still gaps in that binding; impossible to bind a man's soul utterly and entire.

While Tasamin was fully engaged in his struggle with Guthrie, the dead Abbod and dead Askin were beginning somehow to weave a kind of linkage between themselves, a hidden, subtle linkage that Tasamin, entirely focused elsewhere, noticed not at all.

Guthrie made a last desperate heave, plunging himself like a wave against Tasamin's rock, spreading round, going under and over, until, despite all Tasamin's best efforts, he was able to find a way at least partly into the ordinary world, enough to know himself in the tent once more, all too precariously balanced, heaving and gasping, but intact.

'No!' Tasamin cried, stumbling back. 'You cannot!' He raised the skull, which he gripped in one hand now, the other still holding Alia by the wrists. 'I will not allow –'

But no further did he get.

The jewelled skull began suddenly to flash, as did the dead Abbod's on the ground. Guthrie was not sure if he were seeing with his ordinary eyes, or *sensing*, or both at once, but he 'saw' the two skulls each take on a dancing radiance, as if a living flame had been lit simultaneously in each, the two radiances merging into a kind of glowing flower.

'No!' Tasamin screamed at the jewelled skull. 'Ye is mine. *Mine!*'

But there was nothing he could do, it seemed, to halt whatever strange process was begun.

In the shimmer of radiance that danced between and about both skulls, the jewels and gold binding dead Askin's bone prison began to fall away. Slowly at first, one small ruby, a few links of golden chain, a curlicue of filigree. Stricken-faced, Tasamin dropped Alia and clutched the skull possessively to himself, scrabbling in desperate haste with his free hand to retrieve the falling jewellery.

But it was no use. The jewels and gold work unravelled and fell away faster and faster, till the skull was entirely unbound. The twin radiance that enveloped the two skulls flared into abrupt, painful brilliance.

And then was gone.

Simple as that.

Both Guthrie and Tasamin stared, shocked.

Only inanimate, dead bone remained.

Guthrie remembered the Abbod who, back in the Closter on that terrible rain-drenched day of the Sea Wolves' attack, had turned to him and said: 'Trust me, young Reeve. I have seen into this. There is more at stake here than ye can understand.' Abbod Rianna who, with all his abilities, had merely lifted his chin a little higher, baring his neck more cleanly to the decapitating stroke of the Sea Wolf Chieftain's blade.

Guthrie found it suddenly hard to breathe, stunned by this realization.

But Tasamin only glared hatred at Guthrie. 'What has ye done, ye stupid, meddling boy? What has ye *done?*'

Before Guthrie could act one way or another, Tasamin flung aside the now-untenanted skull and leaped for him. Gone was the Tasamin's accustomed elegance. Gone the control. He leaped like a beast, hands clawing for Guthrie's throat, snarling.

The sheer savagery of that leap, hitting Guthrie as he was still precariously balanced on the edge of the ordinary world, carried the two of them plummeting into the *other*.

There were no simple bodily shapes in the *other*. Tasamin no longer had hands and Guthrie no longer a throat to grip. But they remained locked to each other nevertheless, struggling, twisting, falling, in a long, howling, desperate plunge.

No beacon left now. No far-off, familiar glow to draw Guthrie back.

Tasamin was a solid, impregnable weight upon him, smothering him, tearing at him, crushing him. Guthrie could *sense* the blind, hysterical hatred that now filled the man. It was like being locked in a tumbling embrace with a furious wild cat, claws out, slashing and ripping and yowling.

Torn by both the violence of Tasamin's hysterical fury, and by the deconstructive currents of the *other* itself, Guthrie felt his self beginning to come apart. Terror flushed through him.

And Tasamin ...

Tasamin was solid. He had bound his self in jewelled armour, focus and physical embodiment of his iron will, keeping the *other* at a safe distance, walling himself securely away from its terrible currents. That solid, opaque structure Tasamin had built of himself overshadowed Guthrie. Complete and certain control, complete knowing. Impenetrable. Implacable willed.

But the two men were entangled in a forced and unnatural intimacy, and now Guthrie *sensed* beyond the other man's flashing armour all in a sudden rush.

Despite Tasamin's daunting completeness, the seeming invulnerability, Guthrie could faintly *sense* ... something.

Fear.

He remembered Rosslyn telling him: 'A man who passes the nameless gate and denies the *other*, who clings to his old self, is lost. He fears, and lets that fear rule him, and thus has to rule all about him lest the fear destroy him utterly. Like a fish that dams and drowns the river because it fears the current.'

Fear.

Guthrie recalled the verse from *The Book* he had read the day that Rosslyn had sent him off on his own:

> *A man of the way will follow the way*
> *Beyond what he can see or hear.*
>
> *A man who still fears will hold and stay,*
> *And all his way will be filled with fear.*
>
> *A fearing-man will be hard and cold,*
> *A fearing-man will fear to be bold,*
> *A fearing-man will be desperate to hold.*

Suddenly, all Tasamin's strength lay revealed to Guthrie as desperation. Tasamin was horrified at the seeming chaos the *other* embodied. He was cut from the same cloth as Hone Amis: a man who regarded the world with deep suspicion, expecting always the worst, seeing destruction and disaster everywhere. But Tasamin was a man of vaulting personal ambition, having none of Hone Amis's decent commitment to the community good.

Guthrie felt how it must have been, Tasamin learning new skills, new powers, needing new strength to maintain control, weaving his jewelled webs for safety and support, learning yet more new skills, for which he needed more strength ... on and on with no end. The jewelled skull, poor captive Alia ... he sucked strength from them like a leech sucking blood.

Only the unbending strength of his iron will held Tasamin together. His entire life was one long struggle for control.

All this sudden rush of intimate understanding on Guthrie's part took scarce a heartbeat.

He felt Tasamin ripping at him viciously, felt his self begin to come apart like old cheesecloth.

With a final, desperate effort, Guthrie *reached* towards Tasamin's jewelled armour, tearing at it. It was like trying to tear the dried-mud bricks out of a solid building wall with bare hands. But somehow, with desperate strength, Guthrie managed to dislodge one tiny little component.

It proved enough.

The whole structure must have been far more brittle than it appeared, for the small break Guthrie had initiated spread, a little here, a little there, like an egg cracking open, until the entire shell Tasamin had constructed about himself began to break apart.

But this was no process of birth. Agony and terror and rage, that was what Guthrie *sensed*.

Tasamin struggled, raging, wailing, holding on in blind and desperate terror to the disintegrating parts of his self as the *other*, for the first time ever in his life, flooded entirely through his elaborate defences.

All Tasamin's iron strength of will was of no avail. They were too entirely submerged, and the *other* too all-encompassing. Tasamin had never had experience of this, Guthrie realized, had never before been nakedly exposed to the seethe of the *other*. It was too much for him, and Tasamin's carefully guarded self proved as brittle as the will-jewelled egg that had guarded it. All his strength failed him. All his control crumbled.

One last, long, terrible, desperate and furious wail Guthrie *sensed*. And then Tasamin's rending clutch upon Guthrie loosened and Tasamin was torn away into the *other's* endless seethe and turbulence.

Gone.

Guthrie felt his own self beginning to go, as surely as had Tasamin's, shredded into so much mindless pulp. He struggled to resist it, to hold himself together, but he was too far gone in the *other*. The very terror of it filled him.

But in his struggle, he remembered Tasamin, and how all the

man's great strength had amounted to nothing but fatal weakness. Guthrie had a sudden, searing flash of realization: he had shied away from the *other*, tried to reclaim his old self, but even in denying that *other*, he had still used the special advantage it gave him to try to force events for his own best gain.

Just as Tasamin had.

He would not, would *not* take Tasamin's way, Guthrie swore to himself. Not blind strength and brittle will and the useless armouring of I, me, mine ...

He had seen all too clearly where that led.

The *other* seethed about and through him, terrible as ever, but Guthrie ceased fighting it quite so frantically.

And though it surged and tore and howled, there was something else now as well, very faint. Like a strange, soft voice calling to him.

He recalled, suddenly, another verse from *The Book*:

> The way is not clear to the ear or the eye,
> Or the mind's agile fingers, so wanting to pry.
>
> Pathless the way, for what ye await.
> Change is the journey, change is your fate.
> Change is the way through the great nameless gate.

Guthrie felt a strange kind of thrill.

Tasamin had come apart in agony, clinging blindly to his brittle self in relentless determination, refusing change.

Change.

An end and a beginning.

Unless one was too brittle ...

Another verse from *The Book* appeared before Guthrie in his mind's eye:

> *Furled inside its sleek cocoon,*
> *Does the caterpillar not swoon*
> *With very terror at the death*
> *It is facing? And yet, with each breath,*
> *Does it not take on the new*
> *Life so long overdue?*

The new life ... Rosslyn claimed to have endured this terrifying, rending *change* that felt to him like very death. Why could not he, then? Let his self fall finally away ...

Masks, all masks ...

He remembered how the notion of masks had first come to him, sitting on grass, Rosslyn's fingertips closing his eyes, him filling with sudden understanding: just as the world was not the simple, stable, solid place he had always thought himself to be; he was a *being*, a feeling, wondering, alive being, as mysterious and incomprehensible, finally, as the very living world itself. His sense of self, his ambitions ... all only masks over that *being*. He was a part of the world's mystery the way an autumn leaf is part of the wind, or the river part of the fish ...

The time had come to put away masks. The time had come to let the caterpillar die away, terror or no. Let there be a final end to confusion and fear and uncertainty, an end to this constant, wearying struggle to balance two lives, the old and the new.

Guthrie began to let go.

He could feel his old self dissolving. Memory pulsed erratically through him, like a leaking tide emptying from a bay. His father's florid face. Sheets of cold rain. His mother smiling through tears.

It was the end of all things for him, this process of dissolution. It was *change* beyond anything he could properly imagine. He felt a little spasm of the old terror. He would never be the same person again.

But he would still *be*.

He was already changed beyond that old self in any case, and clinging to it would only make him like Tasamin, a bent person, twisted by fear, brittle as a winter reed.

No. He must change entire.

The memories continued to flow through him: the dead as he had seen them piled in a pitiful heap in Riverside; the Sea Wolves' taunting laughter, and his own violent anger.

But distant, all distant. No echo in him now of that anger. It all seemed so utterly inconsequential.

Let it go. Let it all go ...

He remembered Hone Amis in the training yard, shouting at him. The memory brought another: torchlight and kneeling captives, the Militia Master hard-faced and determined, the bandit captive looking up pleadingly.

Guthrie remembered staring into Alia's face by the light of his little fire in the wild hills, and feeling her need for him, and the need of others reflected in hers.

He remembered the sprawled forms of the dead in the rain at the site of the bandit ambush.

He remembered the look of hope in the eyes of the men he had taken oath from.

And he remembered his own part of that oath: *to never misuse you or yours, to never lose sight of the good of the whole, to never forget my position.*

It was like a hook in his guts.

While he yet lived, he was still Reeve, with the Reeve's responsibilities.

It was not yet time for ending.

Guthrie began to strive once more against the *other's* seethe, dipping, climbing ... trying to re-gather his dissolving self in the process, moving through the *other* like a fish through turbulent waters, coalescing slowly, slowly ... until, at last, he was able to feel his proper ordinary fingers, and the coolness of proper, ordinary dirt between them.

He clutched at it, willing the fingers to remain fingers, feeling for the granular texture of the dirt, reaching blindly like a man coming out of deep, dark waters into daylight and air.

Gasping, his heart thumping painfully, Guthrie fell into the tent and half lay in the dirt, paralysed with exhaustion, trying to recover himself.

XXVII

From outside the tent, Guthrie heard shouts, a commotion of men. Somebody screamed, long and shrill, cut off in mid-note.

Struggling to bring himself into proper focus, he rolled to his knees and stumbled up. On the tent floor before him Tasamin lay, sprawled dead, his face frozen in an expression of wide-eyed, staring horror. Next to him lay Alia. She too lay sprawled and staring. But Guthrie saw her chest move, rising and falling in shallow breath.

Outside, the shouting went on.

Guthrie turned and stumbled through the tent's door flap and into the chill outside air.

Day was waning, and the light had the eerie quality to it of autumn evening. The sun hung low and red and swollen in the western sky, gilding the snow of the far peaks. The sky was absolutely cloudless, cold and bright, ice-blue verging to salmon pink on the horizon.

Guthrie blinked, bringing his vision into focus. Before him, two groups faced each other across the camp: Amis's Militia, the green of the hunters to be seen with them on the one side, Hone Amis himself at their head, and Sethir the bandit leader and his ragged men on the other side. There was blood on more than a few, Militia and bandit alike, and several still forms lay on the open space of ground between the opposed forces.

'... and if you do not,' Sethir was saying, 'then he shall be killed.'

'If you *dare* to ...' Hone Amis began. Then he spotted Guthrie. 'Guthrie!'

Before anybody could make a further move, Sethir whirled and leaped upon Guthrie.

Hone Amis and the rest surged forwards in a body.

Guthrie tried to duck away, but, still uncertain on his feet, he was driven to his knees by the force of Sethir's charge. Before he could react properly, he felt the cold edge of a blade against his throat.

'Stand as you are!' Sethir cried. 'Or I kill him now!'

The Militia faltered.

'Kill him, and you'll be signing your own death warrant!' Hone Amis called.

Sethir smiled, a feral flash of teeth through his dark beard. 'I'll be signing *his* first!'

Guthrie felt the blade bite against his throat.

'Back,' Hone Amis ordered his men.

Sethir nodded his satisfaction. 'Good.' He looked about, assessing.

From his kneeling position, Guthrie too tried to assess what had happened. The camp seemed almost evenly occupied, bandit and Militia. No easy way to reckon who might come out the victor in a straight fight here. He shivered, remembering all too clearly the last confrontation. Sethir, too, was obviously uncertain as to what his next move ought to be.

'Put your weapons aside!' he called to the Militia after a little.

Several men started hesitantly to comply, but Hone Amis shouted at them not to.

'I will kill him, man!' Sethir cried. 'Do not doubt that I will.'

Hone Amis looked him levelly. 'I do not doubt it. But you ... do not *you* doubt that I will kill *you* the moment after you do so. And do not, do *not* think you can overbear *me* into giving everything up at your whim.' He waved an arm, taking in the camp, the two armed forces facing each other. 'We are balanced here, bandit. Did you really expect me to throw away all the advantage I have at your mere request?'

Sethir tilted the blade so the tip rested under the hinge of Guthrie's jaw. 'Request?'

Hone Amis shrugged, said nothing.

Despite everything, Guthrie could not help but admire the Militia Master's coolness. He could feel the bandit leader's hand quiver where it held the blade tight up against his jaw.

After a long moment, Sethir let up. He turned a little, beckoned to one of the men near him. 'Fetch Tasamin here. Hurry! What is he up to? Cursed fool and his scheming.'

The man Sethir had beckoned moved off towards the tent from which Guthrie had come, but slowly, obviously all too aware of the way he had become the focus of everybody's attention.

Several of the Militia shifted to intercept him. Hone Amis, after a moment's pause, waved them off.

The man went over to the tent, ducked inside.

375

They waited as they were – Militia, hunter, bandit – silent, uncertain.

Guthrie felt the strain of his uncomfortable position. His knees ached, pushed into the cold and unyielding ground as they were, and the long muscles of his legs quivered. His heart knocked like a hammer in his chest. He felt the complete fool, bent over awkwardly like this on his knees, helpless.

Waiting like all the rest.

The man emerged from the tent, walked stiffly back.

'Well?' Sethir demanded.

'He's ...' the man hesitated, bent closer. 'He's dead, Seth.'

'*What?*'

'Dead! And that girl of his ... dead too, by the looks of her. Laid out on the floor in there like a couple of splayed fish. It's uncanny. And there's that queer skull of his ... all the jewellery's fallen away from it. And there's another skull lying next it now! Fair made my skin crawl!'

Guthrie felt Sethir stiffen. 'If you're lying to me, Alten ...'

'Truth, Seth. Truth as I stand here before ye!'

'The stupid idiot!' Sethir hissed. Guthrie felt him take a ragged breath. 'The great Tasamin. Bah! Letting himself be taken like any fool!' He shook Guthrie, hard. 'I'll make you pay for this, boy! Tasamin was an arrogant arse, but he was *useful* to me.'

'Give it up, Seth,' Hone Amis called, obviously taking his cue from the man by the tent in using the bandit leader's name.

Sethir surged properly to his feet, dragging Guthrie up with him. 'Boh Sethir to you!' he spat at Hone Amis.

The Militia Master made a mocking bow. 'Boh Sethir it is, then.'

'Don't patronize me, Amis!' Sethir said.

'*Hone* Amis, bandit, since we are observing the niceties.' Guthrie could see the look of enquiry on Amis's face. 'And how is it you know me, then?'

'Oh I know you, all right,' Sethir replied. 'I remember you clear.'

'Remember?'

'Aye.'

Hone Amis waited.

'You had me beaten out of the Vale, you and old hard-arse Garth and that pig faced, lying Merith Roul.'

Hone Amis shrugged. 'I remember it not.'

'No, *you* wouldn't. But I remember. Oh aye, *I* remember clear enough. You left the imprint of your boot on my arse as a reminder.'

Again Hone Amis shrugged. 'No doubt you deserved it, bandit.'

'I was *innocent*!' Sethir spat.

The Militia Master smiled. 'Oh, of course. Like all the rest. Innocent as the proverbial day is long. White as new snow.'

'Don't mock me, Amis.'

'*Hone* Amis, bandit.'

It was Sethir's turn to smile. 'Up your arse, Amis.'

The Militia Master flushed and took a step forwards.

'Stop it!' Guthrie cried. Sethir's blade bit against his throat again, but Guthrie kept talking. 'You're like two stupid mountain rams in rut, the pair of you. And for *what?*'

Sethir laughed. 'For life, boy. For life, ambition.'

Guthrie twisted round as best he could so as to face the bandit leader. 'And what *is* your ambition, Sethir?'

Sethir scowled. 'Don't mock me, boy!'

'I do not.'

'I think you know it already.'

Guthrie nodded. 'Revenge.'

'Justice!'

Hone Amis laughed. '*Justice?* You, a rag-tag, murdering bandit talk of justice?'

'Justice is *owed* me, fool!'

'''Tis *you* are the fool,' Hone Amis replied. 'Murder and theft, rape and pillage, *that's* the whole of your ambition. I know your type, man.'

'Oh *aye?*' Sethir demanded. He turned towards the Militia Master, so intent for the moment that he let his hold on Guthrie slip a little.

Guthrie could have squirmed away. In his mind he saw himself diving out of the bandit leader's grip, saw Hone Amis give sudden command, saw Sethir writhing on the ground, skewered with arrows, saw the whole of the camp break out into boiling, bloody fighting. For a long instant, he saw all this, felt the opportunity there in Sethir's slackened grip, ready for him to take.

But he did not.

There had already been too much blood spilled.

'Hone Amis,' Guthrie called.

Sethir jerked himself back with a start, pressing his blade hard against Guthrie's throat once again.

Guthrie tried to ignore the sharp, cold tip of it against his skin. 'Where are they, Amis?'

'Where are *who?*' the Militia Master asked, his face puckered uncertainly.

Guthrie looked at him, intent as he could be. 'You know who I mean.'

Hone Amis suddenly nodded. 'Right. Understood.' He waved a hand behind him. 'Left them back there under guard, where they couldn't do any harm.'

'What's going *on?*' Sethir demanded suspiciously.

'Bring them up,' Guthrie told Hone Amis.

The Militia Master stared. 'Are you crazy, lad?'

'Do it, Amis.' Guthrie ordered. 'Just *do it!*'

'Do *what?*' Sethir demanded. He dug the knife in a little harder, a nasty little twist of the blade that brought blood. 'You'd better tell me what you're talking about, boy, or –'

'Your men, Sethir,' Guthrie said quickly. 'It's your own men that will be coming up here.'

'Prisoners?'

'No.'

Sethir scowled. 'You bring me dead men, then?'

'No.'

The bandit leader shook his head. 'Don't mess me about, boy! What are you trying to say.'

'Wait and see,' Guthrie replied. He looked at Hone Amis, who still stood, uncertain. 'Bring them up, Amis!'

The Militia Master hesitated a moment longer, but then, at Guthrie's unflinching look, he nodded reluctant assent. 'Fetch them,' he called over his shoulder, and two of his men went off through the trees.

'If this is some manner of trick, boy ...' Sethir warned.

'No trick, Sethir, I assure you. Wait and see.'

The bandit leader obviously did not like any of this. His men stood about, nervous as cats, glancing at each other.

'What have you got to lose?' Guthrie pressed him.

Sethir stiffened, then shrugged and relaxed the knife a little. 'No more and no less than you, boy, if this be some trick.'

They waited ... long, slow beats of the pulse.

Then, through the trees, came the shapes of distant, moving men.

Those in the camp stiffened tensely.

Into the camp clearing came three of the Militia, and with them a handful of bandits – unbound, armed, looking ragged but well enough. Guthrie sighed inwardly, thankful that Hone Amis had properly honoured the oath these men had taken.

The bandits in the camp stared at their erstwhile comrades, shocked.

'Ossbert!' somebody called.

The grey-haired Ossbert nodded. He stood as he was, smiling uncertainly. He held a strung longbow in one hand, though he had drawn no arrow from the quiver at his back. 'Me indeed.'

Some of the bandits began to crowd forwards, quite forgetting themselves at the unexpected sight of those they had deemed fallen comrades suddenly appearing like this.

'But how ...'

'When did ...'

'*Quiet!*' Sethir roared. 'Get back to where you were! And you, Ossbert, and the rest of you, get away from those ...' he jerked his head at Hone Amis and the Militia, 'those rat-arsed fools and come back here.'

Guthrie waited tensely. He could see Hone Amis make a surreptitious little hand signal to one of the archers near him, and knew all too well what it would mean: Ossbert's first step back to Sethir would be his last. And then ... who knew what bloody chaos might not break out here?

But Guthrie kept himself still. There was nothing more he could do.

Ossbert shrugged uncomfortably. 'Can't do it, Seth.'

Sethir stared. 'What?'

'Can't do as ye asks.'

'I didn't *ask* you, man. Come here!'

Again, Ossbert shrugged.

'The rest of you,' Sethir snapped. 'Come here!'

The remaining bandits shuffled uncomfortably about, but none left his place amongst the ranks of the Militia.

'What have you *done?*' Sethir demanded, white faced. 'Saved your foul little lives by turning traitor, have you? Is *that* how they found our camp here?'

'No,' Ossbert said quickly. '*He* found out yer camp. The rest followed his trail.'

Sethir glared daggers at Guthrie.

'I am not yer man any more, Sethir,' Ossbert said. 'None of us is.'

The bandit leader spat. 'And just whose man are you, then?'

'His,' Ossbert replied, gesturing at Guthrie.

'Fool!' Sethir snapped, pointing an accusing finger at Ossbert. 'Do you think these prissy Valers will honour any bargain they make with those they call bandits? What did they offer you, silver? To betray your comrades?'

Ossbert brindled, obviously stung, but he kept his silence.

'How long do you think it will be before they slip a blade between your ribs one night?'

Ossbert took a step forwards. 'I have given my oath, Sethir. I was a man whose word counted for something, once. Perhaps I can be that kind of man again. He ...' Ossbert pointed at Guthrie, 'gave me that chance. I will not willingly ruin it.'

Sethir stared, shook his head. 'This is madness. He's put some sort of spell upon you, upon you all.'

'He's given us a chance at what we wanted all along,' one of the other bandits said.

'A better chance than we had from *ye*,' added another.

'A chance,' Guthrie interjected, 'that you can *all* have!'

All eyes turned on Guthrie.

'Tell him,' Guthrie said to Ossbert. 'Tell him how it was.'

Ossbert nodded. 'He took my oath, Seth. I am his man, of my own free will, armed and unbound and willing.'

'As can you all be,' Guthrie called.

He looked around at the gathered bandits. 'You came here to make lives for yourselves. You came here to be men of substance. Well, I offer you what you want. I offer you ...'

'*Shut up!*' Sethir hissed. He twisted the knife at Guthrie's throat, digging painfully into flesh.

Guthrie ignored him. 'I am the ruling Reeve of Reeve Vale,' he said, making his voice loud as he could. 'I offer you a chance to end the bloodshed, a chance to fashion lives for yourselves, homes, fields farms.'

'*Shut up!*' Sethir repeated.

'Yer lying!' somebody shouted at Guthrie accusingly.

'No,' Ossbert put in. 'He took my oath and treated me proper. He is *not* lying.'

'Swear your oaths to me,' Guthrie said, 'and you will be accepted into Reeve Vale. Swear to me and ...'

'Liar!' Sethir snarled. He shoved Guthrie, hard, knocking him flat on his back.'

'*Liar!*'

He dropped on Guthrie, coming down hard on one knee onto Guthrie's belly, knocking the breath out of him.

'No!' Hone Amis shouted.

Too late.

Sethir lifted the blade.

Guthrie saw it descend in a flashing arc. It was like the other time, when he and Alia had inadvertently confronted the pair of bandits in the rainy heights. He saw the death in the glinting metal as it came at him, slow as slow but deadly nevertheless.

He lay there belly up, gasping for breath, the world pulsing about him. The *other* surged close. He felt a roaring in his ears.

The blade went in under his lower ribs, like a white-hot rod, tearing up into him, once twice, again ...

XXVIII

Alia struggled up to awareness.

She felt sick and shaken and confused, stiff and sore, and her mouth seemed dry as old shoe leather. Her mind was full of splintered recollections ... seething chaos and screaming, a web of shimmering gold, flashing gems, ice-blue eyes.

She shook her head, rubbed her vision clear, tried to look about. She seemed to be in a tent. And next to her ... lying next her was ... Tasamin. Dead!

She did not understand.

And then she did.

Recollection flooded through her: Tasamin and young Reeve Guthrie and the falling, falling away into depthless, terrifying dark.

She felt the world quiver uncertainly about her, felt the dark seething that underlay everything, and shivered weakly. She looked at dead Tasamin. With a shudder, she tore the bracelets from her wrists, the necklace from about her throat, shed all the rest of the jewellery he had bound her up in. Only the vaguest memories were left to her of these past days. She seemed to have drifted in a daze, enspelled by Tasamin's foul, jewelled magicking.

Alia ran her hands over her face. A fit of the shivers went through her. She felt soiled, and unutterably weary.

Somewhere, somebody was shouting.

Fuzzily, Alia tried to piece together what had happened. The jewelled skull had somehow escaped Tasamin's control, and Tasamin had plunged with Guthrie into that *other place*, dragging her down with him, and then ... Then Tasamin had seemed to crumble, to simply come apart somehow, screaming, and she had been flung free, rebounding back into the ordinary world with bruising shock.

Tasamin's dead face was solidified in an expression of staring horror, and she felt sickly and shaken to her very bones, and Guthrie ...

382

Were was Guthrie?

Somewhere, somebody was still shouting.

Alia hugged herself. She felt as if her insides had come loose somehow.

Shouting. Still the shouting.

What was going on? She cocked her head. The noise seemed to be coming from outside the tent. Try as she might, however, she could not with any certainty recall what might lie outside this tent. The last clear recollection she felt she could rely upon was meeting with the demon-creature, him lifting her, rushing through the black forest ...

The bandit camp! It came to her in a rush.

She could hear men's voices through the tent's walls, shouting, talk.

Stiffly, Alia rose to her feet. Half bent over, she stumbled to the tent's doorway, lifted the entrance flap, peered out.

The light seemed too pure for her eyes. She blinked, rubbed at them, felt tears. The world felt different somehow, colours, shapes, contours ... It all surged, faded, solidified. Her belly went into spasm.

Alia shook herself, her heart beating hard with fright, tried to focus properly.

There were men before her. Two groups. Bandits and Militia! She saw Hone Amis himself. And ...

Reeve Guthrie!

But standing over Guthrie was the bearded bandit named Sethir, a blade at Guthrie's throat.

It took long moments before Alia could make proper sense of it all.

'Liar!' she heard Sethir snarl. He shoved Guthrie roughly to the ground. '*Liar!*'

Alia saw him pounce, driving his knee into Guthrie's belly.

And then the knife came up.

'No!' Hone Amis shouted.

Too late.

Alia watched, horrified, as Sethir plunged the blade between Guthrie's ribs, once, twice ... Guthrie writhed, trying ineffectually to ward off the flashing blade with his hands. Wet blood flowed from the deep wounds in his chest.

Sethir stuck again, and yet again, grunting with effort and animal satisfaction. 'Rat-arsed son of a shit-eating bastard father!' he cursed. 'Wish that I had been able to do your father, and his father

...' The knife came down again, *fwump*! into wet flesh. 'The whole cursed lot of you!'

Alia stared, unbelieving. The entire camp, it seemed, Militia, hunter, and bandit alike, was frozen by the sudden brutality of Sethir's act.

Sethir rose to his feet, standing astride Guthrie in triumph. He kicked him, hard, in the belly, and again. Guthrie moaned, a faint, gasping sound.

Hone Amis had turned white as any sheet. He opened his mouth to shout some order, but could make no word come forth.

'Now!' Sethir cried. He waved an arm at the stunned Militia, urging on his own men. 'At them! Take them. Destroy them all, and this land is ours!'

But there came the sudden *twung*! of a bowstring, and Sethir stumbled. He looked down at himself in shock. The fletched butt of an arrow stood out from his sternum. He stared at the source of the shot.

Ossbert looked back levelly at him, bow in hand.

'Traitor!' Sethir hissed, clutching at the shaft in him.

Ossbert flinched not at all at the name. ''Tis ye who betray us, Sethir. There's far too much of hate in ye.'

'Kill him, someone,' Sethir ordered. 'Kill him!'

But nobody moved.

Ossbert let his bow drop, lifted his arms. 'We came here to make new lives for ourselves,' he cried to the gathered bandits. 'This man ...' he pointed down to bleeding Guthrie, '... offered us just that new life. And Sethir, Sethir knifes him. With that blade of his, Sethir may have just killed the best hope any of us had!'

Ossbert turned to Hone Amis. 'I am Reeve Guthrie's man, Militia Master. Believe it.'

Hone Amis looked at him with eyes cold as old ice.

'Craven *traitor*!' Sethir cried. He took a step towards Ossbert but stumbled, blinking confusedly, his face white and greasy with sweat.

Hone Amis suddenly roared, as if he had been enspelled, frozen, and only just had broken out of it. There were no clear words, just a great cry of rage and anguish. He raised the long blade in his hand. The Militia, taking their cue from him, moved forwards, weapon to the ready.

But Guthrie, lying in a bleeding heap, cried aloud and raised himself partially up.

All eyes turned on him.

'Le ... let this ...' Guthrie gasped, his voice hardly audible. Bright pink blood frothed from his mouth. 'Let this ... end!'

Men stood poised, weapons out and ready, uncertain.

'Enough of death,' Guthrie gasped. 'Let my death and Sethir's death end things here. Let it *end*! There is room enough in the Vale for all of you.'

'*No!*' Sethir cried. 'He lies, you fools! Can't you see? He *lies!*'

'Shut *up*, Sethir,' Ossbert said.

The bandit leader snarled. 'Come here, lying traitor, and I'll shut *you* up.' He raised his bloody blade. 'With *this!*'

Ossbert said not a word. Drawing his own blade, he moved on Sethir.

The two men circled for an instant, but Sethir was too far gone already, the arrow in his chest grating against bone and what-else with each breath. He gasped wheezily at Ossbert, waving the blade before him in the air. 'Come on. Come *on!*'

Ossbert moved in, ducked under Sethir's clumsy attack, and drove his own blade through the side of Sethir's rib cage in one sudden, hard blow.

Sethir collapsed with a gasp of shock.

Ossbert yanked his blade out and gave Sethir a kick, toppling him in a heap. The bandit leader tried to raise himself, but his strength gave out and he crumpled face first.

Ossbert knelt at his side, grabbing him by the hair. 'Ye were a strong man, Seth. But ye never had the least kindness in ye.'

Sethir glared hatred at him.

'May ye make yer peace in yer next life, Boh Sethir, once of Reeve Vale,' Ossbert said. Then he drove his blade up under the other man's jaw with a wet *cruunch*.

Sethir screamed once, a terrible animal wail, and collapsed.

Witnessing, Alia felt herself possessed of a strange sort of double-vision. She saw men clutch their weapons tighter now, move forwards threateningly, and somehow she could sense at the same time a kind of miasma of tension, like a cloud coiled about them all. She could make out half a dozen different emotions mirrored on men's faces. Events were balanced on a knife-edge.

She pushed herself out of the tent and ran shakily across the camp clearing towards where Guthrie lay on the ground between the opposing forces. 'No!' she shouted hoarsely. She had seen too much destroyed already in blood and violence. 'Stop!'

Men stared at her.

She made the straightest way to Guthrie, knelt at his side. He was all but comatose, wet and slippery with blood, breathing in only the shallowest of gasps. She put her arms about him, holding him up, willing strength into him, as if she were well and conduit together, feeding water to a man near dead with thirst.

Guthrie moaned. His eyes fluttered.

She had pinned her hopes on this man once. And he had let her down. She did not know, quite, what she hoped for now. But the violent, dark cloud she sensed seemed to revolve about him, as if he were the focal point of all that occurred here. And though she could not piece together clearly what had occurred in that disturbing *other place*, she knew from what bits she could recall that he was not the simple, pampered lad she once thought him to be.

'Not yet,' Alia breathed into Guthrie's ear. 'We still need you. Don't you leave us *yet*!' She shook him, gentle-hard. She had heard that a man on the edge of life could sometimes be summoned back from the Shadowland borders by his name. 'Guthrie,' she called into his ear, bending low. 'Guthrie. *Guthrie!*'

Nothing.

There was an angry rumbling from the ranks of the Militia.

Alia shivered. It was too late. She glanced up at the faces of the men near her, seeing uncertainty, grief, burgeoning rage.

She felt the world shudder, felt herself slipping. Her heart beat wildly. It was as before ... plunging into the terrible chaos that Tasamin had claimed underlay all.

Tasamin, who had lied to her, cruelly enthralled her with his magicking.

Alia struggled to make sense of what was happening to her, refusing to accept anything Tasamin might have claimed for truth. She could *feel* the world slipping away from her, as if she were sinking into a great pit of churning, dark water, the ordinary world dwindling away above ...

But all was not entirely chaos.

Near her, she *felt* something move. There was no sight, no hearing in this uncanny realm, but she could still *feel* somehow. What moved near her *felt* like ... it writhed like a crippled eel, half hollow, the swirling currents flowing without it and within it.

Alia did not know how she knew, but she knew: Guthrie! He was sinking faster than she, dropping like a stone.

She reached for him, straining. He was slipping away not just from the ordinary world, but from this *other place* as well, fading like an image scribed in soft sand being washed away by the waves.

He was dying.

No! Alia cried, or thought to cry. She struggled with every bit of what strength remained to her to call him back, reach him back, draw him back to life.

With a sickening heave, she came out into the ordinary world again. In her arms, Guthrie moaned. She looked down and saw his eyes open. He stared about, bleary, shaken, but there.

'You came for me,' he said weakly.

Alia nodded.

Guthrie fell back, shuddering weakly, and Alia's heart faltered. But he lifted himself up a little, motioned weakly, a beckoning gesture with one limp hand, directed at everyone.

The men in the camp closed in, bandit and Militia alike, silent.

'I will take your oaths,' he said hoarsely to the bandits.

Hone Amis surged forwards, protesting.

'I will take their oaths, Militia Master,' Guthrie insisted.

Hone Amis stood stock still, uncertain, his jaw working with anger and confusion.

'And you will abide by yours,' Guthrie added. He gasped, coughing up bright blood in a painful spasm. 'Is that ... *clear*, my Militia Master?'

Hone Amis swallowed, blinked, nodded slowly. 'Aye, my Reeve. It shall be as you say, then.'

For a long moment more there was hesitation. Then Hone Amis gestured to the bandits clustered about. 'It will be as he says. Those of you who wish to prosper at all in this land, make your oath to him now, quickly. Quickly!'

The bandits shuffled closer. 'What ... What do we say?' one asked.

'By my red blood and white bone,' Hone Amis began for them. 'Repeat it, man. Repeat it!'

'By my red blood and ... and white bone,' the man started.

'On one knee, fool,' the Militia Master ordered. 'Down on one knee. Were you brought up in a barn? Where's your respect?'

Guthrie waved such niceties aside. 'Only hurry,' he gasped. '*Hurry!*'

'By my red blood and white bone,' the man said again.

'I swear to be true to you and yours,' Hone Amis led.

'... true to ye and yers,' came the response.

'To your sons and son's sons,'

387

But Guthrie stopped them there, raising a hand weakly. 'I have no sons. And am ...' he smiled, a mere thinning of his lips, 'am not likely to have.'

An uncertain pause greeted this.

'I have seen the good and the bad,' he went on, 'in the Reeveship. There are times when men need somebody to look to.'

Hone Amis nodded. 'It is part of the natural order of life.'

'But it takes too much to play the part as it should be played.' Guthrie sighed. 'Listen to me, all of you. This land is yours to do with as you will. Destroy it. Make it fertile. Cut it into sections. Share it. Hoard it ...'

'Guthrie,' Hone Amis said. 'You tire yourself. We understand. A New Reeve will be found. Your uncle Pell's sister's son is still alive. They're closest to the line, I'd think. And young Tadd is a likely lad I hear. Better than that weasel Malone at any rate! Tadd's had Five Family training. He ought to be able to –'

'Amis! No. No.' Guthrie tried to rise partway but slipped back with an inadvertent grunt of pain. Alia, still supporting him, lifted him a little higher.

'The time for Reeves is past,' Guthrie said.

Hone Amis started. 'What are you *saying*?'

'There's no time for long discussions, Amis. Just listen, will you?' Guthrie gestured at all those gathered near: Militia, hunter, bandit. 'Too much has changed. Too many of these folk come from outside the ways of the Vale. It won't work, Amis.'

'But how else can we ...'

'It won't *work*, trying to force the old pattern upon them. Think of the good of the Vale, Amis. Try to force these folk into the old pattern and you'll have nothing but struggle. It's time for *change*! I've seen what happens when a man fears *change* too much. His entire life becomes one long struggle for control, Amis. It doesn't work!'

Guthrie coughed wetly, gasped, continued. 'The best of rulers utters no word lightly. He is but a shadow, barely seen. The best of rulers hesitates rightly, seeing what he has foreseen.'

Hone Amis looked confused.

'Something Abbod Rianna quoted to me once,' Guthrie gasped. 'In the Closter, it was, that dismal day the Sea Wolves came. I never understood till now ... You can't control it, Amis. Change is upon us all. Let these folk live together, and something good will come of it. It won't be what we've been used to, but it will be good enough.

Better perhaps. The Vale isn't only what it has been. It's what it *can* be! Let it happen, Amis. It's the only way. The *only* way.'

Guthrie slumped back momentarily in Alia's hold again, gasping, then caught himself. 'All of you! This is the only hope you have. Too much blood already. Too much of pain and anger. Do you want a life here? Then you must learn to live with each other, or die. Simple as that. Militia, hunter, the rest of you, *all!*'

Hone Amis looked as if somebody had just kicked him in the gut.

'No more allegiance to one man or one family,' Guthrie said, his voice so weak now that those gathered about had to crowd closer. 'No more allegiance to the way things are *supposed* to be. Things are what they are, and what they become. Live with them, and with each other. Swear your oaths not to me, now, but to yourselves, and your children, and your children's children.'

Folk stared at him.

'Swear it now! Give the oath: by blood and bone and breath ... Repeat it!'

'By blood and bone and breath ...' they echoed, haltingly.

'I swear to be true to ...' Guthrie went on, 'to the hope and the promise of ...'

'I swear to be true,' came the response, 'to the hope and the promise of ...'

All turned to Guthrie, waiting for him to continue.

But it was too late. Guthrie hung limp and white in Alia's hold. Gone.

Shocked silence settled over all for long heartbeats.

Alia stared over the top of Guthrie's still head at the stricken faces all around her. She felt her heart filled with what Guthrie had been trying to say. An end to violence. An end to force. She yearned for it. She took a breath and said, 'True to the hope and promise that Guthrie Garthson gave us as he died.'

After a long, shuffling pause, they took it up, weak at first but ending strongly: 'True to the hope and promise that Guthrie Garthson gave us as he died.'

They stood, uncertain, self-conscious, silently eyeing each other.

Then somebody began the death litany for Guthrie: 'A scathless journey in the darkness, friend.'

Others took it up with him, till all of them were reciting it. 'A scathless journey and a fruitful end. Gone from the world of living ken. Into the Shadowlands ... To begin again.'

It was a strange moment, and one that none there would ever

truly forget. Death and fear and shock, oath giving and unlooked-for beginnings and hope, all mingled into one stunning pattern.

Guthrie lay like a child folded in Alia's arms, limp and white and pathetic.

This was not the ending any had looked to see here.

Men stared about them, at each other, still no less uncertain.

Hone Amis rose finally, blinking tears from his eyes. He stared down at the still form of Sethir, looked about him at the ragged bandits, his eyes hooded with old anger. But he turned back to Guthrie, took a breath, another, shook himself. 'Oaths have been given and accepted here,' he said to the gathered folk. 'Something ... new has had its beginning here, it seems.' He took a long, sighing, weary breath, let it out. 'I will abide by my oath. Will any man here do otherwise?'

He regarded the company about him.

No one spoke.

'Let it be so, then,' Hone Amis said. Then, 'We have a Reeve to bury. Let us do it – together.'

And so they did.

XXIX

Alia perched on a chill rocky rise above the little hollow where the mortal remains of Reeve Guthrie Garthson lay. It was evening, the dawn burial ceremony over long since, and all the rest who had been here gone. She looked down at the small stone marker, dusted lightly with new snow, that was all that remained now for the eye to see. It said nothing, had scribed on it only the star-circle that represented the world's great Powers.

'Gone from the world of living ken,' Alia quoted softly from the death litany. 'Into the Shadowlands ... To begin again.'

Her left palm itched a little, but it was a healing itch now. She scratched it absently, then plucked a tuft of dry winter grass that stuck out above the new snow between two spikes of rock. 'To begin again,' she repeated.

The burial had not been without its tensions. Too many men too recently foes could not set aside all the bitterness in an instant. But there had been a feeling about it ... Even wooden-brained old Hone Amis had seemed thawed a little. Something new *was* beginning. That would be Reeve Guthrie Garthson's legacy.

But what of her?

Alia felt as lonely as ever she had in her life. There were new beginnings, oh aye. But nothing of such beginnings held any real appeal for her now. She had fought to save her way of life, and lost. She remained behind here, alone, after everybody else had left, like a piece of jetsam stranded on a lonely beach by the receding tide. Her choice, to remain – but little other option was there. Her life had been with the hunters, but what the hunters had once had was altogether gone now. What chance she might once have had with the Fey was gone. The person she had once been was gone as well. She felt a great wave of sadness wash through her, remembering the foggy day – only a few weeks back now, though it seemed ages ago – when she had stood in the Heights of the Salter Pass, gazing in all innocence at the half-glimpsed shapes of the Fey. She felt like an entirely other person now ...

The great disasters of the Vale had been resolved – folk could begin to live and prosper again now. But she felt she belonged nowhere in the world any more. The very world itself was strange to her. She was neither fish nor fowl nor good red meat, as the old saw went.

She felt the world shiver into momentary uncertainty all about her and fought to resist it. Too much had happened to her. She did not understand what had happened to her.

Upon the rock at her side, lay a small book, elegantly bound in pebble-grained leather dyed a rich crimson. It had been amongst Gurthrie's few possessions. Alia had felt strangely attracted by it, and since nobody else had shown any particular interest in it, it had come to her. She picked it up now, opened it. About a third of the way down the first page, across the centre of it, in large, elegant, hand drawn letters, was written: *The Pathless Way.* And underneath that, in smaller letters: *The Seer sees but does not seize.*

Alia had read that a half a score times already, and understood it no better now than the first time. She thumbed through the fine parchment pages until a verse caught her eye:

> *Wrinkle veined like an old hand,*
> *A single leaf*
> *rests in my palm.*
> *I bend where I stand*
> *To look at this small thief.*
> *It is gone, my calm.*
> *I am gone.*
> *For I am returned,*
> *And my self is drawn*
> *Back and turned*
> *Into the world again,*
> *Like a leaf caught on a rolling stream,*
> *Or held in a man's hand when*
> *He gazes at it in a dream.*

Alia did not know what to think.

What in the world had Guthrie been doing with this richly bound, nonsensical little book? From where had he got it? There were no structured sections to it, no explanations, no numbers to the pages even, only verse after confusing verse. None of it seemed to make any sense. She flipped on compulsively, read another bit:

> Confusing in its formless form,
> And silent in its noise,
> Whirling like a liquid storm,
> And filled with painful joys.
>
> It has no beginning, no middle, no end,
> Cannot stand stiff, and it does not bend.
> Dark as a raven, light as the sun,
> Made up of many and made up of one.
>
> It cannot be put into words or a rhyme,
> And pathless the way, like a long weary climb,
> Is the route to its wonders, it dazzle and play.
> Pathless the journey, and pathless the way.
>
> Let go of the self, of the wanting and bother.
> Relinguish the self and immerse in the Other.

Alia shook her head. 'Immerse in the Other.' What was *that* supposed to mean?

She started to read yet more:

> The way is not clear to the ear or the eye,
> Or the mind's agile fingers, so wanting to pry ...

but stopped mid-way, for with the words, suddenly, came memory: Tasamin had read that aloud. In a tent. Laughing. It was only a partial recollection – nothing clear remained to Alia of her time under Tasamin's thrall – but she seemed to recall Guthrie and Tasamin and she ... all standing together, then falling, falling into darkness and terror.

Alia shuddered, and felt the world shudder about her.

She did not *like* this! She cursed Tasamin and her own complete foolishness. Though she did not understand what had happened to her, it had a terrible feeling of irreversibility about it. She had taken one unknowing step too far along a path she could not see. And now the way ahead seemed – as the book in her hands put it – pathless indeed.

Sitting there, braced against the frigid stone, Alia felt a deep fragility in herself, in the world's self. She did not understand what she had done to bring about this uncanny change. The world was not the simple, stable place she had thought it to be. All she had ever wanted was to look upon the face of wonder. A girl's simple yearning, that was all. Not this terrible dislocation of spirit. It all seemed too cruel. And, oh, how she did mourn her own lost self here at the end of everything.

Alia gazed down at the little hump of Guthrie's grave. He too had taken one step too far, whatever strange path he might have been following. Alia began to weep softly, for Guthrie, for herself, for all the pain and spilled blood and all the loss of the past weeks ...

And then, through the halo of her tears, Alia saw the earth about Guthrie's grave begin to shift.

It undulated in a slow, strange way, totally unlike anything Alia had ever seen. Almost like liquid, it was, little ripples at first, as if some creature were moving along under the surface of a body of deep water – save it was earth and brown winter grass and snow that rippled.

Alia stared. She felt her belly do a funny little flop, had to swallow, hard.

The earthy 'waves' surged up more strongly. A little bank of snow toppled away from the 'crest' of one wave and, to Alia's utter shock and amazement, a man's arm began to emerge out of the ground. It moved like a swimmer's arm, parting earth and rock and grass and snow like so much water.

Hand and forearm ... then another hand reached out of the earth. Shoulders.

With a surge, the rest came, splashing solid, earthy 'water' in all directions ...

Alia had to swallow again. Merely looking on made her somehow queasy deep in her belly. The world shivered in a spasm of uncertainty. She did not understand what it was she witnessed.

The figure that stood next to Guthrie's grave was covered with earth, like a mole dragged out of its burrow. It looked hardly a human person at all ...

For a heart-wrenching moment, Alia thought it might be some stranger type of Fey, come against all expectations to call her to him after all.

But no.

This was a man indeed.

But what *manner* of man?

Whoever it was stood panting.

Whoever ...

There was only one man it *could* be.

Alia was able to make him out now, face soaked in dirt notwithstanding.

'Guthrie!' she cried involuntarily.

He swivelled, looking up at her.

'Guthrie,' she said again, lamely, not knowing what else to do.

He said nothing, merely stood as he was, panting. He was dressed in the clothes they had buried him in, the same he had died in. Alia could see the rents Sethir's blade had cut through the cloth of his jerkin.

She did not know what to think. Perhaps it was a spirit she was seeing. But he seemed a very earthy spirit, in all senses. He seemed a man who had just exerted himself to the point of exhaustion. As she watched, he sank wearily to his knees.

Alia leaped to her feet. 'But how ... Why ...' she sputtered. 'You're *alive!*'

Guthrie nodded wearily. 'Aye.'

'But *how?*'

He shrugged. 'I do not know how to tell you.' He rose to his feet then and came hobbling up the slope to her.

As he drew closer, she could see through the knife-rents in his jerkin. White skin showed – unblemished by wound or scar.

Alia sat down quickly. She felt herself shaking. 'How ... How did you ... Why are you not ... dead? I saw the blood. I saw you *die!*'

Guthrie lowered himself to a rock with a weary sigh. He was white faced and gasping. 'I'm not ... sure I can explain it to you. I am ... *changed*. I ...' He went silent for long moments, his eyes staring blindly into the evening sky. A long shudder went through him. 'I hurt. I bled. I ... died in some sense, I think. But I came back. The world is ... is not a simple place. It is possible to ... *do* certain kinds of things, things that seem incredible if one does not know about ... about ...'

Alia shook her head in confusion. Almost, it seemed, he was raving. Fevered, perhaps. 'The others have gone long since,' she told him. 'But I can run. I can fetch them back here. Before tomorrow's dawn. I'm certain of it. If you can just last here alone ...'

Guthrie shook his head.

'I can keep you company, then, until you're stronger. Food drink, I have that. We did the journey once together. Perhaps we can ...'

'No, Alia.'

She looked at him, disturbed.

'I shall not be going back there.'

'But you ... you didn't die! Why would you not *return*?'

'I am no longer Reeve, could no more live that role any longer than a fish might fly the heights with the hawks.'

'I don't ... understand,' Alia said.

He shrugged uncomfortably. 'I do not know how to explain it to you so you *could* understand.'

Alia glared at him. 'I'm not *stupid*!'

'Of course not,' he said hurriedly.

Alia waited for him to say something further. Instead, he simply stared off into the distance, his eyes unfocused, as if he were listening to voices only he could hear. It was the same vacancy she had seen in him since their first meeting.

'What do you intend to do, then?' she demanded. 'Just ...' she thought of her talk with Mysha. 'Just walk away?'

He made no reply, seemed not even to hear her.

'Guthrie,' she said, prodding him gently with a finger. 'Guthrie!'

He blinked, shook himself.

'I asked you a question.'

He looked at her uncomprehendingly.

'I *said*, do you just intend to walk away into the wilds and leave everybody, then?'

'Into the wilds? No ... Aye, perhaps. In a sense. Perhaps that's a proper way to put it.'

'But how *can* you just walk off and desert everything you've ever known?' Alia demanded. 'Especially *now*!'

'My old self is dead. Or dying.' Guthrie sighed. 'It was – is necessary. And now ... Now I can make the journey that has been awaiting me.'

Once more, she saw that vacant, *listening* expression overtake him.

'Guthrie. *Guthrie*!'

He came back, blinking.

Alia found herself envying him. Here she was, with nothing, nowhere to go, nothing calling her, stranded and alone and confused to her very bones. And he had everything, and was leaving it. For something he valued more. But what? *What*?

'Take me with you!' she said impulsively.

He shook his head.

'Take me! I have – have nowhere else to go.' She felt sudden tears fill her eyes. 'I have nothing left, nobody ...'

He looked at her, uncertain.

'Take me with you!' she pleaded.

'You have no idea what you ask of me. I go where you cannot follow me.'

'I can follow *anywhere* you go.'

He laughed softly.

'I *can*!'

'Where I am going, there are no paths.'

Alia swallowed. There was something uncanny about him. The very tone of his voice when he said that made her hackles shiver. Suddenly, she was reminded of a verse from the little book. It came to her, perfect and clear, as if the page lay open before her mind's eye: 'It cannot be put into words or a rhyme,' she recited, 'and pathless the way, like a long weary climb, is the route to its wonders, its dazzle and play. Pathless the journey, and pathless the way.'

Guthrie stared at her. 'Where did you learn that?'

'In your book.' She gestured self-consciously to where the book still lay on the rock. 'Nobody else wanted it, so I ...'

He looked at her, a long, searching look. Alia held herself firm under that appraisal, returning look for look.

After a long few moments, he sighed. 'Which, of loss or gain,' he said, 'shall prove the greater bane?'

Alia did not understand.

'Another verse from that same book,' he said. Then he held out a hand. 'Take my hand.'

Alia felt her heart suddenly thump, hard. What was he offering her? There was a fey look to his eyes. Almost, she backed away from him. Almost ...

But no.

Taking his hand, she felt a sudden, shocking jolt go through her. Her senses were torn away by the awful rush of it. The ordinary, solid world was gone in an instant, and there was only that dark, moving confusion that Tasamin had called the Nether Place, the Place of Great Chaos, pulsing sickeningly without and within her. She screamed, or thought to scream, but could feel no mouth to scream with, no ears to hear. She felt herself being torn apart, ruptured into chaos ...

With a cold shock, she was hurled back into the ordinary world. It was like being plunged into ice water from a great height. She staggered back, staring at Guthrie, heart in her throat. She felt the world pulse sickeningly about her.

Guthrie looked at her, unblinking. '*That* is where I go.'

'To the Place of Great Chaos?' Alia shivered. She was soaked in chill sweat, and her heart was still thumping like a mad thing.

'Chaos?' Guthrie said.

'Aye. That was Tasamin's name for it.'

'It is chaos, and not.'

'How ... How did you take us there so sudden?'

He gestured about him. 'It is here, there, everywhere. It underlies all.'

Alia shivered. 'Chaos underlying the world.'

'No,' he said. '*Not* chaos. Something else.'

'What, then?'

He went silent for a long moment, then pointed to the book. 'Over the darkness,' he recited, 'under the light. It has a name yet is nameless. Bright as the day time, dark as the night. It has a frame yet is frameless.' He shrugged self-consciously. 'I know it simply as the *Other*.'

'Relinquish the self and immerse in the Other,' Alia quoted, recalling what she had read only a little while before.

Guthrie regarded her uncertainly. 'Aye. Just so. It is the Closterers' manner of putting it.'

'The book is a Closterer thing?' she asked.

He nodded. 'It is the task they take upon themselves, the knowing of the *other*.'

'Have you become a Closterer, then?'

Guthrie shook his head. 'No. At least ... Perhaps in a small way I have. I knew one. She showed me things. Tasamin was wrong to describe the *other* as brute chaos. Tasamin was wrong about many things.'

Alia was not sure how she felt. She had never wished to believe Tasamin's description. Chaos and terror underlying the world ... It was not what her belly told her lay at the heart of the world's mysteries. Not at all.

But this *Other* was a strange and terrifying place. An utterly mysterious place ...

She looked at Guthrie. Terrifying though the *other* might be – she could still feel her heart hammering – he was prepared to plunge himself into it.

Alia felt a sudden rush of memory and understanding: her strange

398

experiences with the Fey, with Tasamin, with Guthrie; she remembered her disturbing sense of having seen through the world's façade after her interaction with the Fey; she recalled with a shudder the hurtling plunge through the *other* she had been forced to partake in with Tasamin. In her mind, she saw the world like a great onion, each layer another level of realness, human, Fey, others less approachable perhaps. Each real as real, and yet never real at all. Each only one aspect. Each only ...

She thought of another verse she had read. Impulsively, she reached for the little book, flipped through it, found what she was looking for:

> *Face and hands and legs and arms,*
> *Fears and joys and spells and charms,*
> *Warp and woof and nothing more,*
> *Threads to clothe us, nothing more.*
>
> *Tree and rock and cloud and stream,*
> *Are never what they look to seem.*
> *Mind nor self nor leg nor star,*
> *Nothing's what we say they are.*
>
> *Lift the cloth, the threads unwind,*
> *An endless mystery will ye find.*
>
> *Nothing's what it seems to be,*
> *Neither ye and neither me.*
>
> *There's not a river flowing free*
> *But cries its yearning for the sea.*

Alia felt, suddenly, that sense of *yearning*. She wanted to immerse herself, to lose herself, to become a part of something greater.

Endless mystery underlying all ... It had always called to her, that ultimate mystery, a Fey voice in her dreams.

She looked Guthrie straight. 'I would go with you to this *other* place.'

He shook his head. 'You do not know what you ask.'

'I do now.'

He stared at her. 'After what you have just experienced, you still wish to go? With all your heart?'

Alia took a breath. 'With all my heart.'

Guthrie shook his head uncertainly.

'Take me with you,' Alia implored.

He sighed, looked at her. 'I do not think you know what door you are deciding to step through.'

'I know it is a door leading me somewhere *new*.'

Guthrie laughed softly. 'Aye. 'Tis that, indeed.'

'And there is nothing in my old life left to call me back.'

He nodded, sighed. 'I know *that* feeling well enough.'

'Take me with you, then.'

'It will ... *change* you, Alia. Beyond anything you can easily imagine.'

'I am ready for such a change.'

He sighed again, then smiled a small, thin smile. 'If you truly, truly wish it so.'

She nodded. '*Truly*.'

'Come, then.' He stood up stiffly and gestured for her to follow him.

She bent to retrieve the little book.

'Leave it,' he said.

'But ...'

'If we return, we can gather it up easily enough. And if we do not, we shall not need it. Perhaps another will find it, if the need is there.'

'There ... there *is* a return for us, then?' she asked.

'Of sorts. But nothing will be the same, neither the world nor us.'

She nodded soberly. 'Aye.'

'Come.' Walking slowly, Guthrie led her across the slope through ankle-deep drifts of new snow and brittle brown grass, then in through the surrounding pines and onwards, up, always up, but slow. He panted as he walked. Alia closed with him and offered her arm in support. He took it with a smile of thanks. Together, they made their way in silence upslope through the interlaced boughs of the trees until, eventually, they came out at the verge of a high bluff.

The sun was sinking into the west, a glowing red orb. The sky lay soaked in soft crimson.

'Globe of fire, globe of light,' Alia murmured. 'Brightest yellow, shining bright ...'

'Glowing red,' Guthrie took it up, 'at daylight's ending. Glowing red, my sorrows mending. Fire of evening, fire of morn ...'

'Fire in which my hopes are born,' Alia completed.

'Light of morning ...'

'Dawnfire burning.'

'Gone at dusk,' they both finished together, 'but soon returning.'

They laughed together, gently, Guthrie still leaning upon her for support.

'I have not thought of that verse since I was a lad,' he said.

Alia remembered reciting it, standing upon a height such as this, watching the sunset. She recalled, too, the vertiginous fright she had got looking down from that height.

The world shivered a little all about her, and she shivered with it.

Guthrie took her by the hand and led her slowly towards the edge. At the very brink, he stopped and looked down. Alia too, though uneasily.

The drop fell away sheer, a dizzying fall of rock. At the bottom were dark pines and shadows. Alia felt her guts lurch. The ordinary world slipped from her. The strange seethe of the *other* swept up, and, for an instant, there seemed no difference between the fall of rock beneath her feet and the fall of confusion that was the *other*. The two merged into one great, drastic plunge.

She struggled back, gasping, stumbling away.

Guthrie moved not at all.

Alia shuddered, feeling suddenly cold, cold.

'Water, the fish fears not,' Guthrie recited. 'Nor air, the bird. Wings, the Seer has not got, nor fins, I have heard ...'

Alia remembered the verse. 'Yet fly he must, and swim, or ...'

'Or die he must,' Guthrie completed. ''Tis up to him.'

Alia gestured shakily to the edge. 'Do you mean we must ...'

'Leap,' he recited, 'or ye have not got a word to be heard.'

Alia swallowed. She did not know if she could do such a thing. To plunge into the complete unknown ...

Guthrie turned, held out his hands to her.

Alia hesitated for a half score of heartbeats, then stepped slowly forwards and took his hands in hers.

They perched on the edge for one timeless instant, and Alia had the spirit-dizzying experience of seeing both – the solid, familiar world and the great, seething, utterly strange *other*. Her heart beat in terror and strange exaltation.

Then, hand in hand ...

they ...

leaped.

The Book of the Closterers

The Closterers' *Book* is not a book in the common sense of the word; that is, it has no chapters, no pagination, no narrative sequence that may be followed page by page. The contents appear in no apparent order.

The Book is written entirely in verse. Although there is no overall sequence, some of the verses clearly focus on similar subject matter. Such verses have been grouped together in the version below under headings such as *The Way, The Seer,* and so on. This is a practice the Closterers themselves, no doubt, would look upon with the severest of ambivalencies. It seems warranted, however, for the ease of access it allows to the book's contents.

THE WAY

When clear-seeing persons are told of the Way,
They follow, their heads deeply bowed.
To un-seeing persons when told of the Way,
It seems to them only a cloud.
When blind ones are told of the true Pathless Way,
They grin and they laugh right out loud.

If the loud laughing blind laughed never at all,
But flocked here instead to the Closterers' call,
And boasted aloud of the truth they could see,
Unworthy indeed would the Pathless Way be.

One does more and more each day.
In the pursuit of knowing.
But follow the Pathless Way,
The goingless going,
And each day one does less,

Until one reaches fundamentalness.

Trading all for none
Leaves nothing undone.

The five true colours clog the eyes,
And blind us to the wondrous skies
That lie about us.

And five true notes will make us deaf
to talking wind in bough and leaf
That laugh about us.

The five true tastes will blind the tongue
Of very old or very young
And so will rob us.

The name that can be spoken
Is but a token:
A cloud across a star,
A doorway and a bar,
A shackle to be broken.

THE NAMELESS GATE

The way is not clear to the ear or the eye,
Or the mind's agile fingers, so wanting to pry.

Pathless the way, for what ye await.
Change is the journey, change is yer fate.
Change is the way through the great Nameless Gate.

For passage through the Nameless Gate,
For knowing what it is and not,
Simple words for which we wait:
Change the potter, change the pot.

THE SEER

The Seer sees
But does not seize.

Like a star or a cloud
Must the Seer be,
Like a river fast flowing
Along to the sea,

Like a bird on the wing,
Or the wind blowing free,
Like a wide open window
Through which all can see.

Silent and still,
'Tween the stars and the seas
And the crest of the hill,
The Seer sees
A motionless motion,
A soundless commotion,
A greatness receding,
A far-away seething,
Returned with his breathing
Gone silent and still.

A man of the way will follow the way
Beyond what he can see or hear.

A man who still fears will hold and stay,
And all his way will be filled with fear.

A fearing-man will be hard and cold,
A fearing-man will fear to be bold,
A fearing-man will be desperate to hold.

Water, the fish fears not,
Nor air, the bird.

Wings, the Seer has not got,
Nor fins, I have heard,
Yet fly he must,
And swim,
Or die he must.
'Tis up to him.

Leap, or ye have not got
A word
To be heard.

THE OTHER

Over the darkness, under the light,
It has a name yet is nameless.

Bright as the day time, dark as the night,
It has a frame yet is frameless.

Drawing close, I saw not its face.
Following behind, I saw not its rear.
Searching, I could not find its place.
Listening, there was nothing to hear.

Confusing in its formless form,
And silent in its noise,
Whirling like a liquid storm,
And filled with painful joys.

It has no beginning, no middle, no end,
Cannot stand stiff, and it does not bend.
Dark as a raven, light as the sun,
Made up of many and made up of one.

It cannot be put into words or a rhyme,
And pathless the way, like a long weary climb,
Is the route to its wonders, its dazzle and play.
Pathless the journey, and pathless the way.

Let go of the self, of the wanting and bother.
Relinquish the self and immerse in the Other.

Face and hands and legs and arms,
Fears and joys and spells and charms,
Warp and woof and nothing more,
Threads to clothe us, nothing more.

Tree and rock and cloud and stream,
Are never what they look to seem.
Mind nor self nor leg nor star,
Nothing's what we say they are.

Lift the cloth, the threads unwind,
An endless mystery will ye find.

Nothing's what it seems to be,
Neither ye and neither me.

MISCELLANEOUS

The rivers sing their flowing song,
Towards the sea, where they belong.

There's not a river flowing free
But cries its yearning for the sea.

Yer self or yer lived life,
Which is most near?
Yer goods or yer lived life,
Which is more dear?
Desire or yer lived life,
By which do ye steer?

Which, of loss or gain,
Shall prove the greater bane?

The best of rulers utters no word lightly.
He is but a shadow, barely seen.
The best of rulers hesitates rightly.
Seeing what he has foreseen.

The path we may see
Leads nowhere at all.
'I know yer name,' said the man.
But the clouds laughed with rain.

Wrinkle veined like an old hand,
A single leaf
rests in my palm.
I bend where I stand
To look at this small thief.
It is gone, my calm.
I am gone.
For I am returned,
And my self is drawn
Back and turned
Into the world again,
Like a leaf caught on a rolling stream,
Or held in a man's hand when
He gazes at it in a dream.

Furled inside its sleek cocoon,
Does the caterpillar not swoon
With very terror at the death
It is facing? And yet, with each breath,
Does it not take on the new
Life so long overdue?